N.S. BERANEK

LETHE PRESS
MAPLE SHADE, NEW JERSEY

Published in 2016 by Lethe Press, Inc.
118 Heritage Avenue ◆ Maple Shade,
NJ 08052-3018 USA
www.lethepressbooks.com ◆ lethepress@aol.com

ISBN: 978-1-59021-572-2 / 1-59021-572-9

This novel is a work of fiction. Names, characters,
places, and incidents are products of the author's
imagination or are used fictitiously.

Interior and cover design: INKSPIRAL DESIGN.

Library of Congress Cataloging-in-Publication
Data available on file

FOR MY PARENTS,
who taught me with Taxco
that a good story is nourished
by rich detail;

AND FOR ROB,
who gave me Ehrichto.

ACKNOWLEDGMENTS

I COULD NOT have completed this endeavor without the help and encouragement of many individuals. My thanks to Joel Bakrins for being as strong a champion of the written word (especially of "the Scottish play") outside of the home as my parents were within it; to Keith Snyder, my instructor during the 2006 Green River Writers Novels in Progress workshop; to Brian Owens and Joel D. Santner, for expanding the scope of the Louisville Playwrights Festival to include the reading of a selection from an early version of this book; to Kelly Wiegant Mangan, for recognizing when thrift-store finds of the day brought me new insights into character and setting, and for speaking that language with me; to editors Amie M. Evans, Paul J. Willis, R. D. Cochrane, Timothy J. Lambert, Matt Bright, and Krisma, for their expertise and guidance; and, most of all, to editor Steve Berman, who is generous to a fault in nurturing and promoting others' writing. Thank you for believing in me, time and again. Thanks also to Inkspiral Design, for making the book beautiful inside and out.

A SPECIAL SHOUT-OUT goes to my beta reader Christephor Gilbert, who read more drafts of this novel than any human being should ever be asked to do, and gave solid advice each time.

Finally, to my husband Rob, for his endless patience and understanding.

By Ehrichto's estimation the temperature is too cool for relaxing out of doors, yet there are several young men—almost nude, no less, wearing only shorts—lounging on the porch to catch whatever sun can be found. Draped across ultra-masculine brown cube chairs and an equally blocky couch, the boys all have the same basic look: freakishly broad jaws, even broader chests, slim waists, and powerful legs, though the colors of their hair and eyes and skin runs the gamut. Ehrichto isn't surprised by their presence, as his sire does like to adorn his house with art that has a good pulse, but is caught off guard when his reaching for the latch to the iron gate causes the lot of them to jump up and scatter like roaches in sudden light. In seconds they have fled into the safety of the house.

As he expects, the gate is not locked. He knows the front door won't be either. The residents of the house (the modern day rent boys he has just scared away not included) do not require the protection afforded by locked doors and tall fences, because they are all vampires.

O N E

Brick-and-mortar-wise this incarnation of Dorjan's home, dubbed Abaton, is new to Ehrichto, but that has been true on each of his visits. The fact that the members of Dorjan's inner circle—called the kel'an or just the kel, the Berber term for a large family unit or tribe—do not age, necessitates a frequent change of locale before neighbors become suspicious, and authorities are alerted. The kel moves from coast to coast, coming back to the Gulf region every thirty years or so. As when Ehrichto first met them, long ago, they currently reside in New Orleans's Marigny neighborhood, an area described as tattered or chic, depending on whether you ask a tenant or landlord. Large numbers of musicians and other artists, much of the staff from the area's many excellent eateries, and some of the most affluent members of the city's homosexual community all reside within the Marigny's boundaries.

Naturally, each house they choose is grander than its predecessors. This one is massive: three full stories of brick set far back from the street and half-hidden by lush tropical foliage. Though it is dusk, uplights illuminate key features of the structure's exterior, making it possible to see that the bricks are charcoal in color and that the gingerbread is painted a blue brighter than the Mediterranean on a summer day.

Ehrichto ascends the wide front steps, a full flight marked by glass-encased candles with guttering flames, and crosses the deep porch. He doesn't bother to knock; he understands that the porch sitters—*lotus eaters*, he thinks—will have already alerted Dorjan to his arrival.

His sire meets him in the second parlor; Dorjan has a favorite pose: arms folded across his chest, legs crossed at the ankles, and all of his weight resting on one shoulder, which is pressed to the edge of a gleaming, white marble mantelpiece. He has not changed the affluence of his wardrobe. Tonight he has on finely tailored black slacks and an electric blue button-front shirt cut from a silk that will no doubt flow like liquid when he moves. His shoes are so polished that it would be possible to count the arms of the chandelier hanging in the adjoining room just by staring at their surface. His face is tilted toward the floor and his eyes are cast downward as if he is doing precisely that.

"Ehrichto," he says, slowly lifting his head. The color of his eyes is arresting, as blue as his shirt. His skin is pale, a creamy white contrasted by black stubble that gives his chin the appearance of being covered in coal dust. Those hairs are the same lustrous black as the ones covering his upper lip, the same as the hair on his head, and just as densely packed with follicles. The joke has always been that Dorjan doesn't have hair, but rather fur.

Ehrichto believes his sire does not possess the ability to communicate with him by thought alone, but he imagines that he can hear the other's thoughts. In truth the voice in his head is far more his own than his master's. *To what do I owe the pleasure of your company this time?* it asks. It is the question he has most anticipated being asked, the one he pondered all during the flight up from Guatemala and still does not know how to answer.

"Let me get you a drink." Dorjan surprises him by pushing off from the mantel and standing upright. "We have a wide selection today."

"I know. I saw them when I arrived. Thank you, but I'll pass."

One corner of Dorjan's mouth lifts. As the smile spreads, the ends of his moustache achieve equilibrium and reveal very prominent front teeth. The fact that he has again taken to wearing a moustache is, in Ehrichto's opinion, a wise choice, because it both masks his overbite and tempers his aquiline nose. His is not a classical beauty, and yet when he enters a room, everything else in it seems to fade.

Though he cannot see them, Ehrichto is acutely aware of another feature of Dorjan's mouth: his long, sharp canines. The flesh of his neck prickles at the recollection of being pierced by those teeth and a shiver composed in equal parts of dread and desire runs up his spine. He cannot ever forget that bite. Vampires never forget the moment their life was lost and something else took root in their veins.

"Something jejune?" his host asks, sweeping his arm right to indicate a built-in bar on the opposite wall. Without waiting for a reply or request Dorjan crosses the room and picks up a glass already filled with ice. He dumps the contents into the bar's small sink and pours two fingers of whisky from a bottle of Laphroaig. "I assume your tastes have not changed," he says, extending the glass.

"No." Ehrichto reaches for the offered drink but Dorjan pulls it back.

"Then why are you here?"

Ehrichto fears describing what has already happened, back home in Panajachel, and what he thinks is happening there now, because he anticipates being either accused of overreaction, or dismissed as confused or naïve. Even more than that, he can't stand the thought that Dorjan will, once again, insinuate that he harbors secret, tender feelings toward his best and only friend, when he has never had any such thoughts. In the very worst case scenario, he imagines Dorjan implying that he and Nick are lovers. He finds it not unlikely that his sire will assume it was a lovers' spat that drove him away. The thought of being physical with Nick sickens Ehrichto, but he doubts it will ever be possible to convince Dorjan of that. His sire believes only two states are possible between men, outside of the paternal bond: sexual interest or enmity.

Ehrichto's stomach twists into knots. He doesn't want to tell his sire that his progeny blindsided and drugged him, or that he'd caused him to—for the first time in sixty years—miss the first three days of the Feast of Maximón. He doesn't want to recount how, not even twenty-four hours ago, following a disastrous hike through the rainforest to reach the ruins of Chiya, he'd returned home to more bad news.

"Tell me. What happened?"

Intending to gather strength from Dorjan's steady gaze, Ehrichto uses the fingers of one hand to rake the hair hanging in his face back up and over the crown of his head as he raises it. "I was only trying to, to...." he stammers. He stops and swallows hard, forces down the bile rising in his throat.

Dorjan places a hand on the back of Ehrichto's neck. "What did you do?"

"Took his drugs and buried them in the rainforest."

Tiny creases bloom at the edges of Dorjan's eyes. He has always considered Nick a poor choice for progeny.

"I had to. He's crazy," Ehrichto explains. "He drugged me. I was out for three days. I missed the festival." He feels Dorjan's grip tighten. "I had to do something. He won't listen. He won't stop. And he's...he's dying."

Dorjan raises one eyebrow. He looks as if he is suppressing a smirk. "He's a vampire."

"I'm not overreacting," Ehrichto says. "I swear to you, that's what's happening. He's started taking this crazy combination of drugs and it's changing him. He no longer heals. He's nothing but skin and bones." He feels tears threaten to start, and bites his lower lip to halt them. "Please, you have to believe me."

The hand at the back of his neck squeezes harder. Ehrichto assumes it's a chastisement, but when Dorjan speaks the words are kind. "Susem, susem, a memmi," he murmurs, his native Tamazight for *Hush, hush, my son.*

Ehrichto drops his gaze to the hardwood. "He's dying. He is. That's why I....." He falters. There will be a price to pay for Dorjan's help. Steeling himself, he tosses his head to flip the hair from his eyes, and tries again. "That's why I came back. I need your—"

Dorjan stops his words by pulling him forward into a kiss. He tastes just as Ehrichto remembered: a hint of spice and the lingering musk of his last meal. His moustache is soft; the stubble dusting his cheeks rough as sandpaper.

Dorjan brings his other hand up to meet the first, twines his fingers into Ehrichto's hair, and pulls him even deeper into their kiss.

Ehrichto doesn't realize that Dorjan has let go of him again until several moments later, when he feels him gathering fistfuls of the khaki, utilitarian fabric of his shirt. Ehrichto adopted the style of dress from Nick, who favors it because it is well-suited to trekking through the cloud forest. Dorjan grasps the shirt's plackets and jerks his hands wide, easily popping the triple sewn row of buttons.

Ehrichto twists his head sideways to break the kiss. Things are moving even faster than he expected, and he still needs to secure the other's assistance.

"You'll help him?" he asks.

"You will stay?"

He expected exactly that reply; still, the words spark conflict within him: stabbing pangs in his gut vie with a pleasant spike of neural activity in his brain.

"Yes, I'll stay."

Without warning, Dorjan slams the heels of his hands against Ehrichto's chest, knocking him off balance. He falls backward, but only for a second, landing safely on a couch he hadn't noticed behind him. Still, his stomach turns somersaults worthy of a fifteen-story drop.

Dorjan climbs onto the couch and straddles him, placing a knee on either side of his hips and settling his weight so that the hardness pushing out the front of his trousers lies alongside the corresponding bulge within Ehrichto's. Torso to torso, they are separated only by layers of gabardine and wool at the hips and, at the chest, by a thin layer of electric blue silk. Dorjan rests his elbows beside Ehrichto's shoulders. "If things between the two of you are as…chaste…as you claim," he says quietly, "he is a fool, your Nick." Ehrichto turns his head, stretches his neck long, and braces for the bite as Dorjan dips his head low. Instead, breath tickles his ear. "He does not deserve anything you've given him," Dorjan murmurs. "But we have a deal." To punctuate the words he rears his head back and drives his fangs deep.

The pain, at once hot and sharp, causes Ehrichto's entire body to go rigid. He has never forgotten his first because every time he surrenders his arteries to that pain, the sense of being emptied, the chance that he will never rise again, returns; real and, cruelly, satisfying.

Michael drops his shoes on the foyer's white tile and takes a detour right, through the Conservatory. He thinks of each room of the house as having a capitalized title because of the pretentious names his parents use for them, and the extra emphasis his mother always puts on those names in speech—("I'm going to the Kitchen now.") It looks strange, empty, the state it's been in ever since her ill-conceived attempt, eight months earlier, right after they moved in, to own a baby grand. He smiles, remembering how his father went ballistic that day, hollering about not being a Rockefeller and flat-out refusing to listen when Julia said she would try to get her grandmother's organization, Conway Charities, to pay for the thing.

"Well, the WPA people weren't gods," Michael overhears his mother Julia saying as he cuts across the round, cream-colored rug he's sure it's racist to call "oriental." "They knocked down things they didn't want anymore and built what was more appropriate to their needs. It's exactly what we want to do only we aren't being allowed to. And why? Because some lunatic has decided what they built is precious. Well, it's not precious, it's just old."

She relishes opportunities to voice her strong opinions, and argues publicly with everyone, especially his father, except, that is, when it concerns money. His parents try to keep their battles over financial matters quiet so no one will know how little they are worth, but Michael catches the word-bombs they lob at one another, the vicious double-speak they employ after other people turn away at dinner parties. He's pieced together enough of what they've said to one another to know that everything they have is bought on time, that they pay pennies toward every dollar of interest and never a dime toward principal. They own nothing. "We live in a house of cards," he frequently hears his father say under his breath, usually right before commencing to rub his temples, as if his head feels ready to explode.

Michael takes a deep breath before entering the dining room. When he steps through the arch, he finds Julia sitting in one of the high-backed white chairs, thumbing through a glossy, picture-heavy magazine. Their cordless phone is lying beside the magazine on the smoked-glass table top. Two rows of white plaster columns, four columns to a row, comprise the base of the table. Viewed from the street it looks like a film set miniature of the Lincoln Memorial crouched beneath a literal glass ceiling. The day his girlfriend Alyssa first saw it she'd squinted and strained, trying to come up with a positive comment, but had finally resorted simply to "Wow."

He comes to a halt beside the sideboard covered in Chiclet-sized squares of mirror, and waits. Julia stops flipping magazine pages but doesn't immediately look up. "You're going out with Alyssa?"

As if there is anyone else he could be going to hang out with. *Four months and six days*, Michael thinks. It's the amount of time remaining until classes start at the University of Kentucky, an hour and a half's drive away, in Lexington. "Yes. We're having a planning committee meeting for the Thunder party."

Thunder Over Louisville, the kick-off celebration for the Derby Festival, the most important two weeks of every year in Louisville. Michael doubts Julia even remembers there is going to be a Thunder event at school, a prom fundraiser entitled *The, Like, Totally '80s Thunder Party*. If she even heard him when he mentioned it before, he's sure she quickly discounted it. It isn't a real Thunder event, not at all like the fancy black-tie affair she's throwing at the Kentucky Center for the Arts, the biggest deal all year for the charity her grandmother Myrtle Conway founded.

She turns the magazine around to show him the photo she's looking at. It's of a rough-textured stone bowl, dark gray in color like wet concrete, filled with balls covered in tan feathers. It is, Michael thinks, quite possibly the ugliest thing anyone has ever created. It's even uglier than the wooden bowl of polished gray stone spheres which enjoys pride of place on the coffee table in their great room.

He's fairly sure he knows what she is thinking. The color scheme and hard and soft components are the exact opposite of theirs, and their house is chock full of just such patterns, what their architect-slash-interior-designer Angelo de Haven called "the repeating, contrasting patterns which are the hallmark of class and taste." In the den, which is nothing more than an alcove off the great room, chromed bookshelves are filled with books that have crumbling leather spines and brittle yellow pages. Michael always thinks of movies like *Mad Max* and *Blade Runner* when he looks at the den, though he's never seen either one of those films, only their posters.

Here, in the dining room, the stark white columns and smoked glass of the table are reverse-echoed by a hurricane vase filled with bleached, bone-white peacock feathers which dominates the mirrored sideboard.

When his mother flips the magazine closed and Michael sees that the bowl of balls is the issue's cover image, he knows, without a doubt, that she will buy it. "That would go perfectly," he says, though he can't imagine where she will put a second bowl of spheres. Their home is all about clean lines and unobstructed spaces. "The Spartan aesthetic," Angelo de Haven had said. She ignores his remark. When she looks up, he sees her odd smile, a cat-who-swallowed-the-canary grin. "Guess what I bought," she asks in a sing-songy cadence.

He doesn't have to guess; he knows every year around this time she begins making special stops at a real bakery to pick up a pound or two of rugelach, the traditional rolled-dough pastry that is a favorite treat for the Jewish holiday of Passover. She first saw them two years ago in a spring catalog put out by the Gevalia coffee company. Par for the course, she'd paid no attention to the copy about the confection's origins, taking away only that they were seasonal and expensive. Not three days later two dozen of the treats were, literally, on display on their marble kitchen island, showcased within a gleaming glass-domed cake stand.

She believes that because the pastries are handcrafted and many times more expensive than the factory-produced tricolored coconut bars Michael's father keeps stocked for him year-round, it means that he prefers them, which isn't true, but he doesn't want her to know that. He does his best to sound excited. "Rugelach?"

"Six flavors this year. They added walnut-sorghum."

Michael bites his tongue to keep from asking her why the treats are so early this year, not closer to Thunder, as they sometimes are. "Wow."

"Well, go on. Get some."

It's not an invitation but an order. Michael hurries through the next archway and into the kitchen, a bank of stainless-steel appliances at one end of the great room, the space which dominates the back half of their house. He takes several pieces of rugelach from the cut crystal dome on the island, wraps them in a paper towel, then grabs two plastic-wrapped coconut bars and a bottle of Ale 8-1, the spicy, locally made ginger ale that is another favorite of his which his father makes sure to keep in stock.

He realizes his mistake too late, when he reaches the dining room and sees the set of his mother's jaw change. She looks him up and down. Finally, her eyes come to rest on his chin. "Before the dinner," she says, pointing one talon-tipped, red-lacquered nail in his direction. "All of that needs to go."

By "all of that" she means his wispy moustache, dime-sized soul patch and goatee. It's the first facial hair he's ever managed to grow, and has just, finally, started to really be something.

"But—"

"I'm not going to have you looking *that way*," she says. He thinks she is going to say it again, the real F-word. Panic stabs his gut. "Like a gondolier," she says, surprising him. He starts to relax. "Or a—"

"I'll shave." Michael cringes. "Saturday morning, okay? I'll shave."

One corner of her mouth curls upward, and a glint appears in her eyes. "Wonderful," she says, flipping the magazine back open with a flick of her wrist while keeping her gaze on him. Her irises are a frosted shade of blue, far paler than his azure-colored ones. "Well? Go on. You don't want to keep your girlfriend waiting."

THROUGH THE SIDELIGHTS of the front entrance Michael sees Alyssa's zippy yellow Ford Escort enter the cul-de-sac. He throws open the door and is surprised to find his father standing on their front porch, scowling at the mail carrier, who is completely disregarding the stones of their winding front path and, quite literally, cutting a diagonal line across their lawn. The man's heavy black boots tear huge divots from their rain-soaked sod.

Hearing the screen door being opened, Michael's father turns. His scowl fades, replaced by a smile. "Hey there. Are you and Alyssa going out?"

Michael nods. "We have this thing at school." *The Like, Totally '80s Thunder Party* is still a few weeks away; they are still in the planning stages. So far the idea for the night before the event is to set up a projection television, hang streamers, rearrange chairs, hang more streamers, mix up a fruit punch and put it in the refrigerator; distribute unopened packages of snacks, confirm the pizza order, and hang more streamers. Michael despises hanging crêpe paper streamers, but has been informed by Alyssa that an eighties-themed party needs lots of them in order to be considered authentically retro. He wants to ask why they need decorations at all, since it isn't a dance, but he doesn't dare.

As much as he isn't looking forward to taping crêpe paper around the cafeteria in a few weeks, he is even less thrilled about what Alyssa has planned for them after the meeting today. They're going to Cipriani's, the pizza place located at the base of the hill on which both Michael's family's development and the one Alyssa lives in are built, a block or two down Poplar Level Road, just across from the Quarry Plaza Shopping Center and the Kmart.

Michael doesn't dare mention this part of today's plan to his father, because he knows if he does he will be reminded that they pay a personal chef good money to do their grocery shopping and commandeer their restaurant-grade appliances every Sunday afternoon, to prepare a week's worth of gourmet meals tailored to their tastes and nutritional needs. His father will make him feel guilty for wanting to partake, and past experience tells Michael it's a waste of breath trying to get him to understand what it's like to be in the midst of group and unable to take part in the activity in which they are all engaged.

Mercifully, before they can speak further the mail carrier calls out, "Mr. Ferguson!" He comes bounding up their front steps, slopping mud everywhere. "What a pleasure it is to see you!"

Michael takes advantage of the chance to escape. "Bye, Dad! See you in a bit," he says as he pushes past the postal worker. He dashes down the steps and then takes the winding path of stepping stones two at a time, aiming for the safety of the car.

ALYSSA HAS THE windows of the Escort rolled up against the cold and rainy day and she's busy thumbing through a stack of CDs. Michael reaches for the handle of the driver's door and yanks it open.

The blast of chilly air clearly gets her attention at the same time that the sugary scent wafting out from the enclosed space gets his. "Hey," she says as he pulls her out of the car and to her feet. "It's freezing out here!"

He wraps her in his arms and breathes deep. "I remember this outfit."

"You do?"

He nods. Besides smelling like candy, she looks like it. Her mint-green wool cardigan is sculpted to resemble cake frosting and her skirt is the color of bubblegum. As if that weren't enough, she is also adorned in actual candy: a ring with a ruby-red hard candy "gemstone," and a necklace of elastic strung with tart sugar disks. "You wore it on our first day at Danshen."

Her father is his father's boss at Danshen Pharmaceuticals. To please them and to build their résumés for college admission forms, the previous summer Alyssa and Michael had each signed onto be interns for the company. Since they'd been acquaintances for years, dragged to annual company picnics and the like, it was only natural that at lunch on the first day they'd paired up. They'd gone to a hot dog parlor on nearby Shelbyville Road where, despite wolfing down two hot dogs, an order of chili cheese fries, and two cokes, Michael remained hungry, in large part due to Alyssa's Very Vanilla shampoo, sugar body scrub, and bubblegum lip gloss.

"Our first day?" Alyssa asks. "Oh, you mean when you turned around and kissed me without first finding out whether or not I wanted you to?"

He'd been frustrated by the fact that the lunch stand did not sell desserts and eager to get back to the vending machines in the company break room. When they reached the street door and he realized that he'd left his keycard at the intern cubicle, he'd spun on his heel, intending to ask if she had hers, and found her only inches from him. The urge to taste her lips, to see if they were as sweet as they smelled, proved too great to resist.

"You think that was shocking?" Michael draws her closer. "Here's a news flash: that kiss was the only way I had to stop myself from gnawing on you."

"Is that so?"

By way of answering he slips a finger beneath the stretchy string around her neck, pulls a candy disk into his mouth, and bites down. Shattered-candy goodness rains down on his tongue, an intense and vaguely fruity sweetness not unlike Necco wafers. He is about to chomp another but she winds her fingers through his hair and pulls him back as she rises up onto the balls of her feet. Their mouths meet, and an old disappointment twists his gut—the sad reality that bubblegum lip gloss looks and smells far better than it tastes.

EHRICHTO SALVATOLLE LISTENS to the brittle rhythm coming from across the room, the sound of Wren cracking open pistachios. His nephew is stretched out along their tatty green sofa with his shoulders resting against one of its wooden arms. He is half Vietnamese, a product of the American war in that country, and his feet reach only three-quarters of the way to the sofa's far end. His skin is the brown of the wooden bowl that rests on his stomach.

The room is dark, of course.

In a little over a month Wren will turn twenty-five. His father, Nick Krey, Ehrichto's friend as well as the only person he has ever made into to a vampire, has sworn he will share this gift with his son on that day. Ehrichto doesn't see how Nick will manage to stay awake long enough; over the past couple of months he's been barely coherent at the best of times and flat-out lifeless at others. Nick's addiction to narcotics also creates a more immediate problem for Ehrichto. In just a few hours he must leave the house for a week, and travel across Lake Atitlán and up the side of Volcán San Pedro, his annual trip up to the ruins of Chiya, where he plays the role of the Maya deity Maximón for the local *cofradía*, a religious brotherhood dedicated to the god. Ehrichto portrays the deity at lesser festivals and special occasions throughout the year as well, but the Feast of Maximón, held during Easter Holy Week, is far and away the most important.

A few days ago, during one of Nick's rare lucid moments, they'd talked about the importance of his staying sober for this week. He'd assured Ehrichto that he could manage it, and would.

But can I trust the word of a junkie? Ehrichto looks over at Wren and wonders if his nephew is angry with him for still planning to attend the festival, even with things at home as they are. Neither Wren nor Nick has ever understood Ehrichto's relationship to the Nueva Chiya Cofradía de Maximón. Looking at it from their perspective as well as through the lens of time, Ehrichto has to admit that impersonating a deity was a naïve, ridiculous, perhaps even condescending plan, but back when his sire Kabil Dorjan conceived it, the idea had sounded brilliant. The god created by the Maya in the highlands of Guatemala granted favors in exchange for gifts of whisky and cigars—two of Ehrichto's favorite things—and Maya religious practices have always involved bloodletting. As Dorjan put it right before he shoved Ehrichto from the cover of the rainforest foliage and out onto the stone plaza of the ruins of the city of Chiya, *It's as if they knew you were coming. Now go make all their dreams come true and let them repay you in blood.*

Ehrichto has endeavored to make the cofradía members' dreams come true by purchasing milpas on the slopes of the three volcanoes that ring Lake Atitlán, employing members of the cofradía to work the crops on them, even funding a free health clinic in Santiago Atitlán, the town in which most of them reside. The clinic also provided the blood Nick needs. As the Maximón Ehrichto has offered several families the funds with which to send their brightest, most ambitious children to college in Guate, local shorthand for the nation's sprawling capital of Guatemala City, which is located several hours away by bus. He likes to think of it as a symbiotic relationship. He tells himself that even if, as he guesses, they suspect, deep down, that he is not really Maximón, all the good that he does for them will mean that they will allow him to continue doing his impression of their god at various religious events throughout the year. The cofradía need Ehrichto in the guise of Maximón, and he needs the blood they give him.

Ehrichto has been a part of nearly six decades of events dedicated to the god. Soon there won't be a single member of the cofradía who remembers the way it was before he arrived, when his part was played by a wooden effigy dressed in the bright textiles for which the region is famous.

The feast is set to start in just three hours, and it takes time to motor across the lake and to fight through the lush vegetation to reach the terrace on which the ruins are located. Ehrichto will have to leave soon— it would not be unreasonable to leave now—but he is waiting for Nick to rouse. He needs his friend's reassurance that he will stay sober, because Wren's vulnerability requires that one of them be not only with him at all times but awake and alert, to protect him from the hundred and one things that could take his life before immortality is granted.

As if on cue, across the room Wren makes a hacking sound, a single cough he uses to clear the paper-thin skin of a pistachio from his throat. *We need to turn him*, Ehrichto thinks. For almost two years—ever since Guatemala's forty-year-long civil war finally ended and they moved down off Volcán Pedro and into this house in the heart of touristy Panajachel, and Nick unexpectedly began to come unwound—that thought has been developing into something of a mantra for Ehrichto. *It's time. It might be past time.*

Nick's final argument for waiting, that his son might still be capable of a last growth spurt, loses traction with each passing day. *That isn't the real issue anyway. He's scared something will go wrong.* Ehrichto is anxious as well; he does not comprehend how he made Nick into a vampire. There hadn't been time to think, only to act.

"So, what are you two going to do while I'm gone?" he asks Wren.

The pistachio cracking halts. The sarcasm wafting across the small space is almost palpable. "Oh, I don't know, Uncle. I thought maybe we'd play cribbage."

Their family cribbage battles once were epic, but they haven't played in over a year, not since the night Wren overturned the board and sent the pins flying in all directions, several to parts unknown. Though many things could be used for replacements, even the ends of toothpicks or pieces of twig from the courtyard, it has been Ehrichto's intention to buy actual replacement cribbage pins during a business trip to Guate. He has been to two quarterly meetings for his cigar-exporting business since his nephew's little episode, but returned empty-handed both times, having somehow forgotten to inquire after the pins at local shops.

"We used to have some battles, didn't we?" Ehrichto asks. Sometimes, while sitting by himself at this table, listening to Wren typing away at the computer in his room, and trying not to hear the silence in between the keystrokes, the utter lack of sound from Nick's room or the courtyard, wherever his friend happened to be (the deep, deep quiet Ehrichto is still tempted to call dead silence), he is haunted by the memory of family game nights. In cribbage he and Wren would always play as a team, uncle and nephew taking sides against that all-powerful entity known as Dad, trying to together amass 121 points before Nick could reach 61. Deep down Ehrichto understands his insistence that they need actual cribbage pins in order to play and his failure to find any is not accidental. He worries that the rift Nick's addiction has opened between all of them would cause a restored set to go unused.

Wren sets the bowl of pistachios on the end table, sits up, and leans so far forward that his long black hair nearly brushes the floor. He uses both hands to gather the hair into a ponytail and then begins slipping elastic ties off of his wrist and using them to secure the strands. He places a tie every few inches down the length of the thick cable. Just as he finishes there is a noise from the courtyard, a dull thud, as if Nick dropped something heavy on the slate tile flooring. Wren springs to his bare feet but, rather than heading in the direction of the noise, makes a beeline for the door to his bedroom.

"You should be wearing shoes," Ehrichto calls after him.

When he reaches the doorway, Wren halts but doesn't turn around. "Why's that? You think a splinter could kill me?"

"I think that a broken toe can result in a blood clot and that could kill you."

"Mmm, blood clot. Tasty. Has anyone ever told you, Uncle, that you have a one-track mind?"

That his nephew is so blasé about vampirism troubles Ehrichto. He worries raising him apart from other mortals was not the right choice, but what else could they do? It was hard enough keeping him safe without the presence of the world's most dangerous animal. "I'm only—"

"Concerned," Wren says. "Yeah. Have fun with your cargo cult." He disappears into the darkness of his room.

A BREEZE STIRS the hem of Ehrichto's unbuttoned shirt as he stands in the doorway to the courtyard. He's staring at Nick but thinking about the last thing Wren said before dashing off to hide in his room. *Have fun with your cargo cult.* It saddens Ehrichto that his nephew regards the members of the cofradía as an isolated, backward lot. He gives himself much of the blame for that misperception, but he also blames Nick, who disdains all believers. Raised Catholic, Ehrichto finds it hard to fathom that the pair have no real knowledge of that religion or any others, or even a grasp on the concept of faith. Nick once told Ehrichto that his parents, Captain and Mrs. Krey, claimed membership in some Protestant denomination only because in the nineteen sixties not doing so was social suicide. The family rarely attended actual services, a conceit of his father's high rank and the frequency with which they relocated; before he graduated from high school Nick had lived in a dozen places, most notably Japan. Wren has lived in five: Vietnam, where he was born; San Diego, during an ill-conceived period where he was cared for by Nick's mother and the captain, despite their feeling that as a "bastard" and a "mulatto" he was not truly their grandson; Ehrichto's hometown of Louisville, until things there became untenable; and finally Guatemala, first in the shack above Chiya, and for the last two years down here in Panajachel, a one-time hippie enclave and tourist trap on Lake Atitlán's northern shore, a place locals deride and refer to derogatorily as Gringotenango.

Ehrichto's thought—and Nick's, though he might deny it—in choosing to move to Panajachel after the long Guatemalan civil war finally ended, was that it was means to re-acclimating then twenty-three year old Wren to the larger world, which he hadn't had contact with since he was seven. They'd chosen Pana because it was in reasonable proximity to Chiya, yet allowed Ehrichto the freedom of not having to worry that he would run into any of the members of the cofradía on the street as none of them would set foot in such a commercialized town, let alone one located on the wrong side of the lake, the Kaqchikel side. Maximón is a Tz'utujil construct, and the two tribes are sworn enemies.

Nick is slumped over sideways in the hanging basket chair. The syringe used to inject his latest fix hangs forgotten from his forearm. For almost two years, he has been shooting up massive amounts of narcotics, willfully overdosing and dying.

His penchant for slipping into oblivion isn't new. When they met, in a storefront bar in Veracruz in the Sierra Madre Oriental region of Mexico, Nick had been face-down on the table beside a half-empty bottle of whisky. Even being undead, Ehrichto had felt real trepidation when, looking for a flight to Guatemala City and enticed by a flyer tacked to a post outside the bar, he entered the establishment and was informed that the owner/operator of the advertised airline, Machina Airlines, was the apparent drunk in the corner. Nick, though, had surprised him. Not only had he come to enough right then to persuade Ehrichto to withhold his full judgment until the next day, but he'd made good on his promise to be in shipshape form by morning.

When he roused in the early afternoon, Nick had been a new man, not merely up but hyperactive, barking coordinates into an ancient wall phone, and the table on which he'd been passed out the night before was covered in maps and the detailed hand-drawn charts he'd used to construct their flight plan. Back then Nick's nightly binges seemed to be his way of reining in his copious energy. Ehrichto thinks of his friend's behavior in terms one might use when describing a defective motor, as an issue of faulty windings, fraying insulation, or a bad capacitor. Nick has a tendency to spin out of control, to become overvolted, and when he does there is no way to slow him down. The only thing to do is cut the power. Seeing him shut down now, his head and neck smashed up against the basket chair's wicker wall, twisted at a painful-looking, unnatural angle, makes Ehrichto cringe.

He crosses the slate tile of the courtyard in four long strides, extracts the needle from Nick's arm and then tugs on the limb. "Time to wake up."

He wishes he knew why, when they came down into Panajachel, Nick traded the bottle for the needle, alcohol for black tar heroin; why he went from shutting down only after a long manic period to trying to stay permanently switched off. These days there are only thin slivers of time in which the dope has burned off but dope sickness hasn't yet set in, rare moments when the narcotic fog breaks and Nick returns to them.

"I have to leave soon and I need to talk to you."

To Ehrichto's knowledge, Wren hasn't witnessed one of Nick's lucid periods in months. As he did just now, he emerges from his room only when the coast is clear. He will venture out to raid the fridge, flop down on the sofa, or step into the courtyard for a change of scenery only until Nick stirs. Then he heads back into his room. That behavior used to bother Ehrichto, but lately he's been grateful for it. He doesn't want Wren to see Nick this way.

Being vampires, they are supposed to be immutable. Ehrichto hasn't been able to detect a single alteration to his own appearance in the sixty years since his transformation. Nick, though, has an ashen taint to his skin, his eyes have become sunken, and his long blond hair, once shiny as flax, looks matted and dull like used straw swept by the wind.

Though his formal education ended with the tenth grade and the scientific world has made extraordinary discoveries in the interim, Ehrichto has struggled through articles in scientific journals looking for anything that might explain, first, the vampiric state, and second, what is happening to Nick. He's read about so-called lineage reprogramming and the interconversion of cells, some of which can apparently dedifferentiate and redifferentiate as needed, becoming whatever the organism requires. He's read interviews with researchers who have theorized that biological immortality is not only possible but probable, and others who claim that they are on the brink of proving it exists, at least in hydrozoa.

Ehrichto feels that vampires must simply be humans who have undergone a viral transduction and been changed on a cellular level, a natural phenomenon so rare as to be virtually unknown. Their immortality must be owed to the halting of senescence, the aging process, through an acquired ability to endlessly regenerate to a fixed developmental point. It

seems reasonable to assume that if such a transformation can take place
it can also be undone, and Ehrichto fears that Nick's recent behavior has
undone him.

Nick opens his eyes. "Hey…what's going on?"

Ehrichto lets go of him and takes a step back. "I was just trying to
wake you up."

"Yeah?" Nick shifts sideways and sticks a hand down between the
basket chair's thick cushion and its woven wall. "Well, you did."

Worried that he's looking for the syringe, Ehrichto hides the hand it's
in behind his back. Nick, though, pulls out a pack of smokes. He tamps
it on the heel of his left hand several times and lifts his chin, indicating
the round brass tray atop an orange crate set at his feet. "Hand me the
lighter that's on there somewhere, would you?" he asks. "This damned
chair makes it hard to lean forward to reach things."

You have no trouble when you're cooking your drugs, Ehrichto thinks,
surveying the detritus strewn across the tray: a bent and blackened spoon,
a glass of cloudy water, and easily one hundred little squares of tinfoil
covered with black dots, one for each hit Nick has done since the last time
Ehrichto tidied up. One grouping of foil squares has a curious rise to its
center. Brushing the squares aside, he finds the plastic lighter.

"I'll be taking off soon," he says, holding the thing out while Nick
pulls a cigarette from the pack and tucks it between his lips. The sight
causes a hunger-like pang to flare in Ehrichto's solar plexus because he
and Nick used to smoke together most evenings. The last time they did
was months ago now.

Ehrichto knows better than to go back to his room for one of his
cigars and his own, better lighter. If he did he would only be disappointed,
because no matter what Nick says, how convincingly he promises it will be
like the old days, when they used to play cards and have long conversations
as the whisky slowly took hold, it won't be anything like it was, maybe not
ever again. For months Nick's actions have been predictable: after waking
he smokes a quick cigarette and then reaches for his rig. He shoots up,
promptly passes out, and leaves Ehrichto to finish his cigar, essentially
alone.

Tonight though, Ehrichto thinks, *things have to go differently.*

Nick takes the lighter, flicks it to life, and dips the end of his cigarette in the flame until its tip glows red. Then he settles back into the cocoon-like, curved wicker seat. "So," he says, flicking the lighter twice more, just to watch the flame erupt. "Where're you going, anyway?"

They talked specifically about this the last time all the elements aligned and Nick was conscious in Ehrichto's presence. That was just three evenings ago.

Ehrichto tries to squelch the panic fluttering his stomach. "Tonight's the start of the Feast of Maximón, remember?"

Nick's brows pinch closer together. "But it's…. Isn't it January?" He sounds as confused as he looks. "I thought that whole thing wasn't until a week before, uh, before…oh, you know. That holiday."

Ehrichto directs all his emotion into the fist still hidden behind his back, squeezing the syringe so tightly that he pictures its plastic tubing as oval now instead of round. "No," he says, fighting to keep his composure. "It's not January. It's the end of March, and Easter—" he says it pointedly "—is a week away. The Feast starts at midnight tonight."

"Oh."

"What year is it? Do you know? Can you tell me?"

He expects Nick to get defensive, but the other surprises him by seeming to really think about it. He takes a long drag off of his smoke and runs his thumbnail between his front teeth, clearing away imagined scraps of tobacco.

A thin ribbon of smoke wafts upward from the cigarette's smoldering tip, causing him to squinch his left eye shut. "I don't know," he admits at last. "But…what difference does it make?"

Wren's twenty-fifth birthday is in a little over a month, and Nick has promised to turn him by then. Due to his suspicion that it is partly the fear of something going wrong during the turning process which is causing Nick's recent behavior, Ehrichto decides not to mention it now. He brings his fist out from behind his back and unclenches it, so Nick can see what he is holding. "You can't do this while I'm gone," he says. "You just can't. You have to stay sober to see that nothing happens to Wren."

Nick stares down into the crevice from which he pulled his smokes but says nothing. "I know it will be difficult," Ehrichto continues. He tries to bring a little levity to the moment. "But it's not as if the withdrawal will kill you."

I hope.

Nick looks up. Even his irises appear more washed out than normal. They are no longer the cornflower flecked with gold that Ehrichto once found remarkable, and the steeply tilted eye sockets, which a lifetime ago conveyed a sense of gentleness, now seem to broadcast nothing but defeat.

Nick raises a hand and beckons him closer but, thinking he is after the syringe, Ehrichto turns away. He reaches for the wooden cigar box standing at the center of the coffee table. As he does it occurs to him that, at least in this house, the piece of furniture is misnamed. *Heroin table*, he thinks wryly, just before dropping the syringe onto a pile of tiny zip-top plastic packets. Each little re-sealable bag boasts a sticker stamped with a crude line drawing, a trademark or brand that represents the dealer who sold it. The foil packets, too, bear such markings.

The baggie topmost on the pile is marked with a frog. It strikes Ehrichto as an odd choice; usually the images are exceedingly macho in nature. He's seen knives, guns, bolts of lightning, even once—ironically— vampire fangs.

It isn't only the branding on the baggie which is unusual; its contents are strange, too. Rather than the usual small, black, sticky dots common to the foil packets, the little bag is filled with paper thin, translucent curls, peels of some unknown substance. *Eye of newt*, Ehrichto thinks. Intending to say exactly that, he starts to turn around, but before he can, he feels an intense and pinpointed pain in his mid back. Fire shoots up and down his spine and all of his muscles go rigid. A second later, his knees buckle. Fully conscious yet powerless to stop himself, he sinks to a kneeling position. He hovers there a moment, and then the courtyard's slate tile rushes up to smack him in the face, and the world blinks off.

TWO

ALYSSA AND MICHAEL occupy one side of an extra-wide booth at Cipriani's while her friends Drake, Stephen and Rashad fill the seat opposite. Michael considers the three to be her friends and not his because he is still new among them, transferred to their school after moving to the Dream House at the start of what is, for all of them, senior year.

He knows his father fought to delay their move to the new house for the ten months he had left to graduation. He'd thought up excuse after excuse why they should put it off, until finally he'd been forced to come right out and tell Julia what he was thinking—that changing schools and leaving friends behind was difficult, possibly even traumatic, and absolutely detrimental to one's studies, and he didn't want to put their son through it. Julia's reaction had shocked him, but not Michael, who eavesdropped on their fight.

She'd pointed out that colleges looked at transcripts from the first three high school years only; that unless you were trying for an Ivy League school, senior year was considered to be a kind of eight-month party.

For his part, Michael had been relieved by the idea of transferring to a new school, and the chance for reinvention.

"So tell us," Rashad says to Alyssa. "What your top three were."

She has been regaling them with the most hideous of this year's suggestions for a prom theme. "Well," she says. "It's so tough to decide, but I guess I'd have to say the Knight series. That's with a 'k,' mind you. There were some real gems there, ones that mashed up time periods, or geography, or both. Take for example, 'Victorian Knights' and 'A Knight on the Nile.' But then there's also 'Lost in the Knight,' which, admit it, it's impossible not to love. The thing is, of course, how would you decorate for that? And what would you serve? Blood-red punch and gelatin molded to look like brains?" She laughs and looks Michael's way. "I still really like your idea. A photo booth shaped like a spleen."

It pleases Michael that Drake smiles, but his attention is fractured. He keeps one eye on Stephen because a couple of minutes ago he witnessed the guy—heading back to their table following a trip to the restroom—grab a handful of wrapped straws from the wait station. He has the things stashed in his lap, and he keeps—surreptitiously, he thinks—fiddling with them. He is clearly up to no good.

Alyssa squeezes Michael's hand. "You should tell them what ones you decided deserved the title of worst prom theme," she says. She turns back to the other three boys and grins. "These are really, really bad."

Michael does not want to have this discussion with Stephen or Drake, let alone with Rashad. Mercifully, Stephen chooses that moment to raise one of the straws he's been fiddling with to his lips. He takes quick aim at Rashad and blows hard, shooting the hollow paper wrapper straight past Drake and into the side of Rashad's Adam's apple. It flutters to the table top and comes to rest on the declaration *Britney is a fox*, which is carved into the heavily scarred wooden surface.

"Ow!" Rashad exclaims. He tries to jump to his feet, but the move is hampered by the table's deep overhang. He slams his hands down on the tabletop in frustration. "What the hell, man? Grow up!"

Cackling, Stephen tosses the naked straw onto the table. "Damn, dude," he says. "Way to overreact."

Drake nods his agreement. "Seriously. Straw wrapper. Not lawn dart."

At that, Stephen begins to full-out guffaw. He clutches his sides and collapses against the high upright back of the booth. The move saves him from being struck in the face by an ice cube hurled by Rashad. It hits the side of the empty booth across from theirs and skitters across the floor.

"Hey!" Mr. Cipriani shouts from his perch behind the order window. "I got waitresses gotta walk around here with big trays o' food!" Michael fights the urge to roll his eyes. At the present they are the restaurant's only customers, and have already been served. "You gonna be here to fill out workerman's comp papers? You gonna help pay their rent when they can't work? You gonna—" He stops when Rashad exhales loudly, flings himself out of the booth, and stomps over to where the errant ice cube came to rest. He grabs it and tosses it into the sink at the wait staff's station, then looks at Mr. Cipriani.

"We good now, bro?" he asks, affecting a slang Michael imagines he's only heard in videos and on episodes of *Law and Order*. It's no secret among the five teenagers that Rashad's family is the one most well off.

Mr. Cipriani bobs his head once. "We're good," he says.

Rashad returns to his seat, his usual spot, opposite Alyssa. It's also no secret that he is in love with her, and despises Michael for asking her out just days after she broke up with her long-term boyfriend Trey Daniels, who this year is a freshman at Western Kentucky University. Rashad was trying to do the gentlemanly thing by giving her space following the breakup, despite the fact that the idea to end the relationship was hers, not Trey's. Michael, catching up with her on the first day of the Danshen Pharma internship and hearing only that she was unattached, hadn't observed any such mourning period. In fact, as she is fond of pointing out, he'd kissed her first and then asked her out for the weekend.

Drake gives Rashad a shove. "Dude!" he says. "You gotta ditch the whole 'bro' crap."

"He's right," Stephen agrees, nodding. "It's lame."

"Well, you're the expert on that," Rashad shoots back. "Two words: Tribal armband."

Over the Christmas break, and still unbeknownst to his parents,

Stephen had gotten an upper arm tattoo. It was supposed to be an intricate, deep black depiction of razor wire, but, low on funds and impatient, he'd decided to let the friend of a friend who was passing through town do the work. Consequently, the lines of his tat are shaky, the points of the barbs crooked, and what should be broad fields of black are, at best, splotchy patches of charcoal.

"Fuck you," Stephen shoots back. "At least I had the balls to do it."

Rashad scoffs. "Whatevah." He turns back to Alyssa. "Where were we?"

She looks at Michael, causing his adrenaline to spike. "You were going to tell them what your favorite prom themes were."

"They weren't that good. You're biased."

"Are you kidding?" She turns back to the others. "You'll die when you hear these."

Rashad glares at Michael. "I can't wait." There is no doubt in Michael's mind that whatever he says next, the boy will rip apart. The fact that it is the perfect ever ammunition is simply an unfortunate coincidence.

"You know," Michael says. "I need to get home. We should go." He lifts an arm and signals the waitress to bring their check.

Rashad lets out a long, low whistle. "I know *that's* never happened before. Asking for the check? Man must really, really not want to have this discussion." His stare seems to bore right into Michael's chest. "I wonder why."

"It's not that."

"Then tell us fast." He narrows his eyes at Michael. "Don't worry about the check. I'll get it. If you tell us, that is."

Michael knows that continued resistance will only draw further scrutiny; also, that if he tries to substitute some other moronic titles for the ones he'd most ridiculed with Alyssa earlier, she will call him on it. "Fine," he agrees. "But don't say I didn't warn you."

"Dude, what the fuck?" Stephen asks. "Just tell us."

"Okay, one was 'Hot summer Knights.'" He enjoys the lack of reaction it gets. "See? I told you. They're not funny. They're stupid."

"There were better ones," Alyssa says. "Like—"

"'Knights in Bloom.'" Michael hopes if he says a few, she will drop the subject before he gets to the worst of them.

"And 'The Stroke of Mid-Knight,'" she chimes in.

"Wait, what's funny about that?" Stephen asks. "I mean, sure, the whole 'Cinderella' reference is lame for high school, but it's not hysterically bad."

Drake elbows him in the ribs. "Not 'midnight,'" he says. "Knights, remember? With a 'k.'"

"So it's 'The stroke of mid-Knight'? Why's that funny?"

Drake rolls his eyes. "Dude, really? Were you dropped on your head as a baby? Stroke? Like 'strokin'?"

Stephen's eyes widen. "Oh!"

Drake breaks out in raucous laughter. Even Rashad cracks a smile.

Thinking he's dodged the bullet, Michael nudges Alyssa. "Okay, c'mon. Let's go."

"And the best one," Alyssa says. "Well? Go on."

"I…I don't remember."

"Sure you do."

"I don't."

A sharp pain erupts on the front of Michael's shin, from the toe of a shoe being spiked into it. "OW!"

Rashad smiles. "A gentleman always does what a pretty lady asks him to. Stop stalling."

"'Crystal Stars'…?" Alyssa prompts.

Michael winces, partly because of his smarting shin, but mostly in anticipation of the reaction his next words will garner. "And Satin Knights,'" he says.

Maybe, he prays, *broken up that way….*

Drake wrinkles his nose. "The hell?" he asks. "What's a 'satin knight'?"

Stephen shrugs. "Beats me."

Rashad whips a balled-up napkin and hits him in the chest. "Yeah," he says. "A 'satin knight' probably would love to 'beat' you, know what I'm sayin'? Probably would offer to 'polish your armor,' too. Know what I'm sayin'?" He turns and looks right at Michael. "Isn't that right?" The words *You're the expert…*seem to hang in the air between them. It makes the hairs on the back of Michael's neck stand on end. The tips of his ears begin to burn.

He gives Alyssa a shove, to get her to slide from the booth. "Let's go."

"Hey, man," Rashad says. "I asked you a question."

Mercifully, at that moment the waitress arrives with the check. "Tell your mommy and daddy thanks for the dinner," Michael says. He catches the look that passes between Stephen and Drake, and knows the decision he made, though risky, was the right one.

Rashad sits up taller. "What did you just say to me?"

"You heard me." Michael hands Alyssa her coat and grabs his own from the seat.

As they reach the front door Rashad calls after them, "Like your parents don't pay for everything you buy, too! At least my folks don't put everything on credit!"

EHRICHTO OPENS HIS eyes and a thin corona of sunlight, seeping from behind the window draperies, blinds him. He has no draperies—and no window—in his room in Panajachel. He pulls his arm up to shield his face.

Dorjan's scent still lingers on his skin. It makes him smile. He takes stock of his body, noting that in many places he itches, an indicator of muscle and skin tissue knitting back together. Other spots still actively ache, the result of fresher bites, and non-bites, too. It wasn't only fangs Dorjan used to enter his body. Ehrichto's nerve endings still thrum pleasantly from the assault.

His pleasant mood is shattered by a sudden thought: the rest of the kel, who must have been banished from the house on the previous evening, will no doubt soon return.

You will stay? Dorjan had asked, not saying aloud but implying *Even knowing what you do? How we are?*

Decades earlier, Ehrichto had been drawn into Dorjan's realm under false pretenses, the belief that theirs was to be like any other, normal, relationship—namely, that it involved only two, mortal, people. Outside factors conspired to help deceive him: a crackdown on indecent behavior, led by the vice squad, landed Dorjan in jail for two years and scattered the remaining members of the kel around the globe. Dorjan had already decided to make Ehrichto one of their number; he'd therefore had a contingency plan drawn up for him, just as he had for the others, a safe haven picked out to which he'd had Ehrichto spirited away in the middle of the night, while he took the fall for the crimes they all had committed.

Because he'd grown up the son of a cigar factory owner, Ehrichto was working the counter in a tobacconist's shop when he met Dorjan. While Dorjan was being hauled off to jail, Ehrichto was being hustled onto an overnight flight bound for the Cuban tobacco fields. While his lover sat in prison for two years, Ehrichto had overseen the operation of one of his cigar rolling operations on the tropical isle.

It was hubris, mainly, that had led Dorjan, two days into their Havana reunion, to turn Ehrichto without first floating the idea past him that theirs would not be an exclusive—or even human—relationship. The rest of the kel had been around, of course, during the brief time they'd spent together before the vice squad's raid. They were residents of the same apparently former single-family home in which Dorjan lived. Ehrichto had, understandably, assumed the house had been broken up into individually leased rooms during the Depression, as so many former mansions were. He thought the other men residing in the house had been Dorjan's neighbors first, then his friends, and in some cases more than that. Only one member of their rank rubbed him the wrong way: Philip, who occupied the room directly beside Dorjan's and looked at him in a way that stirred the green-eyed monster slumbering in Ehrichto's soul. Anyone could see it if they wanted to: whatever had transpired between Dorjan and Philip, for the latter, at least, was not over. Philip still had designs on his ex.

Or so Ehrichto thought. As it turned out, designs were not necessary. Dorjan turned Ehrichto without stopping to even consider the possibility that he would have a problem with the concept of an open relationship. He seemed surprised to learn that Ehrichto thought he and Philip had broken things off. There was nothing to break off, he said. They enjoyed each other's company and so lived in close proximity to one another to take advantage of that fact whenever it pleased them. It was the same way with all the residents of the house. They were all his lovers. The difference between them and Ehrichto was that their turn to enjoy Dorjan's full attention was over, and his was still happening.

Dorjan couldn't comprehend why Ehrichto would be upset—much less devastated—by the revelation. *We're men*, he insisted. *This is how we are made.* But Ehrichto was devastated. It became clear he would not recover from the shock, would never come around, and that had led to Dorjan's eventual decision to break his own cardinal rule and grant him leave from Abaton. He'd set him up in Guatemala to play Maximón incarnate.

But that was then, Ehrichto thinks, pressing his arm down even harder over his eyes. *This time*....

This time, the situation is very different. He knows full well who Dorjan is—a vampire who believes men are incapable of feeling romantic love. He knows the kel'an is a nest of vampires with whom his sire is intimate, and who are intimate with one another. He knows the group uses sexuality as a lure to attract a revolving door of hangers-on from whom they feed, and with whom they freely copulate.

Movement in the bed beside him draws his attention. He rolls onto his side and lifts his arm, intending to touch Dorjan, to see if he is awake yet and, hopefully, enjoy the illusion for just a little while longer that it is only the two of them in the house.

He gets a start when he sees that the sleeping figure in the bed beside him is not Dorjan. The stranger is towheaded and, for all intents and purposes, chiseled from rose quartz. The shock propels Ehrichto out of bed, not so much scrambling out of it as hurtling over its nearest edge. He twists in mid-plummet, becoming entangled in the sheets, and ends up caught in a pushup position with his palms on the carpet and his feet suspended in midair, bound by trailing linens.

Directly in his field of vision are Dorjan's polished shoes. Ehrichto looks up, and finds his sire dressed in gray slacks and a voluminously cut shirt of lilac-colored silk.

"Well, that was quite a display," Dorjan says.

"I was expecting it to be you. It was a surprise, that's all." Ehrichto pulls his left foot free but cannot free his right one.

"Not a pleasant one or you would have had a different reaction." Dorjan shakes his head in obvious disappointment. "You can relax. He's been here not even one hour. You were out the entire time, and we left you…inviolate."

In his attempt to free his still-trapped limb Ehrichto rolls onto his back. Only then does he realize he is naked. He grabs the sheet and pulls it across his body.

Dorjan drops into a crouch. "Also not pleasant?" he says. "You talk in your sleep." He leans down, looks Ehrichto in the eye. "I do not like to hear you say the names of the men who got away."

There is only one other man, besides Dorjan, with whom Ehrichto has been intimate. If he called out names, plural, it must have been Nick's and Wren's.

"They didn't…they aren't…. How many times do I have to tell you it's not like—"

Dorjan holds up a hand, silencing him. "This is a warning, Ehrichto. If you'd done that a few hours ago, while awake, instead of just now, while dreaming, it wouldn't be Philip who was preparing to go to Guatemala right now, it would be you. But even asleep…." He lets the thought trail off, glares at Ehrichto for another long moment, then stands and strides across the carpeting and out of the room.

Ehrichto stares up at the ceiling and tries to figure out how in the world he is going to manage to keep his promise.

"What the hell was that back there?" Michael snaps at Alyssa as they climb into her car. The whole business about Satin Knights still has him shaking, on the verge of hurling. "Are you trying to get me killed?"

"They were joking."

"No. You don't understand how guys are. That? That was not friendly."

"C'mon. Calm down. They were just messing around with you."

"'Messing with,' Michael corrects. "Not 'around with.' Damn, that's all I need, for you to say that."

"Say what?"

She is not this clueless, and that unnerves him further. The more he considers it, the more the whole conversation feels off to him, not accidental at all but calculated. Planned. He throws a quick glance her way and feels his heart skip a beat, because the look in her eyes is terrifyingly clear, is anything but innocent. As if to quell any lingering doubts he might have about that fact, she says, "What? Are you afraid they'll say that 'messing around' is the sort of thing Satin Knights would do together?"

Michael feels queasy but forces a laugh. He shrugs and shifts his gaze to a point over her shoulder, the blinking neon sign of the adjoining business, a tax preparer's office, and from there down to the lights on the dashboard. "Of course not. That's dumb. They aren't even a real thing."

"Aren't they?"

"No." His right hand is squeezed so tight around the door handle that his fingers are beginning to go numb. It's the only way he can maintain his apparent calm. "Hey, I really do need to get home, like an hour ago," he says. "Can we go?"

CRUZ, GUPTA AND *Lin*, Lloyd Ferguson thinks. *Cruz, Gupta and Lin.*

The phone picks up after just one ring. He hears a click, followed by the sound of an open line. "Greater Louisville Sports Medicine and Rehab," a female voice says. "Can you hold?"

"Yes." There's another click and then the canned music starts, something vaguely current, a song he doesn't know the name or artist of but has heard being played in grocery stores and as the soundtrack to television commercials for a few years. He wishes medical offices still used nineteen-seventies singer-songwriter tunes when they put people on hold.

Cruz, Gupta and Lin.

The music stops. "Thank you for holding. This is Laurie speaking. May I help you?"

He's grateful that the voice and name are not familiar, despite his having been in that office several times.

"Good afternoon, Laurie, my name is Lloyd and I'm calling on behalf of HealthOne," he says, his goal being, always, to say his spiel quickly enough that the representative cannot interrupt him, but slowly enough that it is possible to make out the words, "...as part of our mandatory annual audit for the state's Department of Health to ensure that our patients are able to make an appointment within the required six-week time frame, and I need know what the next available is for a few of your doctors."

As usual, silence emanates from the other end of the line. He uses the time to mull the last few of his words. Maybe fifty or a hundred utterings back "reCHOIR-ed" became "re-KWAR-ed" and now he can't stop saying it. If his wife Julia were to hear, she would have a fit.

"Hold, please."

This time there is no music. As usual, Lloyd wonders if that is intentional, an auditory version of solitary confinement inflicted upon those who dare to add one more thing to the already-full plates of the medical office staff. He has similar thoughts during his day job as a pharmaceutical sales rep whenever he's made to sit in a waiting room for upwards of half an hour despite needing simply the quick signatures of the doctors in order to be on his way.

Not that he ever gets their signatures without at least trying to pitch the company's new wares, the way other reps so often do. Every day he eavesdrops on what purport to be sales pitches but in actuality are commentaries on the weather or on the weekend's prospects for a good game of golf. It wouldn't irritate him if it weren't for the fact that the chit-chat almost never progresses to educating the doctors about new medicines or newly discovered uses for established ones. Too often there is light banter and nothing more.

Lloyd prides himself on always trying to do the job the way it is supposed to be done. Though most of the doctors refuse to even look at him, though they snatch the pen from his hand, scrawl their name on his form as quickly as possible and dash off without a word, he always tries to get his sales pitch out. In his opinion that experience gives him an advantage in the HealthOne moonlighting gig, allows him to be able to get out everything he needs to say without giving the staff member on the other end of the line a chance to interrupt.

Like the doctors on his regular route, the medical assistants on his call list for this job are prone to wandering off without a word of warning. *But at least during this they can't take my pens*, he thinks. Doctors are forever walking off with his Danshen Pharma stick pens, seeming to regard them as just one more of the freebies he has to dole out, along with notepads, pill-shaped foam squeezies, and business-card holders. The phenomenon, universal, has had the odd effect of making cheap Chinese-made stick pens the most coveted item among the sales reps in an industry where trips for four to Cancún are a frequently offered client incentive.

Lloyd hears the phone line reopen. A soft smacking sound tells him that Laurie the medical assistant is now chewing something, most likely gum.

"Mmm, what's the patient's name?" she asks. He pictures her as wearing lavender surgical scrubs, imagines the shapeless v-neck top printed with cartoon cats.

"I don't have an actual patient. There is no patient. It's an audit."

She gives an exaggerated, exasperated sigh. "Well, I can't access appointments without a patient name."

Less experienced staff members often do not know how to access the information he needs without typing in a patient's name.

"I'm certain it's possible," he says. "Ask someone else how to do it."

Instead of pushing hold and once more consigning him to limbo, Laurie drops the receiver onto the desk. The clatter causes Lloyd to jerk the phone away from his ear. When he moves it close again, he hears muffled voices, the clicking of keyboard keys, and finally, more but softer clattering.

"The next available for Dr. Cruz is May twelfth."

Lloyd consults the calendar in front of him. The date is four days outside the mandatory compliance window, which is problematic but not surprising. The Kentucky Derby is rapidly drawing near. In just two weeks it will be time for Thunder Over Louisville. Many professionals, including doctors, take vacation from Thunder Day in mid-April right up to the first Saturday in May, always the date of the Derby. They can be seen escorting their out-of-town guests to the many festival events that lead up to the actual race; occupying the choicest spots at Thunder or packing the stands for the Pegasus Parade; sipping white zinfandel out of plastic cups while waiters and waitresses compete during the Run for the Rosé; or cheering on the Belle of Louisville in the Great Steamboat Race. They also make up the guest list at the biggest fundraising dinner of the year for the organization his wife Julia runs, the venerable Conway Charities. She's scored a real coup for this year's event by managing to secure use of the glassed-in riverfront lobby of the Kentucky Center for the Arts. Tickets for the evening have sold very well.

Everyone is busy getting ready to play host to the visitors from all around the world who will soon descend upon Louisville. Already the city is frenzied; it's hard to get around because so many roads are undergoing last-minute repairs, so many landscaping trucks double-parked, their crews rushing to get spring flowers planted on every median. Wives haul carloads of used clothes to thrift-store drop sites, while husbands unload old tires and broken televisions at the city dump.

The year is flying, he thinks. *August tenth will be here in the blink of an eye.*

Tuition and room and board fees for his son Michael's first semester at the University of Kentucky are due on that date. *The total amount of seven thousand sixty-six dollars must be received by close of business*, the paperwork that accompanied the acceptance letter warned, in order for Michael's student's enrollment to be protected.

"Hello?"

Lloyd snaps back to the present. He looks down at the date he scribbled on scratch paper. "Uh, that's just outside the allowable window," he says, grabbing the computer mouse and scrolling to the proper line on the spreadsheet where he compiles the information. "Don't you have anything earlier? I'd hate to see the doctor fail the audit. There is a fine, you know."

Assistant Laurie types again. "There's an opening for the nurse practitioner April fifteenth at eleven-thirty," she says.

He enters the data. "Got it. Now for Dr. Gupta—"

"I'm sorry. This is taking too long. You'll have to call back later." Before Lloyd can protest, the line goes dead.

He sits, stunned and furious, until the dial tone begins bleating in his ear, urging him to hang up his end of the line. He considers using it to bash the computer keyboard to smithereens, imagines hurling the monitor through one of Julia's precious treatment-less windows.

Seven thousand sixty-six dollars by August tenth, he reminds himself once his temper has cooled. He takes a deep breath, grabs the phone, and begins dialing the next number on the list.

DESCENDING THE STAIRCASE, Ehrichto finds that half a dozen of the would-be European fashion models he first glimpsed lounging out on the

wraparound porch when he arrived almost two weeks ago are occupying
the ornately carved wooden chairs of the grand entry hall. All of them are
still basically unclothed, many sporting little more than underwear, and
each has a plate of food balanced on his bare legs. None of them leaps to
their feet this time, though they do all eye him warily, this stranger who
has been in the house for a fortnight yet never before shown his face in
the public areas. Ehrichto has kept himself confined to Dorjan's quarters.
To his relief his sire has neither challenged that, nor brought anyone in
to join them.

Today, though, things are different. Before heading out of the room
Dorjan had announced it was a special day. He'd instructed Ehrichto to
dress and meet him downstairs.

Ehrichto guesses the young men strewn about the house are also
eyeing him with suspicion because they have figured out that he is not
a stranger after all, nor of their rank; that he is, in fact, one of the kel. A
prodigal son returned home.

Dorjan proves not to be in any of the rooms that open off the
hall. There are only more young men hunched over plates of food. Not
surprisingly, in the dining room a spread fit for an army has been laid out
across the twelve-person table and there is a man dressed in a crisp white
double-breasted chef's coat attending it. The fellow flinches when he sees
Ehrichto and then resumes his work, without inviting him to eat.

Because he knows what I am, Ehrichto thinks, amazed that even after
sixty years, being recognized as a vampire still gives him a little thrill.

He turns to leave but immediately draws back, startled by the sight
of Willem Garrett, framed in the doorway to the entry hall. Willem's look
is anachronistic: he has paired black jeans and a high-collared parchment-
colored shirt with voluminous sleeves. His blond hair is combed straight
back and gelled into place, and for footwear he has chosen the sort of
mid-calf lace-up patent leather boots Ehrichto associates with British
military personnel.

"Hello again, Ehrichto. You're looking well as always."

Ehrichto stares and says nothing.

"I'm sorry I couldn't make it back sooner," Willem says. "There was
business in Prague. Our nightclub there is doing very well." He makes a

show of looking Ehrichto up and down. "Those clothes suit you."

They are Dorjan's clothes, of course. Ehrichto has been wearing his things since shortly after his rude awakening, the evening after their reunion. After he untangled himself from the bed sheets he'd gone looking for his clothes but could not find them. Dorjan informed him later that he'd confiscated the utilitarian items. *I took them*, he'd said. *For charity*. It was unclear whether he'd meant by that that he'd donated them to the needy, or that he regarded divesting Ehrichto of the garments to be a charitable act. Faced with going naked or donning the bed sheet as a toga as his only options, Ehrichto had given in and put on some of Dorjan's less ostentatious wardrobe selections.

This evening he'd chosen a wine-colored Egyptian cotton shirt and black dress pants.

Ehrichto ignores the remark about his attire. "Do you know where Dorjan is?" he asks. "He told me to meet him downstairs."

"I do."

"Care to tell me?"

Willem crosses the room to where Ehrichto stands and circles him with eyes cast downward. Ehrichto's thoughts shift to the man working the buffet, and whether or not he is watching them. The rustle of cling film followed by a metal-on-metal scraping sound provides the answer; the cook is discreetly keeping busy, setting trays of food into warming stands, for the young men in the hall.

Willem stops in front of Ehrichto and lifts his gaze. "What do I get out of it if I do?"

Ehrichto scowls. "Forget it. I'll find him myself." He turns toward the door but Willem catches his arm.

"I'm glad you've returned, Ehrichto," he says. "I like a challenge. So many things around here are too easy, but not you. You're hard." Sotto voce, he says "No matter what you say to the contrary."

Surely, the man at the buffet is straining to hear. "That may be," Ehrichto replies. "But it's Dorjan who is on my mind, not you."

Willem's grip on his arm tightens, becoming a painful pressure. "At the rear of the landing," he says through gritted teeth, "there's a second set of stairs leading down to the underlair. That's where he is." He smiles coldly. "Have fun today," he says. "And think of me."

Every house of Dorjan's that Ehrichto has ever visited has had what passes for a subterranean level. In New Orleans, where the water table is mere feet below street level, it is always the ground floor, the windows painted over and disguised with heavy draperies. For a time Ehrichto wondered if having access to a lightless space was a necessary part of vampire existence, if the underlair's dark corners in fact hid coffins filled with native soil, à la *Dracula*. He'd had a similar thought when Dorjan first brought him to the shallow terrace just below the summit of Volcán San Pedro, wondering if the cliffside caverns dotting the rock face might be a sort of interterranean workaround. He'd been surprised to find that he was being installed in the vine-covered, humble wooden structure built by an ornithology professor for use during his research sabbaticals. It was, Dorjan explained, sufficiently remote and—especially for someone who did not need electricity or plumbing—move-in ready. The ornithologist, he elaborated, had died a few years earlier, and none of his students was interested in roughing it in the cold and damp of the cloud forest, even for the chance to catch a glimpse of the country's elusive national bird, the resplendent quetzal.

The barely there terrace overlooked a much, much larger one, on which stood the ruins of the city of Chiya, the birthplace of the god Maximón. The birdwatcher's shack proved the perfect retreat for Ehrichto and, years later, following improvements to make it possible to cook food and heat water for bathing, for Nick and then seven-year-old Wren as well.

"I'll enjoy explaining to Dorjan that you refused to let me go," Ehrichto says to Willem, who still has a death grip on his arm. "We both know how much he loves to be kept waiting."

Willem doesn't seem cowed. "Yes, we do," he says. "We also know how much he enjoys being told no." He jerks Ehrichto back a half step. "That luxury, which you believe you've enjoyed up until now, is forfeited." He pulls Ehrichto backward again, so that their bodies are pressed together, then snakes his free hand down his front and grasps the hard bulge at his crotch. "When I'm done with you it *will* be thoughts of me that are responsible for this," he says. "I'll reduce you to a gibbering heap on the floor, make you call out my name in front of all of them, turn you half-mad with longing. I am that good." He withdraws his hands so abruptly it feels as if he has pushed Ehrichto away. "Run along for now," he sneers. "You don't want to keep the master waiting. He has a fun day of surprises in store for you."

JUST AS WILLEM described, on the backside of the sweeping central stair there is a second one, its entry tucked away behind the lowest landing, out of view of the foyer. Ehrichto descends the marble steps into darkness.

As with past houses they've had in New Orleans, the lower level of this one is not, in fact, subterranean, not even halfway underground. Like on the two upper floors of the house the windows are heavily draped, but unlike those, these emit no light whatsoever. He guesses they have been painted over as well as masked with fabric. He would not know they were there at all but for the fact that he can feel the sunlight seeping through at intervals as he moves through the room.

He expects to encounter more of the rent boys, and more of the kel, too, but he hears nothing, smells no one. When his eyes at last adjust to the deep gloom he discovers that the space is taken up with deserted pool tables and an equally unattended bar.

Through a doorway on the far wall he enters a room that is only slighter brighter, outfitted as a movie theater, with long rows of bench-like couches. Par for the course (because the kel is not a democracy), Dorjan is seated front row and center with both of his arms stretched along the top edge of the couch's low back. Ehrichto imagines other figures—members of the kel or rent boys forfeiting dinner for the chance to *be* dinner— stretched out along the couch to either side of him, the crowns of their heads disguised by the silhouetted swells of Dorjan's shoulder muscles. Ehrichto has the strong urge to turn and bolt not simply from the scene but from the city. Pictures flash in his mind. He sees himself boarding a plane back to Guatemala, and then at his doorstep, and finally, back with Nick, somehow shaking sense into him, convincing him to stop shooting toxins into his veins. *Maybe if I could just restrain him long enough,* he thinks. *Maybe he could stop.*

"Come in, Ehrichto," Dorjan calls. Still facing forward, he slips his left arm from the back of the couch and pats the seat beside him, proving that that spot, at least, is unoccupied. "Come. Sit with me."

Ehrichto forces himself to make a study of the floor-to-ceiling drape hanging a dozen or so yards from the front row as he makes his way forward. He tells himself it is a nice touch, this nod to the converted vaudeville stages he remembers, the world's first cinemas. He tries not to think what awaits him in the front row, or who might be lurking there. Because it is easiest, he

imagines André Cozart nestled tight to Dorjan's side, sees him pivot to get a glimpse of the new arrival, even hears his genuinely jovial greeting: *Hey there, Ehrichto. Glad you've finally decided to come home.*

As benign as that image might seem, at the same time Ehrichto pictures Dorjan's right hand, dropped just below the sight line of the sofa back, lazily stroking the top of André's bare arm. The thought is almost too wrenching to bear.

Reaching the first row, he braces himself and turns.

"You're alone," he says.

Dorjan gives a rueful smile before turning his head. "No, I am with you." He pats the cushion beside him again. "Sit."

Ehrichto obeys, and Dorjan drapes an arm across his shoulders. Then he pulls him close for a kiss. For a moment Ehrichto is elated, until his inner doubts pipe up and temper his enthusiasm. *This private audience won't last,* he thinks. *You mean nothing more to him than any of the others do.*

The thought makes him ill. He tries to push the sick feeling away, wills himself to focus on the kiss, on the taste of the other man's mouth and the silky feel of his lips. When Dorjan leans back, Ehrichto instinctively starts to move forward, but his sire puts a hand on his chest, stopping him.

Dorjan leans even further back, but keeps his hands up between them, his palms facing Ehrichto, in a clear gesture for *Stay.*

Ehrichto can't figure why on earth Dorjan would seek to put distance between them. "What are you doing?" he asks. A second later he hears a doorknob turning somewhere behind him in the dark, followed by the creak of a seldom-used hinge. Sunlight floods the room. Too late, Ehrichto shields his eyes; even after the door is shut again, the rods and cones protest the sudden assault, rendering him blind.

Dorjan tenses, a subtle shift Ehrichto feels because of the upholstered seat they share. Every muscle in his sire's body goes taut as surely as if he were bracing for a fight. "Maynna?" Dorjan asks, all playfulness now gone from his tone. *What is this?* The seat cushion rocks again as he gets to his feet.

The room resolves itself slowly, pale and inky grays becoming familiar forms. Ehrichto gets a sinking feeling when he recognizes two of them: short-by-Western-standards Wren and still painfully thin Nick. His eyesight continues to return to normal, making it possible to see that the third and final figure is Philip, the member of the kel with whom he has most dreaded being reunited.

The side-by-side comparison between Philip and Nick is shocking. Philip's shoulders are back and his barrel chest is pushed out, making his white t-shirt appear painted on. His faded jeans are artfully ripped, and he has pushed a pair of sunglasses to the top of his head. The arms of the glasses hold his medium-length dirty-blond hair back off of his face. Done up as he is, he might pass for a California surfer dude, if not for the calculating gleam in his eye.

Because of it, the impression he creates is that of a Manhattan hipster feigning the L.A. look in order to land a West Coast record deal. Nick, on the other hand, might as well be a creature conjured by the brush of a master artist in medieval days; some tortured half-human thing let loose from the third canvas of Bosch's triptych *The Garden of Earthly Delights*. His eyes are rolled back in his head, his jaw is slack, and everywhere his skin is so tightly drawn over his bones he most resembles a skeleton standing before them. His wrists are bound with rope, his ankles tied in such a fashion that he is just barely able to shuffle forward.

Dorjan looks at Philip. "I don't understand," he says. "Why did you bring them here? Why have you not fed him?"

"I brought them because I *did* feed him," Philip replies. "Many times. My efforts have had no effect."

"Nothing at all?" Dorjan asks. Ehrichto has never heard his sire sound so surprised, or so alarmed. "It isn't healing him?"

"No. But it's more than that. He looked *better* than this when I arrived." Philip's eyes dart to Ehrichto's and away again. "Whatever's wrong with him," he says, "it's getting worse."

THREE

Beside the front edge of a cemetery is as weird a place for a coffeehouse as the back edge is for a city park with a skate ramp, but the brew the Bardo serves up is tasty and packs such a wallop of caffeine that it is almost as effective at helping Marc to focus as the medicines his doctor prescribes, and he is hooked on the stuff.

The lettering on the glass door matches that which is painted on the plywood shingle hung from rusty chain, cantilevered over the sidewalk. *The Bardo, est. 1992*, it reads, below a character he thinks must be Sanskrit for the same, the state of limbo between incarnations in Tibetan Buddhism. When he pushes the door open, the brass bells tied to its interior handle jangle, announcing his arrival.

The theme of Eastern mysticism is picked up by the eggplant-colored walls, teal cornice, and scattered gold accents. Oil paintings of the Buddha compete for wall space with promo flyers for local bands. An acid-bright print of the Hindu god Ganesh is taped to the back of the cash register.

In addition to being hooked on the coffee Marc has a fascination with the boy stationed behind the register. Even before he saw him ride a board he had the kid pegged for a skater, possibly even one of the ones who've attempted nearby Breslin Park's off-limits cement half-pipe, because he is all lean muscle and scar tissue and spiky dirty-blond hair, and because he has S-T-R-8-E-D-G-E tattooed above his knuckles and sXe on each of his forearms. Marc has run into members of the straight-edge community before; he knows a portion of the skateboarding community is drawn to their modern day asceticism, the way of enlightenment through extreme self-control. In his view the collective of young teetotalers and sexual abstainers is a cult, a late twentieth-century version of hair-shirt-donning monks, or the Puritan movement. He figures anyone fanatical enough to tattoo symbols of a rigid belief system onto multiple locations on his body must be keeping serious demons at bay.

As usual, by the time Marc has reached the counter, the barista/skater boy—who he's learned from eavesdropping is named Jon, sans "h," like the hairband singer—has a tall to-go cup of the shop's daily special prepared. Also as usual, he says nothing at all as he waits for Marc to fork over his cash. Today, though, he never once looks up at him. His attention is focused on his bent arm, and on the crusty patch of road rash that runs from his elbow almost to his wrist.

What is unusual is that Jon is alone behind the counter. Normally, he is accompanied by a fiery little Latina named Lia. Marc assumes she is his girlfriend, though he's never seen the two engage in public displays of affection. Then again, the kid is straight edge, so either he has a desperate urge to kiss her and views giving in to such desires to be a form of weakness, or else he doesn't want to kiss girls at all and has discovered a face-saving way to disguise that fact.

Lia's passion is drawing. Sketches she's done of the coffeehouse's regular clientele are tacked up around the shop. Most are straightforward portraits, but a handful of them are biting commentaries on their subjects. From these Marc has gleaned that the Morticia Addams wannabe perpetually camped out at one of the corner tables is Jon's little sister Danielle, and that she spends her afternoons in the shop doing her homework because their parents, who both work, consider her too young to go off with the goth poseurs who comprise her posse. Marc knows the three older teens only by their goth subculture pseudonyms, which Lia never fails to include in the unflattering sketches she does of them. In the newest and most audacious she recast the three, who go by "Ethereal," "Roman" and "Shelley," as the Three Stooges, making it clear that she regards them as idiots of the highest order. Much to the chagrin of his sister and her friends, Jon tacked up that piece, entitled *The Three Ultra-Goths*, in the coffeehouse's most prominent spot for artwork—just below the menu board.

"Must've been one hell of a wipeout," Marc says, nodding to indicate the massive scab the boy is still picking at, on the underside of his forearm. "You do that over at Breslin on that fenced-in skate ramp?" He has a recurring fantasy of sucking the kid off in the picnic area, exposing the holier-than-thou shtick for what he's sure it really is—overcompensation for the terror struck in him by his attraction to other guys.

The kid looks up but maintains his stony silence. His irises are gray, his skin bronzed from spending long hours outdoors. The bridge of his nose is crooked, likely from multiple bad breaks, and there's a cleft in his chin. Marc pictures him twenty years in the future, pushing forty but still ruggedly beautiful, a bull of the boardroom, the business equivalent of a rock star at a red carpet gala, his muscles barely contained by an expensive suit and his hair shockingly long for an executive. The thought causes a stirring in his groin.

"Breslin Park," he says again, determined to engage the kid in conversation. "Right around the corner from here at Payne and Lexington? C'mon, I know you know what I'm talking about."

The boy's gaze narrows. "Two-fifty," he says.

"Are you telling me you've never broken in there and skated that ramp?"

"Two-fifty."

"What d'ya think I am? A cop?" Marc hands him a five and waits for his change. He would tell the kid to keep it but he's tried that before; it would only be handed back. While he waits something new tacked low on the wall beside the register catches his eye, a clipping from the *Courier-Journal*, a photo of the entries that made it to the finals in the art contest sponsored by a local organization, Conway Charities. The caption reads:

Equine Art Pieces Win Places and Show for Good Cause

Someone has taken a marker to the photo, adding devil horns to the head of the photo's human subject, the charity's president, Julia Conway Ferguson, but it isn't that which has caught Marc's eye. Though she stands directly in front of the table on which the artwork is displayed, making it impossible to see all of the pieces, he can see just enough of the third one from the left to know what it is: one of the headdresses from the production of *Equus* he starred in last year. His adrenaline surges. "Holy fuck." A nervous chuckle escapes his lips. "Baxter's gonna kill me when he—"

"Here."

Jon holds out the change. Marc looks at the photo again, then back at the bills. "You know what?" he says. "Hang on to that. I'm gonna need another coffee."

NICK HAS BEEN brought to Ehrichto's private quarters and propped up on pillows on the bed. Wren sits in a chair on one side of him and Philip on the other, the latter with the right sleeve of his shirt rolled up and his wrist held to Nick's mouth. Wren's gaze never leaves his father, but now and again Philip casts a glance over his shoulder to the conversation area on the far side of the room, where Ehrichto, Dorjan and the rest of the kel'an have gathered to discuss the situation.

The suite rivals many New Orleans apartments in square footage. Despite his having realized almost immediately after turning him that his new progeny did not fit in with the rest of the group, and despite having then set him up on his own in Guatemala, Dorjan has reserved space for Ehrichto in each incarnation of Abaton, in anticipation of this very day. As with previous versions, the room is decorated in shades of deep blue, a move Ehrichto regards less as an effort to make him feel welcome than a bit of sympathetic magic on Dorjan's part, an attempt to convince him he wants what he does not. His theory seems to be borne out by the fact that each succeeding room has used more of the color than the last, and used it more blatantly. This room looks like the interior of a lapis-lazuli mine.

Dividing the room into the bed chamber and seating areas is a wide Byzantine archway adorned in blue, black, and white mosaic tiles. Upon entering the space and seeing the way it framed the bed, Ehrichto's first thought was that it was intended to designate it as sacred space. Now, seated beside Dorjan on a strategically placed couch, it dawns on him that it is a proscenium arch, defining a stage.

The wall behind the king-sized platform bed is painted the color of the evening sky. Under it are layered Afghan carpets of azure and cobalt. The frame of the bed and its button-tufted headboard are each upholstered in black leather and adorned with wide, horizontal, bright gold bands. Lastly, the bed's yellow-gold linens are accented by an enormously scaled, unmistakably masculine ruffle which runs around the turned-down edge of the top sheet. It looks not unlike a giant lasagna noodle has been laid across the bed, and Ehrichto assumes that is intentional. He thinks it is meant as a nod to his Sicilian heritage, and he is thankful that all of his efforts to get Dorjan to comprehend that he was born and raised in Louisville, Kentucky, have failed, fallen on deaf ears. He shudders to think where the other would take things if he once understood that he had a horse theme to work with.

"He's better already," Coronel says, to no one in particular. The newest addition to the kel, he is a complete stranger to Ehrichto, and most resembles him. Though his hair is not as long and he is clean shaven, his hair and eyes are sable-hued and his skin has a similar olive tone.

"I mean, just look at him," he says, nodding toward the scene through the archway. "Don't you agree his color is coming back?"

Perched on the edge of the conversation area's only side chair, Willem sets down the book he has been absently flipping through, a title Ehrichto recognizes from his father's collection of tobacciana. Willem scrutinizes the scene across the room, then turns and looks at Dorjan, who is standing behind the couch on which Ehrichto is seated. "Will it last, though?" he asks. "And why did it happen in the first place?"

Dorjan places a comforting hand on Ehrichto's shoulder. "Those questions we can worry about later."

His idea for how to cure Nick had been to reset his turning by carefully draining and then feeding him. He started the process, and since then the rest have been taking turns feeding their ailing guest, operating on the only theory they can all agree on: that supplied with enough vampire blood, his body will repair itself.

Across the room, Philip stands and begins rolling down his sleeve. Seeing him heading their way, Willem gets to his feet. "I suspect we won't know for some hours yet if this is really working. I'm going to head downstairs for a bite. Ehrichto, why don't you join me?"

Dorjan replies before Ehrichto can. "He's fine here. Let him be."

Philip pauses in the archway. "Going down for a drink?" he asks Willem.

"I am. Are you coming?"

"In a bit. You go on."

"Coronel will go with you," Dorjan says. It's an odd statement. When he gives Ehrichto's shoulder a firm squeeze, it causes trepidation to prickle the skin on the back of his neck.

He and Philip are up to something, Ehrichto thinks. *Again.*

Coronel rises and shuffles out of the room after Willem. When they are gone, Philip steps from the archway. "I hope they didn't leave on my account?" he says.

All Ehrichto can think about is Wren, and the fact that he—and Nick, too, if Nick is even conscious, which at the moment is impossible to determine—is the reverse audience for this second stage the arch frames. He's acutely aware of the deal he made with Dorjan. Because of it, anything at all might happen next and he will have no say in the matter. *Not that I ever did.* In Dorjan's opinion Ehrichto, when he was the greenest addition to the kel, refrained from acting on his true desires merely out of a misplaced respect for, or fear of breaking, social mores. He'd chosen a questionable method by which to free his newly made progeny from society's fabricated restrictions. In bed one night Dorjan took hold of Ehrichto's wrists just before the door opened and Philip entered the room. He'd held them fast while the interloper climbed into the bed. When Ehrichto continued to protest, Dorjan silenced his objections with a kiss.

"That's what you meant when you said today was a special day," Ehrichto says. "You asked me to meet you in the underlair because Philip was on his way there."

He remembers how earlier, after pushing him back, Dorjan had held up his hands, and shown his palms. At the time the gesture was puzzling, but now Ehrichto understands. It was his sire's silent way of proclaiming, *This time there will be no doubt. You will join in willingly.*

Dorjan tried, years before, to make the argument that Ehrichto had participated willingly, because he hadn't fled the bed and the room after Dorjan broke their kiss and relinquished the hold on his wrists. But it had been clear to Ehrichto what Dorjan wanted him to do, just as it was clear, from the look in his eyes, that if he refused even to give it a try, he would be persona non grata among the kel. And it was clear it didn't matter, anyway. His relationship with Dorjan was not, and could never be, what he wanted.

He'd stayed, and afterward withdrawn from all of them, until Dorjan was forced to admit he'd misjudged the heart of his latest progeny, and made arrangements for him to live apart from them.

Feeling Philip slide onto the seat beside him, Ehrichto closes his eyes and drops his voice to a whisper. "Not in front of my family. Please."

The hand on his shoulder withdraws. By the time Ehrichto has opened his eyes and managed to turn around, Dorjan is gone.

"Accept his help and then call him a dog," Philip says, half under his breath. "An odd methodology, but also a ballsy one, I'll give you that."

"That wasn't my intention."

Philip grips him by the chin and turns his head until their eyes are locked. "Like hell it wasn't." Ehrichto tries to break free but can't. Philip leans closer. "Stop acting as if you hate me."

Ehrichto twists his head sideways until he has broken Philip's grip and then leaps to his feet. He moves to stand behind the couch. "I don't hate you," he says. "I despise you."

"I have proof to the contrary."

"You can't possibly."

Philip reaches a hand into his left front pocket and struggles unsuccessfully to extract something. He scowls and withdraws a set of keys, which he tosses onto the seat cushion, then pulls out a small bundle wrapped in a bit of the brightly colored cloth that is the Guatemalan highland's stock and trade.

"Before I figured out I wasn't going to be able to cure your friend over there," Philip says, glancing over at Nick, "I took a little side trip up the volcano to Chiya."

It was Philip who first made the connection between the cigar-loving, whisky-guzzling deity Maximón and the unhappy new vampire in the kel's midst, and suggested to Dorjan that he might be made happy—or happier, at least—if he was allowed to go off and impersonate the god. Philip had discovered Maximón (and the group dedicated to him) decades before, while exploring the ruins of the Maya city of Chiya, birthplace of the myth. He hadn't had a use for the knowledge right then, but filed it away for future use.

"Why would you do that?" Ehrichto asks.

"Dorjan said you buried Nick's recipe book somewhere along the trail leading up to it. I was hoping to find it."

"I burned it."

Philip looks surprised. "No. Dorjan's accent is thick, but I'm certain he said buried."

"I buried the drugs. The book I burned," Ehrichto explains. "I didn't tell him that. I didn't think it mattered."

Philip scowls. "Fantastic. It could've helped us unravel this mess, not to mention also saving me from scavenging through underbrush like a fool. But you didn't stop to think that through, did you?" Ehrichto looks away. "That rashness, Ehrichto, is, by far, your least charming trait."

"What's in the bundle?"

"I'm getting to that. There was no Feast of Maximón this year, was there?"

The abrupt change in topic catches Ehrichto by surprise. He drops his gaze to the floor. "No."

"So I was right. You have managed to undo the second-best situation any vampire could hope to find himself in. That's brilliant. It's a damned good thing you're here, then, isn't it? If you go back there, you'll starve."

Ehrichto resents the insinuation that he abandoned the annual Feast of Maximón, when in reality he was kept from it through no fault of this own. "You have no idea what he's been like."

Philip holds up the mystery bundle. "I found this little gem on a makeshift altar in the plaza." He unwinds the cloth, revealing a taper formed from pink wax.

Far from feeling enlightened, Ehrichto is confused. "It's a candle."

Philip's scowl deepens. "Don't play coy with me." He holds the thing up so Ehrichto can see what is scratched into its surface, a crudely drawn Chi Ro, the symbol of Christ.

It makes no sense that Philip would be so pleased by having discovered the thing. "Why do you think that's remarkable?" Ehrichto asks, just before understanding dawns. "Wait, you think that's a letter, don't you? A capital 'P'?"

And you think it stands for "Philip."

"Hopeless romantic that you are, you had Maria do a love spell."

"For you and me?" Laughter erupts from deep inside Ehrichto. He notes the way Philip looks away, sees the hard set of his mouth, which betrays his embarrassment. "Careful," Ehrichto says quietly, in order to keep Wren from hearing. "Someone might start accusing you of being a hopeless romantic as well. They'll revoke your membership in this modern orgy for an infraction like that."

Philip's free hand grabs a fistful of Ehrichto's shirt fabric and uses it to pull him forward, over the back of the couch. It is all Ehrichto can do to keep from tumbling into him. He struggles to keep his voice calm. "I'm fairly certain you're doing this wrong. You should have come over to this side first."

"Listen to me," Philip warns. "If you keep on this way it's your membership he'll revoke. Do you understand? He will expel you again."

"And you'd hate that."

Philip pushes him away, back to his feet.

"It's not the English letter 'P,' it's the Greek letters 'Chi' and 'Rho' superimposed," Ehrichto says once he has steadied himself again. "I'm surprised you haven't encountered it before, as educated as you are. It symbolizes Christ. Maria used it because she knows it has something to do with Catholicism and I have a history with that religion."

Maria is the great-granddaughter of Itzananohk'u Ujpan Puac, who was the *telinel*, or shaman, of the group at the time of Ehrichto's arrival. Since turning thirteen almost a year ago, she has developed an intense fascination with the herbs, oils and incantations that are the domain of her uncle Acan, the current telinel.

Philip narrows his eyes. "Why would she know anything about your mortal years?" he asks. "You're the Maximón, nothing more." He waits for a reply, but Ehrichto remains silent. "You haven't been telling her about your past, have you?"

"How would I? I don't speak Tz'utujil or Spanish and she doesn't speak English."

Most of the members of the cofradía barely acknowledge Ehrichto. Even in the middle of festivities, most refuse to look him in the eye. Partly, he knows, that is out of respect. Unchecked directness is considered rude among Guatemalans, just as it is among groups the world over, including the secular and Catholic communities in which Ehrichto grew up in Louisville. For the most part, though, it is fear that stills their tongues. Some of the cofradía have seen him heal from wounds that would kill a mortal man, and all can testify that he doesn't age. There is no question that he is not mortal.

Maria alone has always met his gaze, has always seemed to grasp that he is a sentient supernatural being, capable of feeling lonesome if ignored. Even before she could walk she would stare at him for hours. As soon as she was able, she'd begun crawling toward him, and then climbing into chairs to sit beside him. Years ago he'd begun to talk to her, or more correctly at her, commenting on various goings on, or voicing an opinion about one or the other of her relatives, or about the things that were troubling or pleasing him at home with Nick and Wren.

She understands more English than he cares to admit to himself, and he's said far more to her than he should. Even before the last time he saw her he was aware that there were only a few crucial details remaining that she did not know. That night she'd come right out asked him for them, point-blank.

After Nick plunged a syringe of his witch's brew into Ehrichto's neck and knocked him out for days, causing him to miss the start of the Feast of Maximón for the first time in the sixty years he'd been portraying the deity, there seemed nothing left to do but escort Maria safely home to Santiago Atitlán and go to New Orleans, back to Dorjan, to beg him for help. It seemed likely to Ehrichto that he and Maria would never again cross paths. What difference did it make, he'd asked himself as the *motora* cut through the polished obsidian surface of the water, if she knew the last of his secrets? Didn't she have a right to know the truth? After all, she alone had been there that night, in the ruins, waiting for him to arrive.

Staring at him, she'd abruptly asked "¿Cómo se llama de verdad?"

Though he had no aptitude for languages beyond English, his grasp of individual words coupled with the way she'd said it allowed him to decipher her meaning. He considered ignoring her, but felt too guilty for having missed the start of the feast.

"Ehrichto Antonio Salvatolle," he said.

She hadn't missed a beat. "¿Italiano?"

He shook his head and then shrugged. The answer wasn't as simple as that. "My parents were born in Italy. I'm an American."

She asked another question, and must have seen his brow furrow, for she then bit her lip and translated slowly, "How many birthdays?"

They knew he wasn't human. What harm was there in her knowing his precise age? "¿Noventa y cinco?" he said and then, for good measure, restated it in English. "Ninety-five." After that he remembered, and laughed. "Well, not quite. Not until Sunday." He thought a moment, and then did his best to translate. "Mi cumpleaños es, uh, Domingo."

She didn't seem surprised. "Sí. También es Pascua." Before he could ask what she'd said, she asked a different question, one he did know the meaning of. "¿Qué es usted?" *What are you?*

He considered ignoring her, or feigning incomprehension. "I'm not a god," he admitted instead. "I'm…just a vampire."

"I DIDN'T TELL her anything," Ehrichto says to Philip. "What do you take me for?"

"Then how did she know to do this?" He holds up the candle.

"I already told you. That's—"

"I know what you said but you're wrong. First of all, I'm familiar with the Greek alphabet, thanks. Secondly, I know how the thing looked when I first picked it up, which is why I'm certain that what you believe is a Chi Ro is nothing but a 'P' with a scratch through it." Philip turns and glowers at Nick. "Your sidekick over there didn't much appreciate that I was attempting to save his sorry ass, compadre. He fought me and very nearly won. This fell out of my pocket during our wrestling match."

"Let me see that," Ehrichto says, rounding the end of the couch and snatching the candle from Philip's hand. He rotates it until he sees the carving. "Look, this right here is the—" He stops. What he thought was a hastily drawn Chi appears to be exactly what Philip said, a careful capital "P" with a couple of jagged scratches across it.

"I-I don't understand," he says.

WHEN HE STEPPED from the cloud forest into the clearing he'd found Maria on her knees at the center of the plaza, surrounded by a rainbow-hued forest of votive, novena and taper candles. Though her back was to him and she was dressed in the traditional garb which all the women of the cofradía favored, and despite the fact that her hair was braided down her back in their same fashion, he'd known exactly who it was. None of the others would wait days for him to appear, and no one but Maria was brave enough to stay in Chiya alone. Not even her uncle would have done that.

She was praying low, a hodgepodge of Tz'utujil and Spanish with a handful of borrowed words from other languages, including English, sprinkled in like seasonings. His ear caught a string that was mainly in Spanish, containing several words similar enough to their English counterparts that he could discern them.

"...lamento...purgatorio...aflicción...sangre...misericordia...salvación..."

"Ehrichto? What's going on? What are you thinking?" Philip asks, but Ehrichto barely hears him.

HE'D ASKED WHAT she was doing there, where the rest of the cofradía was. She'd answered in a flurry of words until he held up a hand to stop her, and then in more manageable sentences. Not that he could understand them any better, really, but a few words had leapt out, and remain in his memory. "Es la hora de despertar de sueño," she'd said, something about the hour, about time and dreams. "Digo oraciones por su resurrección."

He'd assumed it was all references to Holy Week, to Easter but now he's not so sure.

"What does 'despertar' mean?"

"To become awake," Philip says. "Why? What's going on?"

Ehrichto ignores him and turns to face the other half of the room. "I'm so sorry," he says to Wren, who glares back in reply. "There's something I have to go do. I won't be long, I promise."

MICHAEL FEELS FOOLISH trying to look at Robert without looking like he is looking at Robert. The two are sitting cross-legged on the floor of Michael's bedroom, sharing a joint. Michael watches Robert pull a deep toke. "I like what you've done with the place," his guest says through clenched teeth, nodding with his chin to indicate the walls, which are all but covered by hundreds and hundreds of photos, most of them cut from magazines, some printouts of GIFs taken from websites devoted to the band. Robert's band, and Michael's favorite—the Cure.

Robert passes the roach. Grasping at the notion which is tickling the edges of his mind, the realization that the images papering the room do not belong in this house, that they are from his old room in the house they used to live in, on Donohue, Michael says "Angel food cake" instead of "thanks" and then bursts out laughing, because that's funny, and also because he's high.

Robert begins to giggle, too. Michael grows uneasy. "What?"

Robert stops giggling and lies flat on the floor. "Why did you say 'angel food cake'?"

"It's what the paint in here is called."

"No!"

"Yes."

Robert sits back up. His brow is furrowed. "Are you gonna smoke that?" he asks, indicating the smoldering joint, but before Michael can relinquish it he turns away again, and resumes looking at the walls.

Michael harbors a thrill to know that Robert admires his handiwork. It makes him proud, because the sea of images surrounding them is not some random, easily assembled collection, but rather a carefully crafted display. All the shots are of the singer alone, not with the rest of the band, and most show him at the start of his career, when he was still slim and gorgeous in a spooky, avant-garde way. Michael is pleasantly surprised to find that the singer—who has been prone to picking up weight as he's edged ever closer to middle age—has somehow grown young and slim again.

Rather than almost forty he is once more twenty-something, sporting the more pulled-together, New Wave look he had in the very early days of the band, rather than his current penchant for hockey jerseys, a look that snarkier members of the press have dubbed "Goths on ice."

Michael notices that the singer also no longer looks as if he just clawed his way out of the grave. His poet's eyes are now neatly rimmed with kohl instead of smeared with it, and his hair, normally a rat's nest of dyed black strands, is swept straight up. A well-fitting button-front shirt (kept from being too corporate in feel by its print—a sea of tiny, white, sperm-like paisley shapes swimming across an inky background) completes the look.

Or does it? Michael wonders, gripped by the fear that Robert, who is still turned away from him, might yet be revealed to be wearing the bright red lipstick that in recent years has become his trademark. Michael finds the sight—Jane brand's Reddest, set against the powdered stark white of Robert's face—to be stomach-turning. He can't fathom why the singer ever adopted the look.

Then, all at once, it is no longer Robert, but Joey "Pocket Rocket" Peccorini, first cousin to Roman, one of Michael's former best friend Jon's little sister Danielle's moronic circle of friends, the so-called Ultra Goths. The setting has changed, too. Michael and Joey are in the front seat of the latter's mid-nineteen-eighties economy car, just as they had been on the night of the Blind Cave Fish concert at the Louisville Gardens.

Michael hadn't known the guy was Roman's cousin, of course. He would've steered clear of any associate of that jerk, who loathed him because Danielle had had a crush on Michael since she was eight years old. When he decided to accept the stranger's offer to go to his car and get high, Michael knew only that Joey looked as if his surname might be Corleone or Gotti.

The Cure's CD *Galore*, just released, pours from the dashboard speakers of the rundown car. Every time Michael has the dream, it is the album's single, "Wrong Number," that plays in the background, and he knows why. The radio dial had bathed the interior of the car in an eerie green glow (a green that appeared to have worked its way into the very fibers of Joey's hair), and the coil of the car cigarette lighter they used to relight the joint they passed back and forth and back again was a molten, throbbing orange. They were the same colors invoked in the track's lyrics.

Joey reaches over, just as he had in real life, and grabs Michael's wrist, pulling his hand to the bulge in his crotch. Michael was then, and still is in the dream, too scared to do anything but allow his hand to rest where Joey placed it. After a few seconds, dream Joey roughly shoves it away again. "Jesus, seriously? Are you like totally baked already?" He takes a killing toke from the roach, flicks the remains of it and the still-glowing lighter into the ashtray, and unzips his fly. "Damn, guess I gotta do all the work." He grabs Michael's hand again and guides it back into his lap, past the confines of denim and cotton. "Here."

Michael wraps his fingers around the solid, silky length of Joey's dick, so like his own and yet not his own. All his synapses fire. He can't believe another boy—a real tough guy like Joey, no less, an obviously straight boy—is letting him touch him there.

"Man, pot always makes me horny as shit," Joey says. "Same with you, huh?"

Michael swallows hard, and shrugs, and lies, as he had that night. "Yeah, always," he says, though the truth is just the opposite: smoking pot has always made him deeply paranoid.

"Gives me the munchies, too," Joey says. "How 'bout you? Hungry?" Michael feels Joey's right hand on the back of his head, urging him down. "C'mon, suck my Italian horn," the guy murmurs. "Suck it real good and you'll get the tasty cream filling."

In real life, the line was so awful and cheesy that it jarred Michael from his trance. It does the same in the dream. Wriggling free of Joey's grasp, he fumbles for the door release and tumbles from the car.

Michael opens his eyes and is startled to find himself not, as then, sprawled on the asphalt at the feet of several onlookers, some of them from his school, with Joey back in the car acting outraged and repulsed, telling them that "that little cocksucker just made a grab for me and I shoved him away," but rather back in his ecru room. For a second or two he isn't sure if he is really awake. Then he spies the clock on his bedside table and gets a fresh jolt from seeing that is a quarter past ten. He flips back the covers and is about to spring to his feet when he remembers that it is Saturday. He collapses back against the pillow. Heat radiates from his groin, throbs in time with the song still echoing in his head.

He exhales and climbs from bed, stumbles to his desk, and fires up his computer.

There are two messages in his inbox.

From	Subject	Date
Ernest Rimmer	Meet singles in your area	
		Sat., 4/17/99
Mr. Chauncey Kennedy	URGENT—you must see this now!	
		Sat., 4/17/99

Michael recognizes the first as an advertisement for a so-called dating website which requires users to first verify that they are twenty-one years of age before granting them access. He deletes the file and, though it is almost certainly spam, clicks on the second one, to open it.

"Dear Sinner in Christ, this is the word of the Lord thy God," it begins. He knows he should stop, should delete it, but he can't keep his eye from scanning down the page:"…that the WICKED will not inherit the kingdom? Neither the SEXUALLY IMMORAL nor IDOLATERS, nor ADULTERERS nor MALE PROSTITUTES nor HOMOSEXUALS nor THIEVES nor the GREEDY nor DRUNKARDS nor SLANDERERS nor SWINDLERS will inherit the kingdom of God."

He hits the ESC key, deletes the file, and logs back off the internet. Shaken, he sits a moment, watching cartoon windows fly across his screen and waiting for his erection to fade. Once it has, he gets up and heads to the bathroom, to shave.

WHEN HE OPENS the door and steps out into the hotel's hallway, Ehrichto finds two men standing to either side of a wall-mounted ashtray. A hand-lettered sign taped to the wall to the right of the ashtray reads *Rotary Club Thunder Luncheon* and sports an arrow pointing at an open door.

"When tipped with amber, mellow, rich and ripe." Ehrichto lifts his cigar case so the men will be sure to notice it. "Mind if I join you?"

"Not at all, please do," the taller of the two strangers answers. "And feel free to quote more Byron, if you know any." He wears an ash-brown suit with alternating light and dark blue pinstripes and clutches a fedora by its brim with his left hand; in his right he holds a cigar just a shade or two lighter than the warm chocolate hue of his skin.

"I know only one other by heart," Ehrichto says. "And it's about betrayal, not tobacco."

The stranger's broad smile is flanked by dimples. "Fine by me." He looks to his companion, who, Ehrichto notes, has nothing to distinguish him from a million other pot-bellied, pasty-skinned middle-aged males of Anglo-Saxon ancestry except for the fact that his stark black suit shines like chintz and is too big for him through the shoulders. The second fellow scowls.

"Well, maybe another time," Ehrichto says. He pulls apart the halves of his cigar case, withdraws a slim black stick, and nods to indicate the tall stranger's cigar. "Monte Cristo No. 4?"

"Yes, and worth all the trouble to acquire."

"I don't doubt it." Ehrichto strikes the flywheel of his lighter and begins to slowly rotate the tip of his cigar just above the flame to toast it.

"If Castro would only go on and die, eh?" the fashionably dressed stranger asks, before chuckling. "Then we could smoke them any time we wished."

Ehrichto remembers the night four soldiers arrived by Jeep, put a gun to the head of his right-hand man, Ernesto Famosa y Díaz-García, to press him into service as their interpreter, and announced they were there to take everything for the state. Then they'd grabbed another of his workers, and put a gun to his temple, too. *They say it is your choice,* Ernesto explained. *Either open the safe now, or they will shoot Benito and then you will open it. They say*—He'd faltered then, a cry escaping his lips. Ehrichto had had to urge him to go on. *They say his blood will be on your American hands.*

"I have no love for Castro," Ehrichto says to the fedora-toting stranger. "Still, yours is a rather an odd sentiment, isn't it? Coming from a surgeon."

The stranger's mouth drops open in obvious astonishment. "How did you—?"

The end of Ehrichto's cigar has deepened in color and begun to release its aroma. He holds it in the flame and takes a deep draw, pulling in a mouthful of rich smoke, then smoothly exhales a cloud of white. "Your Rod of Asclepius tie tack tipped me to the fact that you're a doctor. The Cuban cigar and the fine Italian tailoring of your suit said you're a very successful one. The surgeon part was pure conjecture."

The man in the chintz suit thrusts his hand in Ehrichto's direction. "Jackson Harris," he says. "Harris and Miller? Two locations—Louisville and Lexington." The move is such a blatant attempt to steal focus from the doctor that Ehrichto considers not returning the gesture just to watch the fellow squirm. Before he gets the chance, however, Harris seizes his unoffered hand and begins shaking it, rotating his arm like a steam piston turning the wheel of a freight train. "You've probably seen our ads?" the fellow says, his inability to keep from phrasing it as a question strengthening the impression of his being insecure. "We're on all four of the local affiliates, every commercial break from two to four every afternoon."

As soon as Ehrichto can he extracts his hand from the other's grip and extends it to the dark-skinned gentleman, who switches his cigar to his hat hand in order to return the gesture. "Dr. Everett Reilly," the man says as they shake. "Cardiothoracic surgeon, at your service."

"Very pleased to meet you, Doctor. I'm Ehrichto Salvatolle."

Using his real name is an adrenaline rush, and seeing it fail to trigger any sign of recognition in either of his acquaintances' eyes, a disappointment. *It's true that it closed down a long time ago,* he thinks, *but Salvatolle Cigars was a Louisville institution. Can it really be that neither of them—cigar smokers, no less!—has even heard of us?*

"Did you come into town specifically for Thunder, or was that a lucky coincidence?" the doctor asks. He transfers his cigar to his teeth and brushes fallen ash from the band of his hat. A flash of gold alerts Ehrichto to the presence of a wedding ring on his finger.

Well, that's hardly a surprise. "The latter," Ehrichto says. "I had some other...business."

His first trip back to his hometown in more than eighteen years had proven to be a fool's errand. He'd gone to the cemetery not knowing what he might find. Some members of the cofradía swore that Maria's uncle Acan had the ability to change fate with his powders and spells. Who knew if his niece could do the same? Seeing the candle with the letter "P" carved into it and realizing that her prayers had called for the intended to be awakened from the time of dreams, he'd panicked. Hardly aware of what he was doing he'd snatched up the ring of keys Philip left on the couch. One key he'd recognized as his own; not a surprise, given the revelation that Philip harbored feelings for him. Ehrichto had gone in search of the garage and there found the Porsche Carrera he'd left in the kel's care.

Deep down he'd known he wouldn't encounter anything unusual when he got to Louisville and the cemetery where Patrick was interred, that what he was hoping to gain by taking the trip was time to think through everything that had happened in the previous fortnight. Philip was right in one regard—he *did* have a tendency to act first and consider the consequences second. Hadn't he done it not once but three times in that brief period alone? First, when he took Nick's drugs and buried them on the trail to Chiya, then when he burned the recipe book, and finally when he'd run off to his hometown, chasing a ghost.

He hadn't needed to enter the mausoleum to know the crypt was undisturbed. A drift of brown leaves was piled against the outside of the scrolling ironwork door. He made a mental note to tell Richard, through Dorjan's law firm, of course, to clean it up. He wouldn't stand for Patrick's resting place looking like a trash heap.

"Well, this is not how the city normally is," Dr. Reilly says. "Don't get me wrong, I like Thunder and all the rest of the Derby events, but.... Let's just say we collectively lose our minds at this time of year. My fear is you're going to get an erroneous first impression of Louisville."

"You're the only one who's lost his mind," the lawyer interjects. "After March Madness, this is our best time. It should be like this all year long."

It was not Ehrichto's intention to stay in town for any length of time. He'd promised his nephew he wouldn't be long, and already made the deal with Dorjan to return to Abaton for good. Still, he'd been unable to bring himself to simply exit the cemetery and get right back on the highway. He'd felt compelled to make one additional stop.

He was surprised to find the downtown area being set up for a crowd, city workers re-arranging sawhorses to block off certain lanes to traffic, and police milling about on foot, their cruisers parked haphazardly across otherwise deserted intersections. From signs posted in shop windows he'd figured out that Thunder Over Louisville began with an air show at two in the afternoon and culminated after dark with a sizable display of fireworks.

"Oh, don't worry, this isn't the first time I've been to Louisville," he assures the doctor. "My family is from here, actually. But, now, it is the first I've been in town for this Thunder. I gather it's quite a big deal?"

The doctor chuckles. "It's only the biggest annual fireworks show in North America."

The Thunder Over Louisville hype is not what brought Ehrichto to the hotel. He'd been stopped in his tracks by the sight that greeted him at Fifth and Main. For a moment he'd wondered if he was somehow on the wrong block, or if maybe they'd renumbered the streets, any explanation at all besides the obvious and unthinkable, that they'd torn down the Conway Distillery building. But they had. All the buildings on that block were gone, replaced by an angular structure of light brown brick and soaring green glass capped by a rounded, corrugated steel roof. The building looked for all the world like a giant soup can laid on its side.

He was standing, staring at it in horror when a voice to his left said, "I know, right? It's the only decent block in the whole damned city. I so cannot *wait* to get to Man-hattan."

The speech pattern was code Ehrichto recognized. Sure enough, when he turned around he found an attractive young man—perhaps even as young as twenty, it is getting harder to guess ages with so many years of existence behind him—already well dressed and carrying a suit bag. When their eyes met, a hungry, feral look ignited the young man's whisky-colored irises.

"Well, hello there, stranger. Welcome to our fair city. How may I be of service to you?" As if his meaning wasn't already perfectly clear the gent ran the tip of his tongue between his lips. It was a more brazen move than any Ehrichto had seen displayed in public in decades. A part of him wanted to ask, *How did you know?* The other part didn't care. He needed to feed, and Dorjan was right about one thing—sex was a magnificent lure to use to get someone alone quickly.

The name tag pinned to the stranger's shirt read *Marc Payette— Morning Concierge*. He volunteered that he was on his way to work at the Galt House Hotel, next door to the very modern building, and also that if Ehrichto was interested he could find a place for them to have a little fun. Ten minutes later, they'd been in a suite that had not yet been paid a visit by housekeeping.

It was not the same Galt House Hotel Ehrichto remembered from his childhood. Marc Payette rattled off a list of locations the hotel had occupied downtown, as well as the fact that after the original owners shut it down in 1919 it had stayed closed until 1971. The current hotel, therefore, had been named in honor of the original but was in no real way connected to it.

The décor of the lobby was atrocious, all dark wood paneling and deep red fabrics, reminiscent of the riverboat casinos and brothels depicted in the Wild West pictures Ehrichto remembered from decades earlier, but the patrons crowding the space were, in his opinion, far too poorly dressed to be either frontier cardsharps or whorehouse johns.

The worst offender was a man wearing a t-shirt on which was emblazoned the image of a jumping trout, beneath which were the tag lines: *Master Baiter Tackle Shop—Never Leave Empty Handed* and *It's all in the wrist!*

"Sorry about all the Joes clogging up the place," Marc the concierge said as he led the way to the stairwell. Ehrichto hadn't taken his meaning, which must have shown, because the young man had paused, and clarified his statement. "You know," he said with a conspiratorial air. "The Average Joes. Not Starbucks but Cuppa. Surname: Lunchbucket. Husband of Mary, etcetera, ad nauseam." He furrowed his brow. "The dire straights?"

"Let's not worry about them," Ehrichto said. It was the right answer. The concierge had smiled and started up the stairs, taking them two at a time.

Ehrichto did not expect the rooms to be decorated in the same riverboat bordello motif as the lobby but they were. When Marc Payette threw open the door of the second-floor suite—with a bona fide flourish and "Ta da!"—Ehrichto saw the space was crammed with at least a dozen pieces of walnut and brass "Early American" style furniture. The sofa, chairs and heavy draperies were upholstered in a harvest gold, olive and brown tweed version of a fabric he believed was called Herculon, and wrought-iron lamps stood on every table, nightstand or desk. Though every one of the fixtures had been left switched on by the previous guests, the wattage of the bulbs in each was low and their cumulative output all but completely absorbed by the dark furnishings.

"These rooms always get cleaned last," the young man explained. "No one likes them because of the meeting rooms located just across the hall. We get a lot of complaints about noise and cigarette smoke. A lot of the time they don't even get booked, but of course they're booked today. We're sold out."

He threw the deadbolt and reached a hand between Ehrichto's legs. "Now how's about you let me show you some uncommonly good Southern hospitality?"

"I LIKE FIREWORKS as much as the next man," Ehrichto says to Dr. Reilly. "But there's an air show first, at two o'clock, is that right? And the fundraising dinner for the Patrick Conway Memorial Fund?"

"Do you mean Conway Charities?" Dr. Reilly asks. "We're both going to be there, too."

Through the door Ehrichto had heard them discussing the organization, the dinner, and the air show. Hungry as he was, hearing the surname Conway caused him to freeze. What were the odds of that name coming up during such a brief stop, he'd wondered. But it was another name, strung with the Conway, that had led him to grab Marc Payette by the upper arms and haul him back to his feet just seconds after the younger man had sunk to his knees.

"No," Ehrichto says. "I don't. It was originally founded by Morris Conway as a memorial for his grandson Patrick after the latter's untimely death. The name was changed by the grandson's widow much later, after Morris died."

Dr. Reilly and Harris exchange puzzled looks. "I've never heard that," the doctor says.

"My family and the Conways were prominent at the same time," Ehrichto explains. "We had some rather…intimate…dealings."

"Well, we're both friends with the husband of the woman who currently heads the organization," Dr. Reilly explains. "He's the only reason we attend the thing every year."

"Why is that?"

"Because his wife is…difficult." Reilly says. The lawyer snickers.

Ehrichto hears footsteps approaching. He turns and finds Marc Payette heading their way at full trot, leading with his belt buckle.

The lawyer rolls his eyes. "Oh, Jesus. Look what's coming."

"Excuse me, gentlemen," Ehrichto says, turning away from them. He and Marc meet in the middle of the hall, a hundred feet or so away from the others. "All right, you have an appointment for a fitting at twelve thirty, here." Marc hands Ehrichto a scrap of paper on which an address is scrawled. After his eavesdropping, Ehrichto had tasked the concierge with getting him a ticket to the dinner that night and finding him a tuxedo.

"And the dinner?"

"Next on the list."

"It should have been first."

Marc Payette purses his lips. "I'll get you in, don't worry. I'm very good at what I do." He pauses and lifts an eyebrow. "Very, very good." He winks, twirls on one heel, and dashes away.

He is still well within earshot when the lawyer says loudly, "Goddamned little pansy."

Ehrichto sees Marc's footsteps falter just before he disappears around the corner. The lawyer chuckles. "Guess he didn't like that, huh? Well, too bad. I can't stand faggots. Especially the ones that flaunt it like that."

"You'd prefer they kept their proclivities to themselves?" Ehrichto asks, walking back over to join the other men.

"Hell, yes! I mean, not that they really can." The lawyer snorts. "You can always tell when a guy is that way."

Ehrichto taps his cigar against the rim of the brass ashtray. "Is that so?"

"No, it's not," Dr. Reilly says, so forcefully that Ehrichto wonders if the wedding ring he wears might not be a prop. "And even if you believe it is, Harris, as a lawyer you should know better than to make such sweeping generalizations. It's liable to get you sued."

"For what? Finding people like that disgusting? I'm entitled to my opinion."

The doctor glares at him. "And I'm entitled to mine, of you," he says. "I think you're an ass."

"If you'll excuse me, Doctor, I have an appointment to keep," Ehrichto says. He extends his hand to the man. "I'll see you tonight?"

"I look forward to it," Dr. Reilly says as they shake hands.

"As do I."

The lawyer extends his hand, too. Ehrichto looks from it up to his face, gives a derisive snort of his own, and then turns to go. The glimpse he catches of the man's shocked expression is almost enough to bring a smile to his face.

MICHAEL'S FATHER GESTURES to the placard propped on an easel at the base of the stairs that lead up to the Bomhard Theater, the mid-sized of the three performance venues in the Kentucky Center for the Arts. *"Sir Gawain and the Green Knight," now on stage!* the poster proclaims. "Isn't that the play you saw with your class?" he asks. Michael turns and gives the thing a onceover, as if he hadn't already noticed it. "I guess," he says, shrugging.

"What do you mean you guess? How was it? Any good?"

"It was okay."

"What's it about?"

"I don't know." His father's shifting expression lets Michael know he is about to be reminded that English Literature has always been his strongest subject. "This Knight of the Round Table has to go do this thing," he says quickly. "Face his death. It sounds a lot cooler than it was."

"Do you think it's something Alyssa might like? It says here that they have an evening performance next weekend."

Michael is certain Alyssa would love the dress that the actress playing Lady Bercilak wore, would love the catlike way she stalked about the stage while attempting to seduce the noble knight Gawain. "No, I don't think she'd like it," he says. "I mean, it's kind of like *The Canterbury Tales.* The language is archaic. We spent a lot of time discussing it beforehand. I don't think someone who didn't do that would really get it."

Michael's Honors English class *had* spent a long time studying the poem, a unit that turned into an extended discussion about personal integrity, societal expectations, and gender roles. Even so, it had been difficult to get through the story without some of the students having a meltdown about certain events in the plot.

Gawain was a knight given quarter by a lord and lady in exchange for his agreeing to engage in a game with them (an allegory for the chivalric code, their teacher had explained). The rules of the game called for him to exchange whatever he received in the manor each day for whatever his host won while away from it, out on the hunt. It sounded innocuous enough, but it was a trap. The knight's hosts were testing his devotion to the honor code.

Each day after her husband left the manor, Lady Bercilak tried to seduce Gawain. He was duty bound to refuse her more serious advances but also obliged to do as she requested; he therefore had no choice but to accept a chaste kiss from her. To satisfy the rules of the game, he then had to give that kiss to the lord of the manor.

The Gawain unit had created an uncomfortable tension in class. Michael couldn't fathom that a miscellaneous group of kids—not Honors English students but just anyone—would calmly accept the story. Sure enough, the minute the lights began to dim the room had erupted in screams and laughter that had never fully died back down. At first, the kids seated around their class seemed put off by the archaic language. Bored or confused by the story's setup, they'd squirmed and shifted in their seats, whispered to one another, cracked gum, and seemed to Michael to be one enormous, segmented organism with six hundred pairs of arms, legs and lungs, but proportionally little brain matter.

Their impatience grew while Gawain became ever more tightly ensnared. Only when Lady Bercilak pressed herself against the noble knight did their attention finally focus on what was happening onstage. Predictably, a wave of catcalling ensued, the cover of darkness affording the mob anonymity and with it the opportunity to be rude.

Guessing that the thought of one man being made to kiss another would transform the titters he'd heard in the classroom into gales of unmitigated, scornful laughter in the theater, in advance of that scene Michael had slipped far down in his seat, had retreated into his jacket like a turtle in its shell, until the collar was well up over his ears and his hands were buried within the sleeves. He'd hunkered down and prayed for someone to pull a fire alarm or throw something onto the stage and hit an actor, anything that could end the performance prematurely.

He felt tension building in the kids around him as Lord Bercilak reappeared from offstage, presented his house guest with the day's spoils, and waited for the action to be returned. When Gawain leaned in to plant a kiss on his host's cheek, Michael heard kids behind and beside and in front of him collectively gasp in horror. He imagined they expected Lord Bercilak to strike Gawain, or throw him from the castle. When the king only turned and smiled, angry voices rose up from the sea of bodies. "Faggots!" a deep voice shouted. Another called out, "Goddamn! They're *both* queer!"

"Well, speak of the she-devil," his father says, pulling him back to the present. Michael turns and finds Alyssa, dressed in sweats, sneakers and a bright green rain slicker, and carrying a garment bag and duffel, coming toward them across the lobby.

"Hey," he says as she nears. "What are you doing here?"

Her expression is one of mild alarm. "You shaved."

Michael's hand goes to his face. During the few minutes spent thinking about Gawain he'd managed to forget, but now he feels naked again, exposed.

"Uh, yeah. And you're here early. Why are you here?"

"I told you I would be. Why did you shave?"

He gives her a look he hopes conveys *Duh. Why do you think?*

"Well, I'm going to go check on your mother," his father says. "I'll see you kids later." He takes off down the hall behind them, heading in the direction of the shuttered coat check.

Michael doubts his father is really planning to seek her out. The reason they were hanging out at the bottom of the Bomhard Theater staircase is so that they would be able to duck into the hallway just behind it if they heard or saw her coming. They have no plans to show their faces this day, at least until the dinner gets underway and they have no choice. It's their tradition to stay out of the line of fire but within earshot, on the off chance that she should bellow one of their names.

Michael is not at all sure what effect Alyssa's presence will have on things.

"I know you said you would be, but it's so early," he says. "We have hours left just being stuck here."

"So?" Alyssa takes his hand in hers and interlaces their fingers. "I enjoy hanging out with you."

Michael takes the garment bag from her and then extracts his other hand to take the duffel. "I know just where we can stash these," he says. "Follow me."

MEDICINE, MARC THINKS as he yanks open the door of his cherry-red VW Cabrio. He fishes under the passenger seat until his fingers find the small grease-stained nylon barrel bag stashed there.

He is about to pop the childproof cap on a square white plastic bottle labeled *Methylphenidate* when he hears footsteps approaching his car. At the same time, the pager clipped to his belt buzzes. *Sullivan, coming to chew me out,* he thinks. He shoves the bottle back through the bag's zippered opening and drops the bundle into the pile of crumpled fast food sacks filling the passenger-side foot well, then pulls the pager free and checks the number.

Just as he thought, it is his boss, Sullivan. He pictures the man scanning empty cars, looking for him. Expecting to come face to face with him, Marc twists in his seat, but sees only a security guard, still several cars away, checking for the hotel-issued passes that are meant to ensure only patrons and staff get into the garage, not people who have come downtown for the air show and fireworks. It's the reason Marc came down to the garage; to put one of the passes on Ehrichto Salvatolle's charcoal-gray Porsche Carrera.

Images of the handsome Italian flash in his mind's eye and flood his system with even more testosterone. He's already so hard it hurts, but can't stop thinking about the dark intensity of the man's eyes or the deliciously disheveled look he acquired each time his hair fell across them. He can't stop hearing the way the stranger rolled the "r" in his first name. *Eh-rrr-ichto Salvatolle*, he'd said, making Marc think of sexy Ricky Martin, currently taking the world by storm, shaking his ass and singing "Living La Vida Loca" on every screen in every bar—gay or straight—in the known universe.

He listens again, but no longer hears footsteps. There is only the sound of his respiration and the slow drip of rain making its way into the heart of the garage through concrete seams, swelling into droplets and breaking free, an indolent urban waterfall.

The lengthy pauses between the drops makes Marc want to scream. *Medicine*, he thinks again, lurching forward. He digs through the bag once more, locates the square bottle, and claws it open.

Square white bottles have been a prescribed part of his reality since he was fourteen, when his mother's third husband's fly-by-night church failed to cast the devil from his soul and a state psychologist was called in.

He is supposed to take one pill at a time at set intervals but dispensed with that practice long ago. He lifts a hardcover copy of *Harold Prince and the American Musical Theatre* from the stack of library books on the passenger's seat, places the three tablets upon it, then uses a second, smaller hardbound book to grind them into dust. From the hard plastic pocket on the driver's door he fishes out one of several gutted ballpoint pens, and uses it to snort half the drug into his right nostril, the remainder into his left. Then he leans his head back, closes his eyes, and waits for clarity and calm.

His pager goes off again, startling him and sending a fresh surge of adrenaline through his veins. He pulls the thing from his belt and chucks it backward over his shoulder. The action jostles the smaller of the books on his lap and sends it plummeting down onto his foot. Retrieving it, he finds it is Lanford Wilson's *Angels Fall*, one of a dozen of the playwright's works he'd checked out in preparation for the start of rehearsals for the next show he is in, *Fifth of July*. The trunk of the Cabrio is filled with thrift-store finds, potential costumes for his role as Jed Jenkins in the nineteen seventies-set play.

He's based his characterization of Jed on what he imagines local set designer Richard Baxter, who he has worked with on various productions for years, was like at twenty-five, though as far as he's been able to ascertain—Baxter is very cagey about his age—the man was actually closer to forty in nineteen seventy seven. A part of him dreads how the other will react when he finds out he's been used as a model again. The last time Marc tried it, for his role as a chorus member in *Hair* four years ago, Baxter's reception was icy.

He'd been impersonating the man for years, of course, since shortly after they first met, when Marc, then ten, was cast in his first production. Landing the role in *Hair* had simply brought Baxter's attention to the fact that he was part of Marc's vast repertoire of impressions, a trick to pull out of his hat to entertain the masses.

It was mania, Marc thinks, still trying to explain to himself why he'd given such an over-the-top performance during the first full run-through they did for the tech staff. He hadn't been nearly as flamboyant in rehearsal up to that point, but with Baxter watching it had just…happened. He'd burst onto the stage in platform shoes and little 'o'-shaped John Lennon glasses, carrying a cane, had goosed a chorus member made up to look not unlike John Holmes, and then had tried to throw the blame on another member of the cast standing nearby by ad-libbing two words, using many more syllables than were required. "You bay-uh-stud!" he'd shouted. It had brought the run-through to a screeching halt, and propelled Baxter out of his seat. The "conversation" Baxter and the director, Ted, had out in the hall immediately afterward had been conducted at a volume that made it possible for the cast and the rest of the tech staff to hear every word. Baxter had declared it to be not a characterization at all but rather character assassination. When Ted returned to the rehearsal room alone, Marc was certain he was about to be kicked out of the production, but the director had simply—sternly—reminded him that his was not a speaking role, and to do only the blocking he was given. Then he'd instructed the costume designer to radically change Marc's look.

Marc leans his head back, closes his eyes, and reminds himself that his portrayal of Jed is nothing like that ill-thought-out mockery. He's tried hard to capture, honestly, the essence of Baxter. Still, he worries how the other will take it.

Like a fist unclenching, he feels his mind begin to let go of the million fanciful thoughts and fears cluttering it. After half a minute he finds he can take a full, deep breath again.

He sets the copy of *Fifth of July* atop the other books on the passenger seat.

The stack reminds him of the library's limitation on the number of items a single patron is allowed to have out at a given time, the only thing that had kept him from checking out every Wilson script they had. That, in turn, reminds him of the only useful advice he has ever gotten from a therapist, namely to set limits for himself by choosing three or four related actions and to then deal with them one at a time. He reaches across the vehicle and tosses the medicine bottle into the glove compartment.

Three or four related items. Tailor and tux are done. Next up, ticket, and then…. His stomach flutters. *Tête-à-tête.*

MICHAEL STANDS BEFORE the towering glass wall at the back of the lobby of the Kentucky Center for the Arts, gazing out at the Ohio River. "This is just great. It's too cold to go outside, there's nothing to do inside, and there's no food yet."

Beside him, Alyssa shrugs. "It's still more fun than the Galt House was."

"That talk you had to go to this morning?"

She nods. "Only if by 'talk' you mean sales pitch. It was supposed to sell med students on a career in cardiothoracic medicine."

"Dr. Reilly?" Michael guesses. Everett Reilly is his father's—and, by extension, Alyssa's father's—friend.

"Yep. The crazy part was I don't think there were any med students there at all, only guys who want their kids to be med students."

"I take it you weren't persuaded." Alyssa's father likes to pretend to be exasperated by her decision to study law rather than medicine, but Michael is confidant Robert Morrison is extremely proud of his daughter's accomplishments and ambition.

"Actually, it completely changed my mind," she says. "Heart surgery's my true calling after all."

"But don't you faint during blood drives?"

She takes his hand and squeezes it. "So? I like a challenge."

He hears his mother in the distance "Yoo-hooing" someone. Alyssa's grip on his fingers becomes vise-like.

"Oh, no! It's your mother. Quick, where can we go?"

He laughs and doesn't move. "You realize you *just* said you like a challenge, don't you?"

"She isn't a challenge," Alyssa says. "She's the lost horseman of the Apocalypse."

"Horsewoman," he corrects. It reminds him of the suggestion he made, while they were decorating the gym for the Thunder event, that their prom theme should be "Dams and Studs." Alyssa had laughed, wrinkled her nose, and danced around going "Ewww!" He liked making her laugh, so he'd gone on to suggest "Breeder's Cup," which made her squeal and exclaim "You are so wrong, Michael Ferguson!" He's glad he hadn't thought of those theme ideas a couple of weeks earlier. He imagines Alyssa passing along those ones to Stephen, Drake and Rashad. He doubts they would find the same humor in them.

Michael sees his mother enter the lobby on its far side. She doesn't see them. Her gaze is cast upward, toward the second balcony of Whitney Hall.

Alyssa slaps her free hand over her mouth to suppress a laugh, and her eyes bug out. He understands what has caused her reaction. The bell-shaped dress his mother has chosen for the evening is beyond hideous. Made from iridescent blue-green fabric and gathered along the hemline like bunting on a Fourth of July parade route, it looks to him like a billowing dark teal cloud.

He knows there is a word which perfectly describes it, but at present it eludes him. *Cumulonimbus?* he thinks. *A thunderhead for Thunder Day?* He scowls, frustrated with himself.

"She's coming this way! We have to hide!"

Michael takes Alyssa's hand and pulls her to safety behind a massive pillar.

"Oh my god, a circle dress, really?" she whispers. "And I thought petticoats were just for weddings."

The word Michael wants pops into his head. "Caliginous."

Alyssa shushes him.

"No, seriously. That's what that dress is. It's caliginous."

"If that means 'hideous beyond all previous understanding,' then I agree."

Michael laughs. "C'mon," he says, tugging on her arm again. "Let's go look at the finalists for the art contest."

"YOU'RE HERE FOR the charity dinner?" an elderly member of the ushering staff asks as Marc steps through the front entrance of the Kentucky

Center for the Arts.

A ticket to the event for himself was more than Marc could afford, especially in light of the fact that he will certainly be fired for not showing up for work today, but while securing one for Ehrichto Salvatolle, he'd gotten the idea to gain entry to the dinner by impersonating Richard Baxter, whose artwork is a finalist in the charity's art contest. He even had the clothes for it in the trunk of this car—a velvet-lapelled, black polyester tuxedo he'd found while collecting costumes for his role as Jed Jenkins.

Pushing his shoulders back and lifting his chin in order to look, literally, down his nose and through the novelty store half-glasses resting on its tip, he says to the usher, in the most peevish tone he can muster, "My name is Richard Baxter. I am one of the artists whose work is being displayed here tonight." For punctuation, he purses his lips.

She claps her fists together and pulls them up under her chin, a mannerism befitting an excited schoolgirl, which Marc finds off-putting coming from someone with white hair. "Oh, I know who you are! I see your name all the time in the programs!"

At the mention of programs alarm bells go off within Marc and he wonders how many other people will recognize the name, how many know the face. He doubts the phony half-glasses and polyester tuxedo will be enough to keep them fooled for long. It worries him that he doesn't have a cane, a Richard Baxter staple.

Next he contemplates whether anyone will recognize him for himself, the actor who played Alan Strang in *Equus*, David Harris in *Tea & Sympathy*, a chorus member in *Hair*, or one of the many other roles he has had in productions around town.

I must have been out of my mind to believe this could work. He considers turning and bolting from the room, but the possibility of spending the evening chatting up Ehrichto Salvatolle—and, even better, of leaving with him at the end of the night—helps to re-stick his resolve. Marc looks down at the usher. "You've seen my name in programs?" he asks, striving to inject the words with a barely discernible amount of seething condescension, the way Baxter would. "How nice."

The usher doesn't seem to grasp the fact that she should be offended.

"Oh, yes," she says, smiling, her eyes half-moons. "Sally and I—that's my daughter—have seen so many of your shows. I always say to her, I say, 'How in the world does he come up with all those ideas?'" Her eyes widen. "Oh, and now, that mask thingy you did for *Equus*! I was looking at that earlier. My word, but it's beautiful." As a cold sweat begins to break out along the back of Marc's neck, a blush colors her cheeks. "Of course, Sally and I didn't go to see *that* play."

Marc has to stifle a snicker. "No? Pity. You missed seeing a fine performance by this area's best young talent, Marc Payette. Let me tell you, that darling boy is one to watch." He peers over the top edge of the glasses, a move he's seen Baxter do hundreds of times. "And make no mistake, I do watch him, whenever I can. Maybe someday, he'll let me do more." He winks and then turns, intending to melt away into the crowd, but the usher catches his arm.

"Wait just a moment, Mr. Baxter," she says. He turns back in time to see her wave to someone in the crowd. "Mrs. Ferguson!" she calls. "Look who's here!"

THE STATION IS set up on the back patio of the Kentucky Center for the Arts, a triangular swath of concrete defined by the soaring glass back walls of the building, which meet at odd angles, and the grassy public plaza called the Belvedere. The latter spans the area between the Kentucky Center and the Ohio River. Lloyd doesn't envy the people who are literally camped out on the lawn, the entire area now taken up with tarps and tents. It is unseasonably chilly for mid-April, and it has been off-and-on raining all day.

The bartender, too, looks frozen to the bone. "Here you go, sir," he says, smiling in spite of it as he hands over the drink. "Enjoy."

"Lloyd!"

Lloyd turns and sees Dr. Reilly waving. To his right stands Sinclair Whitman; to his left, someone Lloyd doesn't recognize. He makes his way toward them.

"Everett; Sinclair," he says, shaking hands with each of them. Up close, the man he doesn't know looks maybe twenty-five and sports a tuxedo without any lapels, a goatee and moustache, and hair long enough that he has tucked it behind his ears. *Julia will be livid,* Lloyd thinks. *Unless he's rich.* "I don't believe I've had the pleasure." he says, extending his hand to the man. "My name's Lloyd Ferguson."

"We haven't met," the stranger says, returning the gesture. "I'm Ehrichto Salvatolle."

Bingo. You poor bastard, she'll be on you like glue. "As in the cigar?"

"Yes!" Sinclair pipes up before the man can answer. "Atta boy, Ferguson. Knew you'd come through."

Lloyd blushes. "Well, I've always been good with names." Mr. Salvatolle smiles.

"He's the one behind the new Salvatolle's Golden Steeples!" Sinclair exclaims. "You see? I told you that flavor profile was too damned close to the original to be the work of someone who simply purchased the rights to use the name."

Lloyd adjusts his opinion of the stranger's age upward, to thirty, and relaxes further. If he is in charge of the cigar re-release, if he has real money, Julia will have no trouble looking past his unconventional sense of style.

"Mr. Whitman and Dr. Reilly say you're the reason there's twelve-year-old the Glenlivet on offer here," Mr. Salvatolle says. He holds up a glass that looks too cloudy to be a straight shot of the whisky. Lloyd guesses it's a Rusty Nail, and pegs him as a fan of the Rat Pack.

"Guilty as charged." He looks at Dr. Reilly. "If Janice hasn't changed her mind about tonight...."

"She hasn't."

Lloyd isn't surprised. Everett Reilly's wife Janice and Julia mix about as well as oil and water. "Well, then," he says. "I'll have to check with my wife to make sure she hasn't promised the seat to someone else, of course, but it looks to me as if—"

"Hey, Dad," Lloyd hears Michael say, behind him. "They're getting ready to serve dinner. You're supposed to come inside."

"Hey, Dad, they're getting ready to serve dinner. You're supposed to come inside."

The words are strange but the voice so familiar it causes every muscle in Ehrichto's body to instantly tense. When he turns and sees the teenager walking toward him, he feels he cannot breathe.

"Michael, come over here a minute, there's someone I'd like you to meet," a beaming Lloyd Ferguson says. "This is Ehrichto Salvatolle." He says more, but Ehrichto doesn't hear it, because his mind has gone into overdrive.

Patrick!

Bright blue eyes, paper-white skin, curly black hair. Ehrichto has been stopped cold by those attributes a thousand times, each time absolutely certain for half a moment and then crestfallen, left with nothing but a racing mind, a sick feeling in his gut, and a stranger looking at him quizzically.

But this time, far from fading, the impression deepens as he stares.

Patrick! It isn't so much a conscious thought as a resonance in his bones. *Patrick!*

He is stunned to find that the familiar blue eyes staring back at him look struck by the same sense of total disbelief. Frozen. Dumbfounded. Astounded.

Yes, I know! he thinks. *I know exactly what you're thinking! It's impossible! Incredible!* He thinks of Maria, down on the stones of the plaza, huddled over a candle, and a chill runs up his spine. *She did it,* he thinks. *She raised the dead.*

They are supposed to be shaking hands, but his limbs are vibrating like a struck tuning fork. He extends a trembling hand.

When they touch, Patrick's eyes widen considerably. "Hello," Ehrichto says, too eagerly, he is sure. The word sounds inane in his ears.

"H-h-hello."

Beside Ehrichto, Lloyd Ferguson asks, "I hope that I didn't butcher your name too badly?"

"No," Ehrichto answers, and it's true. He isn't sure which is stranger: that the man pronounced his name correctly, or that hearing it evoked no reaction whatsoever from Patrick. It wasn't until he'd glanced up and their eyes met that he seemed to fathom the situation. *Of course he must be in quite a state,* Ehrichto thinks. *First ripped from his eternal rest, and then—*

"Well, I have always had an ear for names," Lloyd Ferguson says. "Comes with the job, I guess."

Patrick tries to extract his hand. Ehrichto keeps hold of it, keeps his eyes locked on Patrick's. Yes, it's really me, he thinks. But now we must pretend we don't know one another. "It's a pleasure to meet you." He gives Patrick's hand a squeeze, and then lets him go. *Can't really touch you in public*, he thinks, as Patrick pulls his hand away. *Don't worry, I remember.*

"It's a…it's nice to meet you, too."

Ehrichto is struck by the realization that the look in Patrick's eyes is wrong. *He's not angry with me, he's frightened! He must not remember. He died and came back. He's feeling lost and afraid.* Ehrichto has to fight the urge to grab Patrick by the arm and drag him from the crowd.

Patrick startles him by turning and darting back into the building.

"I guess there's something important going on," Lloyd Ferguson says. "Shall we?"

Already brushing past the man, following Patrick's lead, Ehrichto doesn't bother to reply.

"IT'S OPEN, DARLING, come on in," Richard Baxter calls from the center of a stack of boxes, a sliver of space located between the drafting table and the southwest window in his floor-to-ceiling-filled office. "I'm so glad you made it after all, though I hope you didn't tell Sullivan to shove it on my account. Anyway, you're just in the nick of time. I was about to start loading up the truck."

"What on earth…?"

Baxter's heart skips a beat. It isn't the voice he expected, but is familiar. He rises up onto tiptoe, trying to see who has entered the room, but the move fails to allow him a clear line of sight. "Jeff? Is that you?" he calls, just before he rounds the end of a wall of boxes and finds his former assistant standing just inside the door. He's dressed like a fashion stylist's version of a longshoreman, in black brogue stow boots, jeans with rolled cuffs, a red flannel shirt, and a black peacoat complete with upturned collar. Jeff always looks like a Ken doll: dressed for a weirdly specific adventure, and usually not anything similar to the moment he's in. It's another reason—on top of his passion for designing sets for the theatre—why people always wrongly assume he's gay.

Busy peering at the contents of an open cardboard box, he doesn't answer or look up.

"What are you doing here?" Baxter asks.

"I could ask you the same thing," Jeff says. He reaches into the box and lifts out a package by its hang tag. "Purple glow sticks? Plastic fangs? Rubber bats? Blood-red candy rings? I'd say either you failed at running a Halloween store in the mall or you're planning a vampire-themed—"

"—rave," they say in unison. Jeff's mouth drops open in astonishment, a reaction Baxter always assumed was just an expression. Jeff stares another moment, then tosses the bag of glow sticks back into the box and lifts a flyer from atop the file cabinet beside the door. "Resurrection Dance Party," he reads aloud. "Oaks Night. Doors open at ten o'clock." He looks over at Baxter. "Isn't it a little sacrilegious?"

"Circuit parties thrown around Easter are always known as Resurrection parties," Baxter says, though he feels quite sure Jeff has no idea what a circuit party is, not being gay or even particularly urbane.

"But it isn't around Easter. Oaks is a month after it."

Oaks Day, dubbed Louisville's Day at the Races by marketers at Churchill Downs, is the day before the Derby, and culminates with the eponymous fillies-only race.

"Close enough for government work," Baxter quips. "And anyway, *that* isn't the party we're throwing. That's the one being done by some outfit from London."

"Kentucky?"

"England," Baxter says. "And I don't think it really is going to be a circuit party. I think they're just using the name to be cheeky." He watches Jeff closely to gauge his reaction. "Do you even know what a circuit party is?"

His former assistant shakes his head.

"It's an industrial dance party with a very, shall we say, focused patronage?"

"You mean gay."

"Yes, darling. Anyway, ours is going to be titled Quarry and will be aimed at anyone into vampires."

"I didn't know there was anyone besides you who was into them."

Baxter feels very exposed. Freakish. "Don't be an ass. Vampires are always in demand. Ever since Stoker wrote *Dracula* it's been one franchise after another. Rice. Saberhagen. Lumley. And that's just the written media. No other monster has been lurking in movie theaters—"

"I get it," Jeff says. The topic has never been one he's expressed even the slightest interest in. "So where are you throwing your rave?"

"In a *quarry*, naturally. There's a massive one under the zoo."

Jeff scowls. "Why go to all this trouble? Why not just go to the one the Londoners are throwing and be done with it? And how much is this going to cost you, anyway?"

"Because it will be fun; because I'd rather go to one that's vampire-themed; and I'll recoup a lot of the cost though the cover charge."

Jeff laughs. "You're not going to recoup your investment with a roomful of kids wearing plastic fangs. Unless...."

"Unless what? What are you implying?"

"Unless this isn't going to be the real deal after all."

Baxter is insulted. "Of course it is."

"With a real light package? A professional sound system? DJs? Security?"

"Of course," Baxter says, acting more miffed than he feels. Jeff's right to be skeptical about the money; Baxter knows he won't get back anywhere near what he's put in, but there's no way he can explain that it isn't about that, so he forces a smile and changes the subject. "How was... Washington state, isn't that were you were?"

Jeff nods. "It was great. Nice people. Good show. A great space. Brand new."

"The set was a success?"

"Oh, damn. I meant to bring the slides. Next time. Yeah, people seemed impressed. I got a lot of nice compliments at the opening night party."

"Wonderful."

Jeff looks around at the piles of boxes. "So. How big is the truck and where do we start?"

"Don't be absurd," Baxter says. "You're not my assistant anymore."

Jeff's smile is electric. "No. But am I extremely nosy. I want to see this thing, and if schlepping a truckload of boxes is what it takes, I'm willing to do it."

"OUR SIGNATURE DRINK," Julia proclaims as she hands Marc a martini glass of straight gin. He watched the bartender—brunet, mid-twenties, not bad looking but so busy making eyes at a female member of the wait staff that Julia had loudly called him out for it—prepare the drink, and knows there is nothing added to the alcohol but flakes of real gold and a dwarf lily. The rim of the glass and blossom are dusted with powdered gold, and Julia's lips are now sparkling.

"A Gilded Lily, I presume?" Marc asks, arching one brow. He doesn't want alcohol, it is the worst thing for his peculiar brain chemistry, but he takes a sip to please her. It's awful, metallic and floral and caustic to boot. He has to fight to keep from wincing. *This*, he thinks, *must be what it's like to lick an iron fence in an English garden. During an acid rain.*

"Are-uhnt they jus' wonder-fuhl?" she asks. Ever since they were introduced she has been attempting to employ a Carolina accent. At least, he thinks that is what she is doing; the effort is inconsistent and atrocious. He wonders how many Gilded Lilies she's already consumed.

"I would like to see my work now," he says. Just before insisting he try the drink of the evening she'd made reference to the fact that the headpiece Baxter created for *Equus* was chosen as the winner of the evening's art competition. She'd assumed he was there because of the congratulatory letter the organization sent inviting him to the dinner as a guest of honor. Marc had been taken aback by that news. For a few seconds he entertained the notion that Baxter might show up and they would have a Hollywood-worthy face off in the center of the lobby, before he remembered that Baxter would never show his face at this or any event Julia Conway Ferguson was attending. He cannot, in fact, attend any such event, because to do so would blow his cover as Angelo de Haven, architect and interior designer of her dream house, to date still the most bizarre of the many odd projects Marc has helped him with.

Julia cranes her neck in the direction of the head table. Marc follows her gaze and sees that the headdress has still not been installed as the centerpiece.

"Soon," she says, slipping her arm through his. "Why don't you come with me to check on things in the kitchen, and I'll introduce you to Chef Anthony?"

Though he's never worked directly in a professional kitchen, Marc has held many jobs—stints as a waiter, as bar back, and the position he held until today, as morning concierge at the Galt House—which have required him to maintain a tangential relationship with one. He finds them intriguing because they are stocked with young, male, thrill-seeker types. Never minding a tendency in the breed toward uber-macho posturing, restaurant kitchens have always been excellent places for him to score fresh meat. Marc has fucked more than his share of coked-up cowboys and commis, but has never yet bedded a chef. He casts another look around the lobby and reminds himself that Ehrichto Salvatolle may not arrive until right before dinner is served. "Mmm, that could be tasty," he says. Julia shoots a sour look his way. He wonders how far he can push her. "Lay on, MacDuff," he says.

The minute her back is turned, he ditches the glass of gin on the nearest table.

THE HEAD TABLE seems ten miles from the door and it feels to Michael as if the entire assembly has turned to watch him re-enter the lobby. He is certain that they are all about to notice the fact that meeting his father's business associate gave him an erection.

It's just hormones, he thinks, trying to convince himself that his present state is owed to misdirected anger, to the fact that just after Alyssa headed for the ladies' room to change for the evening his mother had embarrassed him by grabbing his arm and ordering him to put on his tux.

Michael is used to his body betraying him. He spends much of his daily life doing what he is now: attributing his unwanted physical reactions to chemicals running amuck in his system. He ignores the fact that he didn't get hard until Mr. Salvatolle turned around, and also that the moment he saw the man's face he'd forgotten the earlier incident with his mother.

It's just hormones. It's normal. I'm normal, he thinks as he slips between two groups of guests. The mantra, which he has

SIX

been chanting for years, is inspired by a comment made by his seventh-grade P.E. teacher, who'd said that to be a teenager is to be "drowning in hormones." To Michael it feels like getting caught in an undertow and being dragged to the ocean floor. In truth, he knows it is not "just hormones," or at least that his body is not simply getting confused by a rush of them coming at an inappropriate time. He has already gone through a period of getting turned on by weird, non-sexual but intensely emotional situations, getting hard before taking a test, for instance, or after acing one. Though those things still happen to him occasionally, and though, at seventeen and a half, he gets aroused easily and frequently, the causes these days are almost always sexual in nature, though sexuality itself vexes him. Just as Stephen, Drake and Rashad seem to be, Michael is fascinated by ribald remarks and sexual innuendos, which he views as opportunities to study what he considers "normal" people's reactions, in the hopes of finding the Rosetta Stone of sex. So far, though, none of it makes sense. Every other boy he knows became interested in girls years ago. He's listened to comments they've made regarding the opposite sex but has never understood them. It feels less like not getting an in-joke than it does listening to a stand-up routine being told in a foreign language.

It's not only that he's not interested in girls, it's that the way he believes he's supposed to feel about them is how he feels about other boys. In the locker room, in the hall between classes, even while watching television, he can become transfixed by a nice physique, a stunning pair of eyes beneath a strong brow, even the way a guy walking past smells. Then there's the fact that for the past year and a half he has utilized the x-rated pictures of guys which mysteriously find their way into his email inbox. Lastly, there's the almost-encounter with Joey Peccorini at the Blind Cave Fish concert. Michael always reminds himself that he was stoned that night, as a way to discount how close he came to sucking the guy off. Still, a part of him knows if he hadn't been stoned, and therefore paranoid, the evening would have ended much differently.

Mr. Salvatolle's effect on him, though, is undeniable. *That wasn't anger*, he thinks, wrestling with the implausible notion that he was still reacting to the skirmish with his mother when he met the man.

A lightning-like charge had run through him when their hands touched. Even more surprising than his own reaction was the look that crossed Mr. Salvatolle's face when it happened. His eyes widened and his mouth dropped open in stunned surprise. *He felt it too,* Michael thinks, as the insistent bulge in his pants begins pushing out their flat front in earnest.

His usual tactic for dealing with situations which arouse such wrong responses is to quickly make an excuse to be elsewhere. Whenever, like now, it is not possible to flee, he feigns a sudden and intense interest in the ground while conjuring thoughts of unpleasant things. Trying to employ that trick, he stares at the garish, bright orange carpeting as he winds his way through the crowd, but try as he might all he can think of is Mr. Salvatolle's steady, intense gaze and how he'd leaned forward as they shook hands. Unable to speak, look away, or formulate a complete thought, Michael was relieved when his father spoke and broke the spell.

He recalls the difficulty he had, freeing his hand from Mr. Salvatolle's grip.

He didn't want to let go of me either. Why?

Rounding a group of men who have stopped between two tables to converse, he spies Alyssa, now dressed in a knee-length green satin dress and with her hair styled in fat curls. She turns as he approaches, and he catches and holds her gaze, to keep it from wandering south.

"You look nice," he says.

"So do you."

He hears her father say, "Mr. Salvatolle, I'd like you to meet my wife and daughter. Catherine, this is Ehrichto Salvatolle, a friend of Dr. Reilly's."

Is he going to sit with us? Michael wonders. His heart begins thundering in his chest. *How am I going to get through dinner with him at our table?* He drops his gaze back to the carpet as Alyssa lets go of his hand and shifts to face the stranger. "Hello," she says. "I'm Alyssa."

"Ehrichto Salvatolle," the stranger says and the way he rolls the "r" is both suave and subtle. A moment later he slides sideways and slips between Michael and the person already seated directly behind him at the next table. "Pardon me. So sorry," Mr. Salvatolle says. He presses his body up against Michael's as he reaches for the unclaimed chair to Michael's left. "I hope I'm not crowding you?" is whispered in Michael's ear. "N,n,no. You're fine." *I'm a freak*, Michael thinks. *He's just here to have dinner and watch the fireworks. He doesn't feel the way I do, or think the same things. No one does.* He steals a glance sideways just in time to see a lock of long dark hair dislodge from behind Mr. Salvatolle's right ear and fall across his eyes. After he's seated he tucks it back into place. Then he looks up and their eyes meet again. This time Michael cannot look away.

"Are you going to sit down?" Mr. Salvatolle asks.

There isn't enough room between them to maneuver gracefully. Michael wrestles his chair back, not easy to do because of the carpeting, and then half climbs over it. He gets settled again just in time to hear Alyssa's mother say, "It's always so nice to meet new people." Beside him, Mr. Salvatolle stops smoothing his napkin in his lap. He leans forward and sideways, deep into Michael's personal space, in order to make eye contact with her. "Yes. Yes, it is," he agrees.

Michael leans so far backward that it feels as if the top of his chair will snap his spine. The man's scent fills his nostrils, masculine and inviting, the amber of tobacco mixed with leather and rain. Michael tries switching his focus to the sounds coming from the rest of the room, the chatter of hundreds of conversations and clink of glassware and, underneath it all, a smattering of tinkling notes coming from a piano. He recognizes the song just starting as Béla Fleck's "In Your Eyes."

Mr. Salvatolle and Mrs. Morrison finally end their conversation, and the man returns to his own space. Michael sits back up, grabs the napkin from his charger, snaps it open, and arranges it on his lap.

"You shouldn't have shaved," Alyssa whispers in his right ear.

Michael cuts his eyes sideways and finds her smirking. "Like I had a choice."

"I know, it's just…. Well, I think a gondolier would have been a more appropriate escort."

Michael's stomach does a cartwheel. He regrets telling her about his mother's assessment of his facial hair. *A more appropriate escort for whom,* he wonders, panicky. She doesn't understand the hell he's currently in. "What are you talking about?"

"Your mother told me she thinks this dress is too costumey and I look like a flamenco dancer. And, yeah, I know, the one is from Spain and the other is from Italy, but…."

Michael's about to quote advice she once gave him about holding his own with his mother, when he senses Mr. Salvatolle pushing back his chair to stand. Seconds later Michael's father, Alyssa's father, and Dr. Reilly do the same. Michael scrambles to his feet just as his mother steps into view.

"Good even-uhn-een everyone," she says, using the fake Southern Belle accent she always adopts at Derby time. When her gaze lands on Mr. Salvatolle her eyes narrow.

Oh, no, Michael thinks. He's seen her re-seat people for wearing a tie she didn't like, and something about Mr. Salvatolle clearly upsets her. *The length of his hair, maybe. Or the fact that his tuxedo doesn't have lapels.*

"You must be Julia Conway…Ferguson."

She extends a hand and they shake. "I am. And you are…?" Michael notes that the phony accent has vanished.

"Ehrichto Salvatolle."

She pulls her hand away. "Have we ever met before, Mr. Sal-VOR-torlay?"

Michael winces at her butchering of the man's name. He sees his father do the same.

"It's pronounced sav-a-TOE-lay," the man says. "The first 'l' is silent and the emphasis is on the third syllable." He shoots a look Michael's way. "EhREEK-toe Sav-a-TOE-lay."

Michael holds his breath. His mother hates to be corrected, despises being corrected in front of other people. It's more than enough to be sent from the table.

Instead of flying into a rage, though, Julia blushes. "I do apologize."

She what? Michael thinks, astonished. He feels Alyssa grab his arm, and figures she is thinking exactly the same thing. His father and Dr. Reilly appear equally stunned.

"That's quite all right. It's a Sabine name. I hardly expect a correct pronunciation."

"What kind of name?"

"Sabine. The indigenous people of Italy."

"But you're from here, aren't you?"

Crap, they have history. There's no telling what will happen next.

"I received some of my…early education…here," Mr. Salvatolle says. Again, he casts a glance Michael's way. "My family was once prominent in this town, though that was many years ago. I think my name is familiar to you because your husband has smoked our cigars, Salvatolle's New Golden Steeples. A re-creation of the cigars my father—or, pardon me, I meant to say my grandfather—built the company on." He lifts the glass of whisky he brought with him to the table, and drinks.

"I'd swear I've seen your face before, but…." Her voice trails off. "But that couldn't be, because it seems so long ago."

"You must have met one of my uncles."

"Yes, I must have."

"Where did you grow up, Mr. Salvatolle?" Michael's father asks, mercifully changing the topic.

"New Orleans."

"Oh, New Orleans," Julia exclaims. "There's some lovely old architecture in that city."

Michael feels sure he knows what she is up to. She's hoping to solicit a sizable donation from the stranger before the night is through. He is absolutely certain of it because the last time he overheard her making reference to New Orleans she'd called it "one big, termite-infested crack lab." *Donor Cultivation 101*, he thinks cynically. *How the mark feels about the mission statement is directly related to how the organization makes him feel about himself.*

For almost eighteen years Michael has watched his mother in action, sweet-talking money out of the bank accounts of wealthy people, bestowing it on the less fortunate, and basking in the resultant hagiographic glow. The philanthropy of Conway Charities is felt literally everywhere in the city. The organization has helped make possible such diverse enterprises as after-school basketball programs and artist's residencies that connect noted musicians with aspiring ones. It awards grant monies to authors penning coffee-table books on subjects with a local slant, and has funded many beautification projects throughout the downtown area. He's seen scores of people, mortally afraid of losing the funding the organization provides, grit their teeth and put up with her petulance and shenanigans. He gets that the veto power she has regarding the awarding of grants is a sword of Damocles hanging over the heads of city officials and the leaders of smaller charities, and that fact bends them to her will.

He's always understood that she is fiercely protective of being the director of the charity, a job which is practically a 24/7 affair. But for the first time in his life he connects all the dots and understands *why* it means so much to her.

It's all she's got, he realizes. *It's her only source of power.*

"New Orleans possesses a unique character," Mr. Salvatolle says. "Or, more correctly, several of them."

Dr. Reilly chuckles. "That it does."

"Do you own property there?" Michael's mother asks.

The stranger hesitates. Michael feels queasy. *He's figured out she's playing him and he's trying to shake her. Fat chance of that happening.*

"My family does. I do not." He lifts his glass again and takes another swallow of whisky, before looking to his left at Michael's father. "Speaking of family, the Golden Steeples brand was quite advantageous to both of ours, wasn't it?"

Michael tenses, and sees each of his parents do likewise. The fierce grip his father has on his own glass of whisky turns his fingertips white. His mother lifts a hand to touch the teardrop pearl resting in the hollow at the base of her throat, action which causes the cold diamond solitaire of her wedding set to slip sideways on her finger and disappear from view.

His parents have never talked about it in front of him, but he's aware of the fact that some members of his father's family, which has long been divided into two fractious branches, went to prison. One branch, the one his father comes from, for decades has been comprised of salesmen and middle management for a variety of industries. Many have managed to become comfortably middle-to-upper-middle class, but the other branch was, for a time, filled with big players in the tobacco industry. The tobacco barons in the family had amassed a vast fortune, living high on the hog until an embezzlement scandal toppled their empire, shortly before Michael was born. His mother has a scrapbook filled with newspaper clippings about the trial at which his father's cousin Hunt, uncle Junior, and great-uncle Conrad were convicted of embezzling company funds. The three always maintained their innocence, claiming they were framed by Hunt's personal secretary, a man name Tony de Calle, a Spaniard by extraction. They said that because of his long history of employment as a bookkeeper for various tobacco-related businesses and affable personality they'd given him unusual access to their finances. At the time of their arrests he'd vanished, and many people believed they'd murdered him, or had paid a hit man to do the deed, since no body was ever found. Without one, the police had been unable to open a murder investigation. Tony de Calle remained, officially, a missing person.

Even without being charged with murder, the three accused men had more trouble than they could handle. It turned out that, unlike its bookkeeper, none of the company's money was actually missing. Not only could every penny be accounted for, but the paper trail clearly showed how the three had slyly diverted funds from their business and lavished it on themselves. They'd bought fancy cars and houses and taken frequent trips to Europe. Hunt had even purchased Burley Boy, a Thoroughbred stud horse of such remarkable lineage he all but came complete with a garland of roses.

Worse than those excesses was the fact that all the stolen money had been taken out of the Tobacco Union Workers' Savings and Retirement Fund.

Like most of the newspaper men chronicling the story, the judge in the case seemed to find that the most egregious aspect of the crime. As a demonstration of his outrage, he'd sentenced them as harshly as he could, giving them serious prison time, something Michael later learned was almost unheard of in embezzlement cases.

"No, it was not," Michael's father says, responding to Mr. Salvatolle's assertion that the popularity of Golden Steeple cigars was profitable for both their families. "We weren't involved in any of that business."

Mr. Salvatolle bristles. "'That' business? May I remind you that tobacco built this state? If it wasn't for 'that' crop, we'd still be part of Virginia."

"'We,' Mr. Salvatolle?" Michael's mother asks. "I thought you weren't from here?"

The man turns back to face her. His gaze is withering. "I was born here. I'm as much a Kentuckian as I am a Sicilian or Sabine. Tobacco is in my blood, and I won't stand by and listen to someone refer to it as if it's crack cocaine."

"Well, I was also born here," Michael's father says. "And it isn't in mine. My side of the family has always been in sales, not farming."

"Then we have a second thing in common," Mr. Salvatolle says, backing down somewhat. "I'm a factor. A broker. I deal mainly in cigars, but on occasion I also procure other hard-to-find, high-quality goods for an exclusive clientele." He glances at Michael. "One of my favorite things to locate is pre-Prohibition era whisky."

"Oh look," Michael's mother exclaims with far too much enthusiasm. "The soup is here."

EHRICHTO CAN'T HELP but keep replaying his visit, earlier in the day, to the Conway mausoleum in Cave Hill Cemetery, and the conclusion he came to while there, that the crypt inside was undisturbed. *Was he able to pass through its walls? Is that possible*, he wonders before catching himself and nearly laughing out loud. *Anything is possible. I'm a vampire.*

He steals a glance sideways. Patrick is staring at his bowl of soup as if its surface might contain images that will explain everything that's just happened to him—where he's been; how it is that he's returned; how he came to be at this dinner with a new set of parents; how it is that Ehrichto never left.

That thought stirs the deeper one niggling at the back of his mind, the notion that this is not Patrick, after all; that Maria didn't pull him back from death's clutches; that he is simply one of Patrick's descendants. It would explain why he is ten years younger now than when he died, why he has a new family. It would explain his utter failure to react to any of the details of the past Ehrichto has gone to pains to work into the conversation for his benefit.

All at once the evidence seems overwhelming. *What am I doing? This is not Patrick. Have I lost my mind?* Preparing to make some excuse to flee the scene he begins to gather his napkin into a ball, but before he can toss it onto the table beside his soup bowl he catches movement out of the corner of his eye. Patrick is casting a similar, furtive glance in his direction. Ehrichto's doubts again dissolve.

He remembers the electric charge that seemed to pass between them during their handshake, and that when their eyes locked, Patrick had been rendered speechless, the only time that's ever happened.

He is now all but staring at Ehrichto, who fights the urge to turn and meet his gaze. He doesn't want to do anything to stop Patrick from looking his way, from being flooded with memories of the nine years they spent together. Still, if he continues staring, someone is bound to notice.

MICHAEL STEALS ANOTHER glance at the stranger seated beside him, taking note of his high cheekbones, trim dark brown moustache and goatee.

He has the urge to run a fingertip along the hairs that line the man's upper lip, or to cup his cheek and feel the sting of beard stubble scraping his palm, or to draw him close and taste his—

"Something on your mind?"

Mr. Salvatolle has posed the question quietly, without turning his head. Michael is shocked to realize that he has been staring long enough not only for the waiters to serve them and leave again, but for the man to begin eating and notice that he was not doing the same. He shakes his head and dips his spoon into the broth set before him, though the fluttering in his stomach has morphed into a sensation like rocks being tumbled, and food is the last thing he wants.

"HOW DID YOU even find this place?" Jeff asks, startling Baxter because, given a few moments of silence from the passenger's seat, his mind had put Marc in the truck cab in Jeff's stead. As much as Baxter's always liked his assistant, the reality of the situation comes as a shock. He consoles himself by taking a long look at the younger man, whose face is partially turned away. The minute they stepped outside Jeff had slid a navy blue knit stocking cap over his collar-length dirty-blond locks, completing the longshoreman look. Now he's squinting out the side window at the tired row of houses lining his side of the street, a festival of peeling paint and crabgrass—where there is any grass at all—ringed by fences with missing pickets. Faced off against the Kmart just across tiny Illinois Avenue, the structures seem dubious about their fate.

"The phone book," Baxter says. "I was looking for the number to Louisville Welding and 'Louisville Underground' caught my eye. It sounded like a nightclub, so I called, but the number was disconnected. Naturally, I got in the car and drove to the address in the listing."

"And?"

Baxter brakes the monster truck at the four-way stop at the first and, he knows, final cross street, and points at the scene out Jeff's window. He gives the other a moment to take in the sparse gravel lot, lone mature tree, and rural mailbox. Whatever house once stood on the spot is long gone.

"I don't get it," Jeff says, turning to look at him. An adorable, consternated look has beetled his brow. *Such a waste,* Baxter thinks, *his not being into boys.*

Out of the corner of his eye he catches sight of himself in the rearview. *To say nothing of haggard queens.* It's pure melodrama; in truth, Baxter is happy with the cab's dim lighting, which helps him look much the way he did in his prime, when he danced away night after night after night in New York City's hottest clubs.

Outside the cab, the light has a similar overcast quality. It's been bleak all day, rainy and cold. Why anyone would want to shiver at the riverside waiting for night to fully establish in order to watch half an hour's worth of fireworks is beyond his comprehension, but they will. Most years a half a million people descend on the scene, though he doubts that many will turn out this time, because of the dreadful weather. Still.

"Baxter?" Jeff asks. "I don't get it. What was here?"

Marc would be here, if he wasn't there, Baxter thinks. *Fetching bottles of Evian for the wives of rich men. Or selling pills to them. Or doing god-knows-what-else to secure their money and positive attention.* He scowls. *Only I do know what else. It's a trick question.* The pun restores his smile. *And the answer is....*

"Nothing," he says, enjoying the way his inner monologue segues with their dialogue. *There's nothing Marc wouldn't do for attention.* "There was nothing here, when I arrived. It was exactly the same as now. I stood there, looking around at the gravel, wondering if I might spy the iron ring of a hatch. As if there might have been another whole city beneath the one I was in, and 'Louisville Underground' was the entry point."

"Was there?" Jeff turns back to the gravel lot. "Is there?"

"No. There was just that mailbox with peel-and-stick letters slapped on the side."

"And what did it say?"

From this distance you can barely see that there are letters at all. "Louisville Underground," Baxter says. He throws the truck in gear and they rumble through the deserted intersection. Ahead, there aren't any houses or businesses. On one side there are trees, and on the other, a curving wall of rock.

The road bends to follow it and pitches steeply downward. He pushes off from the steering wheel to keep himself from sliding in his seat. Beside him, Jeff puts a hand on the dashboard.

"But you never give up that easily," Jeff says.

"Of course."

Baxter had first stumbled upon the name in print, but not in the phone book. (Though it was there when he looked, listed just above Louisville Welding, as he's said, and given his line of work he might easily have run across it there.) The mailbox was a compromise someone had made with the post office, a way to spare the carrier from having to make the long trek they now were, down and around, down and around. He got that. What he didn't comprehend was why the law firm of Cozart, Dorjan and Garrett, LLC, didn't just have all mail relating to the property sent to New Orleans, and who it was who emptied that box.

Just then they round the last part of the curve and the road—rock towering above them on both sides now—opens onto a treeless clearing. The headlight beams illuminate a sheer wall of limestone several stories high, protected by two rows of tall chain link. The closest row is festooned with signs: *Danger—High Voltage* and *No Trespassing*.

The rock face is dotted with three massive, pitch-black, perfectly square entrances cut from the rock's striations. Baxter grabs his walking stick from its spot on the floor of the cab, flings open the driver's door, and starts to climb from the vehicle.

The headlights and roof lights of the truck cast two shadows onto the chain link. He hears the passenger's door being unlatched, then the creak of its hinges.

"I don't want to watch you get electrocuted," Jeff calls.

Baxter turns back. The four beams from the truck are blinding. He holds up a ring of keys, blocks the lights with his forearm, and calls back "Silly boy, that's why they make these!"

FOOD REMAINS THE very last thing on Michael's mind. He feels lightheaded, short of breath and—after being caught staring by their guest during the soup course and having choked down several spoonfuls of leek broth in order to make it appear that nothing was amiss—nauseated. He doesn't want to eat anything more for fear that it will come back up.

"What's the drive time from New Orleans, about ten or eleven hours?" Alyssa's father asks Mr. Salvatolle.

Their guest wipes his moustache with his napkin and smiles. "Eight and a half," he says. "At least, in a Porsche Carrera 911, that is."

Michael's father starts to cough, as if hearing the name of the auto maker caused him to inhale a piece of lettuce. "That's…a…very nice…car," he manages.

"Yes. Though it is only a rental."

"Really?" Alyssa's father asks. "Can I ask how much—?"

"Four hundred and fifty a day." Mr. Salvatolle stabs a forkful of spiky, dark green leaves. "Plus speeding tickets, of course."

Everyone laughs.

"Lloyd owns a Corvette," Michael's mother pipes up.

"Also very nice cars," Mr. Salvatolle says.

Michael's father's tone is apologetic. "It's not a Porsche."

"And a Porsche is not a Lamborghini. Each has worth in its own way."

"So, you came in just for the fireworks show, is that it?" Mr. Morrison asks.

"Actually, no, I didn't know about it until I arrived," Mr. Salvatolle says. He leans back in his chair and shifts his weight, making a slight adjustment to his seating position. His right leg brushes Michael's left, contact which sends a shiver up Michael's spine. He gasps, and then freezes. He waits for the limb to be moved away again, but it remains resting against his.

Doesn't he realize that's my leg? he wonders. *How could he not?*

"But from the moment I did become aware of it," Mr. Salvatolle says, still on the subject of the fireworks show, "I've been looking forward to it very, very much." He presses his leg even harder into Michael's.

OhMyGod, Michael thinks, frozen with excitement and delicious fear. His mind reels. *OhMyGodOhMyGodOhMyGod!*

"You see, Alyssa?" Mr. Morrison says. "That's the power of chemistry." He looks at Mr. Salvatolle. "My daughter doesn't regard chemistry as a worthwhile career choice. She's laboring under the bizarre belief that she wants to be a lawyer."

Mr. Salvatolle shifts in his seat, leans forward, and with his left hand plucks his glass from the table. As he lifts it into the air, his free hand comes to rest on the top of Michael's thigh, and reduces Michael's universe to that one point.

"Now that truly is a shame," Mr. Salvatolle says, gesturing with the glass. He sounds anything but let-down. "The Scots say to make whisky you need four things: Good barley, good water, good peat, and a cunning chemist." He emphasizes the last by giving the thigh muscle beneath his fingertips a firm squeeze.

Oh! My! God! Michael thinks again. *OhMyGodOhMyGodOhMyGod!*

Mr. Morrison chuckles. "I like that. I've tried to explain to my daughter that she could do far more good in a laboratory than in a courtroom."

"By making whisky?" Alyssa asks.

"You could cure cancer."

"No, I couldn't," she says. "My strength is in winning debates. Here—" Michael jumps when she touches his arm—"is the scientific mind."

Mr. Salvatolle's hand slips from Michael's left thigh just as, on his right side, Alyssa turns and speaks directly into his ear. "Why are you so tense?" she whispers. "Is everything okay?"

Michael doesn't answer. He looks around at the rest of the people at their table. He's relieved to find that Alyssa's parents look amused, not alarmed. The same is true of Dr. Reilly. His father is beaming at him, while his mother seems not to be following the conversation at all. She is busy moving every piece of dishware in front of her by minuscule increments, business he understands as an indication that the present topic of conversation bores her and should be changed.

He chooses not to look at Mr. Salvatolle at all. "I'm fine," he whispers back.

"Then why are you turning red?"

Michael reaches a hand to his cheek. His fingers feel cool compared to it.

"The kitchen staff may have forgotten to rinse your greens," Alyssa says. "They could be riddled with pesticides. I just read about a case like that. Or it could be botulism."

Michael feels the room start to spin. He puts a hand on the table.

"Of course it could also be an allergic reaction," she goes on. "In which case the kitchen would only be liable if they were informed of a trigger beforehand and failed to eliminate it." She shoots an accusatory look across the table at his mother.

His father clears his throat. "What seems to be the matter? Michael, are you all right?"

"I'm fine," Michael replies. His assertion falls on deaf ears. All eyes at the table turn to regard him, which makes his face go redder still. It crosses his mind that the deep blushing might help to quell the storm gathering in his lower region. *It's a closed system, right? Only so much blood to go around.* He reaches for his water glass but knocks into it. It starts to go over, but Mr. Salvatolle catches and rights it, before even a drop is spilled. More embarrassed than ever, Michael pulls his hand into his lap.

The man says quietly, calmly, "What seems to be the trouble?"

"I...think I'm...allergic to something." Michael casts a glance sideways and sees one corner of Mr. Salvatolle's mouth shift upward. The man raises his hand to his face and thoughtfully rubs the hairs along his chin as he glances around the table. Michael looks around, too, and is relieved to find that everyone is once again engrossed in their own conversations. Even Alyssa is now preoccupied, busy digging through her green satin clutch purse, searching for something.

"Allergic?" Mr. Salvatolle says, at a volume that is barely a whisper. "Is that what they're calling it these days?"

Michael's heart rate soars. He turns just in time to see a crease in the man's cheek deepen, the result of the lopsided, jaunty smile that is spreading across his face.

Alyssa stops rifling through her clutch purse. "I was sure I threw an antihistamine in here, but I can't find it."

Her father turns, his attention caught by the mention of legal drugs. "Nonsense," he says. "Catherine, do you have that E4-18 I gave you the other day?"

Alyssa's mother nods and reaches down to lift her own purse from the floor. "Yes, I think I transferred it to this purse. Hang on, I'll look."

"It's okay with you, Lloyd, isn't it, if we give that to him?" Mr. Morrison asks.

Michael's father halts his conversation with Dr. Reilly. "What now?"

"E4-18. Just one tablet should do it, I think."

Alyssa's mother pulls a foil-wrapped pill from her purse. The minute she does Alyssa snatches it from her fingers, flips it over, and reads aloud what is printed on the foil. "'E4-18.' Great, that's all it says. What is this?"

"It's new," her father replies. "Just about to be released."

"That's not what I asked. What is it?"

"The main ingredient's dihydroxyphenyl-lactic acid. The good stuff, in other words, not like whatever over-the-counter shlock you were looking for a minute ago."

"What does di-fo-hy-phen-whatever do?" Alyssa asks.

"If you'd studied chemistry you'd know."

Alyssa opens her mouth to reply but Mr. Salvatolle beats her to it. "It's one of the key components in the herb known as danshen, is it not?"

Michael's father's eyebrows rise. "That's right, but how did you—?"

"It's also known as Red Sage, Chinese Sage and Horse-Racing Grass," Mr. Salvatolle says. He lifts his glass, downs another swallow of the amber liquid, and says, "That last one, very important. This is Kentucky, after all."

Michael doesn't see what that has to do with anything.

"Its major use," Mr. Morrison says, "is as a treatment for blood stasis."

"Do you really think he has that problem?" Mr. Salvatolle asks. He turns to Dr. Reilly. "Do you?"

"No. I'd say there's a lot going on and he's a bit wound up, that's all."

"So would I." Mr. Salvatolle tosses back the last of his drink and firmly sets down the glass. It's such a decisive move that Michael is surprised, though relieved, when he does not leap to his feet immediately following it. "The scientific name of the plant is *Salvia miltiorrhiza*," he says. 'Salvia' is derived from the Latin 'salvare', meaning 'to save' or 'safeguard', even 'heal', from which we get 'salvation' and 'savior' and—"

"Sav-ah-TOE-lay?"

Michael looks across the table at his mother and finds an annoyingly smug smile plastered to her face.

"Yes. Which is why I know a little about the herb."

"A little?" Alyssa asks.

"I'm no doctor, but I also wasn't born yesterday." Once again the man invades Michael's personal space by reaching across him to pluck the wrapped pill from her hand. "There's no need for this or any other medications because there's nothing wrong with him. Isn't that right, Dr. Reilly?"

"Yes. Granted, he's a bit red, but there's a lot going on."

"I think Everett's right, Robert," Michael's father says. "He's anticipating the coming fireworks, nothing more."

Mr. Salvatolle gives Michael a look. "Aren't we all?"

"E4-18 wouldn't hurt him."

"Of course not."

"Probably not," Dr. Reilly corrects. "But why treat a perfectly natural physiological reaction to a stimulus? The boy's just excited."

Michael expects Mr. Salvatolle to make another sly remark, but he turns toward Michael's father and Dr. Reilly. "So tell me, Lloyd," he says. "How is it that you haven't managed to make a whisky convert out of our friend the good doctor? I notice he's drinking rum."

After he is sure that his father and Dr. Reilly are fully engaged in a conversation about spirits, and Alyssa and her parents are busy regaling Julia with recollections of the trip they took to Baltimore last Christmastime, Michael presses his left leg hard up against Mr. Salvatolle's right one. Then he waits with breath held for what feels like a century.

He has almost given up hope when, finally, the man presses back.

SEVEN

Down in the restaurant's supply room, just off the box-office drive thru, Marc leans against the cool concrete wall and attempts to calm down.

His whole body is thrumming, overloaded with adrenaline. He wishes he had his pills, and a watch, too. It feels as if he has been waiting for hours, but it can't be much later than ten after eight, because that is the time when Wayne Dupree agreed to meet him.

Nothing about the evening is going as he expected it would. First, he'd gotten waylaid by Julia Ferguson while waiting for Ehrichto Salvatolle to show up at the affair. Next, he'd been dissed by Chef Anthony. He rationalizes that it was his weird Baxter-esque attire that put the man off. The look that crossed the chef's face would have been more appropriate had he just found gum stuck to the bottom of his shoe. He'd ordered Marc not just out of the kitchen office, but out of the kitchen, as well.

Before he left Marc had managed to make eye contact with Wayne, a commis of the establishment and his connection for the various drugs occasionally requested by guests of the hotel, and Baxter, as well. Wayne's sources also supply the quantities of Ritalin Marc now needs, far more than the meager amount his doctor prescribes.

Wayne had stopped slicing vegetables long enough to signal "Smoke break 8:10" before a diminutive blonde sous chef took notice and finished her boss's work by escorting Marc all the way to and through the kitchen door.

Back in the lobby, the guests were finding their seats. Marc had scanned the room looking for the handsome Italian and found him just taking his seat beside—he shakes harder, recalling it—Julia's teenaged son Michael.

One year ago, he thinks, remembering the way the naked windows in the back bedroom framed the rainbow-hued sparks coloring the sky. They'd kept him from noticing, when he first entered the room, that Richard Baxter was sprawled across the plastic-encased mattress, drinking champagne right from the bottle.

"It's like launching a ship," he'd declared, startling Marc and making him jump.

"What is?"

"Finishing work on the house. Now it needs to be christened."

Marc knew what he meant, but played dumb. "By doing what? Smashing an unopened bottle on the porch railing?"

"Not the kind of christening I meant."

Had the champagne gone to his head that quickly? Was he really making a pass? Marc kept his cool. They'd bantered back and forth for years, but every time Marc tried to take it to the next level, Baxter spooked and backed off. "Isn't that the job of the people who are going to live here?" he asked.

Baxter rolled his eyes. "Oh, please. I'll wager they haven't fucked even one time in the decade and a half since that boy was conceived. And I imagine that was some missionary style horror."

"I don't want to imagine it at all," Marc replied. "But if the son is fifteen, there's your answer. He'll christen it plenty; probably five minutes after they move in."

"Hey," he hears Wayne say behind him. When he turns he sees that the guy is lugging a bag of trash. Wayne walks to the wheeled bin, lifts the lid, and deposits the bag inside. His well-muscled arms are heavily scarred with slashes from knife cuts and welts from burns, and the tips of tribal inkwork peek from beneath his t-shirt sleeves. Marc finds the look extremely appealing, in a modern-day-pirate sort of way. "I got away as soon as I could," Wayne says. "What's up?" He makes a face. "And why the fuck are you dressed like Mr. Furley?"

"I'm an actor. It's a costume."

Wayne laughs. "Yeah, right. Like you're in rehearsal tonight. It's Thunder and you're a lackey for the hotel industry." He rises onto the tips of his steel-toed boots to grab a black hard pack of cigarettes stashed behind a can of plum tomatoes on the room's highest shelf, taps out one stick, and returns the pack to its hiding place.

"Not anymore."

"What?" Wayne looks genuinely alarmed. "They sacked you right before the Derby Festival? Why? What the fuck did you do?"

"It's not what I did, it's what I'm doing, or rather not doing, right now. I was supposed to do a double shift today but I never officially showed up."

Wayne pulls a lighter from the pocket of his apron, strikes its flywheel, and touches the flame to the cigarette's tip. "Why? Are you out of your mind?"

"What I am," Marc says, stepping closer to him. "Is horny as shit." He tucks the end of the porter's apron into the ties secured around his waist, unzips the fly of his baggy, houndstooth-patterned pants, and sinks into a crouch. Reaching between the folds of fabric, he pulls out the kitchen worker's semi-erect penis. "Now that is an amuse-bouche."

"Amuse-gueule," Wayne says. Unfamiliar with the term, Marc looks up, hoping for a clue, but gets nothing but a smug, cold look in return. "You know the drill," Wayne says. "Break's up when I finish this." He sucks a drag from the cigarette, blows the smoke in Marc's face, and laughs. "Bone appétit."

"As a resident of New Orleans, Mr. Salvatolle, you will no doubt appreciate Conway Charities' Historic Downtown Initiative, the focus of which is on safeguarding our irreplaceable heritage for future generations," Michael's mother says.

"That certainly sounds worthwhile."

Michael catches the slight emphasis the man places on the third word, but the subtle criticism seems to go right over Julia's head. "Oh, it is. Vastly worthwhile," she agrees. "Which is why we've commissioned an in-depth, very costly study that will help determine the needs of the historic corridor."

"Pity you weren't able to save the building that stood right where we're now sitting," Mr. Salvatolle says.

"Where we…?"

"The offices and warehouse for the Conway Distillery," he explains.

Michael cannot breathe. It is not discussed—except in hushed tones behind closed doors—that the Conway fortune was made in whisky. His mother likes to spin the story the same way her grandmother did, making it seem as if the family came over on the boat already well-to-do, but that isn't the case at all. Michael's been able to piece together that they had a modest dairy and ice business in Portland, then a neighboring town and now a neighborhood within the Louisville metropolitan district. When he came of age the youngest Conway, Morris, had ordered a copper pot still to be shipped over from the old country, and had started a small batch whisky distillery. Sales of Conway's Finest eventually surpassed the combined sales of all the other products the family produced, and Morris became one of the wealthiest men in town.

It had all ended with the passage of the Volstead Act, and the start of Prohibition a year after that. Morris's grandson Patrick had died young, though Michael doesn't know how. It's a topic that is off-limits. Morris died shortly after him, and the bulk of his estate went to Patrick's widow, Michael's great-grandmother Myrtle, and her son Donal, as the Patrick Conway Memorial Trust. Somehow over the years, probably a decision of the board of directors at some point, it had been rechristened with the more modern-sounding name of Conway Charities.

They never talk about how the money was made. The fact that Mr. Salvatolle has just referenced it in front of the Morrisons and Dr. Reilly can only mean one thing—Julia will shortly find some excuse to have him ejected from her party, and will then spend the rest of the evening explaining why what he said is ludicrous. Michael braces himself for the start of her tirade.

"Oh, well, all these buildings were in serious disrepair," she says, an oddly lukewarm start to a meltdown. "Perhaps you've seen the ones on the next block? One has no roof, and a tree has started to grow right in the center of it. The ones here were even worse."

"An excellent argument for always acting sooner rather than later to save the city's architectural heritage," Mr. Salvatolle says. He lays his fork and knife on his plate in the four and eight o'clock positions and uses his napkin to wipe the corners of his moustache. Then he reaches into the breast pocket of his jacket and withdraws a leather business card holder. "I'll tell you what. I'll give you my card. Call me as soon as you can with the specifics of saving the buildings on that block, and we'll talk numbers. That's just the sort of project I like." He starts to hand the card across the table to her but stops, lays it down on the table, and again reaches into his breast pocket. This time, he pulls out a pen. "I'm going to put my direct line on here." He scrawls something on the white space on the back of the card. "That way you won't have to go through my secretary." He hands it across the table, then flips over the next card in the stack and begins writing on it. "I'm making a note so I'll remember when you call what this is in regards to…. You know how it is when you're traveling…. Oh, and while I'm at it…." He pulls more cards from the holder and begins handing them out, one to Michael's father, one to Dr. Reilly and—he leans into Michael's personal space a fourth time—one to Mr. Morrison. As he straightens up, he presses a card into Michael's left hand, beneath the table.

It's the second one he wrote on, the one on which he was supposedly jotting notes to himself. Turned face down so that the words he wrote on the back side are visible, it says, *Let's dust out.*

Before Michael can even turn his head, the man pushes back his chair and stands. "Well, this is delicious, but I've had enough," he says. "I'm going to head outside to smoke." He looks at Michael's father. "You know how it is. Nicotine fit."

"Oh, well, we can understand that," Michael's father says. "We'll be out shortly, won't we Everett?"

The doctor nods. "Yes, in just a couple of minutes." He turns his full attention back to Michael's father. "So, anyway, with this new procedure what we're doing is joining an artery and a vein together so that...."

Mr. Salvatolle pushes his chair in and starts to turn away, but Michael touches his arm, stopping him. When the man turns back they lock eyes and Michael says, as quietly as he can, "Nicotine fit? Is that what they're calling it these days?"

The man smiles slyly. "It is indeed," he says. He smiles again, then turns and strides toward the doors to the patio.

There is no way Michael will be allowed to leave the table until he has eaten at least some of his dinner. Just the thought of food has, all evening, made him queasy. Determined to choke down enough to gain his freedom, he grabs his fork and prepares to dig in, but when he looks down, he finds his plate is almost empty. For several heart-stopping seconds he is convinced that he is losing his mind, that he somehow ate the food without knowing he was doing it, but a glance right reveals a pile of cut-up chicken on Alyssa's plate that is so massive it could not possibly have come from just one breast. Hidden beneath her dinner roll he spies another one, smashed flat as a pancake. Utterly at a loss for why she would have done such a thing, he catches her eye and mouths, *Why?* She only smiles.

"I need to use the restroom," she announces. "Michael, will you please show me where they are again?"

Across the table, his mother sets down her fork, lifts her martini glass, and says over-sweetly, "You don't remember where they are, dear?"

Alyssa meets her gaze. "No, I don't. I'm afraid I'm all turned around," she replies, perfectly matching Julia's condescending tone. "Michael?"

Michael scrambles to his feet and wrestles her chair across the carpet. He is grateful to have something normal and obvious to do, but still concerned about what she is up to. Once on her feet, she takes his hand. "Thanks," she says. "Let's go."

"OH, YEAH." WAYNE gasps. He sinks lower, his knees buckling from the pleasure caused by Marc's ministrations. "Oh, *fuck* YEAAAAH!"

He's spent but still trembling when a loud pounding on the street door causes them both to jump. Marc's natural impulse is to clamber to his feet, but Wayne puts a hand on his shoulder, stopping him. "Be cool," he instructs, wincing as he tucks himself back into his pants. "It's prolly a delivery or someone that's lost. I'll handle it." When he reaches the door he just barely nudges it open, not enough for Marc to see any part of the person on the other side, or them to see him.

"C'n I help you?" Wayne asks. The other person mumbles something in reply.

"Yeah, I think I can do that. What's it worth to you?" After a pause, he laughs. "You're not serious, dude. Try a hundred."

Marc figures it is someone looking for drugs. He hopes Wayne isn't planning to carry on an extended conversation with the client. The high their encounter caused is already beginning to fade; unpleasant thoughts threaten to rise to the surface of his mind. Every bit as much as the acrid, rotting food stench coming from the garbage bin at his left shoulder, regret and guilt are nauseating him. He knows what he's just done is dangerous, that he needs to stop having these encounters with Wayne, and with his geology and algebra professors, and with strangers in the park. *This is how people catch diseases for which there is no cure*, he thinks. *Or get pulled into vans, only to be discovered later in dozens of pieces in the city dump, or sealed into the basement walls of a ranch house in the suburbs.*

Wayne takes a bill from the person outside. *Just give him the drugs*, Marc begs silently. He feels trapped and unable to breathe, overwhelmed with the need to stand, to shout, to make something—anything—else happen as a distraction from the panic rising in his gut. He thinks if something doesn't happen soon that panic will end up as puke, all over the floor.

Instead of handing the stranger a baggie or pulling a bottle of pills from his apron, Wayne throws open the door. "I'm letting you in but then you're on your own, got it?"

This time, the stranger's reply is robust enough for Marc to hear. "Absotutely," he says.

Marc has only ever heard one person use the strange term. When the interloper steps through the doorway, Marc sees just the diversion he needs, an answer to his prayers. He scrambles to his feet. "Hey there, Trey," he says, greeting the younger brother of his on-again, off-again boyfriend Neal Daniels as if he runs into him this way all the time. To ensure the other won't misunderstand what he was doing moments before, down on his knees, he wipes his mouth with the back of his hand. "Great timing."

Trey's stunned expression only deepens the naïve-Iowa-farm-boy-lost-in-the-city look which his short blond hair, broad shoulders and humdrum tuxedo have imparted to him. Marc watches his gaze land on Wayne's mid-section, where the still tucked-up apron exposes a slew of slug-trail glossy smudges on the fabric of his fly. Trey's brow knits. Then his eyes widen.

"You know," Marc says. "You probably shouldn't be surprised anymore."

"You rabid fuckin' dog," Trey snarls. He lunges.

Caught between them, Wayne reflexively blocks the advance. Though not as bulky as the former high school quarterback, the commis manages to knock Trey backward and pin him against the cinder block wall. "Dude!" he hollers. "There's nothin' goin' on here. Chill. I'm not queer. I got a girlfriend, 'kay? The little fag's still all yours, so just calm the hell down."

Marc draws a sharp breath, because he knows what is coming. A second later, Wayne is launched backward into the room by a John-Boy-on-steroids-shaped projectile. He lands on his back on the poured concrete floor, with the ex-quarterback on top of him.

"He's not mine, shit-for-brains!" Trey bellows. "He's my stupid brother's!

And as much as I hate his guts, if you call him that name again I'll kick your fuckin' teeth in, is that clear?" From behind the safety of his arms, which are drawn up to protect his head, Wayne nods. "Yeah, man. Shit! Okay. I got it."

Trey pivots to face Marc. "You," he says, getting to his feet again. "What the hell is wrong with you?"

Rather than answering him, Marc turns and bolts for the door to the hall that leads back into the arts center.

RUNNING AND CLIMBING stairs proves tricky in platform shoes. Trey easily catches up to him on the staircase leading up to the lobby, a collection of half flights set in a corkscrew formation.

"Slut," Trey calls, just before leaping onto the stair ahead of him to block his way. "Horndog. Manwhore."

"It's 'Whorella,' thankyouverymuch," Marc corrects. He feints left and then moves quickly to the right, but Trey matches the movement. From far above them come the muffled sounds of several hundred people talking and laughing. "Let me pass."

"Swear you'll stay away from my brother."

Marc laughs. "He's an adult. He can make up his—"

Trey's arm shoots forward. He shoves Marc's left shoulder, almost sending him tumbling backward down the stairs. "Stay. Away. From. My. Brother."

"Is that a threat?"

"Take it however you like." His eyes glint. "You always do."

"Screw you."

"Only one you haven't."

"Careful, Freud, your slip is showing," Marc says. He tries again to push past Trey, but it's like trying to move a boulder.

"What the hell's that supposed to mean?"

"Secretly, you want me," Marc says. He's rewarded with another slam in the chest. This time, though, Trey uses both hands. Marc is rocked back onto the heels of his platform shoes. Gravity tugs at the pit of his stomach. He makes a frantic grab for the stair railing but finds only air, and the resulting adrenaline rush triggers a warp-speed slide show in his mind as he free falls.

HE'S ELEVEN AGAIN, just leaving school for the day, and his stomach is in knots, only it is caused not by freefalling but by the knowledge that his mother's best friend's boyfriend, Bobby Lee, is waiting for him in her trailer, where he is required to go each day after school until his mother gets off shift. The women think the trailer is a good place for Marc to be to do his homework and have a snack after school, precisely because

Bobby Lee is there. They imagine his presence provides adult supervision, but Marc knows otherwise. He imagines the guy pacing the paneled living room, reviewing the details of the X-rated afternoon and evening he has planned for them

THE MEMORY IS stopped by the sensation of a hand clamping, vise-like, around his right wrist, yanking him upright once more. Marc grabs the railing with both hands but remains paralyzed by the adrenaline rush. He feels Trey pull away from him, sees him hurl himself backward onto the steps, scramble to get turned around, and finally, on all fours, dash up the stairs and away.

"How'D YOU REALLY find this place?" Jeff asks.

They are standing in the largest of the three adjoining cavern spaces Baxter commandeered for his event. Moments ago, he'd thrown the switch on the light system. Now brightly colored rays issue from canister lights hung from telescoping towers. They pulse on the craggy limestone walls and distant ceiling of the "room," giving it the appropriate club feel. He wishes briefly that the company handling sound for the event had dropped off their equipment already as well, but then figures that the sort of music the rave/dance party calls for is not something that can be merely switched on. A team of DJs will be engineering the sound during all-night event. "I told you already," he replies, flipping the switch again. The space is once more plunged into near total darkness. Only the truck's roof-mounted beams remain, trained on the nearest wall. "I was looking for Louisville Welding."

"You did not stumble over this in the phonebook," Jeff says. His silhouette is barely visible. He's looking straight up toward the man-made cavern's roof, though it isn't possible to see even three feet above one's head, let alone one hundred. "You read about this somewhere—some *Guide to Lost Louisville* or something—and you came to investigate." He drops his gaze and looks left and right, into the pockets of darkness surrounding them. "I bet the city tricked this out to be a bomb shelter during the Second World War."

They had, actually. The space the city reserved for use as a fallout shelter in the event of nuclear war is located down a different passage, one with running water containing schools of eerie, eyeless, albino fish. There are provisions there for thousands, most of it taken from the army. Baxter found stashes of khaki canvas cots and lockers, field radios, and case after case of B-rations—canned, packaged or preserved foods needing no refrigeration.

Shielding his eyes, he makes his way back toward the truck. The cavern's constant fifty-eight-degree temperature is starting to make his hip ache. He stops to lean against the grill of the truck and let the pain subside.

Jeff comes over to stand beside him. "C'mon, you can tell me," he says. "Is there supposed to be treasure buried in here somewhere?" He laughs. "Or Jimmy Hoffa?"

He's only kidding, obviously, but has stumbled closer to the truth than Baxter finds comfortable. "The only scuttlebutt I've heard is that the company that bought the mining rights from the city overstepped their bounds and got caught. The city shut them down and put up the fencing to keep kids out, because there are some substantial drop offs in here and in some places water deep enough to drown in."

Jeff puts his hands on his hips. "You can drown in an inch of water," he says. "A drunk face down in a gutter, or a kid playing in a storm drain during a spring shower. It happens."

"Aren't you Little Miss Sunshine?" Baxter pushes him out of the way, yanks open the driver's door, and climbs back into the cab. Jeff bounds around to the passenger's side and scurries up into his seat as only the young can. He tucks one leg beneath his body and twists his torso to face Baxter, who can almost hear the twinkle in his eye.

"Too bad they were mining in here. This would've been a great place to stash hooch during Prohibition."

Baxter doesn't believe in ghosts. Still, the words send a shiver up his spine. He turns the key and the engine roars to life. "We should go," he says. "Traffic is going to be hell in an hour."

"MICHAEL! WAIT!" ALYSSA calls as he enters the mouth of the hallway beneath the Bomhard Theater stairs. Her fingers brush his arm but fail to catch hold of him, and he picks up his pace. He is now honestly heading for the men's room, because he feels he is about to be sick. His stomach began doing barrel-rolls the minute he stood up. The sensation is not unlike how he felt the one time he let his ex-best friend Jon talk him into riding a Tilt-a-Whirl, part of the traveling carnival that for one weekend every summer was erected in the parking lot of the strip mall adjacent to their neighborhood.

When the ride finally ended and he was back on solid ground, Michael had thrown up three times, all over the asphalt, in front of God and everyone. Fabric rustles behind him. Alyssa grabs his arm. "Can't talk now," he says, risking a glance backward. "I think I'm—"

He catches sight of a tuxedoed figure half-hidden by the deep shadows of the hall. For a split second he thinks Mr. Salvatolle somehow anticipated this move on their part and came here instead of going to the patio. Then the figure shifts, and Michael sees that the person in question has blond hair. At the same moment, he feels Alyssa tense.

"Trey?" she asks. She lets go of Michael's arm. "Oh my god. What are you doing here?"

"It's that much of a mystery? I came to see you."

"I'm on a date."

"Yeah, you look really nice."

"I just said I'm on a date. What part of that confuses you?"

"We need to talk."

She scoffs. "So not happening. Not after what you did."

"I didn't do anything! How many times do I have to tell you that?"

"The only thing you have to do is leave."

Michael figures he is supposed to do or say something to make the guy go. Before he can begin to think what that might be, Trey begins to beg.

"'Lyssa, c'mon" he pleads. "Please. I didn't do anything, I swear. She asked if I'd decided where I was going in the fall, and she talked up the University of Louisville. That was it. I didn't say anything to her to sabotage his grant."

Last year, Trey's older brother Neal was a finalist for the Conway Charities' Emerging Professionals grant. Everyone assumed he was a shoe-in, but a week after Thunder when the recipient was announced, the money went to someone else. The only thing Michael finds at all unusual about it is that his mother allowed Neal to be a finalist in the first place. He finds the notion that she could somehow have missed his record of social justice activism to be utterly ridiculous.

"You're so jealous of him," Alyssa says. "It's sad."

Lightning fast, Trey's expression changes to a fierce scowl. "Hell, yeah, I'm jealous! You think losing that grant hurt him? Please. He has a ton of scholarship money, and something even better—a whole damned world of people like you, worshiping the ground he walks on." Michael cringes. He thinks the guy should stop now, before he digs himself any deeper, but Trey raises his voice to a comic pitch. "Oh, the poor, long suffering martyr!" he mocks. "'All he wants is to be allowed to love. Isn't he brave for living his life so out and proud? Let's give him everything his heart desires! Let's give him the world!'"

Michael pictures his father and mother and their four hundred guests, seated just on the other side of the stairs, all straining to hear the goings-on. He forgets the rumbling in his stomach when his legs begin to shake.

Alyssa clucks her tongue. "Really? That's how you feel? Wow."

Trey continues to quote his brother's imagined cheering squad. Michael wonders if it is supposed to be an imitation of Mrs. Daniels, who he's met a few times, and whose uber-enthusiastic nature he found overwhelming. "'He was out at summer camp, you know,'" Trey says, still in the painful falsetto. "'He was out in Little League. He founded the chapter of the Gay-Straight Student Alliance at his high school, and he was their first-ever out athlete—out football player, no less! Did you know he's going to be a psychiatrist? That's right—he's going to help gay kids be as out and proud and brave as he was!'" He throws his arms into the air and bellows, "Well, happy f-ing doo-dah! He's gay! Why can't he just go live his life already, and let me live mine? And why can't you let him—" He thrusts an arm in Michael's direction. "—live his?"

Alyssa blanches. "Excuse me?"

"You think I don't know what you're doing, Alyssa? You think everyone doesn't know? Let the kid fight his own battles. He doesn't need you to save him!"

"For your infor—" Alyssa freezes and her eyes grow huge. "Oh, Mr. Ferguson!"

Michael's head snaps left and he sees his father standing at the base of the stairs. The tremor in his legs spreads to the rest of his body.

"You, uh, remember my ex, uh, boyfriend Trey, don't you?" Alyssa stammers.

"We were all just, uh, just…."

"Kidding around," Trey interjects. "Just being stupid."

Michael feels the acid sting of bile in his throat. He studies his father's face in an effort to determine what he did and did not hear and whether or not he buys Trey's assertion.

"Michael," his father says. "Are you all right?"

By way of reply, Michael spews leek broth and masticated radicchio all over the bright orange carpeting.

THE COOL AIR and the crowd, a literal sea of people filling the art center's back patio and the green space beyond it, all the way to the river's edge, stop Ehrichto in his tracks just after he steps outside. Night is falling fast and the sky, bleak all day, now is almost black. Though the air is thick with the stench of beer and greasy fair food, mud, and half a million people, he can still smell the algae and fish of the river and feel its moisture in the air. Somewhere in the darkness a calliope starts up, its steam-driven whistles articulating a lively tune. *Drink Conway Whisky!* Patrick's voice cries in his mind, so clearly that Ehrichto looks left expecting to see his lover exiting the building dressed in jockey silks, the gimmick of a Derby promotion long past.

I can't believe this is happening, he thinks as he reaches into his breast pocket for his cigars and lighter. His hands are shaking badly, something which, before this evening, he hasn't experienced in decades, not even during all the drama with Nick. *Maria brought him back.* He abandons his usual concern over the proper toasting of the leaves, choosing to simply stick

E I G H T

the cigar between his lips and concentrate on bringing flame and leaf together. Just as it seems the thing will catch, a gust of wind blows out his allegedly windproof lighter.

He hears the distinctive spark of a flywheel grinding flint, followed by a vaguely familiar voice. "Need a light?" When he turns, he can just make out Marc Payette's features in the unsteady glow of a dancing flame. The concierge keeps his free hand cupped protectively around the fire as he moves forward. Ignoring the gesture, Ehrichto slips the unlit cigar back into his breast pocket.

Marc releases the lighter's lever and steps out of the shadows. Bizarrely, he is dressed in formal wear three decades out of date, a flared-leg polyester tuxedo with velvet lapels. "Fuck me if I'm wrong," the young man says, loud enough that people further down the patio surely can hear. "But I'd say you abandoned the chicken course because something much more enticing caught your eye." He smirks. "I think you're more interested in the patio menu."

A loud, metallic crack sounds, off to Ehrichto's right. He attributes it to the push bar on the arts center's exit being punched open. *Patrick*, he thinks.

Memories of his lover's jealous rages race through his mind. He knows it is imperative that he get rid of Marc Payette.

"I'm sorry to have misled you, but now you need to leave."

The concierge tsk-tsks. "You don't want to stay out here and watch this silly display. I'll show you real fireworks."

Ehrichto seizes him by the upper arm and pulls him forward a step. "What I want is for you to LEAVE," he says firmly. "NOW." He releases him, turns away, and is immediately disappointed but also somewhat relieved to find not Patrick but Everett Reilly walking toward him. *Good,* he thinks. *He'll be far less threatened by him than by that rapacious little tart.*

Dr. Reilly jabs a thumb to indicate the space behind Ehrichto. "Wasn't that the concierge from next door? What's he doing over here? And why was he dressed like that?"

"I don't know."

"Well, what did he want? What did he say?"

"I don't know," Ehrichto repeats, irritation clear in his tone. "It was something to do with some competition, yet another charity fundraiser."

"A race, no doubt. We race everything during the festival. Stallions, fillies, rubber ducks, waiters, beds...."

"I told him I wasn't interested in his shenanigans and to go away." Ehrichto looks over the doctor's shoulder toward the shimmering lobby. "Where is he?"

"Lloyd? He's not going to be joining us," Dr. Reilly says. "Michael got sick in the bathroom, apparently, and he took him home."

"Who's Michael?"

The doctor looks surprised, then concerned. "His son," he says. "The young man who was seated beside you at dinner. Apparently he really wasn't feeling well and Lloyd.... Mr. Salvatolle? Where are you going?"

Already charging toward the lobby, Ehrichto doesn't bother to reply.

"It's LIKELY TO be the flu, coming on so fast," Lloyd says. He looks over at Michael, who is slumped against the passenger's door with his face turned toward the rain-soaked window. "Just hang in there. We're almost home."

He wishes Michael was well enough to drive, because—as happens frequently these days—the edges of Lloyd's field of vision are gone, temporarily dissolved into a gray blur, the result of stress. In order to get the complete picture of the road ahead he has to move his head far to the left and right.

To his mind, the auditory disturbance he is experiencing is even worse than his ocular one: he cannot get the section of the conversation he overheard between Michael, his girlfriend and her former boyfriend Trey Daniels to stop replaying itself in his head.

...he's gay. I wish he'd just go live his life already, and let me live mine. And why can't you let him live his?

No matter how hard he tries, Lloyd can't figure what on earth—other than the obvious—would have made the older boy say those words, what the three could possibly have been talking about just before he entered the space that would have inspired that bit of dialogue.

The sign for their upcoming exit flies past. "All right," he say, giddy with relief.

Once again, Michael does not respond. Lloyd wonders if maybe he has fallen asleep. He slows the car and carefully guides it onto the exit ramp. At the stop sign at its end, he pauses long enough to turn knobs on the dash and crank up the heater. "You're not cold, are you?" he asks, before pulling right onto Poplar Level, the last major street before their neighborhood.

Was that Daniels kid, he wonders, returning to the subject of the interrupted conversation, *trying to disrupt their date by accusing Michael of being…?* He shakes the thought away and carefully turns the car onto a side street. He gives silent thanks that the street is not as it usually is at this hour, filled with kids holding out against the dying light, zig-zagging across the blacktop on bicycles, scooters and skateboards. The thought of skateboards makes him think of Jon Lewis, and his temples begin to throb.

In most of the residences Lloyd spies the tell-tale blue glow of television. He pictures happy families crowded in around small sets, eagerly anticipating the start of the fireworks, being broadcast by a local affiliate for those few people who refuse to brave the crowds at the riverfront, people who prefer to spend time as a family privately, not putting on a dog and pony show downtown to fund a charity whose true purpose is to make its president influential.

How did he even get in? he wonders, thinking again of Trey. *He wasn't on the guest list. He couldn't have been. His family swore they'd never attend another Conway Charities event after that brouhaha last year, and Julia would never—*

"Um, Dad?" Michael exclaims, at the same instant that the tires on the left side of the car begin to vibrate violently, a warning that the car has veered onto the shoulder, the wrong shoulder, the one for opposing traffic. Lloyd jerks the wheel sideways, then back the other way, looking for the center line. He manages to locate it and get them back to good. As soon as he does, he slows the car to a near crawl.

"Sorry," he mumbles. "We're okay." Michael loudly exhales and settles back against the door.

The road begins to incline; in another minute, Lloyd knows, it will twist into a corkscrew. *Just take it slow,* he tells himself, trying to stay calm, but he feels trapped by the rock face on his right and the guardrail on his far left. He wonders if the rail would be able to stop the car from careening over the side. He imagines the Corvette, flattened to a pancake, lying in the yard of one of the homes at the base of the hill, and that makes him think of the Skeleton House.

LOCATED ALONG THE highway outside of his hometown, by the time Lloyd and his friends were old enough to go exploring it the place was little more than four walls around a room-sized boulder. Whatever furnishings once remained had either been removed by trespassers or destroyed by years of rain and wind and sun. But none of that really mattered; the thing to see was the enormous rock that had come loose during heavy spring rains and landed smack dab on the dwelling. None of Lloyd's friends knew what time of day or night it had happened, or whether or not anyone was in the house when it did, whether anyone had died as a result, because the adults they knew refused to talk about it. In the eastern part of the state space for living had to be taken by force, with dynamite, and people lived with the constant threat that at any minute nature would exact revenge. It was as if they believed talking about Skeleton House would bring another boulder down, this time on their house or car, or the school, or the church.

Lloyd again pictures the Corvette going over the railing. This time his psyche has it land upside down on the roof of one of the houses below them. "We're almost home," he says, trying to banish the image from his mind. "Hey, I'll bet we can see the whole thing from your room."

Michael raises his head. "What thing?"

"The fireworks. You can see downtown from your room, right? Shoot, why didn't we think of that before?"

"Because we've only lived there eight months," his son says, with the deadpan seriousness that is the reserve of teenagers. "And because no way would she ever let us stay home for Thunder."

The heavy emphasis Michael places on the pronoun bothers Lloyd. He has also long despised Michael's insistence on calling Julia either "she" or "her," never "Mom" or "Ma" or even "Mother."

"You have to turn right around and go back," Michael says. "If you don't, it'll be too late and the cops won't let you into the area. All the streets become southbound when the fireworks start."

"I know that," Lloyd says. The idea of having to drive back downtown, and then home again with Julia at an even later hour further unnerves him. He imagines calling his wife and explaining the situation, tries further to imagine her, for once, listening to what he says and then acting as his partner by agreeing to take a cab home, but his suspension of disbelief fails. The only outcome he can foresee is one where the minute the cab drives off she begins berating him for abandoning her, accusing him of weakness.

"If you stay here to watch the show you'll have to wait hours for the mess to clear," Michael says. "You probably won't be able to get back to the Center until like one or two in the morning, and man, she'll be pissed."

"Watch your language."

"What's wrong with 'pissed'?"

The curve of the road tightens. "Just don't say it."

"Whatever."

Lloyd is relieved when he at last sees the stone gate of their development (*Griffin Gate: Where English Gentility and Southern Hospitality intersect*), though the minute they are through it his ability to see grows even worse, because the lampposts of the subdivision are placed so few and far between. Even heading into the development's lone intersection, it is so dark that he can barely tell the cross-street is there. *Just great*, he thinks. *Now I can see basically nothing.*

Just as did the neighborhood and expressway before it, the development feels deserted, though he knows this time that it has nothing to do with the fact that a half million of the city's residents are gathered at the riverfront, and everything to do with the Homeowners Association's ban on street parking, which it claims "invites theft and threatens home values." Lloyd thinks just the opposite is true; he believes that locking cars away behind garage doors fosters insularity and invites crime by making it nearly impossible to tell if one's neighbors are home or not. After their astronomical mortgage, it is the ridiculous mandates of the Griffin Gate Homeowners Association which most makes living in the development a horror for him. The Association is also behind the ugly brick mailbox fortresses at the end of every double driveway; the lack of any sidewalks besides the useless, meandering paths that link driveways and front entryways; and the decision which is most vexing him at the current moment, the one to line the twisting roads with "vintage" street lamps. Lloyd has long felt that the low wattage fixtures give the development the aspect of Mockingbird Lane in the old sitcom *The Munsters*.

Usually the thing that irritates him the most about the development is the Association's pretentious insistence that the hill on which it is located is part of the Original Highlands, one of the city's most desirable residential designations, when in truth it falls just south of the boundary line.

Lloyd steers the car along the curving road as it starts to straighten out. Ahead, he can just barely make out the curve to the right which starts their cul-de-sac. He sees their house, already aglow because its lights are controlled by sensors. Every muscle in his body clenches as he begins to steer the car past the brick mailbox and into the driveway.

"I don't want to watch from my room," Michael says.

Lloyd hits the brakes. "What?"

"The fireworks. I don't want to watch them from my room."

Lloyd tries to sound not crestfallen. "Why not?"

"Because you're supposed to see them firsthand, not from like ten miles away."

"It's not ten miles," Lloyd says. "It's more like—"

"I don't care what it is! That's not the point! It's not the same as being there!"

"I understand that, Michael, but—"

"It's not the same! I wanted to stay downtown! I told you!"

His son's shouting is not doing good things for Lloyd's headache. "I know, but you're—"

"No! You didn't listen! You never listen to me!"

"Dammit, Michael, stop yelling!" Lloyd barks. "You're sick! You're not thinking clearly!"

Instantly, he feels a wall of silence form between them. He realizes his words might be construed as having a different meaning than what he intended. "Wait, that's not what I…uh …."

Michael throws open his door and springs from the car.

"Michael," Lloyd calls. "Michael!"

His Corvette and Michael's Mercedes already occupy the spaces inside the garage. Lloyd pulls the Lexus in behind his own car and throws it into park.

As soon as he does his body seems to turn to gelatin. He slumps forward and rests his head against the steering wheel. For several long moments he just breathes. Then he shifts his gaze so that his slivered field of vision takes in the empty seat beside him.

"What were you three talking about, back there?" he wonders aloud.

The upholstery makes no reply.

It doesn't surprise Ehrichto to find Marc Payette leaned up against the Porsche.

"This is a sweet ride," the young man opines. "How much did it set you back?"

Ehrichto ignores the question. "Where is that house you helped build located, exactly?" he asks.

Back at the Galt House, after he'd hauled the concierge to his feet, the young man had volunteered an opinion about the subject of the conversation on which they stood eavesdropping: Julia Conway Ferguson. The men in the hallway described her as "a handful." Marc's opinion had been somewhat stronger.

"She's a Grade-A bitch," he'd said.

Ehrichto's mind was reeling. He couldn't imagine how such a thing had been allowed to happen. A Ferguson married to a Conway? How had the world not imploded? "How do you know this Julia Conway Ferguson," he asked, the act of stringing the words together out loud making him queasy.

Marc Payette rolled his eyes. "Honey, everyone knows her," he'd explained. "You live in this town, sooner or later you have to deal with her. I don't mind telling you that I've had more than my fair share. I helped a friend build her McMansion."

The young man pushes off from the car, steps too close for comfort. "Why do you want to go there? Take me for a ride," he says, in a way that implies he's not talking about cars. "I promise to make it a very exciting trip for you."

Ehrichto doesn't have time for games. He needs to catch up with Patrick. "You have difficulty focusing," he says. The way the young man flinches tells him it's not the first time he's heard that particular criticism. "The house you helped build for her. Where. Is. It. Located?"

"Out by the zoo."

"How do I get there?"

"Uh, you take 65 to 264 to Poplar Level to...to a bunch of streets all named Sylvan something or other, until you reach...." Marc looks around, spies a road atlas in an open convertible two cars over, and retrieves it. He riffles pages until he finds the one he wants and then points. "Here. It's an ankh, see? The cul-de-sac is the eye. Isn't that wild?"

A chill runs up Ehrichto's spine. *The key to the gates of death*, he thinks. *It's not just wishful thinking on my part, or a doppelgänger. It really is Patrick.* "Where along the ankh is, uh, the ...." He falters, almost overcome with emotion. *I owe Maria an apology*, he thinks. *The blood in my veins can pull a living soul out of death's reach, that's true, but bringing someone back to life after they've died is much better magic. Maya god? No. Maya goddess.* "Specifically, where is the house? What should I look for when I get there?"

"It's the first one on the right after the intersection." When Ehrichto pulls open the driver's door, Marc Payette catches his arm. "But I live a lot closer than that."

Ehrichto feels guilty for having led him on earlier. Though he was mainly after his blood, there was a certain warped attraction to the idea of giving in to Dorjan's view of the male heart, to satisfying some of his baser urges at the same time. But that thought holds no appeal now that he knows Patrick has returned, and there's no time for this sort of nonsense. He must put an immediate end to his interactions with this young man, must disabuse him of his misperceptions, once and for all.

"I've already apologized for misleading you. I don't mean to be blunt but you give me no choice, so here it is: I'm not interested in what you have to offer."

Marc Payette reaches between his legs and gives him a firm squeeze.

"This says otherwise."

Ehrichto grabs his wrist and roughly shoves him away. "You seem not to be aware of what you are, so allow me to enlighten you," he says. "Eau de vie de Marc is a vintage made from the stems and pips, skins, mess and dregs left over after finer runs. From garbage, in other words. It's far too coarse a libation for this god, and I don't accept the offering. What I'm seeking—what I have always been seeking—is *uisce beatha*, the Water of Life. After far, far too long I've just found it again, and I can't waste time here with you. Goodbye."

He slips into the driver's seat and sticks the key in the ignition. Marc Payette stands in the way of his being able to close the door.

"But I'm...I'm recommended at the price! And I've never had any complaints!"

"Free is not a price," Ehrichto says. He turns the key and the car comes to life with a deep, masculine growl. "And the fact that all the village idiots have already gotten drunk on your low wines," he adds, half-shouting to be heard over the roar of the cylinders, "frankly, turns my stomach." He casts a withering glare at Marc as he reaches for the door handle, in order to make the concierge step back, out of the way. It works better than he expects. Looking alarmed, Marc hurtles backward until he is pressed against the next car. It reminds Ehrichto that he does, in fact, possesses the same ability to influence others that Dorjan does, just without the ability to control it. "GOODBYE," he shouts, before slamming the car door closed and throwing the vehicle into reverse.

"MICHAEL?" LLOYD ASKS, giving the closed door one short, sharp rap. He doesn't want to just barge in. He figures Michael is changing his clothes, getting into something not covered in bile and bits of radicchio. "How's it going in there?"

Because of the conversation he half-overheard, not getting a reply is a problem. While downstairs mixing a pitcher of orange juice concentrate, he'd had to sing to distract himself and keep certain thoughts at bay. Now a snippet of the song he was singing is stuck in his head.

He wishes Alyssa and Trey had left well enough alone. He knows he has to find a way to talk to his son, to try to explain that he understands what it's like to be a teenager. He can still recall, albeit barely, the melodrama of being seventeen, filled with the conviction that everything that happened was significant—no, critical—or even preordained. Looking back, he's still surprised to realize how little of what he was obsessed about at that age really mattered, in the long run. *How odd it is to be that age,* he thinks. *Convinced your life will just go on and on, that you have all the time in the world to overcome any obstacle and learn whatever new skill you'll need to get to wherever you want to go, and at the same time worried about everything, conscious of how much you still don't know.*

He looks at Michael's closed bedroom door, and the shadowy hall beyond it.

And then when you get old enough to realize that ninety percent of everything is frivolous, not worth wasting your time on, you find you barely have enough time to deal with the three or four very real crises you're faced with of a day.

How do they do it, he wonders, his thoughts shifting to a couple they know—are acquainted with, really, though Julia makes it sound as if they're fast friends—who take trips constantly, and not quick jaunts, either, but real excursions to Europe, the Far East, the Middle East, Latin America. Other people they know have nicer things than he and Julia do, a bigger (though not a prettier) house, a vacation home, newer cars. They know people who sit on the boards of noteworthy organizations, and also have memberships at every museum and art gallery and theater, who talk about the various exhibits and shows they've seen. *Even forgetting the cost,* he thinks, *where do they find the time?* He looks left at the wall that runs the length of the suspension bridge-like hall Julia calls the gallery because of the roughly half dozen pieces of art Angelo de Haven hung on it, which are visible from the street.

Hell, we've been in this house eight months and I've barely looked at most of these pieces.

At either end of the wall there is an enormous plaster reproduction. *Bas-relief,* Lloyd thinks, pleased he knows the term. The first of the shallow, bone-white works depicts a basket of fruit; the second a Greek god (he can't recall which one) holding a hyacinth by its stem. Between those two works are seven paintings. Looking at them now, he remembers why it is he never looks up here: there is, almost literally, nothing to see. All seven paintings are done in a style Angelo de Haven called Tonalism, a style Lloyd had been unaware even existed up until that point. Afterward, he regretted the loss of his ignorance, for in his opinion the canvases—painted with shades of acrylic so light the images are hardly distinguishable from the gesso beneath—display less artistic merit than the finger paintings Michael made while a toddler. He thinks that if these are some of the movement's best works he would hate to see its failures, and—in the months since he has lived with the works—he has come to think of the adherents of the style as being tone blind.

It's probably a blessing that I never have a chance to look at these, he thinks. *The only good thing that can be said about them is they didn't cost us anything.* He still finds it incredible that the entire lot is on loan to them, borrowed from a private collector who is one of de Haven's other clients. He knows how that game is played, has heard doctors telling one another how to play it. *You buy it for its book value and loan it out because it's ugly and you don't want to have to look at it yourself.* He thinks it would make more sense to buy and surround yourself with things you actually like. But the adult world, he's found, rarely makes sense.

The practice of purchasing art solely as an investment feels like a page from his Uncle James's playbook, an unfair bending of the rules or even outright cheating. It feels suspicious. For a long time he'd wondered if the architect Angelo de Haven was not being aboveboard, if he saw in Julia only dollar signs, a pile of cash to be made. But even after all the expenses of decorating the house were added in, the project was far cheaper than Lloyd ever anticipated and, better still, the mortgage company de Haven worked with turned out to be well-versed in creative financing.

Careful what you wish for, he cautions himself. That morning, he'd received a letter from a law office in New Orleans that called into question the ownership of the land beneath the house. Printed on heavyweight, silken, parchment-colored paper—expensive paper—it read:

Dear Mr. and Mrs. Ferguson,

Our firm was recently contacted by the City of Louisville's Division of Inspections, Permits and Licenses regarding an application submitted to that office by Highlands Pool and Spa, requesting a permit to dig within Platte 23 of the Grecian Gardens Development. All of the land on which the aforementioned development is located is owned by a client of ours, M. Bianchi; therefore we believe this property may have been misrepresented to you as being available for sale, and are looking into the matter. A

representative from our firm will contact you soon to discuss what steps our office is planning to take in order to remedy this situation, and how the matter between you and our client might be resolved.
    Respectfully yours,
    Glenn Cozart, LLC.

All day long he has been trying not to think about that letter and its implications. If the land was not for sale, who have they been paying their money to? Are those funds just lost? Will the rightful owner even agree to sell to them? If not, how will the matter be resolved? Will they lose the house? He doubts their marriage would withstand that ordeal.

It strikes him as grossly unfair that, in a time when anyone with a 401k to liquidate can start flipping houses to earn "TEN DOLLARS FOR EVERY ONE INVESTED!"—as one late-night infomercial he's seen promises—he and Julia should be blocked in their effort to pursue the classic American dream of straightforward dream home ownership. Not buying and flipping, just buying and owning.

We knew it was too good to be true, he thinks. He feels sick to his stomach, angry with himself and with Julia. *We knew there was a catch but we ignored it. We had to. We couldn't afford not to.*

Caveat emptor. Let the buyer beware. He stares at the bleached-out "art." *I should have listened to my gut,* he thinks. *You get what you pay for, and never a dime more.*

He knows only two things for certain. One, that they don't have the money to hire a lawyer; and two, that worrying about it won't solve anything. He pushes the subject from his conscious mind, turns, and knocks on Michael's door again. "Buddy? You didn't fall asleep did you? I found a can of orange juice in the icebox and made that up. Does that sound good? Or too acidic? If you don't want it I'll just get you some water." He knocks again, waits again, tries not to think about how agitated Michael was by the time he got into the house. How like a caged animal he was, pacing back in forth in his room, stripping off his tuxedo and throwing the components onto his bed. He'd changed into jeans and a white button front shirt while Lloyd weighed the options of what medicine to give him. An antiemetic, obviously, but which? A serotonin or a dopamine antagonist? He thinks of his boss, Robert Morrison, stupidly trying to give Michael E4-18 at dinner because he thinks it's God's gift to humankind, and how, deep in conversation with Dr. Reilly, Lloyd hadn't known what was going on with Michael until the whole discussion, mercifully, was squelched by Mr. Salvatolle's citing of the pending fireworks display, and his assertion that there was "no need to treat him, because there's nothing wrong with him."

Lloyd had told himself the man was just being kind, was trying to deflect attention from the fact that Michael was clearly awestruck by him, and overwhelmed. Of course he was. Every man in the place would have killed to be in Ehrichto Salvatolle's shoes. He was young, good-looking, rich. Was there anything better in the world? It wasn't a bad thing that Michael had found a role model there.

Lloyd and Dr. Reilly had succeeded in drawing Mr. Salvatolle into their conversation a few times, but his attention was obviously divided. Lloyd wonders what conversation he and Michael kept returning to all night. He'd seen them whispering back and forth, exchanging little smiles.

Alyssa might as well not have been there.

He shakes the thought away and knocks on his son's door again. "Michael? I found some medicine that will settle your stomach." He waits a few seconds more and then tries the knob, but finds it locked.

A memory from a year and a half ago flashes in his mind, a fragment of the night he told Michael they were moving. His son's response to the news had shocked him. Michael locked himself in his room and began ripping down the rock posters and magazine clippings that papered his walls. A collection it took him years to assemble vanished in moments, leaving the walls dotted with just the torn corners of images and bits of transparent tape.

He paced that night too, Lloyd remembers. He's tried, several times, to discuss the incident with his son, but as he is with so many other topics, Michael remains silent on the issue.

First he wouldn't talk to me. Now he won't even let me in his room, Lloyd thinks, exasperated. He bends down to set the tray on the carpeting outside the door.

When he does, the throbbing in his temples intensifies. He

straightens up, but it doesn't help. He puts his hands to his head, and squeezes his eyes shut.

It's not until he hears a hideous metal-on-metal screeching coming from out on the street that he opens them again. His heart begins hammering his chest. He knows the source of the terrible noise: it's the rotors of the brake system in Michael's car being not-so-slowly destroyed.

His immediate reaction is denial: *That can't be Michael's car. He would've had to climb out the window…using the pine tree? He wouldn't dare!* He doesn't for one minute believe it, though. He understands that his son is no longer in the house; knows also that, in his present state, with his vision so compromised and his head throbbing, he cannot pull a Hollywood-worthy stunt by jumping into the Corvette and going after his boy. There will be no scene where he catches up to him on the eerily deserted streets, cuts him off, and orders him back to the house. Out of self-defense, his psyche conjures a guilt-absolving anger: *I told him to take that thing in to a shop!* He slams a fist against the bedroom door and begins to bellow. "Michael? Open the door right now!" Recalling images from a hundred cop shows he has seen, he throws his shoulder into the door, two, three, four times, trying to force it open, without success.

The fifth attempt causes a sharp, searing pain to shoot through his arm, and it, in turn, triggers a sob that catches in his throat. Waves of raw emotion are unleashed deep within him. They wrack his body and double him over.

He collapses against the door before slowly sliding down it, and ends in a crumpled heap on the carpet, silently convulsing.

ROLLING DOWNHILL, THE Mercedes screams bloody murder. In spite of the abuse his mother heaped on the machine for years, it is still a fine example of German engineering, and one which wants speed, even when the engine is off and he is standing on the brake pedal.

Trying to rein in a thoroughbred is not how Michael pictured making his escape.

In order to get away from the house without alerting his father, he'd put the car in neutral and pushed it down the driveway and out onto the cul-de-sac.

It had seemed his plan was working until he straightened out the wheels and felt the balance shift; only then had it dawned on him just how steep the slope of the road really was, and how soon beyond the intersection the road sharply curved. Now, unable to slow it down, he pictures the vehicle wrapped around a tree and himself standing outside of it, enduring the wrath of his father, who he imagines all red-faced, shouting, demanding to know what on earth he felt was so important that

T
E
N

he would attempt such an insane maneuver. Desperate, he jams the key in the ignition and turns it. The engine squeals in protest, and for one heart-stopping second he thinks it won't catch, but it does.

Just before the first turn, he takes command of the vehicle.

EXITING THE GALT House, Ehrichto struggles to recall the layout of the city.

He's heading west, and wants to go east; he needs a southbound street to get him to a westbound one. Every street downtown goes just one-way. He turns on Sixth and is immediately captivated by the sight before him. The trees lining the street are covered in small, new, light green leaves. Lit by the invisible sun behind the thick cloud cover, they glow with a twilight luminescence. Lights dot many of the windows in the surrounding office buildings, and the taillights of the cars in front of him sparkle like jewels, gaudy red reflected in the rain-slicked street.

At the corner with Market a row of white dogwoods makes him gasp. Seeing them he forgets to take note of new buildings among the old, or the absence of businesses he once knew. All he sees are the trees, their fat white flower clusters nearly obscuring dark branches, and he is overwhelmed by a sense of being home.

Home. Ehrichto has not called Louisville that in a very long while.

By the time he reaches Broadway and turns, he is trembling.

"I'VE NEVER ASKED you why the hell you put your studio in the attic, have I?" Jeff asks.

He had, actually, the first time Baxter brought him to the space, which is not the attic but rather the third-floor ballroom of the largest of the Victorian-era mansions that crowd Belgravia Court, part of the Old Louisville historic district. It was one of a barrage of questions he'd asked on that first visit, and one of many Baxter deftly avoided answering.

Baxter negotiates the space around an overstuffed armchair. "The way you say 'attic' makes me think of a V.C. Andrews novel," he says, sidestepping it again.

Jeff squints at him and smiles. Also as with that first time he has planted himself in front of the window in the northwest turret. Behind him, the sky has turned dark cyan, well on its way to cobalt. It won't be long before the fireworks begin. Thirty minutes after that, the half-million people currently packing the riverfront will climb into their vehicles and begin the crawl back out of downtown. From here, the car headlights will resemble ribbons of white dots and, if history is any guide, the resulting traffic jam won't let up until one or two in the morning.

"Sorry?" Jeff finally says. "V.C. who?"

"You don't know that reference," Baxter says, phrasing it as a statement, not a question. "Of course you don't. You weren't even in school yet when that whole nightmare hit. Plus it's the domain of seventh-grade girls, and you've never been one of those." He arches one brow. "Have you?"

Jeff squints harder, then smiles. "No."

"Thank god." Leaning his cane against the candlestick table he uses as a makeshift bar, Baxter starts to reach for a martini glass, then stops. "I'm going to have a gimlet. Would you like something? I have beer."

"A beer would be great, actually," Jeff says.

After fixing his own drink, Baxter takes a brown bottle from the dormitory-sized refrigerator beside his drafting table and pops the top. He tucks the thing under his left arm and then grabs his glass and cane and—wincing slightly because the chill, damp air earlier aggravated his bad hip—begins to make his way across the jewel-tone Persian rug.

"You didn't want a glass, did you?" he asks after reaching the window and reversing the loading-up process. He holds out the beer.

Jeff accepts the offered bottle. "Nah. This is fine. Thanks." He tips it up and takes a swig, then looks back out the window. "It'll be cool to see the fireworks from here. I'm sorry that I missed the air show this morning."

THE FIRST TIME Jeff visited the house was on Thunder morning two years ago. Having lived twenty years in the house, and even longer in Old Louisville itself, Baxter forgot that everyone didn't know the planes scheduled to take part in the air show were test-flown the morning of it, and sometimes the day before, as well, so their pilots could familiarize themselves with the performance area.

Jeff, apparently, was among those unaware. They were seated on the sofa in front of the fireplace, surrounded by sketchpads and notebooks filled with a lifetime of Baxter's designs for the stage, when the first plane began its approach. Jeff had run to the window as the intense rumbling filled the air. Later, he'd said he'd thought a passenger plane was about to crash-land.

Even flying at what was, for it, a slow speed, an F-16 was an astonishing machine. Its shadow flashed on the houses on the other side of the court. In the same instant it created a sonic boom that felt like being kicked in the chest by a mule. Just as suddenly as it came on it was gone again. Seconds after that, three stories down, car alarms had begun going off, one after another like a string of cheap firecrackers.

Realizing what was happening, Jeff had let out a shout. "Hot damn! That's amazing! I'm never going to watch from the river again!"

The utterance made Baxter's chest feel even more constricted than when the plane was passing over. Before he could stop himself, he'd said "Do you promise?" Immediately he'd cringed, because of a fight they'd had only a few hours before, an incident which had almost shattered their relationship.

Jeff, though, either hadn't heard him clearly or had the good sense to pretend he hadn't. His brow briefly pinched but his grin was unwavering. "What did you say?" he'd asked.

Baxter had held up his coffee mug. "I asked," he said, struggling to remain calm despite the fact that his heartbeat was thundering in his chest, "do you want more coffee?"

"WELL, YOU DIDN'T miss much," Baxter says now. To ensure that he appears nonchalant he begins flipping through a stack of *Courier-Journals*. Preparations for the rave have taken up all his time and put him behind on his reading. "What's the expression these days—'Been there, done that'?"

He's glad that it's too cold today for opening the windows. Though he enjoys the contrast between a crisp, fresh breeze and the heated, smoky air coming from the fireplace, he is not alone in that regard. Lots of people on the court open their windows on cool days, and have smoke rising from their chimneys, and as annoying as he finds it to occasionally hear an announcer describing a ball game from a radio turned up too loud during the summer, what happens on Thunder Day is a hundred times worse. Everyone else, it seems, tunes in to the broadcast coming from the riverfront. He finds the sound ricocheting through the urban canyon to be ghastly.

"I usually don't watch the fireworks from here," he says.

Jeff looks aghast. "What? Why? I'd think this is a great view."

"Oh, it is." Baxter chooses not to explain that watching the show from here makes him a hundred times lonelier than he normally feels, and that the younger man's visits—the many times they've stayed up all night drinking pot after pot of coffee and talking about the aesthetics of design—comprise the best times he's had in this house in the last nearly twenty years. He wishes the younger man was interested in men, but even more than that, much more, he wishes Marc wasn't the complete head case he is. Having good things to share but not being able to do so with the person you most want to is the worst pain Baxter knows. Most years during Thunder he's shut the windows tight, taken a sleeping pill, and gone to bed early.

"THIS IS YOUR place?"

Jeff's reaction that first night Baxter brought him home was not surprising. Three stories of black brick, the house is quite impressive, even imposing, viewed from the walking court.

"Indeed, 'tis my humble abode." Baxter ascended the half-circle steps to the double entry doors.

"Wow. I've…I've loved this building since I was a kid."

Even that wasn't surprising. "I get that a lot," Baxter said truthfully. He tugged the fingers of the leather driving glove on his right hand until he managed to remove it and then, using only his thumb and forefinger, fished a lone key from the watch pocket of his flat-front trousers.

Jeff had pressed his face to the front glass, a child at a candy-store display, which made sense, given that he was studying to be an architect. "So many of these buildings have been broken up, with mixed results," he said. "I had an apartment once that was built around a main stair. The landlord encased it, basically, and made the parlor, study, first-floor bath and kitchen into a one-bedroom apartment shaped like a doughnut.

But this place? I love that from the street it still looks like a single-family home."

What happened next remains one of the highlights of Baxter's life. He'd pushed open both entry doors, the type of exceedingly dramatic move he lives for, and proclaimed "That's because this still *is* a single family home." Then he'd thrown the wall switch and flooded the foyer in glittering light.

As hard as it was to stay silent, he gave his assistant several moments to take in the full scene. The design aesthetic of the space was, on first blush, Victorian. Paintings were hung in vertical rows, three or more works high, stretching up, up, up toward the fourteen-foot ceiling. They all but filled the space between the chair rail and crown molding, leaving visible only little slivers of the ornate paper beneath.

Watching Jeff's eyes further widen, however, Baxter became concerned that perhaps bringing him to the house was a miscalculation. He worried his assistant would be taken aback—perhaps even offended—by the distinctly un-Victorian nature of the images contained within the heavy gilt frames. They were variations on a single theme: angels falling back to earth, an unholy host of lithe, beautiful creatures hurtling downward. In each painting the figure's face was contorted by pain or fear, sadness, anger or—in more than a few cases, because many were depicted not only as anatomically correct but aroused—sexual ecstasy.

"They're, um, they're...wow," Jeff said. When he turned, Baxter locked eyes with him and tried to telepathically convey a message: *You can no longer say you didn't know what was on my mind.*

He swept his left arm wide, indicating the hall beyond the foyer, and asked, "Well? Shall we proceed?"

JEFF TURNING FROM the window interrupts his reverie. "I guess I was thirstier than I realized," he says, holding up his empty bottle. "Can I have another?" Baxter reaches for his cane, but Jeff gestures for him to stay where he is. "I can get it," he says.

There was, perpetually, a line of college students clamoring to be Baxter's design assistant for this or that show he was working on around town. He took them on based on one simple criterion: his level of attraction to them.

He had no qualms about it because he never made a physical relationship a condition of internship, and he never let them have any input on a design.

They got the right to put his name on their résumé and let it open doors for them and nothing more. So what if people assumed an assistant had some small hand in the finished product? He knew the truth. And if things didn't go that far? Well, he still got an office lackey out of the deal. More often than not, though, it was the intern who initiated things. He wasn't sure if it was young people in general or just the ones interested in working with him, but they seemed, generally, to be every bit as willing to use physical means to get what they wanted as he was to use his curriculum vitae.

Jeff was unique in that he did the grunt work of making the coffee and taking out the trash almost happily, without complaint, a far cry from his predecessors, for whom honest labor seemed to be a trigger point for trying to trade up by making a suggestive comment or action. Jeff not only did actual work, he sought out more, finding ways to make himself as genuinely useful as possible. He also listened to what Baxter said, rather than barraging him with half-baked ideas of his own. (Why did twenty-year-old children believe they already knew everything? And when, exactly, had they gotten so dumb? Baxter was only seventeen when he left Louisville for NYC, but he'd already read *On the Road* three times and was able to recite "Plutonian Ode" by heart.)

As much as he liked Jeff, and had begun to rely on him to keep track of incidentals, Baxter had had no plans to break his own cardinal rule by seeking the young man's opinion on the design of the current show, and that decision had led to the fight that nearly ended their relationship.

His intention on the evening he first showed him the house had been to take him out for a nice dinner, as a reward for all of his hard work, but he'd miscalculated his ability—or rather Marc's—to secure a last-minute table for them at the Flagship, the four star restaurant atop the Galt House Hotel.

It wasn't that Marc couldn't do it, it was that he wouldn't. Baxter had found him in the small conference room dubbed the Third-Floor

Concierge Lounge, playing fill-in bartender for an endless line of frazzled-looking executives. They weren't happy when Marc excused himself and stepped into the adjoining storage room to talk to Baxter, and Marc was even less thrilled when he realized Baxter wasn't there to buy pills or a few lines of blow from him, but was seeking a favor. And when he found out he was there with his broad-shouldered assistant? Marc had all but flown into a rage, and had even called security to have Baxter removed from the premises.

Consequently, he and Jeff had ended up at the house, which Jeff had never seen, and revealed he'd admired from afar for years. He weathered the shock of the foyer artwork remarkably well, renewing Baxter's curiosity about his sexual proclivities, and they'd sat down to a meal of leftovers.

It still pleases him to recall how gorgeous the table looked when they walked into the dining room: gloss black plates resting on square white chargers on the black lacquered tabletop; an aubergine napkin pinched in the middle by a brushed steel ring, giving a bow-tie effect, on each plate; and chrome candlesticks with red tapers in a line down the center of the table, an extremely stylish and elegant, yet undeniably masculine, design.

He'd chosen and uncorked a bottle and begun pouring Jeff a glass. "'The wine was Golden Mediasch,'" he'd said. "'It produces a queer sting on the tongue that is not wholly disagreeable.'"

Marc would have easily gotten the reference, but it went over Jeff's head. All things considered, he'd realized in retrospect, that was probably a good thing.

"Is that…from a play?"

"A book, a play, a movie," Baxter answered. He'd moved around the table, and begun pouring a glass for himself.

"Look, Baxter, I—" Jeff faltered, the first sign that he realized Baxter was open to taking things in another direction, and wasn't sure how to react.

"Call me Richard."

"Oh, okay. Richard. Sure." He wiped his palms on his pant legs while Baxter swallowed a mouthful of wine.

"I'm sorry. What did you want to say?"

"Oh. Just that I'm glad we came back here, because the house is amazing, and…. Well, earlier tonight, when we stopped at the Galt House? I totally thought, because you mentioned that guy Wolfgang Huck—"

"Puck."

"Yeah. For like a second I thought we were going to that, what's it called? The revolving restaurant."

"The Flagship." Baxter worried his decision to leave the hotel was not the right one. After his spat with Marc, and the latter's summoning of security, it was clear they would not be allowed to go peacefully on their way up to the restaurant on the hotel's top floor, to try to bribe the maître d' for a table. He'd had serious doubts even before that miscalculation that the plan could even work with the help of a concierge, that connections and money could get one seated on a Friday an hour before closing with no reservation. "Yes," he said, refilling his own empty glass. "I can see how you would have thought we were going there. Are you very disappointed?"

"What? No. I don't care about that. It's just that I was wondering, well…. I was, uh…. What I mean is…." He looked Baxter squarely in the eye. "Is this supposed to be a date?"

A SURGE OF adrenaline greater than any manmade drug coursed through Baxter's veins then. He had to struggle to keep his tone even. "It's whatever you wish it to be," he said with what he hoped was passable nonchalance.

The look that crossed Jeff's face in response was unexpectedly candid and crushing. *Not into geriatrics,* Baxter thought. *Right. Got it.* He'd forced a laugh. "I'm only joking, of course. Don't be silly. This is simply a reward because you've been so very helpful to me on this show." He added the last of the wine to his glass and let the weight of the empty bottle pull his hand toward the floor while he downed it in big gulps.

"I don't know what to say." Jeff's tone implied he didn't for a moment buy Baxter's refutation.

"It's probably best that you don't say anything." That answer was too honest. Baxter attempted to ease the tension between them with humor, but the wine was already going to his head, impairing his judgment. "Relax. There are no hard feelings. I haven't taken the pills for them yet."

The younger man pushed back his chair. "Oh, jeez. I didn't mean to…. If I somehow gave you the impression…."

"You didn't," Baxter assured him. "I was just taking a shot. I thought there might…be some possibility. It's forgotten already, truly. Please, sit back down."

"I mean, I knew, of course, that you were, uh—"

"The euphemism you're searching for is 'temperamental.'"

Jeff began to pace the floor behind his chair. At any moment he would bolt for the door.

"Please sit back down."

His assistant looked stricken. Queasy. "I don't want this to be weird."

Baxter gave an airy laugh. "'This' what? There is no 'this.' I told you, it's forgotten. Water under the bridge."

They'd finally settled down to their respective dinners, leftovers from two different restaurants, but the same dish: linguine in tequila cream sauce. ("What can I say?" Baxter had called over his shoulder as he pulled boxes from the refrigerator. "When I find something I like I try every version of it that I can lay my hands on." It was a comment he later regretted making.)

"You've kept me so busy running errands and doing grunt work I haven't even had the chance to tell you how much I love your design for the show," Jeff said at last. All things considered, Baxter decided not to change the subject, but also not wanting to encourage that line of dialogue, he'd chosen not to respond. After a pause, Jeff went on. "Robert Edmund Jones was one of your big influences, wasn't he? I mean, your work is all about beauty and form, and you do so much with props and always have an opinion about the lighting, but you never touch any costumes, the way Desmond Heeley and Santo Loquasto do."

It was, quite possibly, the nicest thing anyone had ever said to him. A lump formed in Baxter's throat, and that unnerved him. Trying to downplay just how moved he was, he forced a laugh. "This is a first. An assistant who's genuinely interested in my design philosophy."

He expected Jeff to display a cat-who-ate-the-canary grin, but the other looked crestfallen. "You never read it," he said.

The lump in Baxter's throat grew bigger. He had no idea what he was supposed to have read, but figured silence was the best response.

"Oh my God." Jeff dropped his fork onto his plate. The clatter bounced off the walls. "The letter I sent when I applied. The one where I talked about your *Night of the Iguana?* You never even read it."

God only knew why, since they were all the same, but Baxter *did* still at least skim every letter. Invariably there would be a mention he found telling, shorthand put there to clue him in that—wink, wink—the correspondent was gay, too. If the applicant still had one foot in the closet he name-dropped Tennessee Williams, Noël Coward or Edward Albee; if he'd already burned it down then maybe Jean Genet, Harvey Fierstein or Mart Crowley. Not that the sexuality of the applicants *needed* to be telegraphed. Every young man who'd ever applied to be Baxter's design assistant for the duration of a show was gay. He was glad for it, naturally, but he wished they knew that he knew, and didn't all feel the need to relate to him, in three hundred words or less, how they'd first realized it in themselves.

Clearly, he'd skimmed too much, and read not enough. He tried to bluff his way out of the sticky situation. "Of course I read it. I find him very inspiring as well."

"Who?"

Oh, God. Who would Jeff have referenced? He went with the obvious. "Tennessee, dear. Do try to keep up."

The deep vertical creases that appeared above the bridge of the younger man's nose made Baxter think of paintings of Hindu holy men. "I don't care about him!" he said, his rising tone seemingly pulling him up out of his chair.

He whipped his napkin down onto the table. "It wasn't about him. It wasn't even really about the play. My comments were all about your set!"

"My set?" Baxter was confused. He strained his memory trying to recall if a decent picture from that production had made the paper. Most times photo editors chose to run close-up shots of the actors.

"Of course your set. It was amazing. Why would I have talked about anything else?"

That design is one of the ones of which Baxter is most proud. He'd created Puerto Vallarta with cut drops inspired by East Indian sanjhi. It was a beautiful set; the newspaper should have shown it, but he was almost certain they hadn't. *But even if they had*, he wondered, looking at Jeff. *How would he have come across a ten-year-old article? Was he scrolling through microfiche at the library as part of an assignment for school? Could it be that some professor at the university is showing pictures of my work to his class?*

"I'm flattered, but...how did you see my design for *Iguana*, exactly?"

Jeff threw his arms in the air. "IN. THE. THEATER!" he shouted. Then he leaned across the table. "I. WAS. THERE! Which you'd know IF you'd bothered to read my essay!"

Baxter realized just what a terrible mistake he'd made. This was what he'd always wanted, deep down: someone who saw his work as art.

Jeff glared at him. "Did you even bother to *look* at my portfolio?"

"Of course I did."

"Right. I'm the idiot. No, you know what I think?" Jeff thrust an arm backward, pointed in the direction of the foyer. "I think you picked me to be your assistant for this production because I look like one of your angel paintings!"

"No."

Jeff scanned the room as if searching for a coat he hadn't worn. It had been uncommonly springlike for the day before Thunder. "I don't know what *you* were thinking this was," he said, giving up the search and starting for the door. "But I didn't come here to sleep with you so that you'd lie and say I'm the next...the next—"

"Ming Cho Lee to my Jo Mielziner?" The comparison did nothing at all to diffuse the situation. Jeff had spun around on one heel. The look on his face was nothing short of enraged. "GODDAMMIT!" he hollered. "I WANT TO BE YOU! Why don't you get that? Walking into the theater that day changed my LIFE! One minute I was with my aunt in downtown Louisville, and the next—bam!—I'd stepped into Puerto Vallarta."

Again, Baxter felt himself getting choked up. Verklempt. "Really?"

"YES! I've wanted to be a set designer ever since, but in my family that's not an option. I have to study architecture because that's the only thing they can wrap their heads around. That's real. I'm dreading the day they realize I've been over in the College of Fine Arts taking every theatre class I can, instead of the crap—pardon my French—in the Speed School of Engineering. Trust me, the fireworks on the day they figure it out will make Thunder Over Louisville look like kids with cherry bombs."

Baxter no longer had the urge to sleep with him; he wanted to adopt him. "I'm sorry," he said. He wanted to add "I know how it is," but the truth was he didn't. His own parents had been remarkably blasé about his choices, even supportive of them. He always tells people he ran away from home to seek his fortune on the Great White Way, but in reality when he'd told his parents what he planned to do their response had been "If you don't, it will be the greatest mistake of your life."

"My folks think wanting to design sets makes you gay," Jeff said, flinging the last word like a curse, obviously quoting and simultaneously mocking his family. "I expected you, of all people, to understand how dumb that is."

Baxter squeezed his eyes shut. When he opened them again, he looked at the wall over Jeff's shoulder, at the ceiling, at the floor, anywhere but at the younger man's accusatory stare.

"Say something or I'm leaving," Jeff demanded.

"Please don't."

"You have to do better than that, Baxter. Tell me I haven't been just wasting my time organizing your drafting supplies."

"You haven't been."

"No? Tell me you were eventually going to show me your past designs, and recount moments when you had some big revelation about the craft, or just gossip about people you worked with, something."

"My studio is upstairs," Baxter said. "On the third floor. All the models from my sets are there, and my slides and projector, and all my sketchpads. I'd love to show them to you."

"Really?"

Baxter ventured a glance in Jeff's direction. *Yes, really*, he thought. *If you'll stay I'll show you everything. You're what I wanted for years but gave up on ever finding.* "I'd be honored."

For one more terrible minute Jeff hadn't moved. Then he'd exhaled, and his shoulders dropped. "Yeah," he said, nodding. "I'd love that."

BAXTER PICKS UP the next of the newspapers from the stack he's been halfheartedly going through and pulls out the Metro section. The color photo takes his breath away, but not for any reason that could be considered pleasant or good. The picture shows Julia Conway Ferguson standing beside a table on which several pieces of art are displayed. In the very center of the table is the mask he made for Nugget, the primary non-human character in the drama *Equus*, the closest he's ever come to doing something that could be called "costuming."

The caption below the photograph reads: *"Nugget," a prop designed by Richard Baxter for a River City Productions show last fall, is one of the entries in the finals of Conway Charities' annual Derby Festival Art Competition.*

"I'm going to kill him."

Across the room, Jeff turns away from the window. "What's wrong?"

"Nothing's wrong. I'm just going to kill him, that's all."

Jeff crosses the room in loping strides, leans in to view the picture in Baxter's now-trembling hand, and says, "Hey, your work's in an art contest! That's really cool."

"No," Baxter corrects. "No, it is certainly not. It is the very furthest thing

from cool because *I* didn't enter this competition. That mask was stolen. Taken from the warehouse. I even filed a police report."

"Stolen? But—" Jeff points to the line of captioning "—it says 'Designed by Richard Baxter.'"

"That's because he finds this funny."

"Who? Anyone I know?"

Baxter holds up the paper. "I never have asked you. What did you think of the actor who played Alan Strang in this show?"

Jeff winces. "Ooh. Well, I absolutely bought that he was damaged goods, but he came across as really, uh, self-absorbed? It made it hard to empathize with him. Honestly, I kept debating if he was related to the director or sleeping with him."

"Then I'd say yes, you do know him. Rather well, in fact. Though I can't say as you've ever met."

"So now you're a cokehead, too?"

Marc pulls his leg inside the car and reaches for the door handle to pull it closed but Trey grabs hold of the frame, so he tosses the bottle he just killed to the guy and hunches back down over the book in his lap. He covers one nostril and inhales the first of two long strings of white powder. The left half of his brain seems to ignite as Trey struggles to pronounce the name of the drug.

"Methyl...phen...di.... No, wait. Methyl...phen...die...na...."

"Methylphenidate." Marc covers the other nostril, inhales the second line, then leans his head back against the seat and closes his eyes, to wait for the powder's scorched-earth destruction of his nasal passages and beyond to abate, and for it to deliver the calm that makes that pain worthwhile. After the disappointing turn of events with Ehrichto Salvatolle, he's in desperate need of calm. What he doesn't need is some blockhead who doesn't understand that ADHD is a real condition standing over him offering commentary. "It's Ritalin," he says, his eyes still closed. "I have a prescription, okay?"

"Oh, of course. Duh," Trey says. Marc hears him slap a palm to his forehead. "That's why drug reps are always giving out pens. It's so people can crush and snort their drugs."

Eyes still closed, Marc flips him the bird. In response he feels something lightweight impact his lap. His eyes snap open and a surge of adrenaline screams through his system, threatening his promised calm. He grasps the object—it's the empty pill bottle—and glares up at Trey. "Fuck you. I don't care what you think, I *know*. This helps. It's the only thing that does." He whips the bottle into the footwell, leans back against the seat, and closes his eyes again. "Go away."

"It kills me that my brother wastes so much time on you. Just KILLS me."

"Go away."

"Not without answers."

"Airplane. Green. A hundred and sixty-four. Now go away."

"Neal lost out on the Conway Charities grant last year because someone outed him to Julia Ferguson."

The award to which he refers is one for Emerging Professionals. The phrase always makes Marc picture a butterfly in a three-piece suit, exiting a cocoon.

The image falls apart when he thinks of Neal, though. He seems to have skipped the chrysalis stage entirely and been born an adult. Marc opens his eyes again and meets Trey's stare. "With his history of activism? Please. She was *well* aware. The only reason he was ever in the running with that place was because he's *your* brother and at the time you were dating the daughter of Julia Ferguson's husband's boss." He arches a brow. "Speaking of Alyssa, if you still want to hit that, she's probably pretty hard-up. The guy she's dating now plays for my team. During dinner he was practically giving a hand job to the man seated beside him."

Rather than happy or relieved, Trey looks pained. "I know. And I think I just.... I totally did not mean to.... I think I outed him to his father tonight." Marc starts to open his mouth but Trey holds up a hand, silencing him. "If Alyssa hadn't nosed in where she didn't belong.... I mean, dammit, it was bad enough when it was just my parents supporting my brother. At least I could understand that. I was on board with it for the longest, until it became this much bigger thing, PFLAG, and the Gay-Straight Student Alliance, and the Fairness Campaign, and the Pride March, and wanting us all to get trained to be phone counselors for the suicide hotline, and CHRIST ALMIGHTY, when does it STOP? I was so over it already, and then they brainwashed Alyssa. She's now more rah-rah than they *ever* were. She thinks she's going to save the world, one gay guy at a time."

"Wait, are you saying she dumped you so that she could be that little twink's beard?"

"No. We broke up because she thinks I outed Neal to Julia Ferguson at last year's Thunder and caused him to lose that grant."

Marc purses his lips, arches a brow. "You don't think he was Julia's token gay?" He takes delight in positing such an absurd notion. There is no such thing as a token gay, the way there have been token blacks and token women in various competitions for decades. Gay people aren't viewed as a minority in the same way, but rather as an aberration. Homosexuality is seen as a choice, a "lifestyle," like deciding to join a motorcycle gang, or spend one's life savings building a replica Taj Mahal in the backyard, or worship Satan.

To Marc's surprise, Trey's expression softens. "Look, I do get it, okay? How unfairly you all are treated, and how hard it is to fight back. That if you come out you'll get disowned, and probably lose your job, and there's a really good chance you'll get the crap beaten out of you. Or worse, like that case last year."

Marc picks at the frayed edge of a rip in the upholstery fabric of the passenger's seat. The drug in his bloodstream is kicking into high gear, pulling his normally kaleidoscopic thought patterns into single focus, allowing tangential thoughts and flights of fancy to fall away. It's the worst possible time for such clarity, because it leaves him unable to distract himself from real sources of anxiety, and this is one of the worst he knows. He doesn't want to think about what happened to Matthew Shepard. He thinks about it often enough as it is, in unbidden flashes every time he pulls into the lot at Breslin Park; whenever he leaves work in the early morning hours and has to make his way down through this garage to reach his car; and in between classes on campus each time he spies a pack of jocks heading toward him. Every day of his life feels like playing Russian roulette. He finds moments of escape by running headlong into hedonism, but he knows it's simply a matter of time, a toss of the dice. Sooner or later it will be the chamber with the bullet, and that knowledge both terrifies and exhausts him. It's why, more and more, he wrestles for control of the gun and pulls the trigger himself, wanting to just be done with it already.

"Congratulations," he says. "Your peace medal is in the mail."

Trey lets out a frustrated growl and kicks one of the Cabrio's tires. "Why do you always have to be like that? I'm trying to be nice to you, dipshit."

"You want to be nice?" Marc asks, reaching out and grasping the bulge at Trey's crotch. "Let me have a taste of this."

Just as he expects, Trey grabs him by the front of his shirt, pulls him to his feet, and slams him up against the car. "The LAST thing in the world I want is your mouth!" he bellows. His voice bounces off concrete, ricochets around the garage. "I'm NOT gay," he says, the echo of earlier exchanges they've had, in which Marc has insinuated Trey secretly lusts after him. "But if I was? I would NEVER get with a piece of SHIT like you!" Every time he raises his voice he pulls Marc forward and shoves him up against the car again for added emphasis. "What I want to do is kick your fucking ASS for cheating on my brother a couple hours ago with that kitchen jerk!"

"So do it."

For several seconds he thinks Trey will, but the guy only gives a loud grunt and shoves him one more time up against the car, pinning him against it.

"Look, asshole," he says. "All I came down here for is to hear you admit that you're the one who told Julia, okay?"

"You're going to have to enlighten me. What are we talking about?"

"Last year. The grant money he lost out on. It was you who sabotaged him, wasn't it?"

"Why would I do that?"

"Because you aren't half the man he is, and you know it, and it pisses you off."

Marc can't meet his gaze. He looks up at the concrete beam over their head, where droplets of water hang like beaded glass fringe.

"Be a man already and own up to it."

Marc's pretty sure if he does, Trey will lose his shit. There will be blood. "I wasn't at this event last year," he says, surprising himself. "For your information I was with Richard Baxter, helping build that bitch's—" He catches himself just in time. No one is supposed to know it was Richard Baxter who built Julia Ferguson's soulless abode. He'd used a pseudonym because of it, calling himself Angelo de Haven. He quickly backpedals. "That bitch of a set for *Equus*."

"You're an actor, not a tech guy." For emphasis, Trey grabs hold of the silk scarf knotted around Marc's throat, part of his "Richard Baxter" outfit, and twists. "You don't wield a hammer, you wear crap like this mess you have on now, that other people wouldn't be caught dead in."

Marc pushes the guy's hand away and rubs his throat. "You're wrong," he says, "I do both. During last year's Thunder, I was helping Baxter."

THAT WHOLE BUSINESS—Baxter passing himself off as an interior decorator and architect, building a dream house for Julia Ferguson—still strikes Marc as bizarre; he's certain Baxter is neither of those things for real, but just imitates them for the stage. He also still can't quite fathom how his own role in things went from quasi-acting work to general labor. Initially, Baxter had spun it as "a series of telephone improv skits, a chance to practice your accents," when in reality it was just him stringing Lloyd and Julia Ferguson along by pretending to be a schlub in a bank one day, the head of a home loan financing company the next, and so on. But the project fell behind, and he'd seen his golden opportunity. Baxter had been willing to fork over big bucks for actual roll-up-your-sleeves assistance. By Thunder Day Marc felt like an old hand at painting and laying carpet, jobs at which he'd had zero prior experience.

There was still a lot to do that night, one year ago, but the end was in sight. The downstairs rooms were finished, chock-full of the direct-from-the-factory, taste-free, blond-wood furnishings Julia Ferguson believed to be the hallmarks of wealth and class. The walk-out basement was finished, ready for the pieces of furniture they were bringing with them from their current, much smaller house. But the second floor still needed work. That day they'd done a little bit of everything: painted and hung wallpaper, put up crown molding and installed baseboards, laid carpeting. All that was left was to move in some ugly furniture.

Anticipating the start of the fireworks show, Baxter had declared an end to work for the evening and ordered Marc to start cleaning and putting away all their tools. By the time he'd finished and gotten upstairs the fireworks had started.

"It needs to be christened," Baxter declared. Marc was so busy looking at the burst of rainbow-hued sparks beyond the naked windows that he hadn't even seen the guy. When he turned, he got a jolt: Baxter was sprawled on the mattress, gripping a bottle of champagne in one hand.

"Are you referring to the way a ship is launched?"

"I am. It's finished. It needs to be christened."

"First of all, it's not a ship. It doesn't have a bow."

"And that would be alcohol abuse, wouldn't it?"

"You ought to know. You've killed half that bottle in fifteen minutes." Marc exhaled dramatically. "Regardless, we're far from finished with the house. We still have a truckload of bad furniture to unload, remember?"

Baxter gave a dismissive wave. "And we haven't even gotten the window treatments yet."

"That's because there aren't any. Drapes and blinds hinder the ability of one's neighbors to see how well you're keeping up with them. Don't you know anything?"

"'It isn't what you earn but how you spend it that fixes your class.' Sinclair Lewis, *Main Street.*"

"Very nice."

"Thank you. You're still wrong about the house being done, though. We need to install cabinet handles and drawer pulls."

"Oh, no, no no. They break the clean lines of modern design. There's nothing more gauche than giving away that utilitarian things like forks lie behind the vast mahogany expanses of a room."

That had genuinely made Marc laugh. "There's no mahogany in here! Or marble, or chrome. This whole place is lauan and Durham's. It's a set."

Baxter beamed. "I know. It goes right back to your Lewis quote. It looks like a million bucks though, doesn't it? Doesn't it? Damn, I'm good."

"And modest." Marc cast a glance upward, to the crown molding Baxter had crafted by running sheets of foam insulation through a table saw. Coated in polyurethane and painted cream, it was impossible to tell it wasn't wood. No one would be the wiser until they went to remove it. "As good as it looks, if I paid a million bucks for something, I'd be pissed when I found out it was worth a dollar eighty-nine."

"They don't *have* a dollar eighty-nine." Baxter tipped the neck of the champagne bottle toward Marc to emphasize his point. "Hell, they don't have two nickels to rub together."

Marc was well aware that the Fergusons were financially strapped. He had, after all, impersonated a loan officer willing to extend credit to them. During the call he'd had in front of him copies of the paperwork Baxter had doctored up to reinforce the lie. As many questions as he still had about the whole affair, he knew Baxter wouldn't answer them. They'd been over that ground. He'd aimed, instead, for one he might get an answer for. "Why two nickels? I've never gotten that."

"Nickels used to be wooden. The idea is that if you had two of them, at least you could start a fire." He took another long draught from the bottle. "Which is ridiculous. You'd only need one and a bow drill, obviously."

Marc laughed. "Listen to you. Sounding like a damned Boy Scout." He dropped onto the mattress beside Baxter and reached for the bottle of champagne, but the other refused to let it go.

"Eagle Scout," Baxter said. He'd sounded genuinely miffed.

Marc dropped his hand from the neck of the bottle to the bulge between Baxter's legs. "I have a better idea for how we can 'christen' the place."

As always, Baxter had batted his hand away.

THE MEMORY OF being rejected by Baxter triggers echoes of Ehrichto Salvatolle's parting words. *A vintage made from garbage*, he'd said. "I would've done anything to get out of being here last year," Marc says. "I can't stand Julia Ferguson."

"You're here now, asshole."

"I'm here *in spite of* her. This wasn't premeditated. Why do you think I'm dressed like this? I had to make up a story to get in."

"Why?"

"Over at the Galt House this morning I met the guy Michael Ferguson was making moves on at dinner."

"By 'met' you mean…?"

"We were interrupted."

"So you followed him here to get a second shot?"

"You would, with a girl. Hell, you bribed your way in here tonight to get a glimpse of Alyssa and she dumped your ass."

"There's a big difference. While they were having dinner I waited; I didn't run off and help myself to some kitchen schmuck's dick, the way you did."

"Jealous much?" The barb has no visible effect. Marc rolls his eyes. "Look, I'm not trying to marry the guy."

"You're a class act, Fleming, you know that?"

Marc bristles. He's told Trey repeatedly never to use his legal name. He wants to be Marc Payette, twink extraordinaire, wily concierge, all-around fixer, and rising star of the stage and screen; not Mark Fleming, the scrawny, effeminate kid from Shively, who most "real" men want to pummel into the ground and a few want to screw senseless, but only if no one knows. "You win," he blurts, terrified of what other unwelcome truths the methylphenidate in his bloodstream will expose. "I'm the one who outed Neal to Julia Ferguson."

Trey's muscles flex. He shoves Marc higher up the car until he's teetering on the tips of the platform shoes, until they're eye to eye. "You just said you weren't at the dinner."

"I—I wasn't. You remember that interview he gave to *The Letter* right around this time last year? I slipped an envelope with a copy of it addressed to her through the mail slot at the Conway Charities office."

The Letter is an independent newspaper serving the local gay community. Trey was much more blatantly sexual in it than in any of the very open, very out interviews he'd given to *The Cardinal*, the newspaper of the University of Louisville, or to the *Courier-Journal*, the *Lexington Herald-Leader*, and local television and radio stations. In those he was a student athlete who just happened to love other guys; in the piece in *The Letter* did he'd come across more as a guy who loved other guys' cocks.

Trey's grip on him unexpectedly loosens, as the expression on his face goes slack. "I don't understand," he says.

Marc shrugs. It's the very opposite of the twisted-up sensation in his stomach. The gesture has the potential for inspiring violence from Trey, and that sends a burst of adrenaline coursing through his veins. "It's simple. I reached the same conclusion Alyssa did, that Julia didn't know he was gay. It's amazing, really. Her staff must have worked their asses off to keep it from her."

"So you made sure she knew?" Trey asks. He looks more confused and hurt than angry. "But, why? Why would you do that?"

Ehrichto Salvatolle's assessment of him leaps back to the forefront of his mind. "For exactly the reasons you just said. I'm not half the man Neal is, and I know it. I'm trailer trash, born and bred. He's bourbon and I'm moonshine."

Trey's grip tightens again. "He's also your boyfriend."

Marc can do this; he knows he can. He can push Trey over the edge, cause him to lose his shit and go ballistic. All it takes is putting the proper spin on things. "No," he says, smiling coldly. "He's my opponent, and the only way I stand a chance in this world is by taking him out."

He leaves his eyes open as Trey draws back his right arm for a punch.

DOWNTOWN IS A ZOO. Despite there being only half an hour remaining until the start of the fireworks, people are still streaming into the area, hoping to find a space and make it to the waterfront in time for the show. Michael is making better time than most of them because he has been hoofing it for the last five blocks. The Mercedes took the impasse at Broadway as its cue to launch into its grand death scene. It had shivered, shuddered and died. When he tried to turn the engine over nothing happened. The dashboard was black. Moments later a column of smoke rose from the hood. The cops directing traffic were not at all amused, but they'd had little choice but to push the thing up onto the sidewalk while he steered.

Kismet. Fate. Destiny. Michael feels it is all those things and so much more when he nears the corner of Sixth and Main and hears the wet, throaty purr of a race car engine being forced to idle. His eye easily picks the Porsche's sleek silhouette from a long line of sedans paused on Main, cars which, unlike the jam he was in a few minutes ago, are inexplicably leaving the area.

Seeing the vehicle raises a host of conflicting feelings within him. He's excited but also afraid, once more the captive of the dread he feels whenever he attempts to read others' intentions. *What if he* wasn't *thinking what I was?*

That uncertainty threatens to paralyze him, but right at that moment, behind the wheel of the Porsche, Ehrichto Salvatolle turns his head. Their eyes meet and lock, and all of Michael's fears fall away.

Platinum in color, the car has smoke-gray windows and muscular curves. Though he has never been much interested in cars before, Michael is captivated by this one. He understands that it is a sacred thing: powerful, expensive, gorgeous. He is surprised to discover that opening the passenger's door requires real effort, and that when it does give way it makes a sound like a vacuum seal being broken. It calls to mind images from movies, of astronauts opening hatches on the airlock chambers of space capsules.

Two distinct scents, leather and cigar smoke, waft through the open door. As casually as he can—as if he hops into luxury sports cars regularly—Michael drops into the bucket seat.

It is much lower than he expected. He tries his best not to look startled by that fact, tries to focus on the seat's buttery soft leather and the fact that it is contoured to fit his body like a glove, but his overwhelming impression is of being just inches from the roadway.

He is surprised to realize that he can see perfectly well out the windows because of the correspondingly low dashboard, an undulating swath of richly grained, highly polished wood that is devoid of all but the most essential of dials. His eye scans the surface but finds no air-conditioning control panel or radio dial, no pocket for glasses and keys, no drink cup holder. There's only one exception, a small LCD screen mounted low, directly behind the stick shift. It's clearly an aftermarket addition, attached by wires coming from somewhere up under the dash. Otherwise, the machine is clearly meant for only one activity: driving, very fast.

Michael summons the courage to look left. Mr. Salvatolle has his back pressed to the driver's side door. His hair has slipped free from behind his ears again, the way it did at the start of dinner, but this time he has made no effort to put it back. The luxurious dark curtain obscures the left side of his face. His right eye, every bit as dark, is fixed intently on Michael.

Unnerved by such focused attention, Michael stammers out the thing that is foremost on his mind. He is ninety-nine percent sure he understands the situation, but needs that final reassurance. "I, I think I'm…going…crazy," he says.

No sooner are the words out than Mr. Salvatolle is in his space, leaning over the gearshift box which only seconds before seemed a wall between them. Extending his left arm beyond Michael, he braces himself on the frame of the passenger's door. His right hand finds the back of Michael's head; it pulls him up and out of his seat until their mouths meet.

Nothing in Michael's experience compares to the sensation of kissing Mr. Salvatolle. The man's moustache and beard are at once soft and prickly, his lips cool and firm, retaining much of the chill of the air outside the car. He bites Michael's lower lip with sharp eyeteeth, playfully. When Michael gasps, the man's tongue slips inside his mouth and begins exploring the recesses there. The onslaught of sensations triggers a rush of hormones so powerful it leaves no room for doubt in Michael's mind. He wants more. When the man breaks the kiss and pulls away Michael tries to pursue him, but is stopped by the gearbox.

Mr. Salvatolle collapses against the driver's door with his head tipped back, like a drowning man gasping for air. "We can't…do this…here."

"No," Michael agrees. Before he even has a chance to brace himself, the sports car is turning on a dime; centrifugal force holding him in his seat as they peel out from the westbound line of cars. Seconds later they are flying south down still-deserted Sixth, heading into the heart of the city.

ELEVEN

WHEN HE OPENS the door to his apartment Marc gets several unpleasant shocks. The first is from the visual chaos of having too much furniture serving too wide a range of functions, all crammed into one small space; the second comes from the room's sharp scent, the stale smell of sweat leaching from dirty clothing piled about the place as well as from the rumpled bed linens. It's mingled with the raw earthiness of mold. The third shock is auditory: the shrill sound of the phone, not so much ringing as braying. He shoves scripts and articles of clothing and the books for classes he hasn't bothered to attend in weeks from the top of the desk, searching for the offending device, but it eludes him. The fourth time it erupts he dives for the sound, tossing handfuls of adult magazines onto the floor, until he sees it. He snatches up the receiver and hits the talk button twice in quick succession: on and back off. The last thing he wants is to talk to anyone. He switches off the ringer and drops the phone on a stack of papers, watches as the entire thing topples and cascades to the floor.

The commotion jars his computer mouse and halts his screensaver program. He stares at the frozen-in-time image from his email account, a snapshot of what he was doing a week ago, the last time he was here.

From	Subject	Date
MrBB	**Hung masc poz needed to breed slim bttm**	
		Sat. 4/10/99
NoStrings2Nite	**Married Str8/Bi. No games, fems or PNP!!**	
		Sat. 4/10/99
TrucKing	Re: 21yo, 140_, 5'8", 8x6, will take your load	
		Sat. 4/10/99
CollegeBoi	**Fit vers guy seeks mature for mentoring/fun.**	
		Sat. 4/10/99

The rest stop where he and TrucKing met up had felt dangerously quiet, and spotting the orange cab at the end of a long line of idling big rigs far too easy. The adrenaline rush he got strolling across the vast parking lot, so conspicuous in such a place, was major. Just recalling it causes him to shudder. He remembers the sleeper compartment and the trucker waiting for him inside of it, both almost intolerably rank. *It was nearly as disgusting as this place*, he thinks. He makes a promise to himself to spend the next day cleaning up a bit.

Right now he wants nothing but a hot bath and several codeine-enhanced pain relievers, because every breath he takes elicits a scream of protest from his abdomen. He is certain that the beating he took at Trey's hands has resulted in broken ribs. Still, he feels it was worth it, for the metaphorical weight that it has lifted off his chest.

Half an hour after lowering his battered frame into the water that weight unexpectedly returns, in spades. All at once he can barely breathe. He thinks he may be having a heart attack, so he presses two fingertips into the soft spot beneath his chin and monitors his pulse. His fingers feel cold on his skin, and he shivers, though the hot water is causing beads of sweat to run down the back of his neck. He feels out of breath despite the fact that he has been lying down for thirty minutes. He has a strong urge to burp, and tries to, but can't.

Finally, his abdomen—already bruising from the slew of punches Trey landed on it—feels strangely hard to the touch.

Aside from the inability to take a deep breath and the bruising his symptoms are not new, are not anything caused by Trey's powerful right hook.

Even his alarmingly erratic heartbeat: boom, boom, boom—pause—boom, boom—pause—boom, boom, boom, boom, baBOOM, boom, boom—is something he first noticed on New Year's Day, just after leaving a speed-fueled marathon fuck session at a mansion off Frankfort Avenue.

Thinking he might be having or was about to have either a heart attack or a stroke, he'd broken protocol and asked one of the other guys from the party to drive him to the emergency room of the university hospital. The ER doctors had hooked him to an EKG, taken x-rays, even done an ultrasound. After twelve hours they'd released him with an embarrassing diagnosis—panic attack.

When a representative from the campus clinic called three days later and asked him to come in, he expected they wanted to be paid. Though he had no money at all, he went, for the entertainment value and for the opportunity to give a detailed account of his impoverished state, which he thought of as an acting exercise. He felt his suspicions confirmed when he was ushered into the nicely appointed (by university hospital standards) office of one Nadira Bayat, DNP, APRN-BC, but rather than a bill, she'd presented him with the results of a series of blood tests he hadn't known had been ordered.

He wasn't surprised to learn he had the big three—Syphilis, Gonorrhea, and Chlamydia—again, but seeing "HPV" written on the last line gave him a start when his brain misread the "P" as an "I." Dr. Bayat clearly had been banking on that, and she'd laid into him, hard. *If you have contracted these four there is a good chance you are also infected with HIV, but that test takes more time,* she said, as if he lived under a rock and had never seen the PSAs; had never been assaulted with rude literature by sanctimonious lesbians at Pride, or worse, given a dressing-down by a drag queen as he was entering the shower room of a bar, fully primed to receive a hot beef injection from a hunky stranger.

All the village idiots, he thinks, again remembering Ehrichto

Salvatolle's assessment of his lifestyle. *Eau de vie de Marc...a vintage pressed from garbage....*Other voices from the day begin to chime in. *Stay away from my brother...Goddamned little pansy...bone appétit...dressed like Mr. Furley.*

Robert Duvall's voice rings out in his head. *Sometimes they gave a little party before they did it,* he explains, speaking as Sonny Corleone in *The Godfather II,* one of his favorite films. *They went home and sat in a hot bath, and opened their veins, and bled to death.* Then the soundtrack switches. This time the voice is Robin Tunney's, as the character Debra in *Empire Records,* which he's seen dozens of times. *I tried to kill myself with a Lady Bic. A pink plastic razor with daisies on it and a moisturizing strip.*

Carefully, slowly, because doing so hurts like hell, he stretches an arm up to the sink basin and gropes blindly until he finds his cartridge razor. He removes the metal cover and stares at the three rows of blades.

MICHAEL CAN HARDLY believe it when Mr. Salvatolle turns and heads up the walk of the Belgravia Mystery House. Located a few doors down from the headquarters of the charity his grandmother founded, the house was so nicknamed by Julia as a nod to the Winchester Mystery House in San Jose, CA, the sprawling mansion featured on countless television programs about haunted places. The legacy of Sarah Winchester, heir to the Winchester rifle fortune, that house was the result of a construction project undertaken by the young widow after a psychic medium convinced her that the ghosts of people killed by Winchester guns were responsible for the premature deaths of her husband and their infant daughter, and that they were after her as well. There was no way, she said, to stop the spirits, but their actions could be stalled, provided they could be convinced the young widow was building a house just for them. So Sarah Winchester had hired teams of construction men to build a house for ghosts, and just to be sure the ghosts didn't get the mistaken idea the house was complete they'd worked in shifts, nonstop, building and tearing down and rebuilding rooms, until the day Mrs. Winchester died, some thirty-eight years later.

Michael's best guess as to why the house in Louisville reminds Julia of the one in San Jose is that she regards the woman who once owned it, and who has now been dead for almost twenty years, as having been stark raving mad. In typical fashion, she'd blithely ignored every other detail of the two stories. Michael knows the history of the house in Louisville from the many guided tours of Old Louisville he's been on. Tour guides seem fascinated with the story of the reclusive old woman who once lived here. Unlike Sarah Winchester, the homeowner in Louisville was not filthy rich, but broke, and instead of being terrified of the dead, she feared the living. Lastly, Michael's mother ignores the fact that far from having had crews working nonstop inside her home, the old woman who owned this house had for years and years refused to let any workmen inside, even after a large portion of the roof fell in and a tree branch, emanating from *inside* the structure, had breached a back bedroom window.

Though the cold, damp air cuts right through the white button-front shirt and jeans he changed into during his brief stop in his room, and he is eager to get to shelter, this house is too foreboding. Michael's feet feel rooted to the bricks of the walking court's central path.

Noticing that his companion has not followed him the short distance from the common sidewalk to the base of the steps leading up to a darkened porch, Mr. Salvatolle turns back. "It's all right," he says. "They're gone. It's just us." Michael isn't certain whether he means that there are no ghosts or if he is merely saying that whoever now owns the house is gone for the evening, and possibly for the entire weekend. His stomach somersaults at the thought of spending all night, and all day, and all night again with the man.

As if reading his mind, Mr. Salvatolle extends a hand, beckons him forward. "Have I ever lied to you?" he asks. "No, never. And I never will."

Michael takes the man's comment as sarcasm, an in-joke between them. He hopes it will be the first of many, the start of a long shared history. *Never, not once in the entire two hours we've known each other,* he thinks, though he's not entirely convinced the other is being genuine. That doubt triggers a warning deep within him. *What if he's an axe murderer?* he wonders. *Nobody knows where I am.* Far from increasing his fear and leading him to start planning an escape, though, the thought excites him. *No one knows where I am, who I'm with, or what I'm doing,* he thinks. *I can stay here as long as I want and they can't stop me.* In the rush of the moment, that seems worth any price.

Mr. Salvatolle turns and climbs the stair. He pauses at the door to take a ring of keys from his pocket and begins searching through them. At his side, Michael tries to picture what lies on the door's far side. Though the house has never, to his knowledge, been on the Holiday Homes Tour, where paying customers got to walk through the featured homes, plenty of similar houses have, and he has been dragged through them all. Crazy old women, ghosts, and handsome strangers notwithstanding, he feels confident that he knows what to expect, architecturally speaking. Built just after the turn of the century, the structure is a narrow brick row house of Italianate design standing three stories tall, fairly standard issue for the area. Its face is divided into quadrants, of which the top two and bottom left are dominated by large mullioned windows. The last contains the entryway. As Mr. Salvatolle fits a key into the lock, Michael imagines a vestibule and sweeping stair, a parlor off to the left and, behind it, in the corresponding back corner of the house, a dining room. Off that, he guesses, is the kitchen, and on the right side of the house tucked away beneath the stairs, the entrance to a wood-paneled smoking parlor. The first room to the right of the door will be the formal sitting room.

The key turns. The door swings open. Mr. Salvatolle motions for Michael to enter first.

The interior is as black as pitch, every bit as disorienting as the moment during a seventh-grade field trip to Mammoth Cave when the guide switched off his lamp and all the path lights, to let the students experience what being in a cave was truly like. Praying he won't knock something over before the man can switch on a light Michael cautiously sweeps the air with a hand and slides one foot forward, then the other. The space smells exactly as he expected it would, like Murphy's Oil Soap. He wonders who the house belongs to, and how Mr. Salvatolle knows them.

Michael hears the man shut and re-lock the door. Still expecting the click of a light switch, he starts when he feels the man's hands grasp his waist. Their mouths meet again. Unlike the playful one the man bestowed on him in the car, this kiss is filled with desperate hunger. It's a sentiment Michael understands. Grasping Mr. Salvatolle's head in his hands, he returns the kiss as forcefully as he can.

A moment later, mouths still locked together and fingers entwined in each other's hair, they begin to move deeper into the dwelling. Michael is forced backward through the darkness with no idea of what lies in his path. His elbow brushes an unknown object just before his hip and another something collide. Before he has a chance to worry about either thing a wall rushes up to meet his back; he finds himself trapped between it and Mr. Salvatolle, who is still moving forward with force.

A concussive burst makes him jump. It's followed by a dull thud. Michael pictures pottery shattering, a wooden column landing on a rug. The idea that they are tearing the place apart spikes his adrenaline. Whoever owns the house might right now be calling the police. The cops might come and haul them off to jail. Tomorrow, everyone—not just at school this time, but the entire city—could know, maybe will know, what he and Mr. Salvatolle were trying to do together.

If that's the case, he thinks, *I want to make sure it was worth it.* Letting go of the back of the man's head, he contracts the muscles of his stomach and plunges his hands into the sliver of space between their torsos.

THE WHISKY HASN'T done its job, has not chased the scene under the stairs from Lloyd's head. Rather, it's mixed everything up. *Michael's worked so hard to make new friends,* he thinks, taking a deeper drink from the glass in his hand. *And to find the girl, and win her over. If that Daniels kid ruins everything for him, so help me, I'll kill him.* His grip on the glass is much too tight; he is in danger of shattering it and hurting himself. He wills himself to relax. *Maybe I should go lie down,* he thinks. *Try to get some rest until Julia gets home.*

As he expected, she hadn't been happy when he called to say he was in no shape to drive, but what choice did she have but to find another way home? He feels sure she will not take his suggestion to leave the wrapping up of things to her assistants and catch an earlier ride back with the Morrisons, just as he would wager she has never really heard him on any of the several occasions when he said he was having trouble with his eyes.

The image of Michael standing with Alyssa and the Daniels boy in the hallway by the coat check leaps back into his mind. *Tall and broad-*

shouldered and blond, he thinks, the fact that the boy is the antithesis of his son seeming to lend credence to the theory Lloyd has held for the last eight months, that Alyssa is dating his son merely to make her ex-boyfriend jealous. *But not knowing that, Trey thinks he has to sour her on him. So he called him names, and now Michael thinks his whole world is about to collapse.* The pain in his temples flares. *Again.*

He revisits a fantasy he entertained frequently in the months following the fistfight between Michael and his best friend Jon Lewis, which had landed Michael in the emergency room. Lloyd pictures himself behind the wheel of the Corvette, turning a corner onto a deserted street, only to discover Jon skateboarding down the middle of it.

As if on cue he hears a car—in the real world, not the fantasy one—out on the street. It pulls into the cul-de-sac, rolls past their house, turns into their driveway. *Well, what do you know?* he thinks. *She actually took my advice for once, and let someone else from the organization stay to the bitter end.* One of the vehicle's doors opens and closes, and Julia's heels begin hammering a staccato report on the winding stone front path. Then a second car door opens and closes. The rhythm on the walk becomes a jumble.

Alyssa! Lloyd thinks. He attempts to quickly yet carefully deposit his highball glass on the mirrored library table, but misjudges and slams it down. He doesn't have the time to worry, or feel for a crack in the surface. Using the table and sofa as triangulation points, he makes as mad a dash of it as he can, aiming for the bedroom. Before he has taken four steps, however, the front door opens and he freezes.

"You're not coming in," he hears Julia bark. He's never been more grateful for his wife's blunt demeanor.

"But you said that Mr. Ferguson said Michael wants to talk to me!" Alyssa protests.

He had, indeed, told Julia that, when he called to inform her that he wouldn't be coming back downtown. His idea had been to get the girl on the line and then ask her exactly what had transpired under the stairs, what caused Michael's dinner to end up all over the carpeting, and where he might now be headed, but when she came to the phone he'd chickened out. While she repeatedly called out his son's name, he'd disconnected the call.

"That was three hours ago," Julia counters. "I'm telling you now, it's late; Michael is most likely asleep, and you will have to wait until morning. He'll call you when he's feeling better. Good night."

"If he's sleeping where's his car?" Alyssa asks. She raises her voice and calls out "Mr. Ferguson? It's Alyssa. Michael isn't here, is he?"

"His car is in the shop. Now, goodnight," Julia says firmly. Lloyd smiles even before he hears the door slam shut. Neither of them says anything until the Morrisons' car has driven off. "She's right. He's not here," he offers at last. "Also, I'm blind."

"'Blind' as in you should have seen it coming?"

Lloyd's hands begin to shake. He is afraid of the direction her thoughts are taking. "No," he says. "As in I can't see anything. Or almost nothing, anyway."

Judging by the lengthy pause that follows, he infers that his wife has finally, actually, heard him. The stiff rustling of fancy dress fabric and quick clicking of high heels on the foyer's tiled floor fills him with joyful relief. He imagines her flying toward him, throwing her arms around him, promising him it will all be okay, but her footsteps stop short of him and then begin to recede. She stomps away across the carpet in the great room. An abrupt, sharp rattling sound makes him think of tossed dice.

"What are you doing?"

"Throwing out the rest of your drink."

Lloyd puts a hand back, feeling for the wall, but finds only air. "Why?"

"You've never heard the expression 'blind drunk'?"

"That's not what that m—"

"It most certainly is," she snaps. "Don't tell me about alcohol. My family's money was made in alcohol. It killed my grandfather!"

Just as Ehrichto Salvatolle did at dinner earlier, over the years many people have asked Julia about her family's history as distillers, but only once or twice has Lloyd known her to bring up the subject. He finds himself torn by conflicting impulses—on the one hand, to let her speak her piece, whatever it is; on the other, to contradict what he knows is a whitewashing of history.

"Your grandfather was shot by his father."

"By his father the teetotaler," she says. "Who caught him making moonshine."

"Well, that's not what people mean when they say that alcohol killed someone. And anyway, in his case, religion was to blame, not whisky."

Everything he's heard about Tibbot Conway—albeit not much—says that he was an insufferable, hard-hearted man, quick to point fingers and even quicker to make excuses for his own failing.

"The point," Julia says emphatically, "is that alcohol made my grandmother a widow and she warned me about it. For instance, she said that you never drink the alcohol that first comes out of the still because it's pure and will make you go blind."

Lloyd waves a hand. "No, stop," he says. "Just…stop. I don't believe Myrtle said that."

A sharp sound tells him Julia has slammed the highball glass down on the marble apron of the bar sink. "I know what she told me!"

The last thing he needs is to start debating with her, but he can't let this stand. "Then she was an idiot. First of all, the foreshots are weak, not pure and strong. It's not the alcohol that's harmful about them, it's all the other volatile chemicals they contain that—" Pain flares in his temples, doubles him over. "Christ Almighty."

"Sit down."

He knows what she's doing. If he stops now she will rewrite the discussion later on, twist everything around. He grits his teeth and goes on. "Look, give me a little credit, will you? I'm from the eastern part of this state. Where I grew up, you can't throw a rock without hitting a distillery."

"Give me some, too. Who do you think you're fooling? The town you grew up in is practically in West Virginia. The distilleries are all around Lexington. They're much closer to here than to where you're from."

"Well, it's what people talked about all the time, and it's what Everett and Whitman and I talk about now. And at this time of year you can't turn on the television without seeing one news team or the other broadcasting from beside a damn thump keg. I watched a show about it just last week, Julia. What you're saying is wrong. The foreshots, or heads, contain highly poisonous toxins like methanol and sulfur as well as residue from earlier distillations, and those boil sooner, which means they condense sooner, which means you get them first. Drink that and you'll be damned lucky if all that happens is you go blind."

"Which is why you discard that part."

"No, you don't!" Pain again, pulsing in the sides of his head. "You add it back to the heart of the run. The foreshots is what gives a batch of whisky its character and flavor."

"I think you should sit down."

He wishes that, as it so often does, the phrase "Well, that's fine, but," had curtly preceded her words, to give him the illusion, at least, of having won, because he knows this argument is over. Sitting down not only isn't a bad idea, it may be imperative. The only trouble is, he has no idea which way to turn. He takes a few tentative steps, and is surprised when he does not run into the couch.

"Where exactly are you planning to sit?" Julia asks. "In the yard?"

He stops, turns left, and walks into the end table.

"Oh, my lord. You really can't see anything, can you? You're truly blind."

"I told you that. You never listen."

He locates the couch, and begins making his way around its end. As he does he hears her head off toward the bedroom. A minute later he hears water running in the bathroom sink, and figures she is taking off her makeup, preparing to get out of her dress. Realizing he is still in his tuxedo, he slips off his jacket and drapes it over the back of the sofa.

Right after he sits something cold touches his forehead and makes him jump. "This will help," Julia says. "Take it."

"We don't have time to worry about this now," Lloyd protests. "We need to figure out where Michael is."

"Michael isn't blind," she says. She pushes him backward and arranges a wrung-out washrag on his brow. "He also isn't a child anymore. Whatever he ran off to do was his choice. It's on him to deal with the consequences."

BAXTER HAS THE strong desire to give Marc's door several sharp raps with the cobra's head handle of his walking stick but refrains from doing so because it is past midnight and the door to the next apartment stands just across the hall. *My mother and father raised a child with manners,* he thinks. *For example, I would never submit someone's artwork to a competition without their permission.* He neglects to recall that every quarter hour for the past twelve hours straight he has called the apartment and let it ring twelve times; that the only reason he has come here now is because the last time he called, he got a busy signal, the time before that the phone was picked up and then hung up again. That and the fact that Marc's white VW Cabrio is parked on the street not far from the building convinces him that the other is home.

Ever the champion of civility, he makes a fist and knocks softly, before pressing his ear to the door to listen. He expects to hear a frantic rustling and rushing about coming from the other side, but no sounds greet his ear. He knocks again, harder. After a moment, impatient, he calls, "Marc, darling! Come out, come out, wherever you are!" Finally, he tries the doorknob, to no avail.

He looks more closely at it the door, and finds it has five panels set horizontally. Identical to the one across the hall and two further down it, it is obviously original to the Victorian structure. It seems impossible to him that it could have survived so many decades unscathed. He leans a shoulder against it, and feels the panel give slightly. He runs his hand across the surface and feels a jagged ridge beneath the paint, invisible to the eye. At some point someone put their fist through the panel and the landlord, either out of cheapness or a desire to retain the structure's original elements, used spackle and paint to make it appear to be whole again.

He's disappointed by the lack of a challenge, the fact that he will not have to press the button on the back of his walking stick's cobra's head, after all, to release its forked tongue, really a pair of former saber-saw blades filed into what might be hockey sticks for mice, which can be used to pick locks if one is practiced at the art, as he likes to think he is. He considers trying out his skills anyway, then sighs melodramatically, deciding he does not want Marc to know he has such a talent. He gives the repaired panel a good shove, until it falls inward.

He expects the thing to clatter to the floor, but there is no corresponding sound. He reaches through the breach and turns the knob.

"Well, this much is clear," he mutters as he shoulders open the door. "He isn't mysophobic." After he has wrestled it open far enough that he can manage to slide sideways through the gap, he sees why the panel's fall was muffled. A pile of dirty laundry and, judging by their covers, even dirtier magazines all but blocks the entry.

Looking deeper into the room, his first thought is of compulsive hoarders who stack cardboard boxes and plastic bags from floor to ceiling. Then it dawns on him that he is not, as he expected to be, standing in the common area of a multi-room apartment. It's not even a decent-sized studio, but more of a kitchenette. A king-sized bed dominates the floor space; on the left wall a short bank of cabinets hangs above a section of counter so abbreviated that the microwave and automatic coffee maker placed there overhang both ends.

The single basin sink overflows with dirty dishes. There is a dorm-style refrigerator and no oven. The room, he estimates, is a hundred or maybe a hundred and fifty square feet at most, and the fact that it is crammed with enough furniture and personal effects to make a space two or three times larger feel full makes it seem even smaller. It is easily the smallest apartment he has ever set foot in, smaller even than the claustrophobia-inducing studio he lived in for nearly two decades in New York.

On the far side of the bed is the only other door, to the bathroom, where Marc must be. The outright filth surrounding him quickly sours his mood again. Everywhere he looks it greets his eye. Hard surfaces are glazed watery brown with what he guesses—and hopes—is spilled coffee; urban tumbleweeds composed of human hair and grit fill every corner. Plates of rotting food have been randomly abandoned on stacks of papers and books and—his stomach roils at the sight—in the bed.

"A healthy person wouldn't live like this," he whispers, searching for a cleared spot on the floor big enough for his foot. "Almost a bedsit, filthier than even Quentin Crisp could have endured." He uses his walking stick to slide a pile of clothes and scripts aside and takes a careful step, then repeats the action until he is at last at the bathroom door. "Yoo-hoo! Marc?" he calls. "You didn't answer your door so I let myself in. Sorry about the destruction, but honestly, in this mess it's hardly noticeable."

He pauses, listens. It dawns on him that the other might be just waking from having fallen asleep in the tub, might be on the brink of bursting through the door wielding a toilet plunger. "Marc? It's Baxter."

Still, there is no reply. No sound. He uses the cobra's head handle of his walking stick to rap loudly on the door, the way he wanted to do in the hall, then tries the knob. This time, it turns. "Wakey, wakey," he calls as the door swings open.

His first impression is that Marc is sitting in a tub of watermelon gelatin. *I've heard of some weird kinks before, but*—Then he realizes what he is actually looking at and his stomach sinks. "Oh, no." He releases his grip on both the doorknob and his cane and—the pain in his hip forgotten—races toward the tub. "No, no, no, no, no, no, no!"

Marc's head has lolled forward so that his chin is to his chest. The fine golden hairs there are splattered with gobs and flecks of red gore. Baxter starts to reach out but flinches, struck by the memory of touching Ysabella with the intention of waking her, only to realize she was dead. *Cold and terrible*, he remembers, a shiver jostling his shoulders. He takes a deep breath to stick his resolve, then grasps Marc by the hair and pulls his head back. His hand trembles as he touches the younger man's cheek. When he feels warmth there, his relief is so great that he nearly bursts into tears. Then, terror grips him again. *How long does it take for body heat to dissipate*, he wonders. *How long when the person is submerged in warm water?* He pushes the awful thought away, reminds himself that, fancying himself Sherlock Holmes, he'd touched the hood of the Cabrio as he passed it, and found it still warm, too.

"Marc!" He jabs fingers against the younger man's neck, feeling for a pulse. "Marc! Can you hear me? Wake up!" He plunges a hand into the warm, candy pink water and fishes Marc's arms out, one by one. He's relieved to find one wrist uncut, the other merely abraded. *He tried but couldn't do it*, Baxter thinks. His joy is short-lived. *But then where did all this blood come from? Did he...did he cough it up? Did he swallow pills?* He searches around the base of the tub for an empty bottle but finds nothing. "Marc, wake up this instant and tell me what you took!" Baxter looks at his watch. Only thirty-five minutes have elapsed since the last time he called the apartment. *He's still alive*, he reassures himself. *Whatever he took he did it recently. They can pump his stomach. All I have to do is get him to the hospital.*

He pulls the plug to drain the water and reaches for the pile of clothes heaped behind the door. The item on the very top is a tuxedo jacket, circa 1978. Beneath that he finds a shirt decorated with chartreuse, aqua and lemon chrysanthemum clusters. "You've been rehearsing your new role, I see," he says, grabbing a towel from off the pile. He begins drying Marc's arms and torso. "Quelle surprise, you know," he says. "You spent the evening mocking me, and now here I am, saving your miserable, incredible ass." He squeezes water from the fringe of hair on the back of Marc's head, and tries not to look at the shriveled lump of flesh just breaking the water's descending surface. "The funny thing is," he says, drying Marc's face, his shoulders, and chest, "that you don't realize everything you're doing now is a preparation for the hardest role of your life, the one I'm playing now. You'd never, ever believe me but it's true: we're the same, and you are forbidden to die and rob me of the chance to see the look on your face when you realize it. Is that clear? You cannot die. You must stay here with me."

He feels tears threatening to well up but he pushes them down, knowing if he loses it now, the other is done for. As he struggles to work Marc's pants up his legs, he notes that goose pimples cover the young man's skin. *That couldn't happen if....* he thinks, not daring to complete the thought. He actively ignores the fact that Marc's pallor now almost matches the white of the tub.

Looking back through the doorway at the main room of the apartment, he considers his options. Searching for the phone to call an ambulance will eat up valuable minutes, and more importantly he's heard horror stories, albeit mainly at the height of the AIDS crisis, of ambulances which never arrived, or arrived only to leave again, empty, after it was learned the patient was gay.

He feels that avenue closed to them.

"Mary, I'm warning you," he says as he slips arms under Marc's knees and behind his shoulders, preparing to lift him from the tub. "After you make me go through all this, you do not want to die and leave me the last word."

WORDS WERE UNNECESSARY earlier, and insufficient, an unsatisfying use of the mouth. Ehrichto got all the information he needed from kissing, licking and—gently—biting every inch of Patrick's skin. Now, as daybreak approaches, he is exhausted and shivering, left with nothing *but* words, ones which keep forming into questions and bombarding his psyche: *What was the first thing that went through his mind when he realized it was me? How long had he been here with these people? Did he just pop into existence when Maria worked her magic? Does he even know that he did, or does he think he was always here? Does he remember everything from before, or just me? And where was he in between, exactly? Was it heaven? Purgatory? Surely it wasn't…. Is he angry that he's back here with me, or is he relieved?*

"I didn't plan this," he blurts. "I didn't mean for it to happen. I never pictured us here, like this."

Patrick rolls onto his side and props his head on a bent arm. His shirt sleeve is unbuttoned, hanging open rather jauntily midway down his forearm. "Really?" he asks. His expression is one of severe skepticism. "Then what *were* you picturing when you pointed the car in this direction?" A heartbeat later, he grins. The move is so classically Patrick—employing humor to call his lover out as a liar, a coward, a prude—that Ehrichto cannot help but smile as well.

"I meant at a point earlier than that, but fine, you win. I confess—I did picture it. But I didn't believe it would happen."

Patrick laughs; a short, smug burst of sound. "I surprised you," he says, collapsing back against the bare mattress. The sheets, covered in dust, are in a ball on the floor.

"Surprised?" Ehrichto chuckles at the understatement. "You could've knocked me over with a feather. It was all I could do, during that—" Realizing that the dinner at which they rediscovered one another is the last thing in the world he wants to talk about, he stops and changes course, asks something he truly wants to know. "How did you manage to...to get back? And where did you go?"

Patrick raises both brows. "Oh. Now that's not a pretty story. I mean, first of all, I didn't want to leave in the first place, right? But my father gave me no choice."

He didn't want to leave, Ehrichto thinks. *He didn't want to leave me.* His chest begins to swell, but the elation is quashed by the sudden, unwelcome recollection of entering the bothy and seeing his lover uncharacteristically slumped upon the space's sole chair. It had taken a moment for what he was looking at to register: with his left hand Patrick was clutching his lower back, trying to staunch the blood flowing from a deep knife wound there, which was already starting to spread around the sides of his shirt and into view. The heel of his right hand was pressed to the chair seat, his locked elbow the only thing keeping him from tumbling sideways onto the floor. His revolver dangled from the curled middle finger of the same, threatening to drop to the floor. A few yards away, surrounded by his own spreading pool of blood, Tibbot Conway lay unmoving on the cavern floor.

"Your father," Ehrichto replies, nodding. The memory shakes him to the core. As much as he'd disliked the man, seeing Tibbot's midsection shredded by bullets was horrifying, to this day one of the grisliest sights he's ever witnessed. *The possibility that the knife wound Patrick had suffered* was fatal never even entered my mind, he thinks, marveling at his own naïveté. I was much more worried about his soul because he'd just broken two commandments than I was that he would die, because I couldn't conceive of him as mortal. He was the central character of the story I lived in; it didn't seem possible that he could die. And yet, when we were halfway back to the Conway place, that's exactly what he did.

Patrick's death had struck him as a mistake on the part of the universe, a hiccup or rift. He'd thought he couldn't go on without Patrick. I not only did manage to go on without him, he thinks, but I became a thing that can't die. Every year that I've remained above ground while he's been under it has felt more surreal than its predecessors. Nothing has ever made any sense, until now. "Now I understand," he says. It's destiny. We were always fated to meet back up, for good.

"The only thing I could do was bide my time and wait for my chance to slip out and come find you," Patrick explains, continuing his recounting of his escape from death's clutches "When I finally got my chance I went as fast as I could, the whole time expecting to be caught and dragged back. And once I got down there I started worrying that it would be too late when I arrived, that I wouldn't be able to find you in all the chaos. But then I turned the corner and there you were."

"There I was," Ehrichto says. "Here I am." He looks at his lover, at eyes which have always been impossibly bright and blue, and is struck by the realization that, without knowing he was doing it, he has been surrounding himself with their precise shade. He has it as neckties and shirts, as the stone inlay on silver cufflinks, and in a thousand other forms. Dorjan's irises come close to the shade, and Nick's are a watered down version. That color is what kept me in Havana, he thinks, remembering his exile after Dorjan's sentencing, two years of hard labor for "lewd behavior," a punishment Ehrichto hadn't quite been able to believe was still being handed out half a century after it had broken the spirit of Oscar Wilde, who by nineteen thirty-seven was widely understood to have been one of the greatest writers of all time. Much of Ehrichto's grand plan to hop the next plane out of Cuba and go back and fight for his lover, despite Dorjan's command to stay where he'd been sent, had dissolved as he looked around at bright blue buildings and the open ocean beyond them, the same deep blue of his first love's eyes. He understands now that seeing the color had calmed him down, allowed him to follow Dorjan's order and start his life over in the Caribbean nation. "That gorgeous shade of blue," he says. "When our eyes met tonight, I knew it was you and no other."

"Wow."

The word strikes a discordant note for Ehrichto. Instantly, he is uneasy. He tries to push his fear aside. "I…I need a smoke."

Patrick sits up and folds his legs into the position made famous by Indian holy men. "I've been smoking cigars lately," he says, pride evident in his voice.

Ehrichto understands it as his way of burying the hatchet for the odious behavior he displayed in their youth, an apology for having endlessly extolled the virtues of cigarettes over cigars, just to get his lover's goat.

"I'm pleased to hear it. And for my part, I concede that cigarettes weren't just a fad."

Patrick looks uncertain. "Uh, right. Sure."

A fresh surge of doubt washes through Ehrichto. He gives a quick shake of his head, signaling: It's okay. Forget that I said anything.

"Hey," Patrick says, his voice cracking slightly. "You know what keeps going through my head? The song 'Lovecats' by the Cure. Do you know it?" He smiles sheepishly. "I never really thought I'd get to live it. Being with you, here, like this, is so much cooler than I imagined."

The slang word "cool," separated out from phrases like "as a cucumber," hadn't taken hold until the 1950s. Ehrichto remembers its emergence. He knows that for a while before it became a nationwide trend it was employed only in jazz clubs by those persons he still, by default, thinks of as "Negro" musicians. Some habits are hard to break, but he tries.

He knows that if he'd had the chance Patrick would have been a part of that crowd. He also knows he was gone before jazz itself was even born. With that realization the panic that has been gathering inside him wells over. "Cool" was never part of Patrick's vernacular. He looks at the eyes again and prays that if he concentrates hard enough on them he will find a way to rewind the last moments, to rewrite Patrick's incorrect facial expressions and odd word choices, his earlier lapses in memory and knowledge of a song by a band whose members' parents likely weren't even born at the time of his death. Instead of being pulled in by the blue, however, he feels the leaden sensation in his stomach that always accompanies the arrival of very bad news.

No, he thinks stubbornly. *I don't accept this. It is* him. *He has* come *back to me.*

It's no use. A deeper part of him begins openly challenging the notion. *Why didn't he come back just as he was the day he died?* it asks. *Why is he once again the age he was when we met and not twenty-seven?* His gut tells him the whole business is wrong, is off, that it can be ascribed to wishful thinking. *Why would he need a new story, a new family, new friends? No, my first instinct was right: if this were Patrick, returned, I would have found him in the mausoleum.*

He glances over again and this time truly sees the slew of tiny details he ignored earlier, not least among them the blush of embarrassment coloring the pale cheek and the tiny vein twitching just below the corner of one eye.

Nerves, he thinks. *Fear and nerves. Things Patrick never, ever let show.* He grabs the other's forearm and slides his shirt sleeve up toward the elbow, searching for the pale freckles Patrick always referred to as his Irish suntan. In the back of his mind he knows he won't find them. He'd noticed their lack during the night, while they were intimate, but pushed the insight away. He drops the freckle-less arm and stares at the boy beside him.

What have I just done?

He remembers the moment they rediscovered one another, his confusion at seeing fear on Patrick's face. *I told myself it was surprise, and then that he was allowed to be afraid. But Patrick never let anything but confidence show. You could have set off a bomb next to him and he wouldn't have reacted. Even as he was dying his expression remained inscrutable.*

That's why I couldn't fathom that it was as bad as it was. That's why I thought nothing could truly harm him. He acted immortal, and I wanted to believe he was.

"Hey," the boy says, his voice almost cracking. "Did I say something wrong? I'm sorry."

Ehrichto replays the banter they exchanged earlier in the evening. *The pitch rises at the ends of all of his sentences*, he thinks. *Even ones that start out strong end up as questions. Which means his self-confidence is only lukewarm, and that's not Patrick. He also never once said anything to anyone else that could have been recognized as a double entendre. He only said cheeky things to me, privately. And Salvatolle's Golden Steeples rang no bells for him, at all.*

"Say my name."

"What? Why?"

"You've never once used it tonight. Say my name."

"Eric…um…Eh-reek…um…. Oh god, I'm sorry. I don't want to butcher it. How does it go?"

Ehrichto squeezes his eyes shut and drops his head. "I've made a terrible mistake." His eyes fly open again when he feels the stranger—who is he?—touch his arm. He jerks free. "Don't!" He swings his legs over the side of the bed and begins hastily gathering up the various pieces of his attire.

"What? No, wait! I'm just not good with names like my dad is, but I'll get it. Please, just let me hear you say it one more time."

Ehrichto keeps his gaze fixed upon a section of wallpaper coming apart at the seams. The curling imparts a lifelike quality to the gray-green ivy leaves in the pattern that the rest do not have. "It's not you," he says, the cruel joke in the words not lost on him. "It's that you reminded me very much of someone else, and I made some wretched decisions because of it. I don't know how else to explain it except to say that I—somewhat willfully—mistook you for someone else. May God forgive me."

"What? Wait, what are you talking about? You aren't making sense. Please, just calm down, okay? Turn around. Look at me. Please."

If he again sees Patrick's face animated by a stranger his heart will break. Ehrichto keeps his back turned. "It's nothing you did. This is entirely on me. But the truth remains: I don't know you, and you have to leave."

"What?"

Ehrichto feels the young man begin to scramble from the bed. Uncertain what he might do if the stranger touches him again he darts toward the far side of the room. He wants to be alone, to have a chance to think. He recalls his last exchange with Marc, in the garage, and seizes on cruelty as a last resort. "How can you not understand?" he asks. "It's simple. We're done here and I want you to leave. Get dressed and go."

The floorboards creak as the stranger gets to his feet. "But—"

"I said get out! NOW!"

The only reply he gets is a strangled intake of breath, and the start of a low keening. The boy is about to start crying. Ehrichto's disappoint in himself fuels his anger. In the next moment it occurs to him that there is no reason he cannot be the one who leaves.

"Fine," he says to the faded paper on the wall. "If you refuse to go, I will."

"MARC?" MARC HEARS Baxter ask. He squeezes his eyes shut again and lays still. "Your eyes were just open," Baxter says. "I know you're awake. Stop being a shit and look at me."

Marc obliges. When he does he finds Baxter seated in a puce-colored pleather armchair, glaring at him over the tops of his half-glasses. In his lap is the hinged, shallow metal box that contains Marc's medical chart. "So, doctor," Marc says, alarmed to find he is out of breath after just two words. He is further surprised to find that the act of inhaling is strenuous and painful, like what he imagines it is like to draw in the scorching air of a house fire. It also causes a sharp pain outside his lungs, starting on his left side and spreading all the way across his chest. "What does it…say?"

Baxter shoots him a vitriolic look and tosses the chart onto the foot of the bed. "Oh, you know. Everything's peachy. What do you think it says?"

Marc shrugs.

"Fine. Forget the chart. Worry about what I'm saying."

Marc raises his eyebrows, hoping by it to convey *Which is?*

"What the hell happened to you tonight?"

"Pardon?"

Baxter chuckles but doesn't sound amused in the least. "I found you passed out in your tub, blood everywhere, covered in bruises. So far they've determined you have three broken ribs, a collapsed lung, and most likely internal bleeding, because your blood-volume level was insanely low. You were also severely dehydrated. They pumped you full of blood and also some lactated-ringers-something-or-other. Right now they're trying to decide whether they should take a wait-and-see approach or do some sort of scan, and they're trying to contact your mother. I remembered her name is Corrine, but she re-married, didn't she? She's not a Fleming anymore?"

Hearing his real surname causes Marc to wince. When he holds up three fingers, he finds that his arm is caught up short, probably tangled up in an I.V. line.

"She's a polygamist?" Baxter asks.

Marc is pretty sure if he laughs, it will kill him. He folds two fingers down before dropping his forearm back to the mattress. "On her...third husband," he explains. "She's an Archer now." He's out of breath, and has to concentrate on inhaling. "She works at the...Cock n' Bull...Diner in... Charlestown."

"I'll find her."

"No. Don't. I'm fine."

"Mmm, yes. Clearly, that's what you are. In fact it's the first thing I said to myself when I walked into your bathroom tonight. I said, 'Oh look, he's fine.'" He pauses to give the sarcasm a chance to take full effect. "I assured them the only substances you use are Tylenol, enough caffeine to kill a horse, and wild amounts of Ritalin. I think I convinced them that you weren't trying to off yourself. Even the blast of Ritalin they can ascribe to your having developed a tolerance. They're going to put you on something else."

Marc shakes his head vigorously. "Nothing. Else. Works."

Baxter ignores him. "Your dependence on Ritalin doesn't really explain the condition you're in now, though, does it? The bruises. The collapsed lung. Ergo, I'm asking you: What occurred before I entered your apartment?"

"How did you...get in?"

"I will point out that there are drawers full of medical equipment within my reach and you are tethered to that bed. Therefore I will ask the questions and you will answer them."

The news that he is restrained causes Marc's pulse to skyrocket. Ever since the spring his mother dated a born-again Christian who insisted Marc be shunted off to the school associated with his church, and he'd found himself at the mercy of sadists named Sister Bridie and Brother Oren, he has had an intense fear of physical confinement. He tries to move his limbs, but finds they are, in fact, fastened to the bed rails by short lengths of cotton tie. Also, an I.V. issues from the crook of his left elbow. He looks from Baxter to his wrist and back again. "Why?"

"Well, as I already explained, I thought you tried to kill yourself."

"No."

"Mmm. I understand that now."

"No," Marc says again, more forcefully. "Untie. Me. Now."

"First tell me what happened."

"Now!" Marc pulls at his bonds and drums the end of the bed with his heels, effort that quickly uses up all his oxygen and causes him to see stars. He takes a savage breath and kicks his legs harder. He's rewarded with the sound of his medical chart clattering to the floor.

Baxter grabs his ankles. "Stop that! You have to stay still!"

"Nurse," Marc calls, and finds he cannot project his voice beyond a hoarse whisper. "Help, nurse." He gasps for air. "Fire."

"All right," Baxter says, relenting. "You win. I'll untie you. Just shut up and be still." He begins to work on the knot at Marc's right arm. "Just lovely. You've made this almost impossible."

"Scissors," Marc says. He drops his head back on the pillow and closes his eyes. He feels as if he could sleep for years. "Look in…drawers."

"This is hardly the time for that."

Marc raises his middle finger again.

"I just told you no. Hold still. Tell me who attacked you."

"No one."

"Again with the bridge selling? Tell me."

"After."

"Someone was after you? Or do you mean it happened after you left work?"

Marc opens his eyes and yanks his right arm sideways, ripping the knot from Baxter's fingertips. "After…the scissors."

"Oh, for the love of God." Baxter grabs his cane and begins unscrewing the ring beneath the cobra head handle. Marc is confused until he sees the sections of the walking stick separate, revealing a dagger.

After his hands are freed, Baxter asks again, "Who attacked you?"

"Legs."

"As if you could get up and leave." Baxter slices through the two remaining tethers. "Happy now?"

Marc hears him slide the dagger back into the lower half of the cane. "All right, tell me who—"

He's interrupted by a knock at the door followed by the creak of its hinge. "Is he awake?" a familiar and welcome voice says.

Marc lifts his head and his eyes meet those of his ex, Neal. "Hey, there," the guy calls, a smile spreading across his face. "I was hoping you'd be awake. How're you doin'?" Then his gaze drifts and he spies Baxter. Like throwing a switch, his demeanor changes. He crosses the room swiftly, his right arm extended. "Richard Baxter, I presume? I'm Neal Daniels. It's a pleasure to finally meet you."

Baxter says nothing aloud, but a series of emotions play out on his face as the two shake hands. Irritation gives way to a look of fear and finally one of hatred. Marc feels giddy. *You dirty liar*, he thinks. *If you don't fancy me, how come right now you'd like nothing more than to plunge that dagger of yours right into Neal's heart?*

He knows that his ex-boyfriend must see it too, but Neal has been trained to keep his true thoughts and opinions from being revealed. "You're the one who found him, or was with him at the time, is that right?" he asks.

Meaning, Marc thinks, *Why were you in his apartment at one in the morning?*

"I found him, yes."

"He broke in," Marc says.

"I did not."

"Liar."

"Well, whatever the case was," Neal says. "I'm just thankful you arrived when you did." Marc is struck by how much he sounds like a character in a television show. Like he's the actor, not Marc, and is only playing at being a doctor. *Or a human.* He watches a pretended embarrassment blush Neal's cheeks. "Would you, uh, would you mind if I spoke to him alone for a few minutes?"

Baxter glares. Marc thinks he will refuse, but the man gets to his feet. "Canst thou, I wonder?" he asks Neal.

Minister to a mind diseased, Marc thinks. *Pluck from the memory a rooted sorrow, raze out the written troubles of the brain, and with some sweet, oblivious antidote cleanse the stuff'd bosom of that perilous stuff which weighs upon the heart?*

Neal's eyes narrow but his smile stays steady, the perfect, practiced expression of amused bewilderment. "I'm sorry?"

"Cure her of that," Baxter replies, nodding in Marc's direction. "I would applaud thee." He spins on one heel and heads for the door.

THE FRONT GATES of Cave Hill Cemetery stand open. Kicked back in his chair reading a paperback novel, the guard gives barely a nod as the Porsche rolls past, very nearly the only car in motion in all of downtown. It seems that after the late-night street party raucousness of Thunder, the citizenry of Louisville has collectively decided to sleep in.

The quiet chill in the air and overcast sky peeking through the lush tree canopy just inside the cemetery entrance all conspire to make Ehrichto think of home. Then he remembers: the cloud forest atop Volcán San Pedro no longer is home; the cofradía has resurrected the old wooden effigy of Maximón; Nick and Wren are in New Orleans. *And I'm at Patrick's grave for the second time in two days.*

For months after Patrick's death he'd made a daily pilgrimage to the Conway family mausoleum at the heart of one of the cemetery's oldest sections.

He guides the car around familiar curves until he sees the structure, perched atop a gentle hill. He brakes the car at the base of the hill and climbs out.

When he arrived in Chiya, three days late, Maria had, of course, been unable to articulate her thoughts in a way he could understand, to explain why the plaza was dark, why she was there alone. She'd tried, rattling off words so fast they ran together into one long sound, until he'd put his hand up and shaken his head, letting her know she was wasting her breath. He remembers looking left and right and high and low, confused at not seeing snuffed-out torches standing at the plaza corners, or any remnants of the temporary artworks that the women of the cofradía always spent days down on their hands and knees on the plaza stones creating from brightly dyed sand and beans and shells. He expected the surrounding brush to still be festooned with strings of the intricate cut-paper iconography known as *papel picado*. Each year has seen their designs more polluted with his vampiric traits than previously. Last year one showed Maximón drinking blood from a wooden bowl; another had him baring long canine teeth; a third depicted him doing parlor tricks for the faithful—cutting his arm with an obsidian ritual knife and letting them watch his wounds heal at a discernible speed.

Philip would be livid if he knew. They all would.

"¿Dónde está tu familia?" he'd asked at last that day. It was one of the few phrases he knew, even after six decades in the country, and two years in Cuba before that.

Maria pretended not to hear. She pulled a small knife from beneath her waist sash, lanced the meaty tip of one of her fingers, and began squeezing drops of blood onto a thin slip of paper.

"Maria," he said more sternly. "Answer me. Where is your family?"

She shrugged a shoulder but didn't look up from her work. "¿Cuándo regresarán? No sé. ¿Un año?"

One year. His heart sank. "Do you mean they canceled the feast?"

"Se perdió la fiesta."

He didn't understand. "No entiendo."

"Sí. Es hora de despertar de soñar. Digo oraciones por su resurrección."

"All right, yes. It's Easter Week, I know that. I'm also aware that I've missed three days of events, and I'm sorry. What happened wasn't my fault, but I'm here now. I came as soon as I could because I made a promise that I would. Do you understand? I'm here, so if we can salvage some of the festival let's do it. But if not, if there isn't going to be a festival at all this year, then I have to go. My family needs me. I made a promise to them, too, to get back as soon as possible." It dawned on him then how absurd it was to stand there saying how much he needed to be elsewhere. He waved an arm, indicating all the tools of her ritual working. "Put out all these candles."

"¿Qué?"

He'd grabbed a red taper and blown out the flame, to illustrate. "Out. See? Out. All of them. Now."

Maria began a fresh flurry of rapid Spanish. He hadn't needed a translation to get the gist of what she said; he'd seen the expression she wore a thousand times before, on Wren. He suspected it was universal; the petulance of a teenager chafing at a demand made by an authority figure.

"I said blow them all out now," he said. "I'm leaving, and I'm not about to let you stay here by yourself to get attacked by a jaguar. Now, young lady. Let's go."

The hinges on the mausoleum's iron scrollwork door shriek in protest when he pulls it open. He steps inside, steps right up to the base of the long, raised box that dominates the small space, and reads the inscription chiseled into the pale gray and white stone:

PATRICK THOMAS CONWAY
1902-1927

BELOVED GRANDSON, SON, BROTHER, HUSBAND, FATHER, AND FRIEND.

The last two words restart an old war within his breast, gratitude doing battle with resentment. He'd heard rumors at the time that the addition of those two words—*and friend*—had created a rift within the Conway family. Patrick's grandfather Morris refused to back down and omit them; in the end it had boiled down to whose money was paying the stonemason. Ehrichto was shocked the first time he visited after Morris's death and found they hadn't been sanded away. He chalked it up to money, again. The word was innocuous enough for plausible deniability, and removing it would have left the rest of the lettering uncentered, probably needing to be completely redone. Exorcizing him would cost a pretty penny, and so he remained. Ehrichto had realized only much later what the true reason was: upon Morris's death Patrick's widow Myrtle had launched a less physical and more broadly focused pogrom against the husband who failed her by dying young and scandalously. Her aim was not merely to erase any traces of Patrick's relationship with Ehrichto, but to wipe out every last memory of him anywhere.

Maria hadn't been able to tell Ehrichto, while they were in Chiya, that the members of the Nueva Chiya Cofradía de Maximón had solved the problem of his disappearance quite easily, by dusting off the old wooden effigy they'd used in the days before his arrival and celebrating the feast the way they once had, the way that people in all of the other places where the god is revered—Zunil, Antigua, San Andrés Itzapa, Chiquimula, even cities in the U.S.—had never stopped doing.

Entering her family home in Santiago Atitlán and seeing the mannequin propped up in a wooden chair in the center of the main room had been just as much of a shock to him as seeing him entering was to them. Maria's father, mother and uncle had immediately stopped what they were doing and looked to one another, unsure how to handle the presence of a second Maximón. For his part, Ehrichto's thoughts turned back sixty years, to the day Dorjan shoved him out of the dark stand of trees at the edge of the plaza at Chiya.

BORNE ON THE shoulders of a man who was clearly inebriated, the wooden effigy swayed unsteadily. Ehrichto was at once repulsed and fascinated by the thing. True, it was a pagan idol, but its piercing black eyes and thick moustache had obviously been painted onto the clay face with a loving hand, and its mouth had been crafted in a perpetual "o," which allowed it to smoke fat, hand-rolled *sikars*. Over time the Mayan word for tobacco had come to mean the objects crafted from the plant's leaves as well, which they used as ritual offerings. Eventually their creation and the commodity it was made from had spread across the globe.

"It is as if they knew you were coming," Dorjan whispered just a few minutes before he shoved Ehrichto from the cover of the trees with the instruction, *Go make all their dreams come true and let them repay you in blood, whisky, and cigars.*

Itzananohk'u had been dancing with the half-sized wooden man on his back for hours. He was drenched in sweat and looked on the verge of collapse but, strangely, seemed oblivious to that fact. Thoroughly engaged in his chanting, he appeared to be fading in and out of a hallucinatory state as he danced the doll round and round the square. It was, Dorjan had explained, a test of the shaman's powers, his way of proving he was capable of holding the job for another year.

The shove out onto the plaza was timed perfectly. Ehrichto stumbled out and came face-to-face with telinel and effigy. The shaman blinked three or four times and then quickly looked around, as if he thought he was having a particularly vivid hallucination and wanted to make sure no one else saw it, too. Unfortunately for him, it was clear they all did. One by one, the villagers crowding the plaza caught sight of the stranger in their midst and nudged one another, before turning to their holy man, to see what he and the Maximón would do about the interloper.

Ehrichto had to give the man credit; though his eyes were wide as saucers Itzananohk'u managed to swallow his fear. From beneath the old Maximón he bravely addressed the newcomer. Ehrichto couldn't understand a word he said, but could imagine the other was asking the same things he would, were their positions reversed: *Who are you? Where did you come from? What do you want? And why are you dressed like the Rilaj Mam?*

Dorjan had solved the problem of the language barrier by instructing Ehrichto to simply not respond. "Believe me," he'd said. "They'll be relieved to discover they can't communicate with you. No one is ever really happy to have a god in their midst, passing judgment and laying down the law. Is it any wonder they crucified Christ?"

His prediction that the cofradía would try to kill Ehrichto proved correct. After a standoff that felt like it lasted a year but was probably no more than two or three tense minutes, a man had rushed forward out of the crowd with a blade of considerable length already drawn. He drove the instrument between Ehrichto's ribs and upward, aiming for his heart. The pain was intense; it buckled his knees. Seconds later his vision went black.

When he woke again Ehrichto found himself laid out on the dirt at the feet of the seated god. The air was thick with the smoke of smoldering copal resin, and the ceiling and walls seemed to dance in the flickering light thrown by hundreds of candles, but what he was aware of most of all was the body heat radiating from the assembled worshippers.

He took quick stock of himself. His side was still sore but the flesh there itched intensely, an indication that everything was knitting itself back together. The front of his shirt was stiff with dried blood. He'd lost a lot, and repairing damage like that he'd suffered would use up even more. He needed to feed, and knew precisely who he wanted to take a blood meal from—the hothead who'd stabbed him.

He regretted that he could not watch their faces as he sat up, but even after he was on his feet their expressions were priceless. One man even pissed himself. Another made for the door but tripped over his own feet and landed face down in the dirt. The one who'd stabbed him— Itzananohk'u's brother Tlacolotl, Ehrichto later learned—was bragging to a group gathered around him.

They froze with fear when they saw Ehrichto approaching, but the fellow was too busy shooting off his mouth to notice anything amiss. Ehrichto moved swiftly. With one hand he got a fistful of the man's hair and yanked his head toward his left shoulder, exposing the side of his neck. With his other hand he seized the man's upper right arm and pulled him back. He bared his fangs, paused long enough for the inebriated assembly to get a good, sure look at them, and then sank them deep, a perfect hit on the jugular.

IN THE MOTORA on the morning he escorted Maria home to Santiago Atitlán, Ehrichto had, for the first time since that long ago night, removed the Maximón's traditional garb in front of a member of the cofradía. Underneath the heavy black wool suit and wide-brimmed hat he wore a leaf green t-shirt and khaki pants, the mode of dress he'd learned from Nick, who'd learned it in Vietnam.

It was not his intention to stroll into the middle of the Feast dressed in his own clothes. His original plan was to stay in Maximón's clothes until after he'd dropped Maria at the pier on the far side of the lake and made it safely back across the cay and into the stand of trees at the foot of Volcán San Pedro, but after she asked point blank what he was and he told her—a vampire—it seemed ridiculous to leave the god's costume on. He'd slipped off the garb and stashed it in one of the motorboat's many storage compartments. Not surprisingly, Maria had taken his transformation in stride.

"If anyone has ever been capable of magic, I thought she would be," he says aloud, running a hand over the cold marble surface of Patrick's vault. "I felt the same way about you."

After he and Patrick had been together for a while Ehrichto had come to realize that they weren't the only men on Earth who were attracted to one another. If you looked very hard it was possible to find clues that other people felt similarly. You might catch a look exchanged between friends or realize that they spent far more time together than they ever did with the persons to whom they were married.

Some men, of course, never married. Certain professions allowed a man to stay a bachelor without arousing suspicion. The priesthood was one; the military another, though in those days there were far, far fewer people who made a career out of service. Even in secular, civilian life, though, an unmarried man was sometimes ignored. Two bachelors choosing to live together could be explained as a matter of economics, a way to make the best of a bad situation. That sort of concession, though, was only allowed as long as the men in question—if in truth a couple— were quiet about their abnormality, discreet; so long as there was a tacit understanding among all parties that such behavior was amoral, filthy, and sinful. If such men didn't try to convince decent people that the way they lived was right, most people would agree to look the other way. After all, hadn't God given humans free will? If some of them stubbornly chose to ignore His word and go to Hell, wasn't that, after all, their business? Besides, keeping it quiet made it less likely that the idea would spread.

Ehrichto presses his palm flat against the stone. "We could have been like them, Patrick," he says. "You could have convinced everyone that what James said about us was a lie. You even could have done it without marrying Myrtle. You just didn't want to."

Patrick was notorious for his admiration of the opposite sex. A shameless flirt, he was forever casting longing glances at strange women on the street, or familiar ones seated at his table during a formal dinner, or even—he was bold to the point of recklessness—married ones whose husbands he called on for business. He claimed, loudly and often, to be in love with female beauty itself. It was not unusual to enter a room and find him surrounded by blushing women. For a while Ehrichto had taken it to be a clever stratagem designed to quash any rumors about his true desires, but over time he'd come to believe his lover had a dual nature. Patrick didn't merely flirt; he'd actually bedded many of the eligible young ladies in town. Too often when he pulled Ehrichto close he reeked of musk not his own.

The fact that—as far as Ehrichto could ascertain, anyway, and Patrick swore up and down that it was so—it was always females he was with, that he hadn't been with another man since they'd met, seemed significant. Ehrichto assured himself that his lover's attraction to women was merely physical, that he alone had ownership of Patrick's wild heart and wicked mind.

He'd latched onto whatever evidence he could find to make his case. The fact that Patrick had convinced his grandfather Morris to foot the bill for one of the six brand new apartments on St. James Court gave him hope. Patrick had no actual need for one of the newfangled spaces, which were designed for small families of lesser means. His apartment (Ehrichto felt they should just call them what they were: compartments) was almost empty, containing only a settee and rug in the lone parlor, a table and two chairs in the cramped kitchen, a bed in one of the two bedrooms and nothing at all in the second. He let Morris assume he wanted the space for the same reason he'd wanted a car: because almost no one else had one. It was a status symbol. Ehrichto took heart in the fact that he'd insisted on leasing space in the building on St. James, finding fault with every other apartment house going up around town. His flat was less than a block from the Salvatolle family home. Ehrichto thrilled when Patrick promised never to bring anyone else there. Still, he'd memorized the space, fixating on every detail. He developed the habit of making a thousand little adjustments every time Patrick stepped from a room, orienting the chairs to the table just so, straightening the soap on the basin of the bathroom sink, combing the rug fringe with his fingers, so that he could tell when the other had been there without him, and catch him at a lie. Most importantly, Ehrichto began always sneaking back into the building, sticking tiny slips of folded paper into the hinge of the door, tiny traps so very nearly invisible that oftentimes while Patrick was busy with the key and lock, Ehrichto had a tiny heart attack, thinking the last slip he'd placed was not there. In the end, all of his precautions proved futile. As far as he could discern, the biggest threat to his future happiness never set foot into the flat.

No one knew anything about Myrtle Campbell save her name and that she'd come from out east. Exactly how far out she never said. Cattier women whispered that it was really only the eastern part of the state, out by West Virginia, the stomping ground of Hatfields and McCoys. Others said no, it was worse than that—she was being coy because she was from the Cumberland Gap, the region where Kentucky, Tennessee and Virginia all came together. They whispered that she chose to obscure her roots because she was Melungeon, but Ehrichto never put any stock in that assertion. The so-called Melungeon scattered through that area were said to be not just mixed race but triracial, mostly Anglo-Saxon, but—depending on who you asked—also part Negro, Jewish, or Turkish, and, of course, one or another of the Indian tribes native to the area as well.

Ehrichto grudgingly admitted the talk of Melungeon roots was nothing but sour grapes. Other women were jealous because Myrtle possessed both a classic beauty and a charisma that drew most men to her like flies to honey. To his mind, there was nothing mixed race about her appearance at all. She looked as if she'd just gotten off the boat from the British Isles. Her eyes weren't quite as blue as Patrick's, no one's were, but her hair was the same jet black, her skin the same translucent milk white. Someone who didn't know better might easily have thought they were siblings. The fact that Patrick filled Ehrichto's dreams and she made his skin crawl put to rest any last vestiges of doubt in his mind that he would ever be attracted to a female of the species.

Patrick, however, had been instantly taken with her.

They'd met at an anti-Temperance rally. She told him there was a group of some one hundred women out east—truly out east, in New York City—planning to call for repeal, in the unlikely event that Prohibition did get the vote. They'd named their group the Molly Pitcher Club after the revolutionary war heroine who brought water to the troops. They even had a mission statement: "To prevent any tendency on the part of our National Government to interfere with the personal habits of the American people, except those habits which may be designated as criminal." Their goal was to have chapters all over the U.S. ready to spring into action the day after the election, should it prove necessary. Myrtle said she planned to start a Molly Pitcher Club in Louisville.

By Election Day Patrick was a complete nervous wreck, though he hid it from everyone except Ehrichto. The Conways would still have their dairy and ice business if the measure passed, of course, but there was no question that a ban on liquor production would severely, financially cripple them. Ehrichto paid a visit to the distillery office with the intention of giving him relief by taking his mind off the issue for a little while, but it had backfired. Eager to torment his greatest rival, James Ferguson, the heir to the Ferguson Tobacco empire, burst into the room without knocking, through a door Ehrichto thought he'd locked. He'd discovered the pair engaged in an act that, even on his best day, smooth-talking Patrick couldn't possibly have explained away.

A few hours later, while they were still reeling from that disaster, more bad news arrived: the vote had passed. Prohibition was the new law of the land. The Volstead Act ensured that it wouldn't take effect for one year, to give those in the distillery business time to get their affairs in order, and find other work. Morris didn't believe the law would last. He thought as soon as people could no longer buy alcohol, they would begin haranguing their congressmen, demanding repeal. He put the Conway Distillery into overdrive, churning out whisky like mad. He wanted to get as much product as possible into barrels to start aging while the mess sorted itself out. Patrick used the ramp-up in production to explain why he never had time to talk when Ehrichto came calling. He insisted James's knowledge of their relationship didn't frighten him, but he seemed especially busy whenever his grandfather happened into the room when Ehrichto was there. They never talked about it openly, but Ehrichto knew he worried what Morris would do if James decided to tell him what he'd seen. The old man was already nearly apoplectic over the vote to make alcohol sales illegal. Sure, Patrick was his pride and joy, a hundred times more the heir he wanted than his own son, Patrick's father Tibbot; still, would finding out his grandson ran around with boys the way he did with girls be the straw that broke the camel's back? Would he throw up his hands, shut down the business, and write Patrick out of his life? Out of his will?

Ehrichto was distraught. Rather than lessening Patrick's problems he'd compounded them. Desperate yet unable to undo the damage, he began to fantasize killing James and hiding the body. It was easy to do, even for a good Catholic boy, because James Ferguson was clearly almost beside himself with joy, at having not one but two different things to lord over his rival. For weeks after he caught them together he'd peppered his speech with double entendres, no matter who else was around, and smirked until it was all Ehrichto could do not to grab and choke him.

For a fortnight James twisted the invisible knife in their guts, and laughed when they squirmed. Then, apparently, he'd grown bored with the game. He told his father about Patrick's "unnatural" proclivities. Conrad Ferguson, with his son in tow, had paid visits first to the Conways and then the Salvatolles.

EHRICHTO'S WHOLE BODY began to shake when Conrad explained he was there to "do the Christian thing." Then he informed Ehrichto's father, Guglielmo, that his sixteen-year-old son was being taken advantage of by the Conway boy, who was, he explained, at eighteen, already much more worldly wise. He made it clear he thought Ehrichto could be reformed. "We wanted you to know," he said, "so you can put a stop to it, before it's too late."

Ehrichto has to admit his father's method for doing that probably wasn't what Conrad had in mind. The minute the two Fergusons turned the corner at the end of the walk Guglielmo wheeled around and backhanded his son with a tight fist, splitting open his upper lip and dropping him to the hardwood. Ehrichto had instinctively curled into a tight ball and wrapped his arms around his head, which still left plenty of places vulnerable to the sharp kicks and fist jabs his father next inflicted on him. Mostly, though, Guglielmo had towered over him, bellowing, too angry even to attempt to speak English to a son whose Italian was limited to basic vocabulary words and a handful of key phrases, none of which applied in that context. "Non siete più il mio figlio! Non siete più un Salvatolle!" *You are no longer my son! You are no longer a Salvatolle!* "Siete guasti a me!" *You are dead to me!* When he finished yelling he spat on Ehrichto, then grabbed him by his hair and hauled him to his feet by the strands. He shoved him out the front door, sent him tumbling down the front steps all the way to the patch of dirt and scraggly grass beyond the narrow common walkway. He'd just missed going head first into the tree there.

Ehrichto feared his father would follow him, and continue the beating in public, so he scrambled to his feet and whirled around. He was surprised to find his father framed in the doorway, red-faced and huffing, looking not unlike an enraged bull. Guglielmo raised a fist in the air and shouted one final command: "Non ritorni mai qui!" *Do not ever come back here!*

"Please, don't do this," Ehrichto begged, a little over a year later, on the morning of Patrick's wedding to Myrtle. As expected he'd found his lover in the tiny limestone cavern they'd nicknamed the Bothy after the derelict stone houses Morris said were scattered through the Scottish highlands. Weary travelers took refuge in bothies to escape the terrors of the moors at night, he'd said. Before they'd had the flat on St. James, the cavern in Portland, the city just west of Louisville's downtown, was the only place where Ehrichto and Patrick could be intimate. It was no surprise that, one night just before Prohibition took effect, Patrick had spirited Morris's original copper pot still out of their house and set it up in the cavern. He'd sworn there was no way he was going to let the G-men with their axes reduce such a fine thing to scrap.

The still was at full boil that morning, the churning rumble of boiling beer and crackle and hiss of coal being consumed by flame echoing off— and trapped and magnified by—the cavern's limestone walls. Underneath those noises was a steadier, singular one: thump-thump-thump-thump-thumpthump-thump—the never-ending heartbeat of vaporized alcohol rising in

the distillation works.

Patrick used the noise to pretend he hadn't heard what Ehrichto had said. He slipped his suit coat on and busied himself with shooting the cuffs.

Ehrichto increased his volume. "If you do this, I will no longer be able to associate with you. I will not…I will not be party to adultery." That earned him a sneer and a shake of the head, but still no reply. "Please, I'm begging you!" he said, despising the terror that rose in his breast, because Patrick hated any show of emotion. "Please! I can't bear to lose you." After barely a pause he added, more quietly, "too."

That got Patrick's attention. He cocked one eyebrow. "Too?"

"I-I only mean that that I've already lost everything else for you. I don't—"

"Oh, no, you have not," Patrick snapped. "Because of me, I'll grant you, but not *for* me. Never that. I haven't given you an ultimatum the way which you have just done me. 'I will not be party to adultery'? That's curious. It seems to me there are several other Biblical dictums you feel quite free in disregarding." Ehrichto looked away. He heard Patrick cluck his tongue. "Frankly, I'm disappointed in you. Such crude manipulation is beneath you."

Ehrichto took a deep breath for courage and forced himself to look Patrick in the eye. "Listen to me, please. This will all blow over. You needn't marry—"

Patrick held up a hand, silencing him. "First of all, I have always told you that one day I would marry. Secondly, my situation requires a change of plans. Don't act as if you don't understand that. Ignorance is always unbecoming, but on you, Ehrichto, it is particularly vile."

"Your grandfather is disappointed that the fact of our…relationship… became known, yes," Ehrichto said, "but he did not throw you out into the street the way my father did me."

Patrick's eyes flashed fire. "Very sorry about that, are you?"

"What? No, I—"

"It would make things more even between us in your eyes, would it not?"

Ehrichto was aghast. "No! I don't want you to suffer just because I am suffering."

"Don't you? I think it's the real reason you don't want me to marry."

"That's not true!" Ehrichto's legs felt like they might give way. "That's not why at all."

Patrick sneered. "Believe what you want, but know this: I won't make sacrifices needlessly. I won't jeopardize my inheritance when I can so easily put things right. If that's the way you want things to go between us, this association ends here."

The business about losing his inheritance was a lie. Morris still thought the sun rose and set on his grandson. When the shock of Conrad's news wore off, nothing between them had been different. Morris even encouraged Patrick to bring Ehrichto around more often. He was content having someone to regale with his stories and tidbits about the distillation trade. No, Patrick wasn't in danger of being disowned. He was merely twisting things to get his way.

He also wasn't finished with his speech. "Know this, Ehrichto," he said, taking a step forward. In the dim light of the cavern, his eyes appeared navy in hue. "I will marry Myrtle today, and if you show your face at the event and make a scene, or by some other means attempt to sabotage it, I swear I will never so much as look your way again. We shall see exactly what you cannot bear to lose. You may count on it."

Ehrichto's legs shook harder. "You aren't…. You don't understand. Your being married to her will kill me. Can't you see that? I will die a little every day you are her husband when—" He paused, afraid to complete the thought. But if not then, he wondered, when? "When you should be mine." He thought Patrick would fly into a rage, but his lover's expression

softened. Buoyed by it, Ehrichto had pressed forward. "This isn't a childish notion I'm clinging to out of stubbornness. I am in love with you."

A deep scowl replaced Patrick's sympathetic expression. "Don't say that."

"It's the truth!"

"But what can I do with that knowledge? Absolutely nothing. You say it to wound me."

Ehrichto drew back. "No."

"Yes. It's meant to make me pity you. My knowing how you feel can't change anything but how I feel. Can't you see that I'm doing what I must, the only thing I can? You seek to make me sorry on account of it, when it's James your quarrel should be aimed at, or your father, or the whole rest of the goddamned country, for that matter! Take your fight to the imbeciles who cling to pathetic, puritanical fears. It's their idiotic mentality which makes the course of action I take today necessary."

"No, you're…you're twisting everything around."

"Think, Ehrichto. I need not be disgraced by this thing between us. So why do you insist that I should be? My family asks only that I play at being the doting husband and family man. Can you blame them? I am the only son. It falls on me to carry on the Conway name, as it falls on you."

Ehrichto bristled. "I am no longer a Salvatolle, remember?"

"If you went to your father and announced your intention to marry, he would change his mind."

"I couldn't. It would be a lie."

"A venial one."

"Marriage is a sacrament."

Patrick rolled his eyes. "It's perfectly understandable for my family and yours to desire heirs."

Ehrichto didn't care about what the rest of the Conways and Salvatolles wanted. He shook his head, but words lodged in his throat.

Patrick shrugged. "Suit yourself. In exchange for my marrying Myrtle my family has offered to forget what they know about us and look the other way. Not in so many words, you understand, but that's the situation. We needn't stop seeing one another after today. Nothing truly has to change. So then why demand that I lose everything by refusing them this one small thing?"

"It's not a small thing. It's a sacrament," Ehrichto said again.

Patrick's mouth tightened. His lips thinned. "I realize the role of martyr is one you enjoy playing. But I am not fond of the whip."

Ehrichto's reply was not in words, but in a strangled cry. Falling back against the limestone, tears spilling down his cheeks, he began a slow descent, jagged rock tearing shirt cloth and flesh. He doubled over until his forehead was against his knees, wrapped his arms about his head, and began to sob.

Patrick let out an exasperated sigh. "I don't know what I'm going to do with you. Haven't I always been forthright? I told you how it would be but you refused to believe it, because you wished it to be otherwise. As you always do. And now here we are."

Huddled on the floor, Ehrichto silently convulsed, struggling to stem the tide of his tears. He gasped when Patrick grabbed his arms and pulled him to his feet. The other's fierce grip was painful, and the fresh wounds on his back stung, but when his lover leaned in and kissed him, Ehrichto ceased to be aware of anything else. Afterward Patrick said, so quietly that Ehrichto almost could not hear, "If misery loves company take comfort in this: I am in pain, because you are." He took Ehrichto's left hand in his right and laid it on his breast. "You see? It beats," he said, and leaned forward until their foreheads met. "I may be dissolute, but I am not a monster."

"I don't think that," Ehrichto said, as a fresh wave of tears welled in his eyes.

"I could never think that." *I am the monster*, he told himself. *How could I have wished him pain?* "I'm just…scared."

"I know."

"I feel as if I'm losing you."

Patrick slipped his arms around Ehrichto's waist and pulled him closer. "If you don't make it impossible," he murmured, "I will find a way to be with you, always."

EHRICHTO STUMBLES BACK, away from the crypt. *I wanted so badly to believe that with Maria's help he'd finally found that way back that I saw only what I wanted to see. And the awful truth is, he was right; I was doing it back then, too. I saw who I wanted him to be, not who he really was.* A sickening thought settles in the pit of his stomach. *If I hadn't given in that day he would've made good on his threat to walk away and never looked back. For all his smooth talk it wasn't my feelings that mattered to him, it was my need for him that did.*

He pauses before pushing open the scrollwork door. "I was in love with you, Patrick," he whispers without turning back. "I only wish it had been mutual."

"HEY THERE, HOW'RE you feeling?" Neal asks, leaning over Marc's hospital bed.

"Like...crap."

"Really? That's surprising, 'cause you look like death warmed over." Neal forces a smile, pauses, and then grows serious. "Listen, I'm so, so sorry. Trey told me what happened, how he lost his temper."

"He...tried to...kill me." Marc pauses to inhale. "TWICE."

"The bit on the stairs? Yeah, he told me about that, too." Neal shifts his weight from one foot to another. "Listen, Marc, I'm not going to try to excuse what he did, at all. It was wrong. But by the same token, you know how you get. You—"

"FUCK. You."

"Hear me out. You push people every bit as much as he does, you just don't do it physically. What did you say to him? Did you give him the impression that we're still sexual?" The clinical phrasing makes Marc wince. "He told me about the sous chef."

Marc winces again.

"The argument could be made that he felt you were endangering me, and he was just defending his brother." He sighs. "But, okay, let's put that aside for a moment." Reaching out, he takes hold of Marc's left hand and turns it over, exposing the four angry red scratches on his wrist, the worst damage the safety razor could inflict. "Tell me why you did this."

Marc shakes his head. "I didn't." He inhales. "It was...a joke."

With anyone else that would simply be the end of it, but Neal has been trained to sit and wait, for however many hours it takes, until a person becomes comfortable enough (or possibly uncomfortable enough) to open up to him, and give voice to their deepest fears and desires. Images rush through Marc's mind: Ehrichto Salvatolle on the street, in the hotel room, looking fine in a tux at dinner, out on the patio, in the garage. "I met this...guy...last night."

"The one from the storage room?"

Marc shakes his head. "Earlier. A-list." Neal's eyes widen almost imperceptibly, but he says nothing. Marc knows if he lies Neal will see through it, and they'll be here all night. It's best just to get it out now. "He...chose...someone...else."

"I'm sorry," Neal says in his psychiatrist best, an even keel that makes him sound neither insincere nor all that terribly concerned. When Marc looks back at him, he is not surprised to find that the other's blank expression matches his words. It is as if he intentionally withholds any reaction until he hears the complete details of the story. It occurs to Marc that their intended professions are polar opposites of one another.

His mind floods with all the things he wants to say and can't, how this wasn't a normal hook-up, not just another random guy from a bar or the park. This was Ehrichto Salvatolle. Gorgeous. Mysterious. Italian. Loaded. "He was HOT," he says, using all his breathe in an effort to sound emphatic.

"So you got with the other guy out of retribution. To prove you were desirable."

"No, because I was h—" A tickle erupts in his throat and sets him to coughing. Bright specks swim through his field of vision, and he wonders if he will pass out. Finally he regains his composure. "I was. Horny. He's just my...meth dealer."

"Christ Almighty," Neal exclaims. Feeling his hand disengage gives Marc a sick pleasure, the satisfaction of having—finally—evoked an honest reaction from the guy. "What the hell is wrong with you?"

Marc tries not to smile. "You're the doc. You tell me."

"Why was Richard Baxter at your apartment?"

Marc's heart rate soars at the notion that he was right, Neal feels threatened by Baxter. He shrugs because he knows the combination of the gesture and his next words will set his ex-boyfriend off. "He buys... meth from me." It's a lie; he scores speed for Baxter, whose reputation as a former coke fiend is well known. He's never sold meth to him, but it's a better story. Lacking breath, he skips past "You know what I do for a living" and jumps straight to "I'm a concie—"

"Oh that's bull and you know it," Neal snaps. "Your job is to get people tickets to the Broadway Series or reservations for dinner, not to sell drugs to them." His eyes narrow. "And not to sleep with them, either." He turns away, exhales, and turns back. "Look, I get it. It makes you feel special and important to have people asking you to do that kind of crap. You feel needed, but the truth is you're being used. Can you try to understand that? If you get arrested none of your clientele will come to your rescue.

Not only that, but there will be somebody to take your place even before you're done being processed."

"I know."

"Oh, so you're letting them use you? Do you also want to get arrested?"

"'Course not."

"No, no. Let's think this through. What would happen if you went to prison? Well, let's see. There are people there who would threaten you with bodily harm if you didn't do certain things for them, aren't there? Men who would be more than happy to inflict the kind of pain you think you deserve to feel."

Marc's thoughts rewind a dozen years. He's standing at the bottom of the stairs outside Louretta's trailer, looking at her boyfriend Bobby Lee's beat up red Kawasaki motorcycle, which is leaned against the railing. His mother and Louretta work the dinner shift together, and Bobby Lee is supposed to be there to provide adult supervision for Marc after school, to ensure that he does his homework, and to heat up restaurant leftovers for his supper. For as long as Marc can remember his meals have consisted of all-you-can-stand portions of leftover diner food—salt-laden Salisbury steak, green beans from industrial-sized cans, rehydrated mashed potatoes, dried-out discs of chicken-fried steak covered in flavorless white paste flecked with black pepper, day-old pancakes, and the like. A few days after Bobby Lee arrived on the scene, he'd scored points with Marc by throwing the to-go boxes in the dumpster at the end of the trailer park's gravel spur and ordering pizza for their dinner. He'd gone on to slide eleven year old Marc a beer, and then a second one.

Finally, he'd produced a videotaped movie, one of the X-rated type that were kept in a red-neon-trimmed must-be-eighteen-or-older-to-enter back room at the video store.

Halfway through the flick, which featured a middle-aged high school teacher getting blowjobs from his female students in exchange for good grades, Marc unexpectedly found himself pinned to the sofa with a piece of pizza in one hand, a beer in the other, and Bobby Lee crouched in between his legs, giving the girls in the video a run for their money.

"No one ever believes this, but it's a whole lot easier to stay sick than it is to do the work to get well," Neal says, bringing Marc's thoughts back to the present. "Listen to me. What happened back then was not your fault. You didn't make your father walk out on your mother before you were born; you didn't ask your mother's friend's boyfriend to molest you; and it's highly unlikely that he had any clue you were gay. You weren't targeted. What happened wasn't punishment. You were an innocent victim. You still are. But now you have to learn to move past all that. You've got to stop letting what happened then dictate what happens today."

"He liked me...until Michael," Marc blurts, surprising himself. He hadn't realized that on some level he was still thinking about Ehrichto Salvatolle. "Then he called me...rotten fruit." He pictures the last emblazoned on a t-shirt, sees himself wearing it along with the perfect pair of faded jeans, imagines walking into Louisville's most successful gay bar, the Connection, with his shoulders back. He pictures all eyes turning to take in the sight. No doubt some would be amused by the clever self-deprecation of the "rotten fruit" label, and would want to get with him to reward it. Others would ask to sample the merchandise, and deem themselves the clever ones. A third faction would try to convince him not to be so hard on himself, and want to prove that they found him desirable. Regardless, he can't see a bad outcome for the scenario.

"I know being rejected is hard, even in a situation like that, which you didn't want," Neal says, confusing him. Marc realizes the other thinks that his comments about being tossed aside and called names referred to Bobby Lee, not Ehrichto. Before he can interject and correct him, Neal continues. "It always hurts to be thrown over. But in this case it should help you to understand that it wasn't about you. It was about him needing to have someone who was more powerless than you to—"

"No," Marc says. "Not back then. A-list."

"What?"

"A-list. Dumped me. For Michael." He watches carefully, but there is still no recognition in Neal's eyes. Summoning every ounce of breath and strength he has, he says "Ferguson!"

"Ferguson?" Neal asks, his brow creasing. Then his eyes fly fully open. "Alyssa's Michael?" He uses a level of alarm usually reserved for the occupants of buildings on fire. "My brother's ex's new boyfriend is gay?"

Marc lets his head drop back to the pillows. It occurs to him that his situation is being ignored, and he briefly considers being offended, but the fact of Neal's bafflement is far too interesting. Without lifting his head again he says, "YOU didn't know?"

"How would I know?" Neal is silent for a moment, lost in thought. Then Marc hears his chair being shoved back. A second later the other's face looms over him, crowding his vision. "I have to go deal with this, okay?" He gives Marc a platonic peck on the cheek, at the same time squeezing his hand. "I'll be back as soon as I can. We'll fix it, I swear. Okay? Hang in there for me." As he heads out of the room it dawns on Marc that his words sounded neither insincere nor terribly concerned.

THIRTEEN

As HE CLOSES the mausoleum gate, Ehrichto hears two sets of ragged breathing getting louder.

"C'mere!" a deep voice bellows.

"Why should I?" The overly exaggerated lilt in the second person's words suggests they are angry but pretending otherwise. The high pitch indicates a female of the species. "I thought we weren't going to get attached and shit?" she hollers. The vulgarity makes him wince.

Dark silhouettes come into view far to his right. The first is thin and fast, the second thicker and plodding.

"Yeah, so?" the second one replies.

"So go fuck yourself!"

The outburst seems to energize the larger figure. He gains ground, lunges, and manages to catch the female by waist, but she shrieks and twists free.

The sound isn't one of genuine fright but more playful. Ehrichto realizes the two are engaged in a Neanderthal sort of flirting. He watches as they race in figure eights, dodging headstones in the flat, grassy section directly across the narrow road. Just as he expects, the boy catches sight of the charcoal Porsche and abruptly halts.

"Whoa," he manages between gasps. "Sweet!"

Ehrichto always finds determining a stranger's age challenging, but he guesses the young man is past twenty. In spite of his rather stocky build he appears sickly. His face has the pure white pallor of clowns. Even more oddly, given both his apparent lack of health and the fact that he has the beginnings of a paunch, his upper body is sheathed in the fine netting that is usually reserved for the stockings of dancehall girls. His trousers appear to be made of black vinyl and he wears the same style of boot Willem was wearing at Abaton two days earlier, a type that is meant to be worn by a British infantryman. His hair is stringy and unkempt; it looks as if it hasn't been combed—or washed—in weeks. Ehrichto doesn't know what to make of any of it.

"Hullo?" the boy calls. Fear shimmies the word. "Is there anybody there?"

The girlfriend has fallen silent, somewhere in a grove of pine trees far to the left. Ehrichto figures she has found a good spot to hide in and that—confident in her role as the pursued—she will wait quite a while, giving her companion a chance to find her.

It would be easy, he reasons, to slip behind the boy and sink fangs into his neck; easy to leave him, unconscious, behind one of the stone structures. But his collarless, open-weave shirt would not hide the puncture wounds and the pallor of his skin is too troubling, anyway. The loss of even a pint of blood might prove fatal to him.

First do no harm. Dorjan's command echoes in Ehrichto's head. A doctor before he became immortal, Dorjan's primary instruction to those he has turned is the forbidding of the taking of life, even to save one's own.

The thought flashes in Ehrichto's mind: what if he fed anyway? If the boy died, would Dorjan enforce some sort of capital punishment? Would he send Ehrichto to final death? Is it even true that their kind can die? There are rumors. It's what worries him about Nick. But *is* Nick in danger of ceasing to exist? He's not sure anyone knows, not even Dorjan.

Nick. And Wren. He feels bad for having not thought of them even once in the past twenty-four hours. *I'm a terrible friend, a rotten uncle.* He looks back at the oddly dressed boy. *They'd be better off without me.*

The girl reappears in the distance. Ehrichto steps back into the deep shadow beside the mausoleum. Dealing with two people is infinitely more difficult than handling one. She stomps over to the young man and slams both hands into his chest, a move than nearly knocks him over, despite his larger size. "Why the hell are you just standing here?"

Now that she is not running, Ehrichto can see that her attire is equally as strange her companion's. Her skirt seems to be composed of a series of zippers stitched together, and the garment she wears as a top, though resembling a corset, doesn't constrict her movement. Her face is overly made-up, with too-dark lipstick and thick, black, scrolling lines extending far from the outside corners of her eyes. He gathers that it is now fashionable in America to resemble a nineteenth-century street urchin.

"Look," the boy says, pointing in the direction of the car.

"What? What is so goddamned important that you...." The girl turns, flinches, and then begins to look around. "Hello? Who's here?"

"Some rich old fuck," the boy says. "Probably getting his rocks off, watching us." He steps directly behind her, grabs her by the waist, and pulls her backward. He pushes his pelvis against her rear end and begins grinding into her.

"Let's give him a show."

"Cut it out," the girl snaps, but she makes no move to stop him. She continues to peer out into the darkness as he thrusts his hips against her buttocks. "Hello? Who's there?"

The boy slides her tiny skirt upward until it is around her waist. Ehrichto is shocked and nauseated to find that she wears nothing underneath. *Well, that's convenient,* he thinks. "Get up on the hood," the boy urges. He runs his hands over her exposed ass cheeks, which are perfectly rounded. Pale as alabaster, they practically glow in the moonlight. "C'mon, it'll be just like in that old Whitesnake video."

"That was a Jaguar, you idiot." The girl pushes his hands away and yanks the hem of her skirt back down. "I said cut it out."

"Why? That's what we came here for, right?" He reaches for her again, catches her waist, and pulls her backward, tight to him. "Maybe Peeping Tom will decide to join in. You ever have two guys at once?"

"You're a perv!" She twists in his grasp, puts a splayed-fingered hand on his face and pushes him backward. When she takes her hand away again, its imprint is still visible. Ehrichto thinks that her fingers must have been smudged with graveyard dirt until he sees the truth of what has happened—that the boy's sickly pallor is just greasepaint which has come off on her fingers and palm.

All at once, he understands what it is he is witnessing. *Wren was right*, he thinks. He hadn't believed it, of course, but a few months back his nephew had insisted upon the existence of something called computer bulletin board systems, which he explained as a sort of electronic cross between a cork board and a classified ad. Some BBSs, he'd said, were tailored to people obsessed with vampires and various other supposedly mythological, supposedly supernatural creatures. The most fanatical of the patrons of these computer communities, he'd sworn up and down, lived their lives as if every day of the year was Halloween. They decorated their bodies and their homes in fashions inspired by those of a hundred years earlier; listened exclusively to brooding, dirge-like music; and overwhelmingly liked to cut one another with razor blades and "drink" each other's blood, usually as a prelude to sexual intercourse. A few even slept in coffins, and the most extreme among them had had their eyeteeth whittled into sharp points by unscrupulous dentists, though it did not keep them from still needing razors to draw blood from their "willings," i.e. donors.

Ehrichto assumed his nephew was being had. He'd chalked up the young man's gullibility to his long separation from other mortal humans. But watching the girl wipe her hand on the grass in an effort to remove the white greasepaint from her fingers, he realizes it was he who was mistaken.

"Thanks a lot," the boy snarls, checking his reflection in the passenger's side window of the Porsche. "You know how hard it's been to not mess this up? Now it's fucked."

"Yeah? It was stupid. I told you I don't want that shit all over me." She turns her hand this way and that, checking for any remaining bone-white streaks of makeup. "None of that shit better get on my clothes, or you're replacing them."

"I wasn't gonna get it on you. Trust me." The boy slams a toe into the grass. "How would we explain that to Shelley? How am I gonna explain this?" He points at his face, indicating his ruined makeup.

"I don't know, just use what's left and kind of rub it around. I'll tell you when it looks like you just did a shitty job in the first place."

He starts to reach up but she grabs his wrist. "Not now, moron! Sheesh. Do you ever think? Before you get it all over your hands...." She drops into a crouch, grabs his belt buckle, and begins unfastening it. A wide grin erupts on the boy's face. He settles back against the car door as the girl slides his zipper down and reaches a hand inside his pants.

Ehrichto steps from the shadows and clears his throat. "Get away from my car," he says.

"I STILL DON'T understand why you couldn't stay there," Baxter says as they approach the circular entry stair of the black-bricked building in which he resides.

"I told you," Marc says. He's still speaking in measured bursts due to a lack of breath.

"Because hospitals are for sick people? I wonder, what *do* you call a collapsed lung, fractured ribs, extensive bruising, and—"

"Fist. Fight."

"If it was a cost issue, I told you—"

"Staph!" Marc says, coming to a halt. "Don't. Want to. Catch it."

"You do realize how ridiculous that sentiment is, coming from the walking Petri dish?"

Marc holds up a middle finger.

"Mmm. Thanks ever so much for the offer, but this isn't a very good time for that sort of thing. C'mon. It's this one. Right here." Baxter enjoys seeing Marc's eyes grow wide.

"This. Is. You?"

You see now what you've been missing, Baxter thinks. *A wee bit nicer than that hovel you call an apartment.* "No, this is not me. I am a man. This is Blackhaus."

"What?"

Baxter lifts his chin, indicating the front steps. "Do you think you can make it up those?"

Marc nods.

"That went reasonably well," Baxter says when they are safely in the vestibule. "Just a few more." *Flights*, he thinks, but he decides it best to withhold that bit of information. Marc is looking up, taking in the angel paintings.

Baxter pushes open the interior door, but the other doesn't move. "C'mon. We need to get you up and into bed."

Marc turns, and Baxter sees the glint in his eye. "Master plan."

"Honey, if it was, you'd be in this condition after, not before."

Marc smiles and shuffles forward.

THE PORSCHE HAS been retro-fitted with what Ehrichto assumed was a tiny television screen but, when he pushed the power button, turned out to be a sort of electronic map. He remembers seeing a newspaper article about the devices but, not being even in the same country as his car, barely skimming the piece and moving on. As he watches the blip representing the car move ever closer to the roads that form an ankh at the center of the glowing map, he's glad that Dorjan has always had a thing for new technology.

He stops shy of the cross street, pulls the car over, and kills the engine. He doesn't want the sports car's growl to give away the fact that he is here. He doesn't want Patr—he stops himself, tries again—doesn't want Michael to hear it and get into an altercation with Lloyd and Julia Ferguson.

The house is just past the crossbar of the ankh, on the right. All the lights are on, and there are no drapes, sheers or blinds on the windows. Everything inside is visible but all he sees is blond furniture, mirrors, and gilt. There are no personal touches at all. It might as well be a set-up for a magazine. He slips around the side of the garage. The rear half of the house is dark, as is the shallow yard. Looking through the first of three sets of sliding glass doors, he is surprised to find Lloyd Ferguson stretched out on a couch with a washrag over his eyes. But even more surprising, Julia is curled up on the couch that stands opposite his, on the other side of a large square coffee table.

It's not at all what he expected to find. It calls to mind the move Maria's father made right after he turned around and saw Ehrichto, in plain clothes, standing in the doorway of his house. He'd stepped closer to his wife and laid a hand on the small of her back, the same sort of reassuring, protective gesture Ehrichto saw his father make with his mother on more occasions than he can count.

That's all I want, he thinks. *A partner. Someone to love and protect. Someone who loves me.*

Why is that too much to ask?

He doesn't accept Dorjan's assertion that relationships between men can take only three forms: warriors in combat, fathers and sons, or, as with the kel'an, an odd combination of the two: aggression and love transmuted into sexual passion.

I didn't want to fight Patrick, he thinks, *I wanted to merge with him.* Then he remembers: it wasn't Patrick he was with but Michael Ferguson. He feels guilty for having snapped the way he did, and hurt the boy's feelings. His plan is to tell him that he is sorry; to make him understand that the reason it won't work out has nothing to do with anything he did.

But to do that, he first has to find him. Ehrichto scans the scene before him. The layout of the house is very odd. There's a line of rooms he saw on the front half of the house—a grand foyer, conservatory, and dining room all in a row, like a diorama, and there is this one big room on the back half, with front and back divided by a two-story wall. At either end of the structure there are rooms above and below. On the left, as he looks at the house now, the upper rooms are reached by the stair off the foyer. The second floor rooms on the right, situated over the garage and the wide alcove that houses a line of gleaming stainless-steel kitchen appliances, seem to be accessible only by traversing the bridge that runs along the backside of the dividing wall.

He figures the son's bedroom is probably one of the ones at the far end of the bridge, over the kitchen and garage. Then again, it might be room at the top of the stairs, if—as he suspects—there is a master suite tucked behind the two first-floor alcoves on the left side of this massive back room. One alcove is reminiscent of a den, the other of a library, though both are far more like stage pieces meant to indicate such rooms than they are like a library or den in actuality.

He wishes he had Dorjan's improved hearing, or his ability to transmit, without speech, if not actual thoughts then impressions of his desires, in order to influence people to do his bidding. He might then be able to call to the boy, and make him come out to the yard. He wishes he'd inherited something from his sire besides immortality, the way the rest of the kel'an had, wishes at the very least that he hadn't ended up with the genetic glitch of sensitivity to sunlight.

LLOYD FERGUSON STIRS. He reaches a hand to his forehead and squeezes his temples, then pats the washrag over his eyes. Ehrichto steps back into the shadows cast by the shrubbery at the corner of the house, and waits to see what will happen next.

THEY ARE BACK on Donohue, just moved in. Michael is five, riding around and around their driveway on the latest version of the popular, bulbous plastic, vaguely tricycle-shaped riding toy that always makes Lloyd think of the so-called safety bicycles of the last century. He believes he would have a warmer feeling about the toys in general, and this one—a housewarming gift from Julia's father, Donal—in particular, if it was a true miniaturized version of those old bicycles; if it seated its rider high above its oversized front wheel rather than behind it, just inches from the ground. Lloyd has heard horror stories about children being run over by drivers who never saw them because they'd been below their field of vision. It is why, ever since his son tore the wrapping paper off the box and revealed what was inside, Lloyd has sounded like a broken record, admonishing the boy to never leave the sidewalk, to yield at driveways, to stay away from dogs, and every other piece of advice he can think of. In between these outbursts he ruminates on the fact that he never had such a toy himself—or even later on, a bicycle—because where he grew up there was nowhere to ride such a thing. There were no sidewalks or side streets, only gravel driveways and parking lots linked by ribbons of interstate highway. He does not feel deprived; in fact, he feels his childhood was safer for it, but he knows Donal bought the thing for the very same reason he'd bought Julia every conceivable gift when she was a child: he wanted his grandson to have an idyllic childhood because his own had been shattered by the death of his father, Patrick.

Lloyd can appreciate that fact, but he still hates the riding toy. He hates it almost as much as he hates the little boy who lives across the street from them. Jon Lewis is only a year older than Michael but already is riding a bicycle without training wheels. Not only that, he's proving to be some sort of daredevil, continually dragging his bike up the steps of the Lewises' porch and then, peddling as fast as he can, riding it straight off the far end, where, inexplicably, there is no porch railing. Lloyd wonders if that is an indication that Mr. Lewis intended for his son to imitate Evel Knievel, whether he might even have coached him to go sailing over the bushes and onto the lawn. In Lloyd's opinion Jon is a bad influence and his father Jonathon Sr. is an even worse one because he lets his son do such an insane thing. His hope is that the boy's mother, Carolyn, will put the kibosh on the mayhem once she is not quite so absorbed with taking care of their daughter Danielle, who is a handful of a different kind. Prone to whining to get her way and either sulking or screaming when she does not, she is the very epitome of the Terrible Twos.

Like flipping a switch, the dream is gone and Lloyd is aware that he is awake, that he is still stretched out on one of the couches in the great room, eyes covered by a washrag that is now bone dry. Reaching up, he finds one of the corners and peels it off. He wishes he could similarly shed the dream's lingering impression: *Did I overprotect him,* he wonders. *If I hadn't warned him so often about all the dangers in the world, would he have tried to be more like Jon? If he'd managed to be more of his equal rather than his sidekick, the Robin to his Batman, would he not have turned out gay?*

He opens his eyes into darkness. Only after several seconds does he remember that it might not be the case that the room lacks light. *I might really be blind,* he worries, but even as he is thinking it, forms begin taking shape within the void: the coffee table and the large wooden bowl at its center, which is filled with better-than-fist-sized stones machined into perfect spheres; the couch that faces the one he is on; and Julia, curled up on it.

He clears his throat.

"Are you awake?" she asks, sitting up. Not sleeping. Waiting. "Can you see anything?"

"I don't know. Is it dark in here?"

A click, and then light spills from the table lamp at her side. Lloyd is relieved to discover his field of vision is no longer diminished. "Well?" his wife asks.

"I'm okay."

He sees her shoulders drop. Not even a beat, and she says, "See? I told you that 514 was the right answer."

He decides not to point out that the name of the formulation is A5-14, decides to let her bask in the glow of having made the right call. An anti-anxiety medication not yet on the market, the drug has been found to have many unexpected applications, has been used to treat symptoms of lupus and psoriatic arthritis, to ease chronic insomnia, and to help people quit smoking. The last usage is one with which Lloyd has personal experience, the reason why he had some of the pills stashed at the back of his sock drawer. Ten months earlier the drug had helped him kick his pack-a-day addiction to cigarettes.

A memory floods back to him, of going apeshit in the Corvette the day Michael confessed to being similarly hooked on nicotine. Lloyd remembers snatching the pack from his son's hand (they were the clove-laced kind, which Lloyd had heard real horror stories about) and throwing them out the car window. His son hadn't talked to him for two weeks afterward, not one word. He'd barely even glanced his way, which proved something of a relief because his stare had said: *Hypocrite.*

"Alyssa said Michael never came to the phone last night," Julia says. "I assume now that was just your way of trying to get her on the line?"

Lloyd sits up. His brain feels loose in his skull, and sore. Distracted by thinking about it, he is surprised to hear himself answering affirmatively. "Yes. I wanted to ask what she and Michael were arguing about with the Daniels boy," he explains. Seeing her eyes widen, he adds. "Trey. Not the…older…one."

For a brief moment she looks relieved. Then the set of her jaw shifts. "He and I talked at last year's dinner," she says. "Trey. You and Reilly went out to smoke and Michael was dancing with the daughter of your attorney friend, Jackson Harris."

"He's not my friend, just someone I know."

"Oh, he was on my last nerve that night," she says. Thinking she means the ambulance-chasing lawyer, Lloyd is momentarily buoyed. His dislike of Harris, never his favorite person, became intense the day the man dropped a reference to the color of Everett Reilly's skin into a discussion that had nothing to do with race. He finds it heartening that his wife shares his opinion of the man. "I mean to tell you," she says. "Rolling his eyes whenever the girls weren't looking, and wearing this godawful, pained expression, as if just being near them was killing him."

Lloyd realizes she's talking about Michael's behavior at last year's party, not Harris's. "He danced all night in new shoes," he says, despite his own memory of thinking that night that if he'd had the chance, at that age, to dance with a line of pretty girls, he would not have been aware of his feet, even had he ground them to bloody stumps.

"Oh, he was making an absolute idiot of himself out on the dance floor," Julia says. "When Josh Watterson cut in on Alyssa and Trey and asked her to dance, Trey came back to the table and sat down. I figured he might know, because of that brother of his, so I asked him, 'Why do they have to be the center of attention all the time? Is it a brain defect, do you think?'"

A chill runs up Lloyd's spine. "You did not."

"He pretended not to understand what I meant, but I knew he did. All the rest of the evening, every time he looked across the table at Michael, I saw what he was thinking."

"I really don't think that's what he—"

"He saw it. Everybody sees it. Michael makes sure they do."

"That's insane!" Lloyd exclaims. He scrambles to his feet, but the pain flaring in his temples makes him sit back down.

"What, Lloyd? I'm not making this up. It's the same as when he used to wear nothing but black and paint his nails and listen to that gothic music. He does things to bring other people's attention to him, with no regard to whether it's positive or negative attention. I know you think this is just some pop psychology nonsense I got from a drugstore publication, but it's true. Some people feel compelled to constantly be the center of attention. It doesn't matter what kind of attention they receive, they need everyone to pay attention to them all the time."

"Well, it's a real toss-up then, isn't it?" Lloyd says. "Nature or nurture?"

She narrows her eyes. "Tonight he ignored Alyssa and spent the entire evening monopolizing my new donor. Or didn't you notice?"

He had, but he's horrified that she did, too. During the dinner service he'd told himself Michael was simply impressed by the man. Who wouldn't be? But anyone with an ounce of sense could see that it went beyond simple hero worship.

"He's...confused," he says.

"If by 'confused' what you're trying to say is that he isn't actually like that, I agree. No one is. It doesn't make any sense. The human body is designed for reproduction. It's innate."

Lloyd wants to ask, *Then why is it you were never going to be ready to have a child? How come we don't have more than one?* But he doesn't dare. The only reason they have Michael is because five years into their marriage, on Derby Day of 1981, they'd won big at the track, and friends of friends had invited them up to Millionaire's Row to celebrate. Their hosts had plied them with mint juleps, caviar, and cigars, and generally fêted them like royalty. Drunk and high on his vision of the future, the minute they were home Lloyd had steered things toward the bedroom and, once there, neglected—not forgotten—to use a condom. When Julia turned up pregnant he'd lied and said it broke and that he hadn't known how to tell her.

He understands that on some level what he did was wrong, and he's grateful to her for not ending the pregnancy. A larger part of him, though, feels justified. Before they married she'd assured him she wanted children, plural, but she'd put off making real plans to start a family. After Michael arrived she had refuted every positive observation Lloyd made regarding parenthood. Though he was a good baby, not colicky like Danielle Lewis, and then a quiet, well-behaved child, not a destructive monster like Jon, Julia always insisted he was more than they could handle, and that another would have to wait until he was "older."

The year Michael entered kindergarten, more than a decade into their marriage, Lloyd put his foot down, and they began officially trying for a second. It turned out to be a pun, as months of eager anticipation turned into two disappointing, very trying years. When Michael was seven, while searching for nail clippers in her nightstand drawer, Lloyd had discovered birth control pills well within their expiration date, and knew there would be no other children.

"I'm telling you, all of that is an act. A very ill-thought one, but still an act. No one really feels that way."

"You think they're pretending? Who would bring that nightmare on themselves? Except maybe the insane."

"My point exactly."

Realizing if he says the thing that's on his mind he will need a divorce attorney, Lloyd grabs his car keys and heads for the door. "I'm not staying here to have this ridiculous discussion," he says. "I'm going out to look for our son."

EVEN WITHOUT SUPERHUMAN hearing Ehrichto got the gist of the Fergusons' conversation. It doesn't take a genius to understand that the reason Lloyd just sped off in his Corvette, and why he and his wife spent the night in the home's main living space, and were just lashing out at one another, is all because their son never came home last night. But none of that answers the obvious question:

If not here, then where is he?

The street outside the Morrisons' house looks like the scene of an impromptu Ford convention. Alyssa's yellow Escort is in the driveway, and parked on the street are a khaki-green Maverick (complete with black racing stripes down its impressively long hood), and a well-kept, older model F-150. *Good,* Lloyd thinks, as he pulls the Corvette in behind the truck and cuts its engine. *Alyssa's not only awake, she already has friends over. This must be where Michael is.*

When the door first swings open, her bright golden curls are the only thing he can see. "Mr. Ferguson," she says, undoing the snib on the screen door. "He isn't back yet?" She sounds more excited than alarmed.

"You know where he is," he says.

"What? No, I don't."

"You know something. You have to tell me."

"I don't."

Don't know anything? Or don't have to tell me? "I'm his father," he says. "I'm worried about him. He could be in trouble."

"I'm sure he's fine."

Lloyd is about to assure her she will make a terrific lawyer when movement in the living room behind her catches his eye. He cups his hand to block out the sun, in order to look through the mesh of the screen door. Alyssa's ex-boyfriend Trey Daniels is seated on the couch. Beside him, his older brother Neal is just getting to his feet.

"Mr. Ferguson," the latter says.

Oh, no, I don't want any reassurances from the likes of him, Lloyd thinks. He turns on his heel and dashes away from the house.

As he bolts toward the car, he hears Neal Daniels call his name. "Mr. Ferguson! Wait! Please!" Before Lloyd can pull open the Corvette's driver's door, the young man jogs past him to beside it and blocks the way. "Whatever they know isn't specific," he says. "I tried to get it out of them, too, but they refuse to say anything."

"Why?"

"Oh. Well, I have a theory, but it has little to do with Michael."

Lloyd has the urge to tell him that makes no sense, but he thinks better of it and grabs the handle of the car door. He intends it as a cue that Neal should step aside, but the younger man stays right where he is.

"If it's any consolation, they really don't think he's in any danger whatsoever."

Lloyd narrows his eyes. "It isn't. My son is only seventeen years old and he didn't come home last night."

The young man nods. "You're worried. I understand that."

"You don't have the first idea," Lloyd says. He yanks the car door open, hitting the young man in the leg. Still, the other stubbornly continues to block the way. "A friend of mine is a graduate of the school Michael used to attend," Neal says. "Two years older than him. I called him last night, asked if he knew Michael. He said there were some…incidents… involving him."

"One incident," Lloyd clarifies. He is offended by the insinuation that Michael is a bad student, a kid who regularly gets into trouble. "He was in a fistfight."

"Yes. A serious one, as I understand it. He was taken to the hospital?"

Lloyd remembers that the sterile environment of the ER, usually such a comfort to him, lost all illusion of security when Michael was the one on the gurney, when it was his blood smearing the rubber gloves and periwinkle nurse's scrubs. The brilliant attending physician became an exhausted resident just about to prescribe the wrong medication, and every bend in the polished steel I.V. stand was transformed into a harbor for germs. "It took twenty-three stitches to close his scalp," he says. "He had a mild concussion and bruised ribs, but thankfully none were broken." *And following it, he underwent a complete change of personality.*

"According to my friend, there were quite a few events leading up to that one," Neal says. "Comments half-whispered during classes, a lot of shoving and name-calling in the halls, graffiti scribbled on his locker."

The news makes Lloyd's blood run cold. It is precisely the information which countless times he'd asked Michael to provide, even while holding out hope for a different answer.

"I didn't know about those things. He didn't tell us that," Lloyd says. He doesn't say that he'd been secretly relieved each time he asked Michael how things were going at school, and received a stock, "It's fine."

"None of it says anything about Michael, of course," Neal points out. "Just volumes about his classmates." He pulls a folded piece of paper from the back pocket of his pants. "There's also this."

Lloyd takes the paper and starts to unfold it. He wonders if it is an official school document, something Neal had access to through his work as a counselor with troubled youth. The notion makes him silently scoff. *Troubled? Maybe troubled by the fact that they're*—His train of thought is interrupted when he sees that the paper is not a copy of a school document, but rather the printout of a message posted to an Internet chat board. The header lists Michael's real email address. The body of the message says:

> hello. i am mike. i am 15 and i love men. i dont know why
> i just do. i would like any gaysto email me. pleas! Cya.

"My son's strongest subject in school has always been English," Lloyd says, sidestepping the real issue. "He didn't write this." His hands are trembling, making it difficult to refold the paper. Once he has finished he tries to hand it back, but Neal makes no move to take it from him.

"I'm not saying he did. Let me be perfectly clear about this, Mr. Ferguson. I don't know anything about Michael's situation for certain and neither does anyone else. Not you or your wife, or Alyssa, or the kids who were harassing him back then. The only person entitled to say what Michael feels is Michael."

He lifts his chin to indicate the folded paper still in Lloyd's hand. "Regardless, the kind of response this sort of post must have generated can…well, it can change people. Unless he deleted that email account, I'm guessing there's been a steady stream of hate mail and crude solicitations coming in ever since. The important thing now is to find him, tell him how you feel, and make sure that, if he is gay, he doesn't feel that what he's been subjected to already is his fate." Neal pauses and holds Lloyd's gaze for several seconds. "Believe me, it's not."

A light bulb clicks on for Lloyd, understanding triggered by a single word in the note he just read. Only one person has ever referred to Michael as "Mike": *Jon Lewis*. He is about to pull open the car door again, this time hard enough to shove the Daniels boy out of his way, when over the young man's shoulders he sees Alyssa and Trey, framed in the doorway of the house, watching them.

"Tell me something," Lloyd says. "Was she ever really dating Michael, or was it just a…a smokescreen?"

Neal shakes his head. "No, she and Trey are really on the outs. He's been nearly inconsolable over it."

"I can imagine."

Right then the sun comes out from behind a cloud, and causes Neal to squint. "What does your gut tell you? Is Michael gay?"

Lloyd sighs. He lets all the breath held inside him slowly escape. Like the truth. "Yes."

"Have you tried to talk to him about it?"

"Well, I've—"

"He needs to know you're there for him." Neal squints harder. "You are there for him, aren't you?"

"Yes, but in order to for me to tell him that, I first have to find him."

AT THE HALF-LANDING they stop so Marc can rest. "I suppose refusing to stay in the hospital isn't necessarily an indication of insanity," Baxter says, enjoying the opportunity Marc's condition has made possible, the chance to speak to him without being interrupted. "After all, if you really stop to consider it, people in the past didn't have the luxury of a hospital. What would we do if this was a hundred years ago, hmm? Leaving the hospital is far less troubling than your decision, once you got home from the dinner yesterday, to snort the contents of a caplet of oxycodone in an effort to defeat its built-in anti-cholinergic. You made yourself as sick as a—" He stops when he realizes Marc isn't paying attention. He's staring at one of the oil paintings flanking a plaster fleur-de-lys. Painted by an unknown Middle Eastern artist, it is a photo-realistic depiction of a man copulating with a goat.

"I bought that as a reminder of the fact that to this day it is legal for men in Lebanon to have sexual relations with animals so long as they are female animals. Screwing a male animal is punishable by death because, clearly, homosexuality is more frightening than the possibility of creating a cross-species being." He snorts derisively and points to the painting on the other side of the fleur-de-lys, a reproduction of Bouguereau's *Dante and Virgil in Hell*. Dark and romantic, worthy of the Old Masters, it shows two naked, muscular males wrestling while the title characters of the work look on. "This," Baxter says, using a fingertip to trace the curving back of the dominant fighter, whose teeth are sunk deep into his cohort's neck, "is my very favorite work of art of all time. It always makes me think of the Surrealist parlor game Exquisite Corpse."

Marc cuts his eyes sideways and raises one brow, as if prompting, "Go on."

"You don't know it? My. Well, the first person writes a word, and then the second person adds a word to it, and so on, until—"

"Telephone."

"No, that's where you start with a phrase and pass it around, orally, and by the end it morphs into something else."

"Mad. Libs."

"Mmm. Closer, but there you're plugging words into a framework. This has no framework."

Marc glowers at him. "Reminds…you…how?"

"Why does it, you mean? Well, the first sentence that was created using this method—at least as far as anyone knows—was 'Le cadavre exquis boira le vin nouveau.' Translated that's 'The exquisite corpse will drink the new wine.'" He taps his fingertip on the figure in the oil painting. "There's nothing on earth I wouldn't give, nothing I would not do for him."

"Who?"

Baxter looks over, snaps out of his reverie. Marc's skin is glistening with sweat. The effort to reach the third floor is obviously almost more than he can muster. "That's not important right now. We need to get you into bed and get you well." He casts a glance up the next flight of stairs. "Ready for more?"

By way of reply, Marc drapes his right arm across Baxter's shoulders, letting him get close enough to slip a supporting arm around his waist. Then, side by side, they start up the stairs.

THERE ARE NO open spots in the tiny lot attached to the coffeehouse. Lloyd spies Jon's brick-red Toyota Camry and pulls the Corvette in beside it. He bolts from the car, sprints to the closest door and yanks it open, then stops, shocked by the sight greeting him. The wall opposite the door is filled with familiar images—posters, pages torn from magazines, t-shirts and other memorabilia related to the band the Cure. But it isn't simply memorabilia—these are, specifically, the very same items that used to paper the walls and fill the dresser drawers of Michael's bedroom back on Donahue, the ones he ripped from the walls and in the process, tore all the corners from. Glossy 3X5 prints, every one of them a candid shot of his son, have been tacked up strategically to hide the ruin.

The music playing low is familiar, the skritchy-rattling strains of one of the tunes Michael once liked.

"Mr. Ferguson?"

He turns and finds Danielle Lewis dressed in her usual all-black. This time it's a velvet-covered corset and Morticia Addams-worthy sleeves of lace. Her hair is cut Cleopatra-style, in bangs straight across her brow, which is, as usual, powdered white. She's sitting sideways in a booth with her knees drawn up to cradle a book.

Lloyd thrusts an arm out, indicating the wall above her head. "What gives you the right to put his things on display?"

"He…he didn't want them," she says. Her lower lip begins to tremble, and just like that tears well in her eyes. Lloyd isn't surprised or alarmed. He's seen her cry at the drop of a hat a hundred times. *She should be an actress*, he thinks. *That's wasted talent, right there.* Danielle hugs the book she was reading to her chest. "He threw them out."

It would be more accurate to say that Michael threw them out *again*, but no one but Lloyd knows he did it twice.

The first time was a Saturday night, a week after one of their worst-ever altercations. The previous Saturday night, or, more accurately, early Sunday morning, Michael had turned up at the front door accompanied by a cab driver who'd, reasonably, wanted to be paid. It turned out that Michael had snuck out of the house and gone to a concert Lloyd hadn't even known was happening. Just fifteen and not half as worldly as he imagined himself to be, Michael had failed to realize that buses stopped running downtown well before the concert's end time. He'd managed to become stranded, watching other kids pile into cars and drive away. Thankfully, the enterprising cab driver, counting on just such an occurrence, had brought him safely back across town.

Lloyd had rehearsed the exchange that would happen if his son ever pulled a stunt like he did that night, attending a rock concert without permission and then sneaking home in the middle of the night. He'd imagined the dialogue would go something like:

"You did *what?*"

"I went to a concert."

In the made-up scenario Lloyd kept his cool, stayed in control. "You went to a concert. Downtown. At the *Gardens*," he would say, his voice dripping with sarcasm. "Well, it would've been nice if you'd told us that."

He imagined his son would roll his eyes and sneer and say, "You wouldn't have let me go."

"Actually," Lloyd would say, excitement catching in his throat, threatening to ruin his opportunity to reveal himself as, secretly, the Cool Dad, "I might have agreed to drive you there and pick you up."

Michael, of course, would be skeptical. "Yeah, right," he'd say. "You'd never take me to see Blind Cave Fish."

"Well, we'll never know for certain, now will we," Lloyd would smugly reply. "Because you didn't give me a chance." The self-righteous last line was always his favorite part of the daydream.

In actuality, the exchange had been much shorter and nowhere near as snappy. Lloyd had lost it completely and begun yelling, loud enough to wake the tri-state area, even before the cab pulled away: "You did *what?* You went to a concert, downtown, by yourself? Are you out of your mind?"

For his part, Michael had had only one rejoinder, which he uttered again and again at a variety of volumes. No matter what Lloyd had asked, or demanded, or threatened, he'd said only, "I don't want to talk about it."

All the next day, Lloyd had believed that his son's sullenness stemmed from his having been grounded for a month, the Cool Dad having, by necessity, given way to the Strict Disciplinarian. But coming home Monday night and seeing all the color drained from Michael's face, and watching him push food around his plate at dinner, and the fact that asking him about the show itself, and the band's performance, elicited no spark of happiness from him, told Lloyd something more was wrong. Something had happened at the show, or maybe after it, while he was trying to get home, before the cab driver came to his rescue. All of his efforts to get Michael to open up, though, were met with the same brick wall: "I don't want to talk about it."

Rather than blowing over, things got worse. On Tuesday he'd claimed he was sick; Lloyd suspected he was faking it, and letting him stay home seemed like rewarding bad behavior so he had made Michael go to school. By the end of the week his son had dark circles beneath his eyes and had ceased responding to anything Lloyd said. No matter what conversation starter he tried he got nothing in return but a sullen stare.

Because of the conversation with Neal Daniels, he now knows for sure that there were incidents, plural, at Michael's old school. It makes him sick at heart to consider it. At the time he'd only suspected that something bad had happened there, and was contributing to Michael's depression.

The weekend after the concert he'd broken down and done the thing he'd been dreading for weeks: he told Michael they were planning to move, not far away, but far enough that his senior year would be spent at a new school.

Even that seemed, at first, to not elicit a reaction, which was chilling. But a few minutes later Michael had taken the box of trash bags from the pantry and retreated to his room. A minute later Lloyd heard paper ripping, and what he took as the sound of his son repeatedly jumping down from the bed, or from atop the desk. When he investigated he found Michael ripping everything from the walls of his room and stuffing it into garbage bags, which he then hauled to the curb. On his way to work the next morning Lloyd had retrieved them and hidden them in the garage. Surely, he told himself, Michael would change his mind. But a few months later, on moving day, the revelation that they still existed didn't make his son any happier. The moving van rolled out but the bags stayed at the curb.

In hindsight, he realizes it was stupid not to have anticipated that Danielle would go through them. She'd had a crush on Michael from the time she was eight until…well, given that she was right then surrounded by his things, she still did.

"All of this is his," Lloyd says. His legs are shaking. "You had no right."

Danielle starts to open her mouth, but a voice from behind Lloyd cuts her off.

"Mr. Ferguson."

Lloyd turns his head and finds Jon Lewis standing behind him. The boy is flanked on one side by his new best friend, Michael's replacement, a kid named Alan Miller, and on the other by his girlfriend Lia Alvarez.

Lloyd doesn't think, he just draws back his right arm, wheels around, and swings. There's a satisfying crunch when his knuckles connect with the boy's jaw. He doesn't even care if it's Jon or he who has broken. It only matters that he's done what he came there to do.

MICHAEL WALKS THROUGH the open back door of Gear, a head shop thinly disguised as a smoke shop located on Baxter Avenue, just down from the entrance to Cave Hill Cemetery. Like the coffeehouse with which it shares one wall and ownership, it is painted teal and purple and every surface is busy with psychedelic tchotchkes. And also like the coffeehouse, it was one of Michael's regular haunts back in the day. *Before the fall out*, he thinks sarcastically. The term is one his father once used when trying to get him to talk about what had led to the fistfight he and Jon had, which hadn't so much as ended their friendship as announced it to the world. *Fall out? That's like referring to a tsunami as a wave.* They'd come to blows after Danielle spread the rumor that she and Michael were secretly dating. Not only that, but that they'd done it, all the way. She was only trying to help, of course; and it had, for a little while. But naturally Jon had found out, and he'd confronted Michael, and demanded that he denounce the rumors. The decision to not do so is what had triggered their fistfight, another problematic term because it makes it sound as if they'd been evenly matched, and also like Michael had even tried to hit back, which he had not, out of guilt.

The girl on shift at Gear that morning is slumped behind the counter with her elbows resting on the glass, and her eyes raised to the ceiling, where a spiral of prismatic Mylar lazily twirls in the incense-laden air.

When she sees Michael, she straightens up and smiles.

"Hey there, little Robert." The nickname makes him wince. On the night of the Blind Cave Fish concert he and Roman, one of Danielle's stupid friends, had each turned up wearing hockey jerseys, because they both idolized the Cure's Robert Smith, and Robert had been wearing the things onstage for a couple of years. Roman's jersey fit him the way Robert's did, but even the smallest available size had been more of a dress on Michael's bony frame.

Someone in the line they were both queued up in, running along the side of the Louisville Gardens, had noticed the contrast and hollered "Hey everybody, look! It's just like Elvis postage stamps! You can vote for Fat Robert or Thin Robert!" The look Roman gave Michael turned his blood to ice. It was most of the reason why, when the guy directly behind him in line starting chatting him up, and suggested they go to his car and smoke a joint while the line cleared, Michael had accepted the offer. He'd had no idea that the guy was Roman's cousin Joey, recently arrived from Chicago, or that the only reason the guy had started talking to him was to lure him into a compromising position, which Roman planned to make sure certain people there that night saw. By Monday morning it was the talk of the school.

"Haven't seen you in here in a while," the counter girl says.

Michael shrugs. "That's 'cause I haven't smoked in, like, almost a year."

"Wow. You mean just cloves or—?"

"Anything."

She bobs her head. "Yeah, I was thinking you look really straight now."

He bristles until he realizes she means conservative as opposed to liberal, an abstainer not a stoner. He looks down at his wrinkled white button-front, ironed jeans and unmarked tennis shoes. When he was a regular here he'd worn practically nothing but Cure shirts, painted his nails black, and teased his hair into a careful rat's nest.

"That's cool, man," the girl says. "It's all really bad for you." Then her eyes widen and she slaps a hand over her mouth, holds it there for several seconds. "Please don't tell Sheila and Bear I said that," she begs.

"No, no. I won't," Michael assures her. "I totally wouldn't."

She looks relieved, then puzzled. "So, um, what'cha come in for, if you don't smoke?"

Michael picks up two tins of spice-laden cigarettes and a cheap plastic lighter. He sets them on the counter followed by the twenty his father gave him for emergencies, before urging him to try never to use it.

At seventeen he isn't old enough to buy tobacco, but that has only ever been a problem a few times here, always with newly hired staff. He hopes his agreeing not to rat on the counter girl will make her amenable to his plight. "I need 'em bad," he says.

"I hear you," she says, taking the bill from his hand.

SURPRISINGLY, JON LEWIS doesn't seem inclined to fight back. After Lloyd clocked him, he'd staggered back and put an arm out to keep Alan Miller from lunging.

Lloyd's hand seems functional, though it will, no doubt, swell to the size of a grapefruit and be hard to explain on his route tomorrow. Keeping one eye on the boys, Lloyd asks Danielle, "What happened at that concert?"

The three kids exchange glances. For a moment Lloyd thinks he is going to witness a repeat of the Alyssa/Trey dynamic, but Alan Miller twists free of Jon's grasp and says, "What, at Blind Cave Fish? He made a grab for a guy's dick."

Jon shoves the guy hard on one shoulder. "Joey was high, idiot. They both were. Who knows what really happened?"

"What *happened* is Michael's idea of smoking a joint and Joey's were two different things."

"Joey's a space case," Danielle offers. "You can't believe a word he says."

"Oh, c'mon," Alan protests. "The Cure?"

"Robert Smith isn't gay. He's *married.*"

The boy snorts. "So? We're talking about Michael. No guy who likes girls puts nothing but pictures of another guy up in his room. You know and I know he offered to do the tube steak boogie for Joey."

The pieces of the puzzle fall into place for Lloyd. "It was you, not Jon," he says as he pulls the piece of paper he got from Neal from his back pocket. "You put this garbage on the Internet." He unfolds the paper and shoves it toward the boy, who calmly reads it.

"Oh, yeah, I remember this," Alan says, nodding. "But I didn't write it. Wish I did."

Lloyd is startled when Danielle scrambles out of the booth and snatches the paper from Alan's hand. He reaches for it, but she backs away too quickly.

Her eyes grow huge.

"Michael didn't write this," she says.

"I know that."

"They took it down. They swore they would and they did. I double checked."

"Who?" Lloyd asks.

"The...the website."

"Wait, you posted that?" Alan asks. "Damn, that's *cold*."

"No! I, I just vented. I was mad. Ethereal's the one who posted it." Lloyd assumes "Ethereal" is one of the older kids she began hanging out with about a year before Michael and Jon's friendship-ending fight. The two girls of the trio had looked at least Michael and Jon's age. The boy seemed even older.

Lloyd had wondered at the time what was wrong with the Lewises that they let their fourteen-year-old daughter hang around with a young man who looked possibly old enough to buy alcohol, and clearly didn't have a job. How could he, dressed the way he always was?

"I made them take it down as soon as I found out," Danielle says, looking up at Lloyd. "It was only there for like twelve hours."

Jon shakes his head. "Dani, I've told you. Nothing ever really gets deleted from the Internet."

"I didn't know it was still up anywhere, I swear. Please tell him I'm sorry."

Lloyd feels his shock turn to loathing. "I thought you *liked* him."

She stamps a foot and shrieks. Lloyd remembers that as an infant she'd wailed like a banshee, for hours. He could hear her, even all the way across the street. It was her carrying on that had put the lie, finally, to Julia's assertion that Michael was a colicky, inconsolable child.

"I did! I loved him! I was the one who was always there for him!" She turns and glares at her brother. "Even after the Blind Cave Fish concert it was me who stood up for him. He was supposed to be your best friend, but you abandoned him. After you beat him up, that is."

"I was protecting you," Jon shouts. "Your reputation was being trashed!"

"And I told you, it wasn't your business!"

"Hell yes, it was! You're my sister!" He turns and punches the wall, leaving a sizable dent, then spins back and glares at her. "If I'd had a clue you were masterminding the whole thing, or that your sick friends were gonna post some piece of crap illiterate message making him out to be some kinda perv looking for hook-ups with strange guys, believe me, it's your ass and theirs I would've kicked, not his!"

If he was my son, Lloyd thinks, *I'd be looking into military schools. If they were my children, I'd send both of them.*

"That wouldn't have done anything to stop it and you know it!" Danielle says. "Only one thing did."

"What?" Lloyd asks.

Alan Miller surprises him by answering. "Paducah."

"I don't understand."

"You know, when that kid Michael Carneal shot up Heath High School? Everyone freaked out then. They thought, you know, that the same thing could happen here."

"Michael would never do anything like that," Lloyd says.

"I wouldn't blame him if he did." This time it's Jon's girlfriend Lia Alvarez who has spoken. Everyone else in the room turns to look at her. "This guy I know who goes to the Catholic school right near there told me some of his friends saw Michael sitting by himself at a bus stop. They'd heard the shit that was going around about him, so they grabbed him and tried to pull him into some tall bushes beside this house. My friend said he didn't know for sure what they had in mind, but he could guess, and he had a change of heart. He started arguing with them, and managed to hold the other two guys off long enough that Michael was able to get away."

"Once Paducah happened, all that kinda crap stopped," Danielle says.

"No," Lloyd replies, snatching the computer printout from her hands. "It didn't. You just couldn't see it anymore." He holds the paper up, right in front of her face. "This is not love," he says. "It's hate." He looks from her to her brother to Alan and finally Lia. "All y'all" he says, not caring how horrified Julia would be if she heard, "can go to hell."

FIFTEEN

MICHAEL SITS ON a bench a block from Gear on Broadway, jonesing so hard for a nicotine fix that his hands are shaking and jostling the small white paper bag in his hands. What he said to the girl in the shop was a lie; he never stopped smoking, not really. For a while after he confided in his father and had his cloves thrown out of the car window he'd just gone back to hiding it. And then—Michael still can't quite fathom that it's true—his father had decided to teach him how to smoke cigars.

The cigar thing came about after his father received a gift membership in a cigar-of-the-month club offered by the last real old-timey smoke shop in town, Kremer's, from one of the doctors on his pharmaceutical sales route. Dr. Reilly had given him the yearlong membership on one condition: Michael's dad had to agree to quit smoking cigarettes.

He'd never asked Michael whether or not he stilled smoked. Instead, out of the blue after dinner one night, he'd proposed they try out the cigars that had just arrived. Afterward, he'd mentioned about a hundred million times that he was giving up cigarettes in favor of cigars. He might as well have followed it up with "Hint, hint." The next month they'd not only repeated the ritual, but midway through the month he'd produced cigars not from the subscription service, ones he'd stopped at Kremer's to buy. Now they sample a new stogie once a week, and compare tasting notes.

At first Michael feared that his father might use the one-on-one time to pester him again about the whole business at school, but he hadn't. The sessions proved to be all about the cigars, about learning to dissect their flavor profile, or reading an article in a magazine that detailed how they were crafted. Mostly it was a time just to sit and share space without saying anything at all. In all honesty, it was a relief. But the thing Michael likes best about the whole thing, even more than the fact that it makes him feel like an adult, is that it drives his mother crazy.

Michael looks over his shoulder, hoping for a bus. He needs to light up, but not here, and he needs to get back to Belgravia Court. He wonders if Ehrichto has returned yet. He tries to think of what to say to convince the man to give him a chance. But what can he say? That it isn't fair to not want to be with him just because he looks like someone else, someone who caused Ehrichto pain, maybe broke his heart? That's not something you can easily overcome. A few minutes later the hiss of air brakes being released makes him jump. He scrambles off the bench and hurries toward the accordion style doors of the bus.

To Marc, the bed is heaven. Like the air of the house only stronger, its sheets—blood-red linen with an astronomical thread count—are permeated with a deep smoky scent, not as from cigarettes or even cigars, but rather like that of a camp or forest fire, a primeval, primal scent. When asked about it, Baxter had explained there is a fireplace in the attic den, just one more flight up. He'd said that he uses it often, and offered to get it going again, but the bedroom was warm enough, and they'd agreed that moister air would be easier for Marc to breathe. Another thing which has helped is that, per doctor's orders, he is lying on his wounded side. Counter-intuitive, the advice has not only made breathing easier, it has considerably lessened his pain.

Or maybe, he thinks, *that has to do with Baxter's being freer with the hydrocodone than the ER nurse was.* He remembers that the attending physician wrote him a prescription for a sleep aid. He has only a hazy recollection of waiting in the car while Baxter was inside the pharmacy filling it, and once they got into the house, of lingering downstairs long enough to take the first dose.

What Marc saw of the house on the way up here was incredible. In his opinion the décor is the perfect mix of wood, leather and steel; bright colors and black; ultra-modern and classical design. He can't wait until he feels well enough to really take it in, but right now what he wants is sleep. He pulls a fistful of sheet fabric over his face to cover his eyes. Seated beside him on the king-sized bed, Baxter chooses that moment to uncross and re-cross his legs, and then launch into a fresh discussion topic. It is his persistent questions, on a variety of topics, which have thus far made falling asleep impossible for Marc, despite the drugs.

"Was it that you couldn't take the pressure of being queer?"

Though he knows Baxter can't see it, Marc rolls his eyes. "No."

"Good. I'm glad, because that would break my heart. I've always viewed it as a saving grace, myself. I think if I'd been born straight I would've jumped off a bridge long ago."

Marc has the urge to say *Please, go do it now.* Thankful that the meds have reduced what was a searing pain to the mere sensation that his lungs are being sandblasted, he gathers his breath and says, "Why?" The action of trying not to fall forward is wearing Marc out. He flops onto his back. Instantly, it becomes harder for him to breathe.

"You're supposed to stay on your side."

"Can't." Marc pulls air through his nostrils. "Too hard with the bed tilting."

He feels Baxter scramble from the mattress. "You should have said something." Marc considers attempting the Herculean task of turning onto his other side, turning his back to the man, but figures Baxter will only then move around to the other side of the bed. There is no way to escape him. "Damn it but I have a knack for making things difficult for you," Baxter says.

Sensing where this change in conversation topics is going, Marc shakes his head. "No."

"Don't argue with me. It needs to be said. When I was driving you to the hospital that's what I kept coming back to, over and over. I should've realized. I should've stopped it."

How? How were you supposed to know it when, out of the whole shitload of husbands and boyfriends my mother and Louretta paraded through my life, one decided to get all up in my business? Marc can't say all that, so he says "You're...psychic?"

"No, not psychic, seasoned. I knew there were people like that in the world. When you returned after your hiatus from the stage, I knew immediately that something wasn't right. You were different."

"I was...older."

"Too much older, too fast," Baxter says. "You hate me for it, don't you?"

"You didn't do anything."

"That's exactly why you hate me. You don't have to admit it. I know. I've always felt it."

"I *don't!*" A flutter of breath threatens to erupt into a cough. Marc concentrates on stifling it.

"But you do think I should have called the police."

Marc tugs fistfuls of his own hair in frustration. *No! What the hell could they have done? Arrested Bobby Lee and charged my mother and Louretta with neglect? Put me in a foster home with god knows who? It was over by the time I came back to the theatre. The only thing calling the cops would have done was make things worse.* "I'm glad you didn't," he says. They glare at one another. "One question."

"What?"

"Why didn't you ever give in?"

Baxter looks confused for a moment before his face twists into a mask of horror. "You were a child."

Marc nods. "You know when I really could've...used your help?"

"When?"

"Pentecostal. Prison. Camp."

Far from tickled, Baxter looks ill. "If I'd had *any* idea that's where you were," he says. "I would have rescued you."

Marc feels exhausted. He gestures for Baxter to come closer, and is relieved when the man obeys. He takes his hand and squeezes it. "I'm not a…child anymore." He tries to pull Baxter's hand toward his crotch, but the man wrenches free and crosses the room.

"Why? Not?" Marc calls.

"You don't understand."

I understand you want to fuck me. You won't admit it, but you do.

Baxter laughs, but the sound is anything but funny. "And so here we are, arriving at the last station on our route, the much-dreaded pity fuck. Just put me out of my misery."

"Listen," Marc hisses. "I. *Want.*You."

Baxter sneers. "Word to the wise, my dear. If I ever find you unconscious again, I don't care if you're bleeding out, foaming at the mouth, or turning blue, there will be, shall we say a small delay, before the paramedics are summoned."

The corners of Mark's mouth turn upward and his eyes widen. "Always…knew you…were a…sick bastard."

The minute he says the word, he knows what Baxter's reaction will be. Sure enough, the other stalks back across the room, leans down over him, and without masking the twang that is part of his natural speaking style, says, "What I *am*, dear, is a cock-sucking bay-uh-stud and a son of a bey-utch." He straightens up again, pushes his shoulders back, and raises his chin high.

MICHAEL HAD HOPED that by the time he got back to the house on Belgravia Court Mr. Salvatolle—*Ehrichto*, he thinks. *Eh-REEK-toe*—would have returned, but when he turns onto the walking court from Sixth, the street where the bus let him off, the windows of the taupe-painted Italianate are still dark. The sight deflates him, slows his steps, and twists the knot of fear in his stomach more tightly. He worries that the man isn't ever going to come back, that he stormed not only out of the room but out of the city, all the way back to New Orleans. Then he reminds himself that the man said at dinner that he'd come into town for business, not Thunder. He'd had no idea any of that was even happening. It was just dumb luck that he'd ended up at the arts center. He tells himself the man is away at a meeting, never minding that it's Sunday. He tells himself Ehrichto will come back here before he heads home.

A grassy median stands between two narrow sidewalks, one running in front of each row of houses. In line with the front steps of Ehrichto's house there is a tree. Michael leans against it and pulls one of the tins of clove cigarettes from the white paper bag. He tucks the bag beneath his arm, tears the cellophane from the tin and tucks a slim white stick between his lips. It feels right there, feels natural. He fishes the lighter from his front pocket and thumbs its flywheel to bring flame to life, then touches the tip of the cigarette to the fire and inhales savagely, pulling spicy smoke deep into his lungs. The tip of his tongue goes numb almost instantly. He silently wills the rest of his body to do the same, but as usual, it defies him. He leans his head back against the tree and tries not to think of his father and how disappointed he would be if he found out he'd gone back to smoking cigarettes.

Or found out about other things, he thinks, but deeper down he knows that's just childish, wishful thinking. The time for worrying about that is over. After yesterday's debacle—that stupid, stupid fight between Alyssa and Trey beneath the stairs at the KCA—his father has to know.

What the hell was that, anyway? Michael wonders. He'd known Alyssa knew, or okay, suspected; technically she couldn't know what he hadn't even really, deep down, been one hundred percent sure of himself until last night, but the thought that she was dating him because of it, like she'd always known—suspected—chills him to the bone. What did she think he was, a charity case? He chuckles bitterly at the irony of it: Conway Charities. Then he feels like puking.

He pulls a vicious drag from the cigarette. He feels bad for breaking down and buying them, feels like he has betrayed his father, and let himself down, too. He really had stopped smoking cigarettes, eventually, hadn't had one for six months.

Quitting them got easier when his father started letting him smoke a cigar once a week, and then once every few days. The fact that the only place that would sell cigarettes to him was on the other side of town also helped. The switch hasn't been bad, and he's enjoyed another aspect of the trade-off, getting to spend time hanging out with his dad. He'd liked their drives last summer, during his internship, too. They'd carpooled together, because why not? It was on one of those rides home that he'd admitted to his dad that he sometimes smoked clove cigarettes and confessed his fear that he was growing dependent on them. He hadn't expected his father to go ballistic, just the opposite. He'd thought he, of all people, would have been able to relate. He expected sympathy and advice, not to have the tin he was holding snatched from his hand and thrown out of the window of the moving car. He hadn't expected to be subjected to a damned tirade about the evils of cigarettes.

He thinks of last night's drive home, after dinner, after the awful scene under the stairs. Mostly he thinks about the fact that his father hadn't said anything about what he'd overheard. In a way it's a relief—how awful would it be to have that conversation?—but in another way the silence is worse. It says to him that the subject matter is something so bad that his father can't even bring himself to acknowledge it when it's right in front of him. It's like what you're taught about meeting a wild animal in the woods: Don't look it in the eye and don't take off running. If you just turn and walk away calmly the chances are better that it will leave you be.

Michael is careful to flick his ashes onto the pavement, despite the soggy ground beneath his feet. Thursday after dinner his father had made him laugh by imitating their mail carrier, who'd apparently been all freaked out because somewhere on his route a business had burned to the ground after someone threw a still-lit cigarette into the mulch. His dad had been really funny—Jon would say "mad funny," as in "he has mad skills"—riffing on the mail carrier's pith helmet and galoshes and being just this side of apoplectic about the divots the idiot always makes in their lawn because he refuses to stick to the stepping-stone path. But he'd been more than snarky; he'd been proud, too, when he related how at one point the mail carrier looked past him, through the open front door, and stared longingly at the foyer. It had made his dad really, really happy to possess something other people only dreamed of owning.

Michael has a moment of snarkiness of his very own, imagining both of his parents finding help in getting over their horror at having a son who likes boys, in the fact that Ehrichto is rich with a capital "R." Porsche-driving, mansion-on-Belgravia Court, old-money rich.

The cigarette is all but gone; he takes one last drag and stubs it out on the inside of the tin's lid, and then pulls out another. He was not a chain smoker before, even in the heyday of his addiction, far from it; cigarettes were precious things. But it seems somehow appropriate and necessary now to immediately light up again. He places a pristine stick between his lips, and flicks his lighter.

A radio goes on, in a building further down the court. The pounding notes of the Stones' "Miss You" are hollow and tinny in the open air. Michael figures a U of L student is the one blasting the music, enjoying the fact that Central Park—not *the* Central Park of course, but a much smaller one, also designed by Frederick Law Olmsted—is just half a block away. Most of the former mansions are broken up into oddly arranged apartments, studio spaces made from former front parlors and foyers, with bathrooms crammed below stairs, stained glass over the bathroom sink, a former servants' stair turned into a serpentine pantry. The buildings that are still whole are often on the Christmas homes tour, or available for viewing during the famous St. James Court Art Show, and Michael's been dragged through more of the residences than he cares to recall.

It's not quite as cold as yesterday, and thankfully not raining, but it isn't warm out, either. Michael lets his cigarette hang James Dean-jauntily from the corner of his mouth, so that he can slip his fingers into the front pockets of his blue jeans. Smoke wafts up into his left eye as he looks up at the darkened windows of the Salvatolle residence. He'd never been in that particular house before yesterday, and he'd give his right arm to be back there now. Squinting like a gangster in a two-bit mob flick, he sings along with Mick, and then says, "Seriously, what's the matter with you?"

"I'm sorry. Was that directed at me?"

Michael turns around. Ehrichto is leaned up against the front railing of a house with his head down and his hair hanging free, totally obscuring his face, a curtain of darkest brown. He tilts his head slightly as he lifts his gaze and at the same time drags a hand over the crown of his head, pulling back half the strands. The eye trained on Michael is the same deep, deep brown.

The hair alone makes him look like a bad-boy English rock star, Mick Jagger to the millionth power, but he is also dressed like one. Last night's tuxedo has been replaced by a burgundy-colored shirt with French cuffs, black jeans, and gloss-black wingtips.

The fact that he's there is such a great relief that Michael's knees threaten to buckle, but he manages to steady himself. "Yes," he says, though in point of fact he can't recall what he said a moment ago, to know how it relates to what the man just asked him. He means it this way: *Yes! He came back!*

Hands in his front pockets, Ehrichto hip-chucks himself away from the wrought-iron railing and takes several long strides forward, closing the distance between them.

"I'm glad you came back," he says.

Michael's heartbeat stutters. His speech mimics it. "Y-You are?"

"I want to apologize for my behavior yesterday. It was unfair."

"No."

"Yes. I wanted to tell you that I did not intend to—" The stuttering is contagious. He stops abruptly, seems to skip over difficult words. "And then throw you out."

"I know."

Ehrichto pulls the rest of the curtain back, tucks those strands behind his ear, and looks earnestly at Michael. "I'm not…I'm not like that, really. Not monstrous. Not…dissolute."

It's a word from English class. More rock star stuff, a word for describing rakish earls. "Okay."

He's so close Michael can count the hairs of his sparse moustache. His eye goes to the thin white hairline scar beneath them. He'd noticed it yesterday but had no chance to ask. Before he can do so now Ehrichto notices him, noticing. He brings a hand up self-consciously but Michael catches his forearm. After a pause, the man pulls free.

"You should go home," he says. "Your father is worried about you." He puts too much emphasis on "your" and Michael gets it: who gave him the scar, and why.

"I didn't mean to make you uncomfortable. I'm sorry."

"Yes, well, now we're even, aren't we? Go home." He starts for the house.

Michael follows. "But I want to be here with you."

Ehrichto reaches the front steps and ascends them two at a time. His keys are already in his hand. He slides one into the lock.

"Tell me why that isn't possible," Michael says, reaching his side as he shoulders open the heavy mahogany door.

Ehrichto pauses on the threshold but doesn't look back. "Many reasons."

The answer sours Michael's stomach. "Name one."

"You're too young."

"I wasn't last night. Not then but now? Talk about dissolute. That's the definition."

"I thought you were someone else. What's your mother's father's name?"

"Donal. Why?"

Ehrichto throws back his head and laughs. "Incredible." He steps into the house.

Expecting him to block the path, Michael launches himself through the doorway, and ends up at the center of the vestibule. "What is? What's incredible?"

Ehrichto remains beside the open door, his hand still on the knob. "You can't stay here."

"Because I'm too young? Or I look too much like someone who broke your heart?"

"We don't know one another," Ehrichto says. "We share nothing in common."

"We have one thing."

Ehrichto's eyebrows go up. "Crudeness is unbecoming."

"Mind out of the gutter," Michael says. "I'm talking about love."

Ehrichto chuckles. "Love? Is that what you think this is?"

"Yes." Michael crosses the foyer to where Ehrichto stands and pushes the door closed.

It's while walking down Santa Monica Boulevard in sunny California, accompanied by Anthony Kiedis, lead singer of the Red Hot Chili Peppers, that Marc remembers the bag of drugs stashed under the passenger's seat of his car. The fluid nature of dreams remakes Louisville into the California town on the outskirts of Los Angeles. Turning to the singer, whose idea it was to venture out to score some blow, Marc says,

"We have to go downtown." The sound of his own voice startles him and lets him know that he is dreaming. Hearing Baxter reply, "I'm sorry, I don't speak noddish," from somewhere close, as close as Kiedis, also helps to draw him back to consciousness. He feels Baxter's fingers press against his forehead, sampling its heat. "They said to keep an eye out for fever. I don't think you're running one." He retracts his hand. "All right, now what does that mean, 'Weftaga donton'?"

"My car." Marc remembers that, just before thinking of his bag of drugs, he'd spotted Ehrichto Salvatolle leaning in the doorway of the Viper Room, which—if his copy of *Guide to West Hollywood* is to be believed—is on Sunset, not Santa Monica. He is dreaming. He opens his eyes to see Baxter leaning over him, looking worried.

Marc shakes his head. "My car is still downtown. I need my bag."

"Ah," Baxter says. "You don't remember that after we left the hospital we stopped at your car and I took everything out of it, including, of course, your bag of goodies. You brought quite the party mix."

The only drug Marc cares about is his Ritalin. He remembers hitting it hard, killing a bottle that was supposed to get him through several more days.

He'd taken the oxycodone when he got home because it was what he had, stuff he kept around because it was easy to unload, a fast way to make money.

"I did too much," he says aloud. "I crashed."

"No, you think?" Baxter chuckles. "On a lighter note, several of the outfits from the trunk I simply *adore*."

Marc waves his hand.

"I don't have the faintest idea, though, why you bought them. Let me see, what could it be? I know you were thinking in terms of costumes; you don't have the good taste to like those styles, or the balls to wear what you honestly like. So the question is, costumes for what role? Jed is a botanist in small town Missouri, for heaven's sake. You've outfits that would only have been appropriate at Studio 54." He raises his eyebrows and tips his head sideways. "Which, who knows, might be foreshadowing. Keep going as you have been, and you're going to end up like Steve Rubell."

Marc groans.

"*Pour the T*," Baxter says. It's the title of a collection of one-acts they worked on together for the Shout! Theatre Company, STC for short, a group dedicated to producing shows relevant to gay culture. The "T" of the play's title stands for both "truth" and "T-cells," and is a nod to Michael Kearns's *T-Cells and Sympathy*, which itself, of course, is a reference to the classic stage play *Tea and Sympathy*. It's also a derivation of the seventies-era gay slang expression for gossiping. To say that one is "pouring the tea" means he is telling the hard truth someone else doesn't want to hear.

Baxter adjusts the thin blanket around Marc's shoulders. "Are those Ambien kicking in yet?"

"Mmm-hmm." Just before letting his eyelids droop, Marc stops and says.

"But I...need my pills. Can you...call it in?"

"Already taken care of. Now get some rest. It's the best thing for you." In the pause that follows, Marc thinks he can feel the man debating whether or not to say what else is on his mind. "You know, the doctor said you'll need a couple of weeks to a month of bed rest, which means there's no way you're going to be able to do *Fifth of July.*"

Marc holds up two fingers. "Two weeks...just right."

"It's true there are two weeks left to opening night," Baxter agrees. "But listen to you. You can't say four words at a stretch. How are you going to rehearse? Even if they recast you as Ken Talley so you could go around in forearm crutches, I don't see how it's going to be possible."

"It will."

Marc hears Baxter cross the hardwood to the bathroom. It's obvious from the sound that the man is walking on his tiptoes rather than on the massive soles of his platform shoes. Still, the sound seems deafening. The squeak of the medicine cabinet door is the same, and also the rattling of pills, as Baxter busies himself with putting bottles onto shelves. Alphabetically, Marc guesses. Bored, he looks around the room, from the window beside the bed to the dresser in the corner to the doorjamb and back again, everything within his field of vision. He is about to close his eyes when movement pulls his gaze back toward the corner. He finds Freddie Mercury leaning against the dresser, his arms folded across his chest, his left leg crossed over his right. He is rocking several of his classic looks at once: the motorcycle-cop moustache and leather jacket of his latter days as well as the shag haircut and spandex bodysuit that made him infamous. His form is framed by luminescent white light. It's only after several seconds that it dawns on Marc that it isn't light after all, but the glowing feathers of an enormous pair of angel wings.

"Oh, *shit.*"

"Everything okay?" Baxter calls.

Thinking that if the other will come back into the room the singer—who he assumes is there to escort him to gay heaven—will vanish, Marc raises his voice as best he can. "C'mere!"

"Just a sec—"

"*Now!*"

"All right, all right. Don't get your panties in a wad, I'm coming already." Baxter's voice grows louder as he nears the doorway. "And don't go taking that the wrong—" He halts, and Marc feels the energy of the room shift. *This is really happening*, he thinks, panicking. Then another thought occurs to him. *Or maybe none of it is real. What if Baxter isn't really here? What if I'm still in the tub?* He hadn't tried to slash his wrists, just scratched them deep enough to draw tiny pinpricks of blood, and he hadn't cut down the vein but crossways. Still, just before climbing into the tub he'd coughed up blood, and when the water reached chest-height he'd felt something deflate, and breathing became a chore. But the pill he found in a desk drawer, and opened, and snorted was already taking effect, and he'd been unable to either lift himself out of the water or catch the drain pull chain with his toes. *What if*, he thinks, *Freddie really is the Angel of Death? What if I'm still in the tub and I just died?* The only hope is Baxter. He looks right and sees him standing ramrod straight, shoulders back, making full use of his platform-shoe-enhanced height. He holds his cobra-headed walking stick at an angle across his body, ready to strike. "Who are you and how did you get in here?"

Whaaat? Baxter doesn't recognize Freddie? Perplexed, Marc turns back to the stranger and gets a shock: it is no longer anyone he recognizes. The man in the doorway is a stranger with Freddie-like attributes—high cheekbones, medium-length jet black hair, and a thick moustache which balances a slight overbite and a nose that's too large for his face. His skin is a hue magazines love to call "café au lait" and his eyes are almond-shaped, but his irises are bright blue.

"Don't you know who I am?" the stranger asks Baxter. Also unlike Freddie, he doesn't lisp, and has a pronounced Middle Eastern accent. "I know who you are."

"You're in *my* house."

The man raises one brow, and his lips purse in obvious amusement. Only when he uncrosses his legs and pushes off from the dresser he is leaned against does Marc notice he is wearing white slacks and a black button-front silk shirt.

"It's in your name, but it isn't yours, yes? It's his, and he is mine. Which means…."

Baxter gasps. A loud clattering causes Marc to start, and sends his pulse skyrocketing. He realizes Baxter dropped his walking stick. A clomp-clomping tells him Baxter is charging the man. He thinks he means to push him over the railing, but he runs right past him.

"Is he here?" Baxter shrieks. "Ehrichto? Ehrichto?"

Man, I am tripping hard, Marc thinks.

"Well, that answers one question," the stranger deadpans. "This broken thing in your bed is not meant for him."

Heels on hardwood again, as Baxter re-enters the room. "You're Victor Dorjan." He pauses. "Why are you here? Where is he? Is he back?"

Wait, Baxter knows Ehrichto? Holy shit.

"Those are all good questions," the intruder, Victor Dorjan, says. "But you should be asking what took me so long."

Baxter takes a half-step back, and the expression on his face changes from indignation to—Marc is astonished to see it—terror. He can't recall ever having seen Baxter look so afraid before. Sad, plenty of times, but never terrified. "I don't know what you mean."

"It's really too bad I had to keep it from him. It's been such an effort on your part, I know." Baxter makes a noise like being punched in the gut, and staggers back another step. The stranger seems unfazed. "Good thing I'm his lawyer as well as his lover and—" He cuts his eyes sideways, regarding Marc—"other things."

What the hell is Ehrichto doing running after Michael Ferguson if he's got that at home?

"You...you kep' it from him?" Baxter asks. Marc's ear catches the dropped 't', the same lazy pronunciation for 'kept' that Lloyd Ferguson and half the rest of the local citizenry use. "He doesn't know about any of it?" Baxter asks. "Nothing? Not the house? Julia? The bothy?"

"Now he does. Despite my best efforts he ran back here chasing ghosts, and found one."

What I'm seeking—what I've always been seeking—is uisce beatha, the Water of Life, Marc recalls Ehrichto saying after the dinner. *I've just found it again, after far too long; I can't waste time here with you.*

"Are you saying he is here?" Baxter asks. "Where? I have to see him. Please, I have to speak to him." He sways unsteadily. Marc wonders if it's just because his cane is still on the floor, or if he is getting ready to pass out from the shock.

"He's next door, in the house he grew up in. He spent last night there with someone he believes is Patrick Conway."

Uh, oh, someone in continuity is gonna get fired, Marc thinks. Concentrating hard in order to get his mouth to work, he manages to say, "Not Patrick. Michael."

Baxter steps to beside the bed. Marc is surprised to find he is now wearing a gray wool fedora and his silk scarf has been replaced by a knitted version, which is knotted stylishly about his neck. He opens his mouth to speak, but like in those old chop-saki flicks, the audio comes late. First, his lips move, then his voice says, "What did you say? Wake up. You're mumbling."

Marc concentrates hard. "Not. Patrick," he says. "Michael. Conway. Ferguson. He picked him up. Last night. At Julia's dinner."

Baxter sways again, this time right out of the frame of Marc's vision. He hears a sound like someone dropping a fifty-pound sack of potatoes onto the hardwood, but before he can wonder about it he realizes he's walking along a city street again, only this time he's not in seedy, sunny Santa Monica, but Manhattan in winter. The entire scene is rendered in black and white. Someone begins vocalizing very near to him. Marc turns his head left and finds that the someone is Sting. Before he can react, the proprietor of the corner market they are nearing darts out from the door of the shop and drops to all fours. He begins trying to reclaim the potatoes scattered about on the snowy sidewalk, collecting them in his greengrocer's apron. Marc checks the doorway of the shop, and the doorways of the businesses further on, hoping to find Ehrichto in one of them, but he isn't there. Then he sees Baxter, seated on a park bench just a little ways off. He still sports the fedora and scarf but has added a long coat and gloves. It dawns on Marc that they are inside Sting's video for the song "Englishman in New York." He turns to the singer, walking beside him. "You gave him his own video? That's great. He'll never shut up after this."

He cocks his head, to check that Baxter heard.

SIXTEEN

Before he has even shut the front door Lloyd calls out "Michael?" A glance up the stairs reveals that his son's bedroom door is still closed, locked from the inside. He mounts the stairs anyway, grabs the knob, and tries the door.

When he turns around, he sees Julia standing in the conservatory.

"He hasn't called?" Lloyd asks.

"No. But the city did."

Lloyd thinks of the letter he got the day before from the New Orleans-based law firm, which he has not told her about. *They wouldn't call about that on a Sunday.*

"What did they want?"

"It was the impound lot, letting us know they have his car. The man said it looks like it overheated. It was pushed up onto the sidewalk on Broadway."

I don't want to watch the fireworks from my room, Michael had pleaded with him the night before. *You're supposed to see them firsthand.* The idea that Michael managed to make it back to the crowd of half a million people, though, is not a comforting one.

He hurries back down the stairs and makes a beeline for the den. He pulls out the desk chair, drops into it, and shakes the mouse to call the monitor back to life.

"What happened to your hand?"

Lloyd looks down. The knuckles of his right hand are abraded, his fingers a little swollen. "I was in a fight," he says.

"A fight? Good lord. With who?"

"Jon Lewis."

It is not just his imagination. Julia's eyes widen and the tiniest hint of a smile turns up the corners of her mouth. "Well, you came out of it remarkably unscathed."

"I did, didn't I?" He decides not to tell her the boy chose not to fight back.

"That's all you're going to say? You aren't going to tell me why you went looking for him, or anything else that happened?"

Lloyd pulls the folded computer printout from his back pocket and hands it to her. "I got that from Neal Daniels. I thought Jon wrote it, but it turns out one of his sister's friends was the culprit." He turns back to the computer screen. The screensaver has started back up, so he shakes the mouse again, and a deep blue field dotted with icons appears. The crinkle of paper tells him Julia is unfolding the note as he clicks to open the browser. He types in the administrator password and wonders how it is that he's always managed to convince himself before now that it would be an unacceptable violation of his son's privacy to do what he is about to do now. He clicks to log in under Michael's account and types in the admin password again. Julia sets the paper on the desk.

"They posted that on the Internet," Lloyd tells her. "Danielle swears they took it down the next day, and who knows whether they really did or not. But you know how they're always saying nothing ever really goes away once you put it out there."

"What are you doing?"

"I want to see if he's getting bombarded with hate mail. If he is, we're canceling this account."

"'Hate mail'?"

"Exactly." He positions the cursor and clicks to open his son's email program.

From	Subject	Date
JoinMe	Re: I am Mike	04/18/99
Mutual Jo	Just wanna	04/18/99
HOTNHORNY THICKNHARD	Drain it NOW!	04/18/99
Toys4Bois	Re: I am Mike	04/18/99
Five Star Meal	Let me feed you	04/18/99

"That's lovely," Julia says. It feels very strange to look at this sort of thing with her present. Hand shaking, Lloyd moves the cursor again, and clicks to view the contents of the sent mail folder. It takes him a moment to realize that the most recent post is almost a year out of date, and that all of them, save one, is addressed to "LivingDeadGrrl6," Danielle Lewis's internet handle. The other was sent to her brother, whose email name is "Str8Edge4Life." That one is dated a week after their friendship-ending fight. He clicks to open it. It reads simply,

Go to hell.

He feels proud of his boy, and of himself, too, for having gone to the coffeehouse and decked the little bastard, for having told the lot of them the very same thing Michael did, via cyberspace.

Julia shifts her weight, and rests one hip against the edge of the desk. "Have you ever stopped to consider, Lloyd, that maybe they were doing him a favor?"

All the breath goes out of him. "You're not seriously proposing, are you," he asks, "that having that cretin crack his skull open was good? Or that their posting this note and making his life a living hell for what—a year—was a boon?"

"Well, it went too far, obviously, but yes, I think they were trying to teach him a lesson."

He blinks. Pain flares in his temples. "What lesson would that be?"

"That that sort of behavior is unacceptable."

In spite of the pain it causes, Lloyd slams his hand on the desktop. "The only unacceptable behavior is what they did to him! They terrorized him, Julia! He's been in a living hell!"

Julia grabs the mouse and clicks the back button once, twice, until the inbox is displayed. Then she clicks on one of the unopened emails. The picture that pops onto the screen causes Lloyd to lurch backward. It depicts an officer leaning against a police car with his fly open, while a man made up to look like a teenager in a backward ball cap, t-shirt and torn jeans kneels on the asphalt in front of him.

"What about that behavior, Lloyd?" Julia asks. "Are you okay with that?" Before he can reply she clicks to close the image and slides the cursor to open another one.

"Stop."

She ignores him and clicks again. The picture that leaps onto the screen this time is of a man spread-eagled on a skylight, naked but for a necktie and glasses. A second man, wearing only a yellow hard hat and boots, stands behind him. Lloyd stares at the image for several seconds, as his brain tries to make sense of the image, to resolve why it is that he cannot see the lower half of the construction worker's right arm. And then he understands.

Without consciously deciding to do so he lashes out, shoves the monitor hard enough to send it over the side of the desk. It jerks when the cord goes taught, hovers in mid-air for a split second, before the plug pulls free from the wall and the unit crashes to the floor. There's a loud pop as the interior tubes shatter, followed by a burning plastic smell.

"I'll take that as a no," Julia says. She circles behind him, steps over fragments of the broken casing, and disappears into the hallway leading to the bedroom.

"You're certain you're all right?" Victor Dorjan asks after Baxter is back on his feet.

"I'm fine," Baxter says. "Where is he? I want to see him."

"Not surprisingly, I knew this," the man says. "I'm sorry but that's not possible right now. I told you, he's busy."

"Getting busy," Marc pipes up behind them. Baxter opens his mouth to respond, but a voice from the parlor below interrupts him.

"Uncle Baxter?"

Despite the fact that so many years have passed and the voice addressing him is deep, unmistakably that of an adult, when Baxter looks over the banister at the room below, he expects to find a seven-year-old little boy. It confuses him to see, instead, a man of twenty-five, standing near the royal-purple fainting couch in the parlor.

Intellectually, Baxter knows that the toffee-glazed skin, epicanthic folds over the eyes, and ruler-straight burnt-umber hair can belong to no one else.

Still, it's too incredible. "You're not…you can't be Wren, can you?" he asks.

The familiar stranger nods.

"But," Baxter holds out his left hand, palm toward the floor of the stair landing, waist high. "You were…"

An awful, sickening thought seizes hold of him then, one he has never before allowed admittance to his conscious mind. He wonders if Ehrichto and Nick are also mortal, after all, not vampires at all but a pair of ordinary joes like himself. The idea that in the eighteen years since he last saw them they may have grown fat and wrinkled, with strands of silver running through their hair, similar to his own—or even no hair at all—is too terrible to contemplate. He forces the notion back out of his mind.

Wren looks as every bit as queasy as Baxter feels. "What *happened* to you?" he asks, aghast. Then he turns and looks to his left, to an area of the room not visible from the stair landing. "Dad? What happened to him?"

A miracle steps into view: Nick, looking gaunt and distinctly unwell but no older, really, than he did the last time Baxter saw him. His forehead is not lined; his wiry build has not been desecrated by a paunch; his hair is still full, still hanging well past his shoulders, though it lacks the luster Baxter remembers. When Nick spies Baxter a broad Cheshire cat grin breaks out across his face, but no crow's feet mark the corners of his eyes. "Hey, Richard," he says. "Been a damned long time."

No shit.

Wren stops waiting for his father to answer his question. "*Why* do you look so different?" he asks Baxter.

"It's been eighteen years. People change." He doesn't mean to, but he puts extra emphasis on the word "people."

Beside him, Dorjan steps forward and leans over the railing. "This," he says to Nick, "is why you don't raise children without exposure to mortal kind."

He lowers his volume and, without turning his head, addresses Baxter. "He swore to me that he never told you. He said you've simply always known."

It's very nearly the truth. From the first moment their eyes met, Baxter regarded Ehrichto as a god among men.

He can't say why the notion took hold that there was something more than human about him, but every day brought new indications that he was correct. Ehrichto never ate, unless whisky and cigars counted as food; he could go from pleasantly drunk to stone-cold sober in the blink of an eye; he grew restless and irritable but never tired and lay down for only a few hours each day, always when the sun was highest in the sky. Finally, there was the assignment he'd given Baxter, right after he bought the house on Belgravia. He'd asked him to befriend the old woman living in the once stately Italianate mansion next door, and convince her to let him bring in workman to save it from certain ruin.

The dwelling turned out to be a living museum, a prop man's dream. Most things in it had been untouched for decades except by dust, water from a multitude of leaks, and the mold slowly overtaking everything. The place fascinated Baxter even before he noticed that one of the figures in the photos on the front parlor mantle looked remarkably like his new friend, Matteo Bianchi, the alias Ehrichto was using in those early days. It turned out the figure in the photo was the old woman's brother Michelangelo, who'd died during the influenza epidemic of 1917 while stationed at Camp Taylor, but Baxter took note that more than one of the photos was not centered, in a day and age when photos were rare and careful things. Further examination revealed, always, the hand or toe of someone who'd been indelicately cropped from the shot. When pressed the woman—Ysabella Salvatolle—revealed she'd had another brother. When asked his name, though, she'd spat on the hardwood and said only "finocchio," the Italian slur for homosexual.

Even with all of that, he'd never asked directly, and Ehrichto had never volunteered the information. They simply looked at one another, and silently acknowledged that they both knew the truth of the situation.

They'd met in 1978, in the bathroom of the nightclub the Downtowner, on the site of what was now the Connection nightclub complex. Conscious of no longer being in Manhattan, where people cut their coke right on the bar, Baxter had been seeking the privacy of a stall to do a couple of lines of blow. The last thing he needed was to get arrested.

The first stall was in use. The sound of fabric rustling and low moaning, just discernible over the thump-thumping of the bass line pumping through the bar, as well as the fact that two sets of feet were visible beneath the door, told him the men inside had come to the bathroom seeking privacy for a different purpose. It was yet another quaint small-town tradition with which the denizens of the Big Apple had all but dispensed, in favor of screwing in the dimly lit corners of bars, or wide-open dungeon-themed back rooms, or shower rooms, or bath houses.

Baxter tried to give the bucolic couple space, but that was easier said than done. Someone had been sick in and on and around the toilet in the far stall, so he'd headed back to the middle one. Just before he reached it the door of the first stall swung inward and the handsomest man he'd ever seen emerged.

Conscious of a hierarchy that put movie-star types like the stranger at the top and men like himself nearer the bottom, Baxter dropped his gaze, and saw that the back of one of the stranger's hands was smeared with fresh blood.

He looked up again and spied dark flecks on the man's shirt. Though they might easily have been another fluid, and no person in their right mind would have made the leap he did, he'd lifted his gaze higher still, to search the corners of the man's mouth, but found them clean. Scanning upward again, he found himself locked in a penetrating gaze.

Coming out of the memory, Baxter finds himself fixated once more, this time by the sight of Dorjan's gleaming fangs. He realizes that he's never seen Ehrichto's—or later, Nick's—bared fangs. Yet somehow he'd known exactly what it was he was looking at, that night in the men's room of the Downtowner. Call it instinct, or maybe radar; he'd known beyond a shadow of a doubt just what Ehrichto was, and that he would do anything for him.

"A Renfield," Dorjan says. "And here I thought Bram Stoker made you up."

Baxter steps beside him and leans his elbows on the railing, too. Peering down at Nick, he says "I know exactly how you feel."

"WHAT ARE YOU staring at?" Michael asks. "Bug doing the backstroke?"

Ehrichto looks up and realizes he has been standing in the doorway, dumbly staring at the water glass in his hand for who-knows-how-long. It's half-filled with red wine, exactly the same manner in which his father always drank the stuff, glass after glass, from the moment he walked through the door after work until he'd finished his last cigar of the day and was heading off to bed.

Ehrichto hadn't stopped long enough last night to think about it, of course, but the entire experience of being back in the house feels odd to him, though not nearly as odd as it felt in 1978, when he drove into town from Lexington on a break from settling an old score. Under the guise of Matteo Bianchi he'd gotten a job as a bookkeeper for Hunt and James Ferguson, in order to frame the latter for embezzlement and finally get some measure of revenge.

It was strange walking back into the house after so many years. After buying the much larger house beside it he'd sent Baxter and four-year-old Wren next door as scouts, instructing Baxter to befriend his sister Ysabella, then in her mid-seventies. Though he hadn't outwardly aged in four decades, when he finally did walk back through the door their father had thrown him out of Ysabella hadn't for one instant been fooled, and time hadn't softened her heart toward him at all. She didn't buy the story that he was his own grandson. Right off the bat she'd called him the same names their father had so many years earlier, and crossed herself, though the latter surely was owed to the fact that he still looked thirty-five.

He feels a hand on his elbow. "Are you okay?" Michael asks.

"I'm fine," Ehrichto assures him. "There are just a lot of memories."

He knows he keeps getting lost in them, and that's rude, but he can't help it. The house is full of triggers. Little movies keep playing in his mind. The worst—or best—happened when he walked into the kitchen looking for glassware. He'd been hit with a flood of wonderful images then, memories of his mother moving about the room as she cooked, the sun streaming through the window over her shoulder. What aromas used to waft from the oven, he'd recalled, what flavors. He still misses the flavors and smells of his childhood, as well as the sound of her laughter, and her smile. He was her baby, and he'd stayed that way, because Francesco, who should have been four years his junior, was stillborn, and when he was eight his mother and the last baby, the one that followed Francesco, died together during labor. Reeling from the shock, Ehrichto's father had refused to give the baby a name, allowing a headstone to be placed on the grave that reads "Baby Boy Salvatolle," a thing which bothers Ehrichto on several levels to this day.

Aside from those two horrific events his memories of his mother are all good ones, great ones. He wonders how different his life would've been if she'd lived, if there'd been another or even two other boys to carry on the Salvatolle name after Michelangelo died. He wonders how it would have all turned out if he, rather than Ysabella, had stayed in the house to care for their aging father, if he'd been allowed to be the bachelor uncle instead of forcing her to be the spinster aunt? He thinks he could easily have resigned himself to that fate.

"You're not thinking about him, are you?" Michael asks.

Him who? Ehrichto wonders. Then he realizes the younger man means Patrick. "No," he says, astonished to realize it's true. Because he inhabits a body so similar in appearance, every few minutes the stranger—*Michael,* he thinks—does something physically reminiscent of Patrick that causes his heart to leap in his chest. But he also, truth be told, does many more things that aren't at all like him. He has his own expressions, a different speech pattern, a unique laugh. "No, I was thinking of the song," Ehrichto says, lowering his glass so that Michael can see the bit of sunlight dancing on the liquid's surface. "See? Not quite a rainbow, but it still made me think of it."

"Which song?"

"'I'm Beginning to See the Light,'" Ehrichto says, by his exasperated tone implying *Which one do you think?* "The Kitty Kallen version, of course. The others are good, but—" He stops when he sees the lost expression on the young man's face. "You don't know it?"

Michael shakes his head.

Sometimes the fact that he isn't Patrick is so clear it borders on startling. Earlier, he'd asked to use the restroom; a few minutes later Ehrichto heard the water running and, over it, little exclamations of pain. When he investigated, he'd found the boy trying to wash his hands by running them first under the hot tap and then the cold, back and forth. "How are you supposed to use a sink like this?" he complained. It had practically blown his mind when Ehrichto stoppered the sink, half-filled the basin with tepid water, and dipped his hands to wash them. "You've never seen one like this before? I thought you'd been in a lot of these houses?" Ehrichto asked, because Michael had mentioned being dragged through many of the surrounding homes by Julia. Michael explained that the other houses had been retrofitted with a pipe that brought the hot and cold streams together. For a moment the episode was comical; ultimately, though, it drove home the fact that, for all intents and purposes, they were from different worlds.

And that was even leaving out the fact that Ehrichto was no longer human, which of course he couldn't reveal, though Michael would never believe it if he could. *What was I thinking when I let him back in here?* he wonders. *Why am I letting him stay and wander around, getting more and more attached? Granted, my delivery yesterday could have been better, but wasn't it kinder to be honest? Isn't it cruel to drag it out?* He braces himself for the terrible scene he's about to inspire. "I like you," he says. "I do. But this won't work."

The grip on his arm tightens. "Because I don't know one song? So play it for me. I love music. Let me hear it."

"That's not the point. You're seventeen, and—"

"And a half."

Ehrichto smiles. "Yes, well, that makes all the difference, doesn't it? Listen to me. I'm…older." He imagines being arrested, a fate like Dorjan's: years trapped in a prison cell, starving. He feels grateful, for a moment, that at least it would be due to the age discrepancy, and not for the simple fact of being a male with another male.

"I don't care how old you are," Michael says.

Ehrichto pulls his arm away. "It's not enough."

"I think I'm in love with you."

"We don't know one another."

Even as he's saying it, Ehrichto sees the hole in his argument. He'd fallen in love with Patrick the moment he rounded the corner of Fifth and Main and saw him up on a makeshift stage for a Derby promotion. Dressed in bright blue jockey silks that matched his eyes, and riding a barrel mount as if it were a thoroughbred stallion, he'd held the assembled crowd in thrall with his smooth salesman's patter. By the third and final day of the promotion, Ehrichto knew Patrick's sales pitch by heart. He'd said it along with him, under his breath, at the back of the crowd.

"Tell me what you want," Michael says. "Tell me and I'll make it happen."

Ehrichto scowls. "It isn't about what I want. It's about what I don't."

"Fine, what *don't* you want?" Ehrichto doesn't answer, and Michael begins to beg. "Just tell me, please!"

"I don't want to be someone's dirty little secret. I've been that before. I won't be it again." He stops Michael from turning away by grabbing hold of his shoulder. "If the bell rang right now and it was your father at the door, what would you do?"

Michael recoils.

"That's what I thought. You wouldn't tell him about us, about me, and what we did together last night. You'd do the same thing everyone else does—lie about all of it, or avoid the topic. You wouldn't tell him what you just told me, that you think you're in love with me. You couldn't." All his anger vanishes and Ehrichto feels empty. "I'll never have that, and it's all I've ever wanted."

He expects the young man to apologize, and begin making excuses, but Michael says, "Yes, you will. I'll tell him."

Ehrichto feels real panic then. He doesn't want to be the cause of the other's undoing. "No, don't," he says. "It will destroy everything for you."

"There isn't anything else."

"Of course there is. You can be happy, and you should be."

"Not without you." Michael steps closer, grasps the back of Ehrichto's neck, and pulls him down into a kiss.

Ehrichto likes kissing this boy, likes believing they can stay like this forever, hidden away from the world, and somehow it will all work out. He likes daydreaming that he will find a way to get out of the promise he made to Dorjan, and won't have to return to the kel'an. But thinking of them is like a splash of cold water. Nick. Wren. He'd promised Wren he would be back soon.

He pulls back from Michael, breaks their kiss, but Michael refuses to release him. Ehrichto mutters, "You have to let me go." He pushes the boy away.

"You don't want us to be together?"

He does. Already, Ehrichto misses his touch. "It's complicated."

"What? You have a boyfriend?"

Is it kinder to let him believe it? Ehrichto wonders. "I wouldn't call it that."

Michael looks pained, but rallies. "Is he the one I remind you of?"

"What? No. That was…he was…a very long time ago."

"Is he your age, this not-boyfriend?"

"Older."

"You're not in love with him," Michael says. He sounds very certain. "You're not happy with him. If you were you wouldn't have just said what you did, all that stuff about what you don't want. He doesn't treat you like his 'dirty little secret'?"

"No." *He makes me feel like one of a million, instead of one in a million.*

"Okay, but you just said you want to be with someone who isn't afraid to let other people know what you are. And people only *want* things they don't *have*."

That's true, but moot. "I can't leave him. I'm sorry."

"Can I use your phone?"

"I'll drive you home."

"I'm not calling for a ride," Michael says, glaring at him. Puzzled, Ehrichto directs him to the phone bench at the far end of the hall. "It's rotary dial. You have to put your finger in the—"

Michael stops him with another withering stare. "I know."

"Hey, it's me." Michael's speaking at an outsized volume, obviously so that Ehrichto will be able to hear. "Listen, you know the guy from dinner, Ehrichto—" Something the person on the other end of the line says makes him pause. "What? Why would you think that? I'm fine. I'm more than—" He's interrupted again, and this time, the pause seems to suck all the air from the room. "Oh my god. Okay. I'll be right there!" He half places, half drops the receiver back into its cradle and turns toward Ehrichto. What little color he had has been drained from his face by bad news. "I have to go home," he says. "There was a fire. Our house burned down this morning."

IT WAS MOST likely a faux pas to drive Michael all the way back to the scene, but the girl from dinner, Alyssa, had told him on the phone that his father wouldn't leave the site, despite his having run up the stairs during the conflagration and thrown his body against the bedroom door until the frame cracked and the lock gave way, just to make sure that he wasn't inside. He'd looked under the bed and in the armoire and the built-in closet, too, before he was convinced; then he'd run down the bridge-like hallway to the guest suite on the far side of the house. Ehrichto had seen for himself, just that morning, while spying on the house from the yard, that there was no stair connecting those rooms to the main floor, and Michael reiterated the point. In hindsight it was a really stupid, not fire-safe design. Ehrichto wondered how anyone had been allowed to build such a thing.

He stopped a good distance from the Corvette, which was parked haphazardly in the gravel right after the cross street of the ankh-shaped roadway. He'd ventured into the intersection only because he expected there to still be a host of emergency vehicles crowding the cul-de-sac, blocking his car from view, expected lots of flashing lights, and shouting, and general confusion, but it was all over by the time the Porsche rolled up. The pavement was still soaked and the spot where the house once stood was blackened, charred, with what amounted to little more than kindling poking up here and there. Lloyd Ferguson was seated atop the grassy mound at the heart of the turnabout, looking—well, like a man who'd just been through a fire.

Ordinarily, one would go over to a person in such a state and express sympathy and offer assistance, but given the greater circumstance the standard rules didn't seem to apply. It was bad enough Michael had been AWOL for nearly twenty four hours, and that he'd pulled up to the scene in Ehrichto's car. If Ehrichto got out too it would only drive home the point that they'd been together, and that seemed bad form.

It was cathartic for him, though, to see the man's expression go from confusion to surprise and then relief and elation. Ehrichto got choked up when Lloyd Ferguson leapt to his feet, threw his arms around his son, and tears began running down his soot-covered cheeks, leaving clean streaks in their wake.

He'd felt like an intruder, watching them, so he'd thrown the Porsche in reverse and backed away from the scene. Now he's speeding around the curves of the hill they live on—another stupid design, he thinks, imagining a ladder truck trying to navigate this narrow corkscrewed two-lane road. It's no problem for the Porsche, of course, is even somewhat enjoyable, and he increases speed as he goes. He's going so fast that when it registers that someone is standing in the road there's no time to simply apply the brakes. He swerves left toward the sheer rock face, but there isn't enough room, so he veers right, only to find the same problem. Finally, out of desperation, he spins the wheel, and prays he doesn't end up too far in either direction.

The car has hardly come to a stop when Dorjan appears in the driver's side window.

"I hope you don't always drive in such a manner," he says, loud enough to be heard through the glass and over the idling engine. He walks around to the passenger's side and climbs in. "This is an old joke, yes? You went out for a pack of cigarettes and got lost?"

"That's just an expression," Ehrichto says. "And I was on my way back."

"An idiom," Dorjan says. At first Ehrichto thinks he meant to say "idiot," as in "Do you think I am such an idiot that I would believe that?" but he follows it with "Blowing smoke," and Ehrichto knows perfectly well what he means: *I don't need you to tell me what I mean to say, and I understand that you're lying to my face.*

A hand clamped at the back of his neck pulls him over the center console and practically into Dorjan's lap. Their mouths meet and their teeth clash, knocking together like ram horns. Part of Ehrichto is turned on by the idea of having no choice, but deeper down he knows this isn't what or who he wants. His left hand finds purchase on the passenger's door as his right locates the seat back. He pushes away.

"No," he says. "I can't do this. I'm sorry."

"You made a promise, memmi."

"I know, and I shouldn't have. It's not what I want. I'm not like you."

"What about your Nick?"

Nick. "How is he?"

"You should be asking how he will be if you walk away from me."

It's an empty threat, and Ehrichto knows it. He's always known. The code in his sire's DNA that drove him to become a doctor is greater than that which made him a vampire. The kel'an operates under only one commandment, to never take a life. Dorjan may not like Nick much, may wish Ehrichto hadn't turned him, but he will never let him go to his final death if he can help it. The threat is just a game they play, an imaginary line drawn in the sand that Dorjan tries through various methods to get Ehrichto to cross. He went too far once, after misreading the signals his progeny was sending. By first physical force and then emotional coercion he'd brought Philip into their bed. All the apologies in the world couldn't make things right between them after that, but time has at least smoothed the rift.

"I've done all I can to help him," Ehrichto says. "Are *you* going to let him perish?"

"You know the answer already."

"Yes. So how is he?"

"Much better. Not perfect, but that's not a thing I can control. You are drawn to not perfect, I think." Before Ehrichto can object, Dorjan says "Tell me about this young man. Michael?"

"Fine, but we should get out of the middle of the road first." Ehrichto jockeys the car forward and back until it's once more in the correct lane. "All right," he says as they start down the hill. "So, here's what's been going on."

"Oh, thank god," Michael's dad says over and over, in between burbles of relieved laughter and bursts of tears. "Thank god. Thank god, you're safe." He's clutching Michael so tightly that it's beginning to be hard for him to get a breath.

Then the shock of it all begins wearing off, and Michael starts to cry, too.

The glimpse he got of the scene before he was engulfed in his father's arms revealed that the house is simply gone. It looks like an enormous charred playpen, a perimeter of black sticks surrounding a pile of weird charcoal, such a foreign sight that he couldn't muster up any emotion for it, but now it's sinking in: their house is gone. Everything in it is gone. All of his clothes. The bowl of stone spheres. The ugly sideboard covered with bits of mirror. Their computers, though that thought is a relief.

As terrible as it is, he'd kind of like to look at the destruction some more.

He tries to pull away to do so, but his father's hold on him is too tight. "Dad," Michael gasps. "I'm okay, all right? I'm here. I'm fine. Calm down." He pushes back again. This time, the arms wrapped around him oblige and he is released.

His father's forehead, cheeks and chin are red, like cooked lobster or a really, really bad sunburn. His hair and clothes are singed in spots and covered in soot. In between sobs he sputters and coughs. Alyssa had said he'd run all through the house, not willing to assume Michael wasn't there. Michael tries to picture the rooms engulfed in flame. He looks over at the site, but it isn't much help. He thinks of the mailman, and wonders if his dad tossed a cigar into the mulch. He can see him doing it just to show the guy up.

"What happened?"

"Say again?" His dad points to the side of his head. "Speak up! My ears are ringing! Fire is loud!"

Michael supposes it makes sense. A roaring fire, and all that. "*How did it start?*"

"In a wall socket behind the bookshelves in the den," his dad shouts. "Did you know they weren't really books?"

Michael had known that. Shortly after they moved in, after he'd noticed that the titles were grouped by color and height, so that from a distance the den looked like a section of a law library, he'd discovered that the books higher than head level all had really odd titles, stuff like *Paraguayan Fly Fishing Techniques*. The most surprising thing, though, was that those titles were also nothing but spines glued to lightweight boards, something he found out when, bored beyond reason, he tried to take down *Diseases of the Eye*. "Really?" he says. "That's weird."

"There's also no hydrant." His dad gestures to indicate the cul-de-sac and Michael turns to look. Sure enough, there isn't one, something he'd never noticed before. "There's one in Alyssa's subdivision, but they had to string several hoses together to make it reach," his father explains. "Which took time and wasn't as powerful."

"Sure." Michael notices his father is trembling, and then that his own arms are covered in goosebumps. While it isn't nearly as cold as yesterday, it's by no means warm. "Hey," he says. "What are we standing here for?"

His father laughs, and wipes his nose on his shirt sleeve. "I don't know. It's not like we can go in."

"Are we're gonna stay at Grandpa's?" Michael asks. It's the only logical solution, because his father's family lives three hours east, practically in West Virginia. The only other option he can think of would be crashing at the house his mother's organization uses for their offices. That, he realizes, would be great, because it's right around the corner from Ehrichto's house.

"Yes," his father says, nodding. He holds out the keys to the Corvette. "I think you should drive."

"Cool." Michael takes the keys and starts for the car, but before he's taken two steps he feels his father catch hold of his arm, and he knows, instantly, what's coming next.

"Wait. Before we go. Are you...are you okay?"

Michael hasn't turned around. He shrugs, and then nods.

His father tugs on his arm, trying to turn him around. "I'm not talking about the house."

Michael forces himself to turn around and look his father in the eye. "I know." He nods again. "I'm okay." The exchange is too awkward; he decides a little bit of untruth is okay in this instance. "We just talked."

"What?"

"Talked," Michael says. "We just talked!"

"Oh. Good." His father lets out the breath he was holding, and looks as if a weight has been lifted from his chest. Concurrently, Michael feels that weight settle into the pit of his own stomach. As if he sees it happening, his father straightens up. "I don't mean 'oh, good' as in...well, what I mean is...." He puts a hand to his forehead, but winces and takes it away again. Michael guesses that, just as with a traditional sunburn, his reddened skin hurts. "What I mean is I'm not ready to deal with that much yet."

Michael looks at the ground. His father squeezes his arm, which causes him to look up again.

"But you are—" he swallows hard—"gay, aren't you?"

Michael considers lying but nods instead. "Yeah."

"It doesn't change how I feel about you."

"I know." But he hadn't.

"You can talk to me. I promise I won't go crazy like I did with the whole smoking thing. I may not know what to say immediately, but I'll listen. I love you more than anything in the world."

Michael glances at the Corvette. "I love you, too."

"Okay, then," his dad says. "Man, it's freezing out here. Let's get in the car."

THE MEETING CONVENES in Baxter's bedroom. Dorjan introduces the vampires, though he doesn't say that's what they are in front of Marc. Baxter recognizes several of their names as making up the law firm of Cozart, Dorjan and Garrett, LLC. All the paperwork Baxter has seen for the firm over the years has listed their given names as Glenn Cozart, Victor Dorjan, and William Garrett, but Dorjan states his colleague

Cozart's name as André, his own as Kabil, and Garrett's as Willem. The last is every bit as blond as that name would imply and very stylishly dressed, while André Cozart looks to be of either of Hungarian or Czech background. He has flame-red hair and the monstrously broad sort of jaw beloved by Hollywood casting directors and modeling agencies.

The only vampire whose name Baxter doesn't recognize is younger than the rest, in his early twenties like Marc, not close to thirty, as the others all appear to be. He also is obviously of some Latin extraction. His coloring is not dissimilar to Ehrichto's. His name is Coronel Figueredo.

Brunet, blond, redheaded. Baxter looks at Dorjan. "A man for all seasons?"

"Wouldn't you, if our roles were reversed?" He smiles, though not broadly enough to show his teeth. "You ought to sit down, Richard. I don't want a repeat of this morning."

Baxter gives an indignant sniff. "There won't be one."

"I know, because you're going to sit down." The man looks at André and then points to the chair in the far corner. "Get that and bring it over here."

Marc pats the edge of the bed. "Sit here. I won't bite."

"We will," Willem Garrett says. He climbs into the bed beside Marc and leans over him. "Do you like being bitten?"

Baxter braces himself for the display he knows is imminent. This is Marc's forte, after all. Emotionally, he's still twelve; will likely always be twelve. Baxter says to Dorjan, "Marc isn't like you and me."

"It would seem no one is."

"He's broken."

"We can fix that," André Cozart says, as he deposits the chair beside Baxter.

"I'm not talking about his physical wounds." Baxter locks his gaze with Dorjan's and drops his volume to a whisper. "I mean emotionally, he's broken."

"Mmmm, aren't we all?" Willem asks. He drapes an arm around Marc's shoulders.

For his part, Marc looks confused. "Aren't what? What did Baxter—" He pauses for breath. "...say about me?"

Willem ignores him. He pulls Marc closer. "Did something bad happen to you? You can tell Uncle Willem all about it. Or better yet, why don't you show me?"

"This isn't healthy," Baxter says to Dorjan. "Please, you don't know him like I do. He's traumatized. He doesn't act of his own volition, only reacts, to things that happened to him when he was a child."

"Willem, that's enough," Dorjan says. "Leave him alone."

"But—"

"You heard what I said. That's Richard's house. We don't enter without his permission."

Baxter glances over in time to see the look that flashes in Marc's eyes.

"That's...not what I meant."

Dorjan raises one brow. "No?"

"I have an idea," André Cozart says. "Why don't we concentrate on why you called a meeting that includes the two of them." He cuts his eyes right and left, indicating the two mortals in the room.

"Because it mostly involves them," Dorjan says. He gestures at the chair. "Sit, Richard."

"I'm—"

Dorjan draws his hands into fists. "You serve at my pleasure, and right now it would please me if you sat down."

Baxter sits.

"These two," Dorjan points from Baxter to Marc, "have gotten us into some legal hot water. Nothing we can't manage, but the matter will have to be handled with great delicacy."

"What happened?" André asks.

"The house Philip designed burned down this morning."

Baxter is lost. He looks to Marc, but finds he looks the same. He raises a hand, reminiscent of children in school. "I'm sorry. Who's Philip?"

From the doorway, a familiar voice replies, "I am." Jeff steps into view.

Baxter leaps out of the chair, stepping backward until he hits the wall. "I don't understand."

"I'm sorry I had to mislead you. He sent me to see what you were up to," Jeff says. "I needed an in, and it wasn't hard to figure out that what you really wanted was a protégé. Plus, I'm an architect. Playing a wannabe set design student wasn't too much of a stretch.'"

"You *were* an architect," Dorjan corrects. "A century ago. You told me you'd kept pace with it. You said you were capable of pulling this off."

Marc snickers at his choice of words. Dorjan glares at him before casting a glance Baxter's way. "I see now what you mean," he says.

Baxter, though, is much more concerned with Jeff. "Philip, is it," he asks.

"If you want to get technical it's Philippe," Jeff replies. "Philippe Edward Xavier Dundon, seventh bastard son of Bernard Xavier Philippe de Marigny de Mandeville." He steps all the way into the room and takes a bow. "My father was the so-called unbacked mustang they shipped off to London thinking it would calm his pyrotechnic nature. My half-siblings and I are proof of just how erroneous that belief was."

"Sounds like my father," Marc says.

"Does it?" Philippe/Philip/Jeff narrows his eyes. "Was he a French nobleman too? Did he throw lavish parties for visiting dukes and counts, one of them a future king? Did he inherit a plantation at the tender age of fifteen? Did he—" He ducks just in time to miss being clobbered by the vase Baxter snatched from the dresser top and hurled at his head. It hits the door frame and shatters, raining glass shards across the floor. Philippe/Philip/Jeff looks down at the mess, then up at Baxter. "What the hell was that for?"

"For telling me you weren't gay!"

"I was in character! Jeff isn't gay!"

Baxter folds his arms. "How convenient."

"You screwed plenty of assistant designers. What you wanted was a protégé, so I gave you one."

Baxter sees a hurt look cross Marc's face. "Oh, don't even…. You've had everything in this town that moves." He pauses, reconsiders. "Twice."

"But you said he doesn't operate the same way you do," Dorjan says. "He has no volition, isn't that how you termed it? It implies that you do, therefore your trysts are the only ones that matter."

"They would if we were a couple, but we're not," Baxter says, his eyes still locked on Marc's. "We never have been."

"Whose fault?" Marc croaks. He turns and bats his eyes at Willem.

"I've tried."

"Enough!" Dorjan glares at them. "Richard, sit back down. Philip, find a seat. We have serious business to discuss. As I was saying, the house burned down this morning."

Recognition dawns. "The *Fergusons'* house?" Baxter is glad, after all, that he is seated.

"Yes. And now the city is involved. Apparently there are permits missing, and things weren't done to code. The wrong materials were used, there was no hydrant, and on and on. In general the workmanship was... questionable." He turns his gaze on Jeff. Philip. Whoever the hell he is. "And that's a very kind assessment."

"I thought the builders he was paying off to do the job would fix the things I was unfamiliar with," Philip explains.

"You were wrong." Dorjan looks at André and Willem. "On top of everything else, nothing was insured. They made up a dummy insurance policy, purportedly worth one million dollars, from a company that doesn't exist." Philip opens his mouth, but Dorjan cuts him off. "I advise the three of you not to speak again until you're asked to do so. Is that clear?" Philip, Baxter and Marc nod in unison. "Good. Because this would be a very different sort of a meeting if one of the family members or emergency personnel had been killed." He glares at each of them in turn. "Now, here's what we're going to do. The two of you—" he points to Baxter and Marc—"are going to reprise your roles as Angelo de Haven and the insurance agent, bank manager, and whatever other characters you created in order to pull this off, while the rest of—" He stops when Nick appears in the doorway.

"'Scuse me," Nick says, crossing the room. "Pardon me. I'll just be a minute." He slips past Baxter and disappears into the bathroom.

"Who is that?" Marc asks. Seeing Dorjan raise one brow, he back pedals.

"Oh, sorry. Forgot."

It strikes Baxter as odd that Nick and Marc have never met, and stranger still to think that Marc is two years younger than Wren.

The toilet flushes. The bathroom door opens. "Thank you, folks," Nick says. "I'll leave you be." At the doorway he stops and turns back.

"Hey, Richard, where's the nearest bar in here?" He mimes taking a drink.

"One more flight up. On the wall opposite the windows."

"Thanks muchly." Nick disappears around the corner of the doorway and clomps up the stairs to the Lodge.

"As I was saying," Dorjan continues once the racket has stopped. "We are all going to play whatever roles are necessary in order to get the city off our backs, anything it takes to be allowed to rebuild that house the correct way."

"Better than. It was. Before," Marc says, his lack of breath chopping his words into manageable bites. "Stronger. Fast—" He catches Dorjan's scowl and flashes a lopsided grin. "ADHD."

Dorjan clears his throat. "In theory, we have the million dollars of insurance money to make it happen. In reality, we're eating the cost of the rebuild. If we can do it for less, obviously that would be good. But by 'less' I do not mean an outlay of a buck twelve."

"So no Styrofoam crown moulding this time?" Philip asks, before looking at the floor. "Sorry. It's contagious."

Baxter raises an index finger. "Excuse me, I have an important point to make."

Dorjan narrows his eyes. "It had better be."

"We can't rebuild on that site."

"Why not?"

"Because it's on top of the cavern where—"

"No, it's not," Philip says. "The cavern where that happened was across town in Portland. Trust me, when I realized that's what you were up to I made sure of it. I wouldn't let you do that to him."

It dawns on Baxter for the first time that building the house above, and throwing the circuit party in, the place where Patrick died would not only get Ehrichto's attention, but would also cause him great pain. He can't believe that in his desperation to draw the other back he'd overlooked that fact. "Oh, God."

"That knowledge won't leave this room," Dorjan says. "He'll never know what you tried to do. And for that, Richard, you owe me... everything."

Baxter nods.

He jumps when a scream pierces the air, followed by a flurry of footsteps descending the stairs. Wren flies around the corner into the room, looks right at Baxter, and exclaims, "Quick! It's my dad!"

MICHAEL'S GRANDFATHER LIVES on the south end of town just off of Dixie Highway, an area his parents never set foot in if they can help it. Five years ago, after Michael's grandmother died unexpectedly in her sleep, the victim of a ruptured brain aneurysm, he'd sold their two-story brick Cape Cod out by Bowman Field, the house Michael remembers from all the Christmases and Halloweens of his childhood. The neighborhood that house was located in was famous for their holiday displays. The residents went whole hog, and Donal and Jean were no exception. They owned several life-sized animatronic figures—among them a witch bent over a bubbling dry-ice cauldron, a Santa, and an Easter Bunny—but Michael's favorite was always the vampire. Every year they set Count Dracula up in front of the plate-glass window in the living room with a backdrop painted to resemble a crumbling stone wall and a red-tinted floodlight at his feet, so that the little kids rolling past in the backseats of their parents' cars would be sure to get a good look at him.

Michael's parents thought the whole affair was tacky. Michael has always found it impossible to imagine his mother growing up in such a place, with parents who were into restoring muscle cars and going on cross country trips in their Gulfstream RV, folks who didn't see any value in eating dinner at a Michelin-starred restaurant, but loved Shoney's, or ate off paper plates while camped in front of the television. He isn't surprised at all that Julia and his great-grandmother Myrtle became close. Everything he's heard about his grandfather's mother tells him she and his mother—both his parents, really—were cut from the same cloth, a fine linen to his grandparents' flannel-backed vinyl.

As out of place as Lloyd and Julia always seemed in the house near Bowman Field, they are infinitely more so here, in the seven-hundred-square-foot clapboard one-story home Donal purchased after Jean's death. Just having to visit him for a few hours a couple times a year has been painful for them. The thought of all of them living within the tiny space for an extended period boggles Michael's mind.

When he steps through the doorway, he finds his mother seated on the couch, looking angry, and his grandfather camped out in his recliner, staring at the can of Old Milwaukee in his hand. Hearing the door, they both turn. Michael doesn't expect the reaction he gets from his mother, who gasps. Her hand flies to her mouth, and then she's up and across the room, hugging him, before he can process what is happening.

A few seconds later the love-fest is over. "I told you," she says, releasing him and turning to address his father. "I told you he wasn't home." She turns back to Michael. "Where were you, all night long and half the next day?"

"Julia." It's Donal. Michael's grandfather grasps him by the shoulder, turns him around, and pulls him into an embrace. Theirs is not a hugging sort of family. It's the longest hug Michael's had from him since he was maybe seven or eight years old. Finally, Donal steps back, and Michael sees that he still clutches the can of beer in one hand. "You gave all of us a scare."

"I'm sorry."

The man ruffles Michael's curls. "It's all right. You hungry? I can make sandwiches."

"No. Thanks. Maybe later."

They all stand there, at a loss for further topics of conversation, though Michael's mother's expression seems to say *I know exactly where you were. Don't think you're getting away with this.* He notes the items piled up on the end of the couch: his mother's fur coat; three pairs of high-heeled shoes; her jewelry box; and the wooden case containing his great-grandmother's silverware. He looks from the pile of stuff to her, and conveys a silent accusation of his own: *So that's what you did while Dad broke down doors looking for me?* She seems to get the message, and looks away.

BAXTER'S MIND IS consumed with flashes from the past, memories of five year-old Wren pushing his way through the sea of partygoers—a veritable forest of denim- and polyester-clad legs, with lit cigarettes and alcoholic drinks dangling like fruit on low-hanging limbs. Curious and protective, Baxter had trailed him all the way to the house next door, where Ehrichto was hiding out, misanthropic as usual on a party night. Wren burst into tears as he ran up to him. "It's my dad! It's my dad," he'd cried, as Ehrichto, obviously puzzled, scooped him into his arms.

Baxter has never seen Ehrichto transform into a bat or a wolf but that night he became a linebacker, tucking the child under one arm and taking off at a run, superhuman as any other parental type when a child's heart is in danger. The sea had parted for them—and for Baxter, who followed in their wake—until finally they were upstairs in the room Nick had claimed for his own. He'd been half in the bed and half out of it, and his eyes were rolled further back in his head than Baxter knew was possible. Traces of white powder were visible on his nostrils and the back of his left hand. Seeing it, Baxter's whole body had started to shake. On a few occasions back in Manhattan at the clubs people had dropped dead after trying coke for the first time. It was too much for certain hearts. Nick's usual drugs of choice were opiates and alcohol, both downers, but earlier he'd asked what the high from coke was like. He'd said he wanted to try it, and, like a fool, Baxter had indulged him.

Baxter and Ehrichto have never spoken about the night Nick was— Baxter has read up on it since—in a state doctors term "technically but (potentially, anyway) temporarily dead." His lips and nail beds looked cyanotic and he was unresponsive, classic signs of sudden cardiac arrest. Ehrichto thrust Wren into Baxter's arms and ordered him to take the child from the room. Though only five and small for what Baxter considered normal size for that age, owing to his being half-Vietnamese, Wren was hard to contain because he was hysterical. He didn't want to leave his father. It had taken everything Baxter had to get him next door to Ysabella's.

When Baxter, Dorjan and the others reach the Lodge Nick is face down on the Oriental rug, surrounded by five empty pill containers and an equally empty bottle of whisky. Dorjan stoops down and picks up one of the pill bottles. "Who gave him these?"

No one comes forward. After a second, Baxter realizes why. "They came from the bathroom," he says. "He interrupted us and went in there, remember, looking for drugs."

"He flushed the toilet to cover up the sound of taking them from the cabinet," André says.

Baxter feels like a fool for not realizing the obvious: vampires don't use toilets. He figures the others feel the same.

"So we've solved nothing where he is concerned," Dorjan says. "Wonderful." He begins rolling up one of his sleeves. "All right, boys, you know the drill." Baxter, too, starts to unbutton one of his cuffs, but Dorjan shakes his head. "Not you."

"I want to help. I have to help. It's my fault." He doesn't say "again" but feels it hanging in the air between them.

"No, it's not. But more importantly, our blood is different than yours, and yours is spoken for already."

"What?"

"I told Ehrichto to wait in the underlair and I'd send you down after our meeting."

Baxter's mind reels. Ehrichto is downstairs, in this house, waiting for him, apparently without the company of Michael Ferguson, at last. The past few hours have been hell for Baxter, knowing he was next door, but being forbidden by Dorjan to go to him.

"You do still want to see him again, don't you?"

Oh, hell yes. Baxter guesses he is now allowed to speak. "Can I? Now?"

"YOUR MOTHER IS a little strange," Michael's grandfather says, "But she does love you."

Michael nods. "I know." She *had* looked genuinely relieved to see him. For several seconds, even.

They are sitting at the kitchen table, where they'd silently convened after it became apparent that neither of them could fall asleep. Michael has been relegated to the couch, his grandfather to the recliner because Michael's parents have been given the only bed in the house.

"She said last night was the big dinner down there at the art place," his grandfather says, by "down there" meaning downtown, which is due north. Michael wonders if he's ever even set foot inside the Kentucky Center for the Arts. He guesses not.

"Yes, sir."

"Said you ran off right after it and stayed out all night."

Michael stares into the glass of milk on the table in front of him. He wonders what else his mother said about him, and whether or not his grandfather suspects that the thoughts that were keeping him up a few moments ago were not about their house burning down, but the revelation that Ehrichto has a boyfriend back in New Orleans, someone he said he "can't leave." Someone he'd said was even older than himself, though Michael can't hazard a guess at Ehrichto's age. Between twenty-one and sixty-five is all the same gray zone to him; there's "adult" and then there's "old."

"You do that a lot?"

"Sir?"

"Run off. Stay out all night."

"No, sir. Never before." He doesn't want to have this conversation, but there is one he does. "Do I look like someone in our family?"

His grandfather exhales. Michael thinks he's mad at him for interrupting what was meant to be a teaching moment, but the man pushes up out of his seat and heads off into the living room, coming back a minute later with a shoebox in his hands.

"You do," he says as he lifts off the lid. The box is chock full of photos and one yellowed envelope. He takes out the envelope and from it extracts three black and white prints with scalloped white borders mounted on card stock. He looks at them a moment and then hands one to Michael.

It might as well be a mirror. Michael stares a moment, then flips it over to read the inscription written in fountain-pen ink faded to a pale purple: *Patrick, 1919.*

Michael has been to Cave Hill cemetery, of course. The last time was five years ago, when his grandmother died. He knows the particular hill where his ancestors are buried, headstones rising out of the grass just below its crest.

He's peered through the gates of the mausoleum, has seen that it holds only one stone sarcophagus. He'd wanted to go in but his mother stopped him, saying sharply, "Forget about that. It's locked. Come back over here."

"Who was he?"

"That's my father. Your great-grandfather."

In the second photo Patrick is older and more dressed up, his curly hair tamed with what once was called pomade and now is product. An older man with a hawkish nose and beady eyes stands beside him. On the back of this photo there's a sentence written in, Michael thinks, the same hand as before. "Wedding day, 1920. Patrick and Tibbot Conway."

The third photo shows Patrick sitting on a lawn, looking in the direction of a woman and small child, who are a few feet away.

"That's me," his grandfather says. Michael recognizes the woman as a much, much younger version of his great-grandmother Myrtle. "That's the only photo I have of all of us. He was killed not long after that."

The word leaps out at Michael: *killed.* It's the first real clue he's ever had for why his mother, who was so close to her grandmother, never talks about him. Is it too painful? Or unsavory? "What happened to him?"

"His father Tibbot was insane, that's what. He regarded his son as damn near the Antichrist."

"He killed his own son?" Michael asks. Then it occurs to him that he's never heard that name—Tibbot—until now. He doesn't recall ever seeing it chiseled into a headstone. "He's not buried with everyone else, is he?"

"That's right. He's next door, at Eastern Cemetery. If Morris had his way I think he would've been dropped in the river. After Patrick was laid to rest he went home. Refused to go to the second funeral."

"He wouldn't go to his own son's funeral?" Michael asks. Then it registers with him, the fact that the ceremonies were back to back. "Wait a minute," he says. "They died on the same day?"

"That's right. They killed one another. Tibbot stabbed Patrick in the back; Patrick pulled a gun and shot him. It was self-defense. Nobody but my mother ever held it against him, but then, she was bitter about a whole lot of things where he was concerned."

The house where nothing has ever been updated, and Ehrichto's having been at ease there; the weird directions he kept taking the conversation in at dinner, like calling himself a "factor" instead of a broker, or slipping up by saying "my father" before correcting it to "grandfather"; and, of course, everything this morning—can it really have been only this morning?—in particular apologizing for having thought Michael was "someone else."

Now it all makes sense. Sort of.

"Can I...can I hang onto these for a little while?" Michael asks. "Please?"

Three hours later, when his grandfather starts to snore, Michael, still wide awake and fully dressed, slips off the couch and out the front door, heading for Belgravia Court.

IN BLACKHAUS THE underlair is a one-hundred-year-old unfinished basement comprised of rustic limestone walls, a brick floor, moss, mildew and mold. It's as dank and dark as any basement ever has been. Why Dorjan would instruct Ehrichto to wait for him there—and why the latter would agree—is a mystery to Baxter, and yet here he is, as promised. He is turned partially away and his head is bowed, his long locks obliterating any chance Baxter has of glimpsing his profile.

"Richard," Ehrichto says.

Baxter's knees threaten to buckle and send him tumbling down the last few steps but he manages to make it the rest of the way, all the way to solid ground. "You're here. You're really here."

"I didn't mean to be away for so long. I was angry with you, but we were all to blame."

He doesn't want to turn around because he's afraid to look at me, Baxter thinks. *He's heard what a hideous, pathetic creature I've become and he—*

Ehrichto tosses his head back to throw back the strands of

his hair and turns. If he's shocked by what he sees, it doesn't register on his face, and Baxter is amazed by his own view: Ehrichto is as handsome as ever, and as young.

Overwhelmed with joy, he's speechless.

"I need to feed, Richard," Ehrichto says. "That's why he sent you down here."

"I know." Baxter steps forward and reaches for the knot of the decorative silk scarf around his throat. Ehrichto moves around behind him, slides one arm around his neck, and grabs the wrist of that arm with his free hand.

Baxter recognizes the move from the wrestling films and magazines he watched as a teenager. It's a chokehold. He grasps Ehrichto's forearm with both hands. "No. I want to stay awake." Ehrichto relaxes his arm but doesn't withdraw it. Baxter leans back against Ehrichto's chest and tries to drink in the feeling of being embraced by him. Any pain is worth this experience, these few moments in his arms, even knowing they are happening for the wrong reason. "Please," he begs.

The other's grip unlocks. His arm slides down to across Baxter's chest. "I had good reasons to not tell you what I was," Ehrichto says. "Partly it was for my own protection, but it was also a way to spare you from this." He pulls Baxter more tightly to him. It feels for all the world like a hug. "What I'm going to do isn't pleasant."

"It's the price of admission, though, isn't it?" Baxter slides one hand along Ehrichto's forearm until he reaches his hand, interlocks their fingers, and gives a squeeze. Ehrichto returns the gesture. Baxter tilts his head sideways, stretching his neck long. "Do it," he says.

Baxter feels breath on his neck, followed by the velvet brush of lips. He has a split second of pure joy before the stabbing pain. Fire erupts in the juncture of his neck and shoulder, the worst pain he's ever felt. It's hot and sharp, like the touch of an electric current, and not a fleeting sensation but a persistent, relentless one. It drains him of energy almost instantly. All of his muscles involuntarily contract. His vision begins to tunnel. For a few seconds after he is blind he hovers in darkness, conscious only of the pain and of Ehrichto's arm, still across his chest. He thinks one last time that it's like an embrace.

EHRICHTO HAS JUST finished laying Baxter down atop a steamer trunk and some cardboard boxes when he hears footsteps descending the stone stair that connects the underlair and the walking court.

Through the clouded window of the interior door and, beyond it, the bars of the wrought-iron gate, he sees Michael step into view. The young man cups a hand to the glass and looks in, but appears unable to see anything in the basement's deep gloom. "Ehrichto?" He tries the gate, but it's latched. "They said you're down here. Can you hear me? Let me in."

Michael would've gone to his childhood home next door first. There's no reason for him to come to this house, no reason for him to know Ehrichto owns both. He can only imagine that the "they" to whom he refers are Nick and Wren, that the two were exploring the old house, taking in sights neither has seen in almost two decades, when he arrived on that doorstep. An odd thought strikes him, the idea of Wren standing in the kitchen doorway reminiscing about a woman cooking there, the same way Ehrichto was doing yesterday. Only for Wren that woman would not be Ehrichto's mother but rather his sister Ysabella. It strikes him as nothing short of bizarre.

After he'd gotten Nick and Wren settled in the converted birdwatcher's shack on the side of Volcán San Pedro, Ehrichto had tried to make his mother's recipe for arancini, balls of rice coated with breadcrumbs and fried, because Ysabella had made them for Wren many times. Despite his having been born during a war, Ysabella was the first person Wren had really known who had died, and he'd been distraught over the loss.

The timing of her death struck Ehrichto as prophetic. On the very day he'd turned the evidence of James Ferguson's supposed embezzlement over to authorities, and concluded his yearlong quest for revenge, Ehrichto had come home from Lexington and found his household there in mourning. Ysabella had died in her sleep a few hours before, Baxter said. He, Nick, and Wren were grieving.

Ehrichto wasn't sad so much as left feeling hollow. The last of his family members was gone, perhaps gone on to all be reunited, but he remained in an earthly limbo, neither fully alive nor dead. Nothing he'd said to his sister over the last few months of her life had done anything to change her attitude toward him. He hadn't magically undone the past and reinstated himself in the family of his birth any more than—he saw it only then, after her death—his taking down James Ferguson's empire would undo the fact that he'd exposed Ehrichto and Patrick's relationship and nearly destroyed it in the process. Ruining James's life and the lives of his descendants wouldn't change the fact that the other had robbed Ehrichto of his place in his family and in society, or reverse his father's disdain for him. The satisfaction he was so certain revenge would bring hadn't simply failed to blossom, or been quashed by Ysabella's death; it had never existed. Nothing had changed except for the fact that he'd ruined the lives of two innocent men and their wives and children in order to get back at James. He felt deceived, tricked into engaging in the very sort of cruelty he despised. He'd never hated himself more than in that moment.

The memory of that realization triggers another. *I'm the one responsible for this, too. It's my fault. Baxter wouldn't have masterminded building that house for Michael's mother if he hadn't been trying to draw me back here. He was betting on my being so outraged by finding that name— Conway Ferguson—on the legal documents that I'd have no choice but to return to investigate. He was so desperate to pull me back because I abandoned him for nearly two decades. I held onto the grudge about what happened to Nick for far too long. I became oblivious to the fact that Richard was here all alone, aging and dying.*

I drove him to it.

"Ehrichto?" Michael calls again. "C'mon. I know you're in there. Open up."

It was me, not Maria, or Baxter, or anyone else who brought him—no, not "back." Rather "into being." That was all my doing.

On that awful day, Derby Day of 1981, Wren had been hysterical, unable to understand why, as Baxter explained it to him, Ysabella wouldn't be waking up ever again. His seven-year-old mind had no way to process the notion of "never." Baxter was unnerved. Nick was glum. Ehrichto recalls being overwhelmed, utterly at a loss and compelled to go to the vestibule.

It seemed only right that the room would have been transformed by his father into a shrine to his eldest son. It's the same room where, each year, the family erected their St. Joseph altar, which was meant to ward off barrenness of the crop variety. It isn't hard to see the analogy between a harvest of wheat and one's offspring. In fact, the house itself had been intended as a sort of totem. Ehrichto's father had surprised his mother with it after the trauma of losing Francesco. It was meant to take her mind off the tragedy.

Aside from the weeks when it held the St. Joseph altar, the vestibule table was crowded with photos and mementos of the children who lived. After Michelangelo was killed in the influenza epidemic, it had become a shrine to him. Baxter mocks it with his collection in the entryway of the house next door, filthy works Ehrichto could never, will never, bring himself to call "art."

Michael rattles the gate again. A dull thud and a startled cry of pain inform Ehrichto that he has grown impatient enough to give it a swift kick.

"Ehrichto?" The voice is Dorjan's, coming from the stairs at his back. "What are you doing?"

"I'm the one. I did it."

"Did what, memmi?"

"Caused all of this. Him. The day Ysabella died, we were next door, and they were so distraught, all of them. I felt so…helpless…and so empty. I'd just pulled the trigger on my plan with James; I'd known innocent people were going to get hurt, but for months, for a year, I'd told myself that I was justified. After I called the police, and pointed them to the evidence they would need to put James away, I…I wasn't happy, exactly, but I did feel smug. Then I walked into that scene." He shakes his head, recalling the sour feeling in his stomach when he saw their faces, and heard that his sister was dead. "It felt like God killed her just to punish me, like he took away my last remaining family member as revenge for what I'd done."

"Ehrichto…." Dorjan chides. He doesn't believe in the Anglo-Saxon idea of an all-knowing, judgmental deity. The tribe he was raised in had its own ideology and, ironically, matriarchal hierarchy. He liked to say he didn't begin to understand the mindset of the Abrahamic ones.

Ehrichto doesn't let himself be dissuaded. "My father started to go off the deep end when my mother died," he says. "He threw over St. Joseph and started seeking help from other sources. For a while it was Mary, then Jesus. When my brother died he latched on to St. Michael. He was Michelangelo, after all. I really think he'd become convinced that we were being targeted, and that God and the saints needed to be appeased. Not that it would bring my brother or any of them back, but…." He shakes his head again. "He began collecting paintings glorifying the archangel Michael. He filled the walls of the vestibule with them. People—especially that he did business with—thought he was losing his mind."

"Death can have that effect," Dorjan says. "I've never been a fan of it."

"The day Ysabellá died I went into my father's shrine to St. Michael and said a prayer," Ehrichto explains. "I still remember it. 'St. Michael, guardian of lost souls, I ask for your intercession, that Almighty God might be moved to have mercy on me, a sinner. St. Michael, assist me to find peace.'"

Across the room, at the door to the outside, Michael reaches through the bars of the wrought iron gate and raps on one of the panes of glass in the interior door.

"Perhaps it worked," Dorjan says. He's being kind. Ehrichto knows he doesn't believe in any of it: Fate. Romantic love. Original sin. "Go open the door and find out."

"What if he doesn't have free will?"

"What is it that you desire, memmi?"

Before today no one has ever asked him that, and now it's happened twice. First Michael, and now Dorjan. All day, Ehrichto's psyche has been wrestling with the answer. "To love someone who is in love with me," he says.

"Then go open the door."

"I thought you didn't believe in such things?"

"I don't, but you do. And so does he." Dorjan lifts his chin to indicate the door. "Go let him in, Ehrichto, before he finds a rock and breaks the glass."

"Hey," Michael says when the interior door opens.

Ehrichto doesn't reply. Releasing a latch on the wrought-iron gate, he pushes it open.

N·S· BERANEK   289

"Why are you over here? Why aren't you next door," Michael asks, stepping inside. He wants to ask who the two guys were who finally answered the door after he rang the bell four times and pounded on the glass of the sidelight. One had looked like the love child of Iggy Pop and RiffRaff; the other was younger, and likely half-Asian, with ruler-straight medium brown hair and the kind of eyes that attach directly to the bridge of the nose. That second guy, who Michael thinks wasn't much older than himself, had been sporting a tee bearing the iconic logo of the Misfits, Glenn Danzig's old band. Danzig's song "Mother" is one of Michael's all-time favorite tunes not written by the Cure, and the reason why, when the guy opened the door, by way of greeting Michael had said, "Cool shirt. Is, uh, is Ehrichto here?"

Now he follows Ehrichto deeper into the dimly lit basement. His eyes are still adjusting to the gloom, and he can see very little. "Why didn't you come to the door sooner?"

Ehrichto shifts his gaze. Michael lets his follow. He sees a man passed out on a stack of boxes. His collar-length hair is a mix of silver and dark strands, and his face looks…familiar.

"What's *he* doing here?" Michael says.

Ehrichto looks as surprised as Michael feels. "You know him?"

"That's…Angelo de Haven," Michael says, as the realization dawns. "He designed our house." Ehrichto seems oddly relieved by that news, but Michael's uneasiness grows. The fact that the house burned down last night, and de Haven is here, unconscious, twists his stomach into knots. Something isn't right. "How do *you* know him? Why is he here? And what's wrong with him?"

"His real name is Richard Baxter," Ehrichto says. "I've known him since before you were a gleam in your father's eye."

All things considered, the expression is unsettling. It occurs to Michael that during the course of conversation at dinner two nights ago Ehrichto had mentioned being involved with an effort to restore some of the historic properties in New Orleans; also, that a person who made his living designing homes would have a lot to recommend him to someone concerned with such matters. Hadn't Ehrichto said his partner in New Orleans was "older"? Jealousy washes over him. "That's him."

"Who?"

"Your not-boyfriend from New Orleans."

Somewhere not far off in the darkness a creak sounds, wooden boards shifting beneath weight, rubbing together. "No," a voice says. "That would be me."

A man steps into view. He's taller than Ehrichto, and broader, and looks to be of Middle-Eastern descent. The way he carries himself and the cut of his collared shirt announce that he's wealthy. Powerful. In charge.

Shit, Michael thinks. *That's why he didn't answer the door right away.*

"My name is Victor Dorjan."

"I'm Michael."

"Yes, I know." The stranger looks him up and down, and then turns to Ehrichto. "Not what I would have expected."

Michael remembers the revelation he had the day before: *You aren't happy with him. You* want *because you don't have.* "Then you should've done your homework," he says.

The stranger turns back, seems to reconsider him, smiles condescendingly.

"How's that?"

Michael holds out the photos he got from his grandfather. Seeing the stranger ever so slightly flinch when his gaze falls on the close-up shot makes him giddy. Without a word, the man hands the photos to Ehrichto, whose reaction is much stronger. He begins to tremble. "Where did you get these," he asks. Before Michael can answer, Ehrichto does it himself. "Donal."

"I look like my great-grandfather, but you really did know him, didn't you," Michael says. He realizes how crazy it sounds, but at the same time he's sure that it's true, somehow. It's the only thing that makes what happened between them make sense. "You thought I was him." He takes a breath, to steel himself. "What *are* you?"

To his right, Angelo de Haven—correction, Richard Baxter—moans and shifts positions. When he does, the right side of his neck becomes exposed, revealing two small puncture wounds. *Vampires*, Michael thinks, buoyed that the fantastical beyond belief yet somehow also wholly plausible theory he'd come up with seems to be being borne out. His heart races with excitement.

Ehrichto is still staring at the photos in his hand. Michael looks to the other man. Dorjan. The not-boyfriend. "Are you vampires?"

Ehrichto's head snaps up. Then he looks to the other man.

Dorjan's the head vampire, Michael realizes. *That's what Ehrichto meant when he said he's not his boyfriend but it's complicated and he can't leave him.*

"You have quite the imagination," Dorjan says. "You must watch a lot of movies." He grins, an action that strikes Michael as forced. He and Ehrichto exchange a long look. "I'll leave you two alone."

It's only when Dorjan begins to ascend a set of steps that Michael realizes he was standing on a staircase all along. When he reaches the top he pushes open a door, revealing a glimpse of the room beyond, which is nearly as dimly lit as the basement. Before he steps through the opening he calls back over his shoulder, "It really is quite a remarkable resemblance, memmi. Who knows? Perhaps it is the hand of your God after all."

Michael waits until the door is closed. "You're a vampire, aren't you? Is he your Master?"

Beside them Richard Baxter moans and falls silent again.

"I told you it's complicated," Ehrichto says. "I'll explain everything later."

Michael has questions now. "What did he mean by 'the hand of God'? I'm right, aren't I? He's the head vampire? That's why you said you can't leave him. Are you like Kiefer Sutherland? I guess you would be. And then I'm like Michael, right? I mean, I am Michael. Well, you know what I mean."

"I don't have the slightest notion what you mean, actually."

"How old are you? Can you make me one? Did you grow up in the house next—"

"Michael?"

"Yes?"

"I said I'll explain everything later. Right now, there's something much more important I need to do."

"What?"

"This." Ehrichto grasps the sides of Michael's face in both his hands and leans down until their mouths meet.

"Excuse us, gentlemen, I need to speak to my family alone for a few minutes," Ehrichto says as he enters the room that has always been Nick's in this house.

Just as they did back in New Orleans, the kel'an have been taking turns feeding Nick their blood, and Wren is sitting beside the bed looking worried.

"He's still quite unwell," Willem offers.

"He's strung out. Taking five bottles of prescription psychoactive medication at once tends to have that effect." Ehrichto steps to the dresser and sets down the bottle of Laphroaig and three rocks glass he brought with him. He sees Nick's eyes widen. He waves an arm in the direction of the door. "Please, leave us."

"You're mad," André says, nodding to the whisky.

"That may well be. Only time will tell."

André, Willem, Coronel and Philip exchange uncertain looks but then, grudgingly, exit.

The minute they are gone Wren asks, "Uncle, what are you doing?"

NINETEEN

That's the first thing he's said to me since Guatemala, Ehrichto notes. *We're moving in the right direction already.* "I didn't get my birthday toast this year, so I thought we'd have it now." This year, his birthday fell on Easter. He always hates when that happens, but this birthday had been especially terrible because he'd been at Abaton, holed up in Dorjan's quarters, hiding from the rest of the kel, while Nick and Wren were in Guatemala, just days away from, quite literally, he knows now, wrestling with Philip.

There is a method to his madness. He has just returned from driving Michael back to his grandfather's. It's still so odd to think of Patrick's son Donal now being an old man, the grandfather Michael says he barely knows because the fellow isn't a social-ladder climber like his daughter and son-in-law, and simply being kin wasn't enough of a recommendation to earn him more than a token place in their child's life.

He breaks the tax stamp on the bottle and pours a finger of whiskey into each glass. "Here's how this is going to work," he says, setting down the bottle but making no move to pick up and distribute the glasses. "If you say something worthwhile, you can take a drink. Since I'm the birthday boy, I get to determine what counts and what doesn't. Deal?"

He knows the look that crosses his nephew's face, even before Wren scoffs. "I'll pass," he says.

C'mon, work with me here. "121," Ehrichto says. Wren's brow furrows.

"Proof?" Nick asks, his eyes taking on a decided glimmer.

Ehrichto doesn't answer. Wren's a smart boy; he has faith that he'll work it out, will realize that his uncle is talking about their old cribbage strategy, two against one, the only possible way to beat Nick, who is also no slouch in the intelligence department. He picks up a glass and turns to his friend. "How about you, Nick? What do you say? Deal?" Nick holds out a hand but Ehrichto doesn't move. "Ah, ah, ah, ah. Question first, worthy answer, and then the reward." Nick shrugs his grudging consent.

Ehrichto doesn't hold out much hope of this game lasting very long so he cuts right to the chase. "Why does the idea of me turning Wren bother you so much?"

A few years earlier, when Wren first started to suggest in earnest that it was time for his father to make him immortal, and Nick first balked at the idea, Ehrichto had pointed out that he would be right there, should something start to go wrong, and then had suggested doing the turning in his stead. His friend had turned and shoved him, hard enough to knock him backward, the first time Nick had ever struck him.

"I'll rephrase the question," Ehrichto says "My blood is in your veins. Why can't it also be in his? Why must it be you who turns him?"

Nick narrows his eyes until only slivers of cornflower are visible. "Shut up." His voice is a dog's growl. "Shut your damned mouth now."

Ehrichto feels the warmth of the sleuth who has found the culprit. He started to figure out what was really going with Nick a few hours ago, while listening to Michael frantically attempt to bring him up to speed on all the important details of his life that he'd missed. Right after their kiss in the underlair he'd started talking, fast. He'd rivaled Maria in the rapidity of his words. And just as when she got excited and carried away, most of what Michael said had been a blur to Ehrichto's ears, sentences filled with cultural references he didn't understand and names that were unfamiliar to him. One sentiment, though, had stopped him cold. Michael explained that when he'd asked to use the phone and called Alyssa, he'd been planning to tell her where he was, who he was with, and exactly what they'd done together, as a way to prove to Ehrichto that he wasn't ashamed of him. Before he could, however, she'd dropped a bombshell of her own—the news that while he was away his house had burned down.

Michael had branched off from there, detailing the abuse he'd suffered while attending a different school than his current one. He cited the psychological abuse and threats of physical violence that had been heaped on him by his former classmates as an explanation for why, when they met, he'd been pretending to have a girlfriend, as if Ehrichto couldn't possibly understand why anyone would need to resort to such action.

Looking back now, he realizes there was a kernel of truth to that notion. The closest he'd ever come to making such a move himself was his decision not to correct his fellow navy men when they'd misheard the name he called out while asleep, and assumed he was pining for a lover named "Patricia." But wasn't that, truly, the same as showing up at a dinner with a girl on your arm? Didn't it stem from the same fear that led a man to marry someone he wasn't in love with, in order to secure some level of protection from the world's scrutiny? Ehrichto had gotten on his high horse and lectured Patrick about the sanctity of marriage, but the reality was that Myrtle wasn't some dewy-eyed, desperately in love schoolgirl; she was a calculating woman looking to improve her station in life through a fortuitous marriage. He's almost certain she hadn't known anything about Patrick's relationship with Ehrichto before they wed. But if she had, he wonders, would it have changed anything?

I couldn't tell her, Michael had said, after explaining that he'd feared, early on, that Alyssa suspected he wasn't interested in her romantically. *Even after I realized she knew and didn't care, that she was just trying to help, I couldn't tell her she was right. If she'd told anyone—not intentionally, I knew she would never do that, but accidentally....*He'd let his voice trail off but the implication was clear. If she knew and let it slip he might have been in real danger.

Ehrichto understands that sort of paralyzing fear, and he knows Nick does, too. They'd ceased being client and pilot and had become good friends almost immediately, yet they'd known each other for two years before Nick felt comfortable enough to tell him he had a son: Nguyen Hai Yen, who was being cared for by his parents back in San Diego. The child's name, he said, translated roughly to Good Luck Sparrow. The boy's mother had named her son after a bird as a way to tie him to his American fighter-pilot father. Nguyen was pronounced "Win," which was similar to "Wren," a bird, and so when he arrived stateside Nick had renamed him Wren Krey.

At first, Ehrichto's feelings had been hurt. He felt Nick hadn't trusted him enough to confide in him that he was a father. But Ehrichto had secrets of his own he hadn't shared, and still wasn't inclined to reveal, so he'd let it go.

Even after he was forced to turn Nick to keep him from dying, and had to reveal to his fledgling that he was a vampire, that they were both vampires, he hadn't been able to tell Nick the deeper secret of his homosexuality.

I just couldn't. The stakes were too high, he thinks, echoing Michael's explanation about keeping his truth from Alyssa. *Even after everything we'd been through together, Nick might have hated me for it.*

He hadn't. When the moment finally came, one night in Guatemala, Nick had laughed and shaken his head and said, "Yeah, no kidding, Einstein. I've known that for a while."

"Fine, we'll start with an easier one." Ehrichto swirls the liquid in his glass. "Let's talk about April thirtieth." It's the day they've always celebrated as Wren's birthday. "That's the day he arrived at your parents' house, after being airlifted out of Vietnam," Ehrichto says. "Which is, in a poetic sense, a 'birth day,' I'll grant you, but it's not his real one. You don't know what the real one is, do you?"

Wren looks at Nick. "Dad?"

Nick makes a grab for the whisky glass but Ehrichto seizes hold of his wrist. "Answer the question if you want the whisky. You don't know what his actual birthday is, do you?"

Nick winces. "No."

Ehrichto relinquishes the glass. Nick tosses back the contents, and holds it out for more. "Next question," Ehrichto says, before snatching the bottle from the dresser top. He takes the glass and starts to refill it. "Your father loves you more than life itself, Wren," he says. "He gave up his naval career in order to care for you, but things didn't go exactly as planned. He didn't have a wife, or even a girlfriend, and this was before there were such things as daycare centers. He had to leave you with his parents while he worked to build his one-man airline into a thriving business."

"I know that," Wren says. He should; they've told him the story many times.

"To say your grandparents didn't approve of his decision would be a gross understatement. It didn't matter to them that he did the right thing by you by sacrificing himself. They couldn't see that he lived up to all the moral standards they'd said for years that they stood for, but didn't. And more remarkably, that entire time he had an ace up his sleeve that he couldn't even use."

Nick narrows his eyes. "Don't."

Ehrichto sighs. "He *should* know."

"That's my call, not yours."

Wren perks up. "What are you talking about? What ace up his sleeve?"

"Nothing," Nick says. "Don't listen to him. He's on a fishing expedition." He glares at Ehrichto. "If you say anything more, Ehrichto.... This friendship is over. We are finished. Broken."

"I believe there are more important things than our friendship. Stopping you from killing yourself is one of them. Your having the relationship with your son that you deserve is another."

"Will somebody please tell me what's going on," Wren says.

Ehrichto holds up the bottle. "Tell him and you can have all of it right now." Nick surprises him by striking out and knocking the bottle from his hand. It hits the carpet with a thud, and liquor begins flowing out onto the floor. Their gaze locked on one another, neither Ehrichto nor Nick moves for several moments. "Fine," Ehrichto says at last, turning away. He puts several paces between them, turns, and says to Wren, "He's not your biological father."

An instant later he is on the floor with Nick on top of him, attempting to crush his windpipe with his bare hands. His field of vision diminishing, Ehrichto hears Wren screaming for Nick to stop, and feels the vibration of the floor as the members of the kel rush into the room. Nick is pulled this way and that. At last his grip loosens, and he's thrown sideways onto the floor.

"You had no right," Nick bellows. "No goddamned right!"

Wren stands in the center of the room, looking dazed. "Is it true?" His voice sounds small and frightened as he turns to Ehrichto. "How do you know?"

"Because." The word comes out as a croak. Ehrichto rubs his smarting throat as he sits up. "I've put together little things he's said over the years. And keeping secrets is a learned skill albeit a dangerous business. Human or vampire, the lies will eat you up inside."

"Then who is my dad?"

Across the room Nick stops trying to break free of Willem and Coronel's grasp, as if defeated.

Ehrichto pities him. "What you mean is who fathered you. That I don't know. I can only assume it was one of the men in his unit, someone willing to walk away and abandon you."

A terrible silence floods the room broken only when Nick murmurs,

"His name was Coburn. I-I tried to get him to understand, but he was a real rat bastard. He was so…blind to it." He pulls free of the others' grasp on his arms and struggles to sit up. "You were my responsibility, ultimately. I wasn't going to leave you there. We all knew what would happen. The minute we were gone the Viet Cong would come rushing in and shoot everything in sight, including orphans. Especially half-American ones. I had no choice, I had to get you out of there. I told my commander you were mine. He didn't for a minute believe me, but my men backed me up."

"Even my real father?"

Nick flinches.

"Wren," Ehrichto says, taking the young man by the arm, and giving him a firm squeeze. "Nick *is* your father, just like I'm your uncle." He gestures to indicate the kel'an, and Dorjan, who is now leaning in the doorway, watching the little drama unfold. "We are all your family. Dorjan put his blood into my veins, I put it into Nick's, and he's going to put it—along with his own—into yours…."

"And then we're all going to live happily ever after?" Wren asks. His expression shows doubt.

Ehrichto feels a hand on his own arm, pulling him back. He's surprised to find it is Dorjan, come up behind him. "I misjudged him, your Nick," he whispers in Ehrichto's ear. "And you, as well. You make me proud, memmi."

Wren crosses the room to Nick, drops to his knees, and throws his arms around his father's neck.

"I think he'll be all right now," Ehrichto says. "No more running in fear from this moment, though he may never speak to me again."

Dorjan drapes an arm across his shoulders. "He will. You'll see."

"Well, even if he does, now that the cofradía no longer need me to be their Maximón, I have no way to provide for us. We can't all move into Abaton."

"The cofradía still need you to provide all the things their wooden god can't," Dorjan says. "Jobs, medical care, money for education. I'm sure that's worth a little blood to them, even if, after all, you're nothing but a vampire."

"They've never taken me up on the last one," Ehrichto says. "I was hoping Maria would finally be the one to go to college. I had this crazy vision of one day hiring her to be a chemist at our Guatemala City operation. Now, who knows?"

"You still have a few years to convince her. As for the more immediate problem of how to feed the two of them...." He pulls a folded paper from his pocket and hands it to Ehrichto.

"*The Quarry Dance Party. Oaks Day, under the Louisville Zoo,*" Ehrichto reads. He notices finer print at the bottom of the sheet. "*A vampire-themed rave for the ages.* What is this?"

"The second answer to your prayers. Maybe there's something to your saints, after all." Dorjan steers him toward the door. "Come, let's find Richard. I'll let him explain."

TWENTY

THE SCENE IS one Ehrichto never thought he'd see in his hometown: hundreds upon hundreds of mostly twenty-something young people gathered together, dressed in black or jewel-toned velvet clothing trimmed in fishnet and lace. Some of the outfits are high-collared while others have plunging necklines, and there are some floor-length hems but also skirts that might be better classified as wide belts. There are impossibly high heeled shoes and British combat boots of the kind Willem and the boy from the cemetery favor, and shaved heads alternating with long, artificially dyed locks, some bright red, some purple, and here and there a head of green or blue or bleached bone-white, but overwhelmingly the patrons have chosen black. Flashes of silver glint from the dark hollows of their belly buttons, or the centers of their tongues, riches glimpsed only during laughter, or sex. In short the scene is almost exactly the way Ehrichto pictured it would be after Dorjan explained that Richard was planning to host a goth rave in the former limestone mine Ehrichto hadn't known he'd inherited.

Richard had first learned of the existence of the space, and the Salvatolle family's ownership of it, while turning out drawers and poring over scraps of paper in Ehrichto's childhood home. He'd found out more by squinting at microfiche in the library, and talking to WWI veterans in the Camp Taylor neighborhood, and other means of sleuthing he'd employed during the nearly two decades when he had nothing better to do.

Ehrichto was astonished to learn that he'd not only inherited ownership of the quarry but much of the neighborhood surrounding it. It was all part of a purchase his father had made as a consequence of his meltdown following Michelangelo's death. Outraged when the city announced plans to divide the old Camp Taylor site into tracts and sell it off, Guglielmo had decried the plan to anyone he could convince to listen. Ultimately he'd proven to be among a handful of individuals with a serious interest in acquiring the land. The vast majority of people were looking for acres to develop, land on which to build homes and businesses, but there was widespread fear that the Spanish influenza bug still lurked in the soil, and could reinfect people without warning. After setting aside a large chunk of the space to be the Louisville Zoo, city officials had been only too happy to unload the rest—including a million square feet of underground space—on those they saw as suckers.

Only one other buyer could back his hopes with actual cash. He'd developed the subdivision where Alyssa Morrison and her family now lived, on the opposite side of the hill from where the Ferguson's dream home was located. Guglielmo, meanwhile, had done nothing with his share. He considered the land sacred. It was the spot where his firstborn child, his eldest son—and hundreds of other young men—had been cut down in his prime. He sank his life savings into the purchase, and it had come to Ehrichto upon Ysabella's death. The city considered the underground rights worthless, since all the limestone that could be had already been removed. They'd thrown them in to sweeten the pot before realizing there was no need: Guglielmo was a motivated buyer.

Ehrichto looks out at the quarry's dance floor and scowls. The young adults crowding the space aren't dancing so much as writhing, or gyrating, or perhaps suffering a collective epileptic fit. He blames the strobe lights Baxter installed all around the room. *And this so-called music*, he thinks.

He has hated the song currently playing since back in the days when he made the drive over from Lexington on Thursday nights in order to attend Richard's original "vampire" parties. On those evenings Blackhaus looked and felt like Halloween, every normal light bulb extinguished, replaced by black-light fixtures. Their guests all dressed in leather and fishnet, à la Dr. Frank N. Furter, and Bauhaus played on endless repeat on the turntable in the front parlor. Ehrichto still despises that the musicians used the name of the art movement as the name of their band. He thinks Pretentious Art-School Caterwaulers would have been a more apropos moniker.

Richard's parties were little more than orgies. By the end of each evening every corner was filled with copulating pairs, trios or even larger groups while, invariably, other guests—as high as kites on cocaine—would run from room to room, shrieking just to hear their own voices. Still others were tucked away in upper rooms they'd stolen off to in order to shoot up. Those ones Ehrichto sought out, because it was easy to feed from them while they were "on the nod," junkie parlance for the comatose state achieved after a high. They were easy and plentiful targets, and he was thankful to Richard for hosting the soirées. Still, by the ends of those nights the house always resembled the scene of a sarin gas attack, and he was relieved when he, Nick and Wren left for Guatemala and the whole sordid episode came to a close.

He'd thought the desire to spend weekend after weekend dressed like an extra from a film by Hammer Studios was something peculiar to Richard's theatre friends. Even after Wren stumbled upon the existence of vampire BBSs Ehrichto hadn't dreamed there could ever be an event like the one he is currently viewing. He certainly never imagined he would be at such an event, accompanied by someone who views it as a pinnacle of human achievement.

"God, I *love* this song!"

It's Michael, arrived at last. Ehrichto plasters a smile he hopes isn't too anemic-looking on his face and turns to greet him. He's surprised to find that it isn't Michael, after all, but some random partygoer who has made his way up onto the deck reserved for the kel'an. The articles of clothing he wears are so clean and crisp they must all be brand new, bought specifically for the occasion. Enormous white sneakers engulf his feet, his denim trousers are a rich, never-washed black, and his equally dark t-shirt is screen-printed with the image of a man holding a guitar, though unlike with most such shots the figure is shown almost in silhouette, his back partially turned to the camera. The pose heightens the impression for the viewer that the neck of the guitar emanates from his crotch, and draws an obvious connection between the instrument and a certain part of the male anatomy. Ehrichto grimaces at the vulgarity.

Like the figure on the shirt, the young man, whose face is turned toward the floor, has teased his hair into a gravity-defying rat's nest. Ehrichto guesses it must have taken an entire can of hairspray to pull off such a feat, though why one would want to do such a thing he cannot fathom.

The boy raises his head. It's all Ehrichto can do not to stagger backward.

"Well? What do you think?" Michael asks, looking at him imploringly. His eyes are heavily lined with kohl. His weak smile falters. "You hate it, don't you?"

"No, no," Ehrichto says. "I just wasn't expecting.... It's a surprise, is all."

"You hate it. I'm sorry. I brought other clothes. I'll go change." He starts to turn toward the stair, but Ehrichto catches his arm.

"I don't want you to do that. Just give me a minute or two to get used to it."

Already, the black circles Michael has drawn around his eyes aren't half as unsettling. "It's...good. I like it."

The huge smile that brightens Michael's face then erases any remaining dislike Ehrichto has for the style.

THIS, NO CONTEST, is the coolest event Michael has ever attended, or known existed. It blows away every story he's ever heard about the Sextacy Ball tour that came through town four years ago, featuring My Life with the Thrill Kill Kult and Lords of Acid. It's better, too, than the descriptions of the Marilyn Manson and Nine Inch Nails show three years back at the Louisville Gardens, and it makes the Blind Cave Fish concert he snuck across town to attend look like a Sunday school field trip.

One of the strangest things that's happened in the past two weeks was when two guys his own age, out in Colorado, donned all-black clothing and shot up their high school, killing a dozen students and one teacher, and none of Michael's classmates had so much as looked askance at him.

He wonders how Danielle and her crew fared. Then he thinks that they will kick themselves for missing this event tonight—if, that is, they *are* missing it. He hasn't ruled out the possibility that they are here somewhere, four little black and white specks in a sea of the same. He watches the crowd of attendees as they, almost collectively, do the bending-over-backwards-and-forwards-like-Peter-Murphy dance.

"I am not enamored of this tune," Ehrichto says.

"What?" Michael shouts: "You can't dislike this song. It's against the law!"

"Arrest me, then. I have only less contempt for it than I do for the one where they scream the Lord's Prayer in Latin and reverse."

Michael loves the song "Stigmata Martyr" almost as much as he loves "Bela Lugosi's Dead," but neither song can hold a candle to "Double Dare," in his opinion. He can't imagine why anyone—especially a vampire—would not like this music. He gestures for Ehrichto to lean down, so he doesn't have to scream. Trying to be heard over the music is already threatening to leave him hoarse or even speechless tomorrow. Ehrichto leans close, and Michael says into his ear, "We are seriously going to have to work on your music appreciation skills."

TWENTY-ONE

EHRICHTO CAN'T FIGURE out when it happened, but he's fallen in love with Michael. Did it happen while they were at the Derby Festival chow wagon by the river, after Michael ate an entire serving of cotton candy in three minutes flat and for twenty minutes after that sang snippets of songs by his favorite band, the Cure, trying to prove that Ehrichto *did too* know their music, despite his insistence that he did not? Was it on the double date they went on with Alyssa and her no longer ex-boyfriend Trey, at the Great Balloon Glow? The fairgrounds had had a magical feel, what with the brightly colored hot air balloons all around, and the flickering light from the flames heating the air that provided their lift. Michael had been very animated that night as well, laughing with Alyssa and jabbing her in the ribs before whispering in her ear, which led, every single time, to her turning and looking at Ehrichto, making it obvious that they were talking about him. That Michael was talking about him, making his feelings for him plainly known to her.

He thinks that if Michael had been able to make the phone

call he wanted to that second evening, that would have been it, the I-am-in-love-with-him moment. But Michael had been unable to execute his plan, which left Ehrichto in doubt for a little while longer about whether the relationship could ever provide him with the things he wanted and needed.

"I can't decide," he says. They are sitting on a couch at the back of the elevated deck, well away from the railing where, earlier, they stood watching the crowd on the dance floor. It is almost two in the morning, and though the rave's patrons are just getting started, Michael is clearly tired, not used to staying up this late. His eyes keep threatening to close against his will.

"About what?"

"If it happened bit by bit or all at once," Ehrichto says. "I do, though, know when I knew for certain that it had happened. It was just after you arrived tonight. You were so anxious about my reaction to your outfit, and then you grinned. Right then, I knew."

"Knew what?"

Ehrichto leans down and kisses him. "How much I like you." He kisses him again. This time when they part he hears Michael's stunned-sounding whisper: "Oh. Wow."

MICHAEL KNOWS THEY will sleep together again soon. Part of him wants it to be now, now, NOW! The other part, though, is glad Ehrichto suggested they slow down, and not do it again right away. After the whole I-thought-you-were-someone-else business, it would be weird. It's weird enough as it is, to know so little about Ehrichto in most regards, yet so much about him in that one. Michael thinks the past two weeks have been really good for them, have been the chance they needed to get to know one another better. Although if Ehrichto doesn't give that aspect of their relationship the green light again very soon, Michael thinks he just may die of frustration.

There's also the matter of finding enough time and privacy to do it justice. He prays their spending an entire night together again won't have to wait until fall, after he has (officially, anyway) moved into a dorm at the University of Kentucky. Until that time there's only so much covering for him that Alyssa and Trey can do, and only so much pretending that he doesn't know what's really going on that his father can.

Michael needs to tread carefully around his dad for another reason. Under no circumstances can he be allowed to find out that Angelo de Haven / Richard Baxter and Ehrichto know one another. Michael knows Ehrichto is very worried that, after they've been together long enough that they feel they can safely tell him they're a couple, his father will find out that it was an associate of Ehrichto's who was behind the one-million-dollar check the Fergusons received from the "insurance company." His fear is that Michael's father will view the money as a bribe, a fee he's been paid for allowing Ehrichto to sleep with his son.

"All right," Ehrichto says, before reaching over and giving Michael's leg a squeeze. "We need to get you back to the house to change out of those clothes and then I need to get you to your grandfather's." The cover story Alyssa, Trey and Michael concocted to enable him to be here is that they are all working as catering assistants (read: hors d'oeuvre tray bearers) for the celebrity-studded Barnstable-Brown Derby Eve Gala. The Barnstable twins are his mother's charity event arch-rivals, and the most anticipated guests for the event this year are Rod Stewart, Stevie Nicks and Norman Schwarzkopf. Julia had thrown a fit when he first announced his plans for the evening. Then she got a familiar glint in her eye. He knows he will have to call Alyssa early and pump her for juicy details, because he was allowed to attend only as his mother's spy.

He lets Ehrichto pull him to his feet. "I'll have to take a shower to get the gel and stuff out of my hair," he says, wrapping his arms around the man's waist and looking up at him. "No one else will be there. You could join me."

Ehrichto smiles. "Ah, but you told your parents you'd be home by three and it's nearly two now."

"I told them 'probably three.' You know how those things go. I'll just say that my new buddy Rod decided to play a few tunes for everyone on the piano. That's a once-in-a-lifetime opportunity, how could they be mad about that?" *Besides*, he wants to say, *they know I'm really with you. They've known for the past two weeks that every time I've gone out I was lying through my teeth.* "Oh, I know," he says. "This is even better. I'll say that I was serving canapés, one thing led to another, and Rod said he has some cousins in the States who are named Conway. I'll say they were distillers, and I'm pretty sure we're related."

"Not just related. You're his doppelgänger."

Michael's stomach drops. "No, not...." He can't bring himself to say "To Patrick."

"I meant to Rod Stewart."

Ehrichto looks flustered. He's realized his faux pas. "Oh, I-I don't know who that is," he says, obviously trying to make a joke. He has a strange, very dry sense of humor that Michael often doesn't get.

Michael doesn't want to talk about his great-grandfather, mostly. There is one thing about him he's been dying to know. And since Ehrichto already brought him up....

"Did he have facial hair? A beard? A moustache?"

For a heart-stopping second he thinks Ehrichto won't answer, but the other says, "No. Those things were only fashionable for much older men."

Michael grins. "Cool, because I had a goatee and moustache until like right before we met. My mother made me shave them off for her party because she thought they made me resemble a gondolier."

Ehrichto raises a brow. "What a lovely euphemism." He doesn't look amused.

"I know, right? Anyway, what I mean was I could grow them back. Unless you don't like that idea."

"On the contrary, I think it's a capital one," Ehrichto says, so quickly that the sour feeling in the pit of Michael's stomach intensifies. *He needs something to keep from seeing Patrick when he looks at me.*

It's not exactly rocket science. It's nine-tenths of the reason Michael decided to resurrect his old goth persona for tonight. Patrick certainly never looked the way he does now.

That thought triggers another. Michael looks down at his nails, which are painted black. "Oh, crap. I forgot to buy nail polish remover." He pauses. "Do you think Baxter has any?" The minute the words are past his lips he regrets them.

"No," a stern voice says from the darkness off to his left. "Baxter does *not* own nail polish remover. Nor does he have any padded bras or pantyhose. This is because Baxter is a *man.*"

"Sorry," Michael calls. Inwardly, he bristles. *Well, excuuuse me,* he thinks, like Steve Martin on old episodes of SNL, ...*for thinking that a guy who wears under-eye concealer and heels—oh sorry, platform shoes—might occasionally paint his nails.*

As they reach the landing the music fades and the sea of bodies on the dance floor ceases to move. There's a moment or two of awkward silence followed by giddy laughter and a few random whoops of joy. Then feedback screeches through the speakers and makes everyone jump. Just starting down the stairs, Ehrichto and Michael halt.

Lights slowly come up on the stage at the far end of the crowd, revealing two figures—one male and one female—standing before microphones in stands. Ehrichto puts a hand on Michael's shoulder, signaling him to pause there a moment. He wants to see what it is that Baxter has planned to have happen next.

A lone voice rises up out of the silence. Each note is drawn out, clear and pure, a reverent, holy sound that transcends gender. Since neither of the figures has raised their head, it's impossible to know which one of them is singing. It reminds Ehrichto of the Muslim call to prayer, or the music of Sufis, songs meant to bring the listener to an ecstatic, holy mind. He casts a glance Dorjan's way and sees his eyes are opened wide.

The singer lets the note they are holding slowly extinguish. The stage slips back into darkness. Silence falls over the room.

Just before Ehrichto signals Michael to resume his trek down the stairs new music—bright, bubbly, thoroughly modern—begins pouring from the sound system. Michael's head whips around. His eyes are huge, as is the smile that breaks out across his face. He grabs Ehrichto's hand and begins pulling him down the stairs. "C'mon," he shouts. "This is the Cure! It's 'Friday I'm in Love'!"

"How are you feeling?"

Baxter knows he knows the voice, but the name belonging to it escapes him. In the place he just returned from there were no names, no faces or bodies. There was simply existence.

"Do you know where you are? Who you are?"

A different voice asks "Do you know who I am?"

"Ehrichto."

Baxter opens his eyes, and is startled to find a crowd staring back at him. It takes him a moment to remember all their names: Ehrichto, Kabil Dorjan, Nick, Jeff—correction, Philip—Willem, André, Coronel. Far off to his right, seated on another sofa, he finds grown-up Wren, and a pang of hot envy flares in his breast. Wren will be twenty-five forever. *Why didn't Ehrichto turn me twenty years ago? I could be an eternal forty-one, and not be condemned to eternity looking so old.*

"That was pretty trippy, huh?" Wren asks.

Baxter nods, and the room spins. For several anxious seconds he thinks he may be sick. Dorjan slips onto the seat beside him. When their eyes meet, the unpleasant sensation ceases. "Is that better?"

"Yes."

"Everything is fine. You can relax. You're one of us now."

"Forever," Philip adds.

"I was just telling Ehrichto that I'm going to borrow you for a while," Dorjan says. "He and Michael need time to be alone, to really get to know one another, and I need you to help me throw a party like the one last night in every city in which we own a house."

"How many is that?"

"Well, let's see. Prague, Sardinia, Stockholm, New York, Rome...."

"Rome fell through," Philip says. "And the deal in Austin is still pending."

"About a dozen. I think you'd like Marc to be your assistant, yes?"

Marc has made an amazing recovery—Baxter doesn't know if the kel'an had a supernatural hand in it or not, though now that he's one of them he supposes he can ask—but even so, just as Baxter predicted, he'd had to drop out of *Fifth of July*. "Yes, I would, but won't that be difficult?" Dorjan has made it clear that Marc is not to be told the truth about what they are. The way he termed it, they'd met their quota of broken things when Ehrichto turned Nick.

Since being outed by Ehrichto as not Wren's biological father, Nick has been the man Baxter remembers. He's gone back to downing a single bottle of whisky every night, staying cognizant of his surroundings and full of hell most of the time.

"You're the only one who can answer that."

"Are you asking if I'll be able to withstand knowing that he's sleeping with all of you?" Baxter gives a snort. "It would only be unsettling if he wasn't. I wouldn't know how to react."

"Good." Dorjan stands and holds out his hand. Baxter isn't sure it isn't just his imagination, but when he gets to his feet his hip doesn't hurt, not even the tiniest twinge, the first time that's been true in years. "Go find and invite him," Dorjan says. "And then start packing. We leave in the morning."

"Of course," Baxter says, half under his breath. "It's the day after

Derby, the time when the world departs from Louisville."

"Only this time you're part of the world."

"The race is today?" Wren asks. "I'd like to see it. Can we go?"

Baxter laughs. "Only on television. You can't get near the track today."

"Where? Churchill Downs?" Philip asks. "I have a box. We can all go."

Wren turns. "What do you say, Uncle Baxter?"

"What do I say?" Baxter crosses the room to stand beside Dorjan. "I say 'Lay on, MacDuff, and damned be he who first cries, "Hold! Enough!"'"

Dorjan smiles and throws an arm around Baxter's shoulders. "Fair warning," he says, as they start for the door. "I do not believe in damnation, and it is never, ever enough to suit my tastes."

"I'm the same."

"I know." Dorjan tightens his hold on Baxter. "That's why this is going to work out very well, yes?"

ABOUT THE AUTHOR

Born and raised in Chicago, N.S. Beranek was an Assistant Propmaster in regional theatre for nineteen years. She lives in Louisville, Kentucky with her husband, Rob. This is her first novel. You can find more about her writing and musings online at **nsberanek.com.**